HERE, NOW

SYLVIA BOURGEOIS

Coastwerks Press
Fanny Bay, BC

Here, Now is a work of fiction, but deals with real issues including stillbirth, injury, and death.
For more content warnings, please go to
https://sylviabourgeois.com/content-warnings/

For Charlie.
Who called me Boss and showed us
the value of hard work.

Port Neville
PACIFIC
VANCOUVER
ISLAND
OCEAN
Sointula
Alert Bay
X Camp 1
X Camp 2

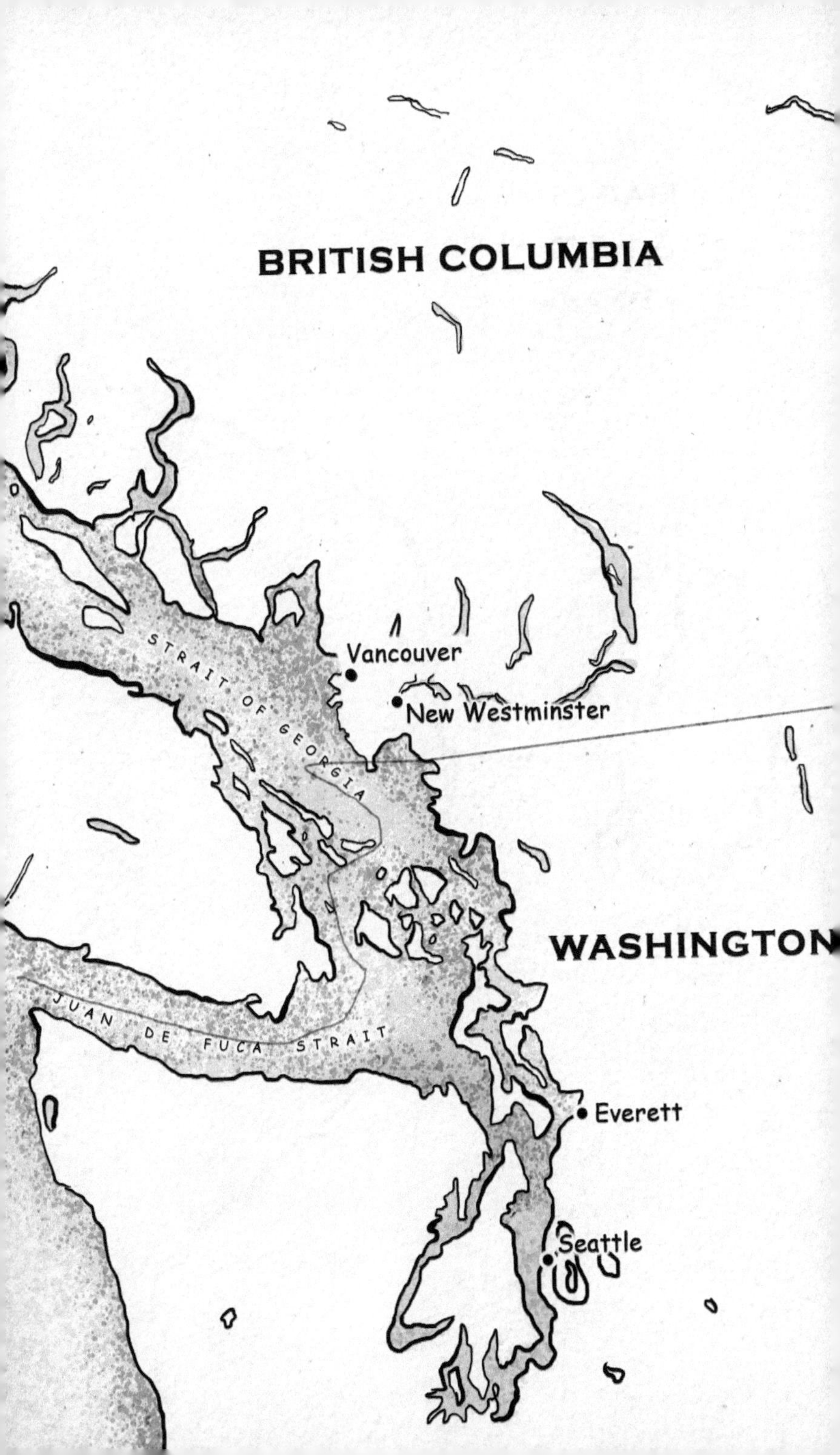

BRITISH COLUMBIA
WASHINGTON
Vancouver
New Westminster
STRAIT OF GEORGIA
JUAN DE FUCA STRAIT
Everett
Seattle

MAP OF
CAMP 2
~1924~
NIMPKISH

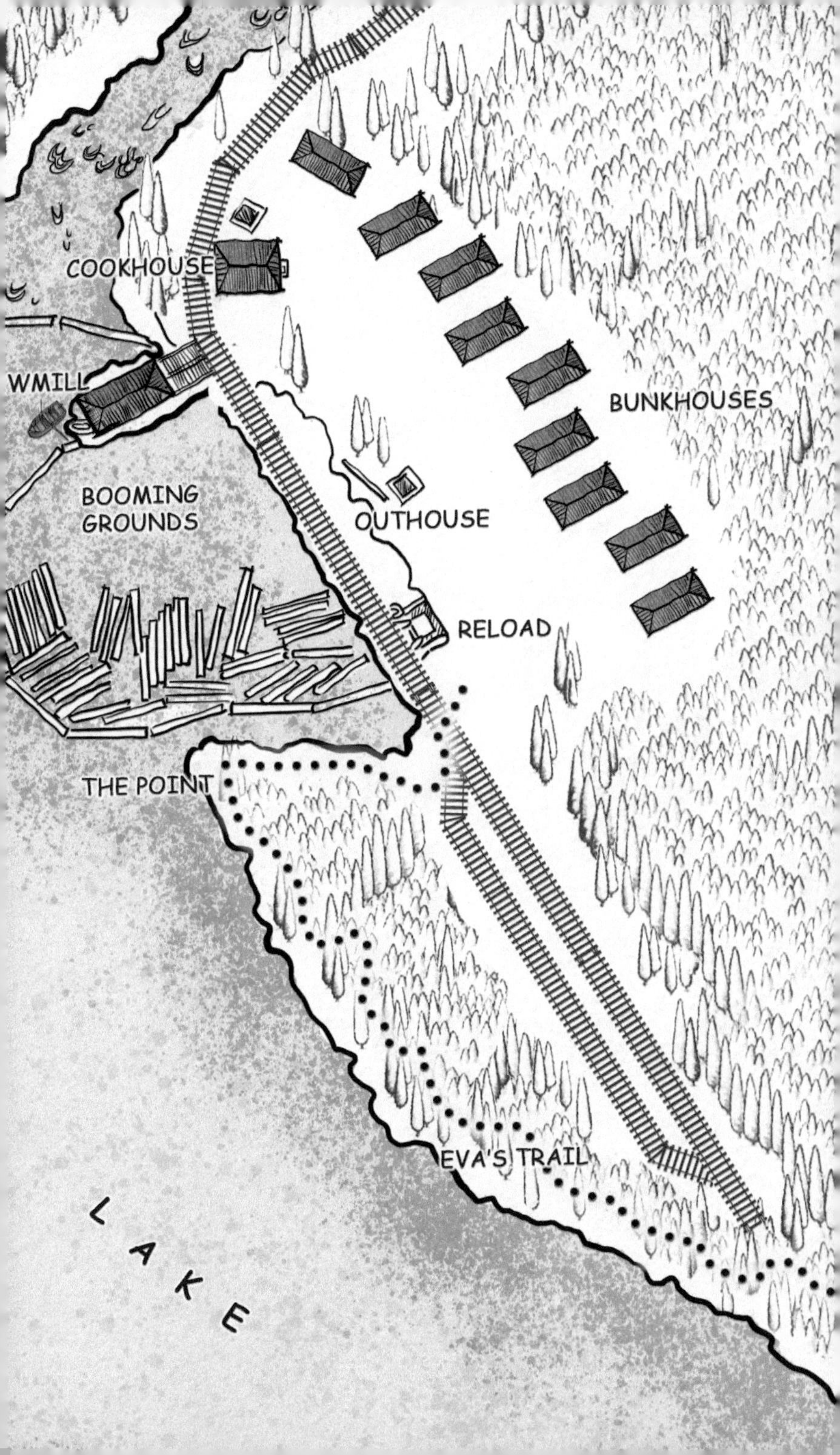

COOKHOUSE
WMILL
BOOMING
GROUNDS
OUTHOUSE
BUNKHOUSES
RELOAD
THE POINT
EVA'S TRAIL
LAKE

CHAPTER 1

I've always preferred trees to people. The forest has a predictable rhythm, and doesn't judge or criticize. This afternoon, I will make history as the only woman in America to earn a Master's in Forestry. It's a day of celebration, but first I must survive a luncheon with Mother. Her outdated aspirations for me are simple: a church aisle and vows. But today she'll witness me at a different altar, my academic achievements replacing her traditional dream.

Outside Seattle's Olympic Hotel, an elegant couple slips into a taxi under the enormous American flags flanking the ornate awning. I duck off the sidewalk and up the marble steps where the doorman pulls open the heavy door. I'm late for lunch with my parents and my new openwork pumps click across the terrazzo floor of the bustling lobby. Two stories above the well-dressed crowd, a 300-pound crystal chandelier sparkles. The room couldn't be farther from nature's hushed clarity, but the echoing grandeur runs a tingle up my spine.

Mother will detest everything about this day: the hateful hotel jazz, the arid academia, and my modern flared heel. I grin down at the gleaming black patent leather, kicking out from under my silky sheath dress with each hurried step. I spent almost four dollars on these shoes, and wearing something I love gives me a surprising satisfaction. Maybe

I should have let Mother shop with me, but then I'd be in respectable shoes. I roll my shoulders back, shaking the self-doubt she instills. Today's celebration belongs to me and the Class of 1924. Mother ought to be pleased I didn't just polish my sturdy work boots.

At the tea room I announce myself, and a tuxedoed steward leads me to my parents. Mother nods, remaining seated, then comments on my paleness, eyeing my new shoes with a frown. Predictable, but still so irritating. Father heaves his large frame up, enveloping my small hand in his huge ones, his entire face shining with love, and I beam back. Without his sedate support, I would not have persevered to this graduation. He's gentle and supportive in every way Mother is stiff and severe.

We settle in, Mother's customary monologue beginning with the weather, which she declares to be typically west coast. My father and I murmur responses as she covers the family and neighbourhood news. Meals were so much easier when we were a table of four. Tony always redirected Mother's diatribes with easy humour, and the absence of my big brother's joyful spirit stabs at my stomach even more on special occasions.

Above us, palm fronds rustle in the carved, dark wood second-floor planters. From the corner, the piano player beats out "Maple Leaf Rag", muffling the drone of voices and the tinkling of silver. The upbeat ragtime reminds me of Thomas. He brought me to this hotel's public pre-opening a year ago, where he spun me into a lively foxtrot. It was a lovely night, before all the recent confusion between us. Mother and Father later attended the December opening gala, of course, as did many of Seattle's citizen bond-buyers. The city's older, wealthy crowd helped finance the hotel's ridiculous luxury, and demanded more subdued musical choices.

Mother glares over her shoulder, clucking her tongue and shaking her head. "I wish they wouldn't play this rag — it's indecent." She leans over, squinting at me. "You should get more rest. And stay out of the sun." Her fingers flutter off the table, as if she's going to brush the purple shadows under my eyes. But she deposits her hand back onto the white tablecloth, maintaining distance, and continues. "You know, most girls would kill for your natural dark curls and porcelain complexion. They wouldn't go traipsing in the bush, letting their hair frizz and skin freckle." She sighs, peering at the spots scattered across my nose and cheeks.

"Yes, Mother." Nodding in agreement, I work the tongs to drop a sugar cube into my tea, counting down seconds with a silent exhale. She pivots, sharing news that Alice, the daughter of a country-club friend, has applied for the front desk position at Father's car lot.

"Can you believe? It's so unbecoming for young ladies to work, especially those who needn't." Mother's lips pucker in distaste. Her comment refers to Alice, who works out of boredom, not need. But Mother's words are an attack on my goals, a topic she touches on every time we meet. Under the table, I clench my napkin, gritting my teeth. Next, she gushes about Alice's husband's promotion, which he secured because the woman in that position got married. Her wedded state caused her firing. I raise my eyebrows, unable to restrain my disbelief. My mother's bias against progress and women's independence is infuriating. But she's saved from my response by the returning steward. He places a silver platter in the centre of the table and removes the cloche cover with a great flourish, revealing an enormous selection of tea sandwiches.

The smell of sardines, olives, and pumpernickel wafts over me from the tray and a queasiness fills my throat. I look away from my parents, pretending to admire the architecture, swallowing down the bile. My brain scrambles to find a logical excuse, but the mounting evidence is pointing to just one cause of this daily ailment. I quash these thoughts, unclenching a fist from my crumpled napkin and laying my palm against my lower belly. No. Not today. Tomorrow. I'll think about it tomorrow.

"There's a handsome new fellow working for your father. As manager. His name is Harold." Mother smiles her match-making smile as she expands on Harold's attributes and how well my father's car lot is doing. "He's a Hewitt. Good family. Right, Jim?" My mother looks pointedly at my father, who's been working through the sandwich tray. He swallows a salmon bite, sensing commentary on his never-ending appetite. So he answers amiably.

"Harold's doing a fine job. Fine job." Father nods at both of us, leaning back against the velvet chair. "Going to be the best month since the Great War, June is. A good month." Father smiles and reaches for a tigereye sandwich. "We can thank those speedy new Buick roadsters, we can." Mother expects my father to say more, but when he doesn't, she lists the new engagements her golf friends have reported. So many daughters doing what's expected of them. After detailing the plans for four summer weddings, she dabs her lips with a napkin. Her critical gaze lingers on my hands, where the gritty traces of my beloved spruce seedlings stain my fingernails.

"Honestly, Eva! Your hands. It'll be a wonder if you ever get married. Why won't you wear gloves?" Mother's exasperated question punctuates her list of not-so-subtle critiques of my life. My back stiffens and I start to reply, no longer willing to contain my exasperation. But Father catches my eye, raising a glass of Virginia julep. I clamp my lips shut, drawing in a slow, steady breath. There's nothing to be gained by speaking my truth.

"To Eva. And her education. And her firsts. We wish you well, my girl." Father's toast diffuses the tightness in my chest and we clink our frosted glasses. I move the mint sprig onto my side plate and savour the lemony sweet cider mix. After his first sip, Father shakes his head in disgust. Five years of prohibition and he still can't stomach the fruity replacements respectable establishments are forced to serve.

"Thank you, Father." The lump in my throat surprises me. Mother has showered me in criticism, but Father's acknowledgement saves the tenor of the day, and I'm grateful. My choice of profession has puzzled scholars, colleagues, and friends. They don't understand my connection to the land. Nature is authentic and unpretentious, never imposing norms. It's people who put up barriers where they're not needed. Today, I celebrate the tenacity that got me here. Setting my mother straight can wait for another time.

Chapter 2

Father guides his sparkling new 1924 Buick touring car from downtown Seattle to the lush green grounds of Washington University. This morning's drizzle leaves the cobblestones damp and the gloomy skies match Mother's expression. Once we've parked, the rumbling six-cylinder silenced, I gladly leave my parents and walk to the College of Forestry's stone, ivy-covered building. In the first-floor lobby, my classmates gather, donning black gowns. Our group is small, with only twelve students receiving degrees this year.

The boys pause when I enter, greeting me with wolf whistles. They've only seen me in faded trousers and worn work boots, nothing like this lacy silk sheath. I shake my head, laughing off their brotherly comments on how well I clean up. Already wearing their plain black gowns, they jostle each other in front of the mirror, securing their mortarboards and placing the russet-brown tassels carefully on the right.

I feel Thomas's gaze on me before I turn around. He looks stunning in his gown, the russet hood framing his dark features and bringing out the gold in his hazel eyes. I hate that he makes my heart skip. Today signifies many changes. I can't imagine not seeing Thomas every day. We've been colleagues for years, and other than Millie, he's still my closest friend. But on Monday, he starts work in a downtown office, for his father's lumber business, whereas I have yet to land a job. A heaviness returns to my chest.

"How was it?" Thomas asks, his features softening. He knows I just had lunch at the Olympic Hotel with my parents, and how awful my mother can be. "Looks like you survived." His gaze lingers on my new shoes and sheath dress before his eyes meet mine, sending another buzz beneath my skin. I look away, taking the gown he's holding out for me. The russet hood matches his, since we're the only two from our college graduating with a Master's today.

"Draining," I say. Thomas chuckles at my exasperated tone as I wriggle into the gown and smooth it over my dress. "But the hotel is gorgeous. Ridiculously opulent. And stunning." Thomas hands me my cap, as I tuck stray fronds of my dark, wavy locks behind my ears. The mortarboard is floppy and difficult to place, but soon we agree we're both presentable. Thomas looks at me a little too long, head tilted and his jaw clenched. His soft eyes have lost their laughter, now looking hollow and I feel heat rising up my neck. I wish we could turn back the clock, to change that troublesome night and his subsequent proposal. Before those events a few months ago, there were never awkward silences or pained glances with Thomas.

When one of the boys announces it's time, our jovial group walks toward the indoor pavilion. Thomas keeps pace next to me, but we're both quiet, speaking only when the chatter of our classmates is directed at us. I wonder if Thomas is also considering how a portion of our everyday life is ending today. His camaraderie has been a steady comfort, and there was a moment I thought I wanted more. He's smart, handsome, and finds my penchant for order amusing. But I need to establish my career before I consider marriage. Without thinking, I press my palm against my middle. Then I wrinkle my nose, burying the heaviness that fills me whenever I relive that day. Straightening, I meet Thomas's gaze again, but he doesn't return my smile.

We enter the pavilion through the back entrance with other excited graduates. A temporary wooden floor covers the dirt of the arena where we sit on folding chairs in rows beside a stage. Our friends and family face us from the stands, usually filled with sports fans. We settle into our class's designated seats and I scan the crowd for my parents. When I catch my father's eye, he grins and nudges Mother. She acknowledges me with a nod but quickly turns back to a woman in a fashionable hat beside her, who's introducing a young man in uniform. As he rises to take mother's hand, she stiffens visibly, clutching her other palm against her breastbone. She sees my brother Tony in that soldier.

Tears prickle as Tony fills my thoughts again. He should be sitting up there with my parents, celebrating my triumph, like he did the summer he taught me to ride his bike. Our birthdays were just a week apart, and I had begged for a bicycle. But it was Tony, the boy, who received one. Even at nine years old, I was discouraged from adventurous, unladylike pursuits. Unwrapping a baby doll with real eyelashes, I stifled the urge to throw it across the room. But Tony saw my defeat and dragged me outside, tackling my frustration.

As a lanky preteen, my brother jogged alongside me with a wide grin, holding the padded leather seat of his shiny blue two-wheeler. I wobbled, fell, and skinned my knees. But Tony cajoled me until I shook it off and got up, gaining confidence under his unwavering encouragement. When I finally balanced and the world around me became a blur of sunlit greenery, his cheer echoed through the quiet neighbourhood. I'll never forget his infectious laugh and the pride on his face as he patted me on the back. If only he were here now. My big brother would support me through this mess I've gotten myself into.

The lights dim and I'm drawn back to today's ceremony. It begins with the valedictorian speech by a fellow I don't recognize. As students from other colleges walk across the stage, I clap absently, mind wandering. My gaze lands on my mother, who's scanning the crowd. A sharp pain stabs my chest. She was so proud of Tony. His quirky grin and endless energy were easy to love. Mother's still trying to understand how she raised such a tomboy. She deserves a daughter who gushes over the latest fashion and delights in whispered gossip. Instead, she got me, who prefers tromping alone through towering cedars in grubby overalls. I wonder how she'll twist today's events into a tale suited for her country-club.

Finally, it's our class's turn and I applaud the boys loudly. Thomas and I are last, and when my name is announced, I carefully cross the stage in the blazing spotlights. As I smile and shake our Dean's hand, accepting my diploma, Thomas's wolf whistle penetrates the roar in my ears. I flash him a grin over my shoulder, but see only the glare of electric lights. Standing tall, I beam at the audience, expanding my lungs to their fullest through a deep, satisfied breath. From the shadows, my father's cheer rises above the rest. Off stage, I pause at the bottom of the steps, feeling dizzy, gripping the stair rail with a trembling hand. Things are moving too quickly. My shoulders curl forward and I try to swallow the ache in my throat.

Behind me, Thomas's name is announced, and I force myself to turn. He smiles and waves at the stands where his mother claps enthusiastically, her heavy diamond bracelet glinting in the faint light. She is impeccably dressed; her feathered cloche hat and luxurious fur stole befitting a woman of her means. I look for Thomas's father, but expect his absence. He'll be at work, managing his lumber empire. Mrs. Clark catches Thomas's eye and blows him a kiss, her intricately beaded dress shimmering and a proud smile filling her face.

He hops down the steps, stopping to offer his elbow with a grin. The gesture loosens the lump in my throat, and I laugh. As he guides me back to our seats, I consider the canyon-sized gap between my mother and Thomas's. Mrs. Clark exudes modern sophistication, whereas Mother, just a few rows away, emanates a deliberate conservatism in her dark hues and modest pearls.

Soon after we take our seats in the folding chairs, the University President makes his final address. As the speech ends, his voice breaks through the fog in my head. He's saying something I've heard before.

"...reach for the stars, but don't forget to recognize opportunities that are right in front of you." The President's loud monotone drones, and beside me Thomas stiffens. He had used the same words the night of his heartfelt proposal, trying to convince me that feeling safe and whole with another person *is* love. His plea then, to see what's right in front of me, was an echo of the President's phrase now. My fists clench in my lap and a surge of sickness hits me, uncontrollable this time. I stand abruptly, pushing past my classmates into the darkened aisle, and stagger toward the back door of the pavilion.

I burst through the heavy doors and into the bright sunlight before I double over, crouch, and heave next to a towering fir. My palm grips the rough bark as tea and sandwich bits hit the grass. I pull a handkerchief from my pocket, dread clenching my gut. Slumping onto the lawn, I lean back against the trunk, eyes closed. This tree is a *Pseudotsuga menziesii*. I repeat the scientific name over and over in my mind. Picturing the quirky genus and species words signals how agitated I am. I've had this habit as long as I can remember, complicated syllables distracting my thoughts from my choking anxiety. *Pseudotsuga menziesii*, I think, slower now, taking another deep breath of the fresh summer air. My head is ringing, but my belly feels better. Then the crunch of gravel makes me squint toward the sky.

Thomas stands a few feet away, his brows narrowing in concern as he moves closer. When he sees the mess in the grass, his lips purse.

"Are you alright? Are you sick?" Thomas kneels beside me, his eyes searching my face. He leans forward, hands inches from me. But I refuse his help with a raised palm.

"Don't. I'm fine. It's nothing."

"You're not fine. Let me—"

"Don't." My voice sounds harsh and I close my eyes again, needing to block out the comprehension flashing across his face. I've been able to read his thoughts for years. And he thinks I'm pregnant.

Chapter 3

I know he's correct. Of course he's correct. But if I admit this to Thomas, it becomes real. So terribly real. And I'm not ready. Not today.

Thomas stills, and when I finally look up, his expression is now an unreadable mask. Bracing against the tree trunk I stand, tucking my handkerchief in my pocket and brushing bits of grass from my gown.

We're saved from our heavy silence when the doors push open and a noisy flow of smiling graduates spills out. Thomas and I join the bustle to return our cap and gowns, then walk to the parking lot.

My parents greet us with bright smiles. Thomas's position as the heir to a lumber fortune explains mother's deference. Father, on the other hand, genuinely enjoys his intelligence and character, and asks what his plans are now that he's finished school. Thomas says he's taking a local role with his family's company, but expects to be posted to Canada soon. He's worked up on Vancouver Island every summer break, spending time in the company's logging camps, learning the ropes and getting to know the crew. Father nods, impressed, and Mother inquires after his family. Thomas gives her a friendly but non-specific update, and I silently admire his ability to deflect.

"Are you leaving together? Now?" Thomas turns to me, hopeful eyebrows raised. "Or will you take a last walk around campus with me?"

"Oh, Eva's in no rush." Mother gushes as Father opens the door of the Buick for her. "You two go have your walk." There's no one I'd rather spend time with, but a walk with Thomas will reveal the truth. He won't let me lie to myself.

"I'm sorry," I say, looking up at him. "I promised Millie and the kids a visit this afternoon." Mother lets out an audible sigh and I curse her, and my cowardice.

"Well... call me... if you need... anything." Thomas steps close, his voice upbeat. But his eyes reflect deep concern. He stuffs his fists into his pockets, watching me climb into the backseat on the far side of the car. "I hope to see you around soon, Eva."

"See you around," I say, unable to meet his gaze. Oh, Thomas. An ache fills the back of my throat as we drive away. It takes all my strength to hold back tears and not look over my shoulder. But I'm a career woman now, and need to be independent. And that starts at once.

Father drops me off at Millie's house, a bright white clapboard two-story with a steep shingle roof, dormers, and a covered front porch. My childhood friend's home is perched on a slight slope in a new tree-less, restricted community. I walk up the path between two patches of young grass to the porch stairs, pushing Thomas's pale face from my mind, determined to enjoy this visit. The intermittent thwacking of hammers reaches me from the lot across the street, where a Dutch building crew works on Millie's neighbour's house.

At the top of the stairs, I cross to the front door, knock once, and let myself in.

"Millie? I'm here!" I unpin my hat and hang it on the coat rack, calling down the hall, then walk toward a fragrant whiff of onion and garlic. Millie's in the kitchen with the two-year-old twins, stirring a tomato sauce, one child on her hip and another gripping the hem of her skirt.

"Eva!" Millie drops young Eddie from her arms into mine and stoops to pick up Lizzie. "How was the graduation?" she asks, dropping the wooden spoon and leaning her tiny bottom against the tile countertop.

"Long. Good." Eddie pounds his pudgy fists against my tender chest and I rub noses with him. Giving his stout body a tight squeeze, I move him to one hip and tickle his bare feet. Eddie squeals, squirms, and slides down my skirt, saying he's "gonna show Eva my twuck".

"And lunch? Tell me all about the hotel. We haven't been there yet." Lizzie wiggles out of Millie's grasp as well, and she toddles off to "bwing dolly". Millie watches her leave. "They're so clingy now, since the baby's been born. There's always someone with sticky fingers hanging off me." She tastes the sauce on the stove, wrinkles her nose, and peers into the spice cabinet. I dip a spoon into the burping tomato concoction, sniffing it before gingerly taking a lick. Millie is a terrible cook.

"Salt, definitely. And more pepper. Maybe a teaspoon of sugar." It's doubtful anything can hide the scorched flavour, but I try to be helpful. Millie works so hard to please her husband, but her non-scientific brain just can't grasp how to make an edible meal.

I sit on a wooden chair at the kitchen table, glad for the distracting bustle, as Millie plies me for the hotel's ritzy details. She won't be satisfied until she can paint a picture in her mind, so I share every sight, sound, and smell of the lunch. Millie sits across from me with her elbows on the table, eyelids half closed, chin resting on her hands, reliving my morning. When the baby cries from the second floor, she sighs. Millie takes off her apron and goes upstairs just as the twins toddle back into the kitchen.

Smiling, I kneel on the linoleum to admire their treasures. Toddlers are fascinating, with their big heads, unsteady gait, and earnest language. Eddie's new dump truck is dark green rolled steel with red wheels, sturdy enough to support his weight. After assuring him it's the best toy truck I've ever seen, he places his chubby hands on the dump box rails and runs the toy down the hall, making engine sounds. I cringe, thinking of the damage the sharp edges could do to ankles and plaster.

A hollow thunk on my knee turns my attention to Lizzie, who has thrust her doll onto my lap. The head, arms, and legs are a hard, shiny, skin-tone composite, with delicately drawn features. Unblinking blue eyes stare up at me and a white-painted tooth peaks out from the baby doll's dimpled grin. It's dressed in a navy sailor's frock with cream satin trim, just like the doll I unwrapped on my ninth birthday. I make a silent promise to gift these children toys that cater to all — puzzles or sports gear or books. Nothing that confines them into narrow future roles.

"Help?" Lizzie holds out a matching bonnet. I place it over the fake moulded hair and tie the satin ribbon under its chin. Smiling over at Lizzie, I rock the doll, its cotton-filled body soft in my arms. "Baby hung-gwee." Lizzie pushes the doll's head into my chest. I look down, visualizing my possible pregnancy and its outcome — a child. The realization brings on another wave of nausea and I lurch upright, dropping the toy from my lap onto the floor. Lizzie grabs it and runs after her brother, unruffled by my distress.

My breath comes in gasps, and I lean over the sink, vomiting for the second time today. I wait for the queasiness to settle, then run cold water and rinse my mouth. Fear floods my gut again. If I'm pregnant, it changes everything. Forever. As I splash water on my face, Millie walks up beside me with the baby. She sniffs, her nose wrinkling, and I turn away from her questioning eyes, yanking open a drawer for a tea towel, rearranging my face into a neutral expression as I dry it.

"Are you sick?" Millie asks, motioning me into the living room.

I shake my head and follow her. "No. Probably just something I ate." I swallow the sour taste in my mouth as I lie to her. She shoos the twins outside, easing onto the plush new davenport to nurse little Flora. Millie cocks her chin, lifting a single eyebrow. She sees my deflection but doesn't confront me as she struggles to get the baby to latch on under the nursing cloth. When Flora finally settles and feeds, Millie looks at me with narrowed eyes.

"Did you see Thomas today?" She watches me closely for a reaction.

"Of course." She knows he was at the graduation, so I give her nothing else. But part of me aches to share everything with Millie. I need help to figure this all out. My friends and family got acquainted with Thomas over the past year. He accompanied me to parties and events over Christmas. They all adore him and the sudden end to our courtship perplexes everyone. I've never provided details because if they knew Thomas proposed, they'd chastise me for refusing such a suitable match. And if Millie knew I was pregnant, she would push for what she views as the inevitable conclusion.

"When do you see him next?" Millie asks.

I glare at her. Everyone's a matchmaker today. "It's over with him. I've told you that!"

"Level with me, Eva. I don't understand. You were goofy for him until a couple months ago. What happened?" I shake my head again, crossing my arms, but say nothing. "Thomas loves you. You know that, don't you? He'd be a wonderful husband." It's Millie's turn to shake her head as she clucks her tongue.

"Why does everyone want to marry me off?" My voice raises, quivering, as I get up and pace the oriental rug. "I just got my Master's, for goodness' sake. I'm going to work. Have a career. I do not need a man!" My heel pounds onto the floor with the last word. "I've already got an interview next week in Everett."

Millie looks at me with a thin smile, biting her cheek. It's the expression she wears every time she tells me that for someone so smart, I can be pretty stupid. But today, instead of sharing whatever observation she has on her mind, she changes the subject. And I soon see why — more matchmaking.

"Will you come to our Fourth of July cookout? On Friday?" she asks. "I could use a hand. And Leo's friend Herman will be here." I scowl at her in disgust. She hasn't heeded a word I've said.

Leo is Millie's husband, a young banker she met while volunteering for the Red Cross during the flu epidemic. He's fond of saying pneumonia brought him the love of his life. Leo's still frail from his illness, but steady and kind. He takes good care of Millie, and though I don't fully understand it, she's happy. The chaps Millie tries to set me up with are gentlemen as well, but awfully boring. They spend their days in windowless offices with ledgers, and are clearly looking for wives. Millie knows that's not for me, but presses on. I think she hopes that if she introduces me to the right man, I'll settle down next door so we can raise our families side by side.

Flora sputters, and Millie bounces the baby over her shoulder. Through the front window, I watch the twins tumble on the lawn. Across the street, the building crew wraps up for the day. I imagine a houseful of my own children. In a different life, I could be heading over the road to cook my husband dinner and freshen up, awaiting his arrival. A shudder runs along my spine and bile rises in my throat again. I haven't fought through years of schooling to wear an apron in suburbia. But a single foolish drunken choice might force me to throw it all away.

I bring a shaky hand to my forehead, considering my options for Friday, before Millie comments on my glazed look. My mother will also host her annual Fourth of July picnic. So I can either spend the day at home answering questions about why I'm not married. Or be herded into Millie's kitchen with the other wives who will debate baked pork chop recipes and the effectiveness of Borax soap chips. A loud burp splits the silence of the living room, and then Flora gurgles. I force a smile over at my friend.

"I'll be here. To help out. But no matchmaking." Turning from the window, I wag my finger at her as she expects. At least coming here lets me sneak off without the guilt my mother would lay on.

A smile lights Millie's face. My help lets her be a better hostess, which she appreciates. She holds Flora up and I take her, cradling the baby to my chest and cupping her head with my palm. I drop a light kiss on her fluff of hair, inhaling the sweet scent of powder, milk, and soap. Another chill runs through me as I imagine her as mine. I need to get away from here.

After handing Flora back to her mother, I stab my hat onto my curls, and give the twins hasty hugs goodbye outside. Walking down the front path and into the summer evening, I'm even more agitated than when I drove away from Thomas this afternoon. I'm used to feeling like an outsider, and it no longer bothers me. For half my life, I've plotted a route to become an independent career woman.

But if there's a child growing inside me, every stitch of my plan will unravel. I've never felt so unprepared, and it's terrifying.

CHAPTER 4

On the long walk home from Millie's, I deliberate feasible actions, playing each option to its conclusion. It's the first time I let myself consider the enormity of the mistake I've made, but running the problem through a logical sequence is calming.

By the time I hang my hat on the coat rack, I'm eager to list my thoughts in my little red notebook. The aroma of frying onions reaches me from the kitchen and I shout a greeting to Mother before bounding up the stairs. I dig my notebook and a pencil from the bottom of my haversack before flopping onto my bed. The faint scent of lavender drifts from the sheets as I lay on my belly, propped on my elbows.

Leafing through the pages, I skim past dozens of previous lists, most of them related to my Master's thesis on Sitka spruce seedlings. On an empty page, I draw out a table.

ACTION:	PROS:	CONS:	COMMENTS:
Medical termination.	Fast. Easy to conceal.	Dangerous. Illegal. Where to go?	Remember Mel — EEK!
Adoption or Maternity home.	Provides a healthy baby to a family. Place to stay, guidance.	Endure pregnancy to term – ugh! Move away from Seattle.	Who would be with you for the birth? Research places to go / costs.
Have the baby and raise it myself.	None – I don't want a child!	Harder to find a job with a child. Mother ??! Responsibility – I'm not ready!	This is only on the list to cover all the options. NO!
Get married.	None – I don't want a child or a husband.	Turns a nine-month mistake into a lifetime mistake.	This is only on the list to cover all the options. NO!

I reread the list, tapping the pink eraser against my lower lip, pondering the page. Eventually, my pencil stills and I sit up, crossing my legs. With precise movements, I strike through the last two options, then circle the words 'NO!' in thick black spirals, denting the paper.

It's absurd to derail everything I've worked for, to raise a child. Unlike Millie, who's dreamed of herself with children since the fifth grade, I've never wanted that. Employers would be even more reluctant to offer an opportunity to an unwed mother. And it's unfair to the child — I know nothing about caring for them, not to mention the stigma of growing up a bastard. Schoolyards can be poisonous places. I shake my head. No, keeping the baby is not an option.

But neither is getting married. That would extend my current indiscretion into a long-term blunder. I sketch a large three-dimensional X next to the words 'lifetime mistake'. Marriage for me is like trying to grow a seedling in the shade — a doomed experiment.

I circle the first two choices on the list, swiping graphite dust off the page, and imagine each series of actions. If I can find someone to do the procedure, I'll want a friend with me. And if I move away to give up the baby, I'll need help with a cover story. Both require me to confide in someone.

For the umpteenth time this week, I ache for Tony. Flipping to the last page of my notebook, I pull out a faded photo of him, grinning at the camera. He's bundled up wearing a striped knit cap, standing tall on tube skates. The frozen reservoir blurs behind him and he grips a hockey stick with his new padded gloves, pride in his eyes. I still wonder if he would be alive today if he didn't love hockey so much.

"What would you tell me to do, big brother?" I run a fingertip along the bent edge of the photo, whispering the words and smiling softly. He'd say take it step by step. Tony always teased that I wanted everything all at once. I can hear the chuckle in his kind voice. "One step at a time, sis."

Right. So what are those steps? I consider this question. I have to see a doctor — best to confirm the pregnancy. Then choose a way and enlist someone to help me with this mess. Without Tony, Millie and Thomas are the only ones I'd trust with this secret. But I don't need to decide all this right now. The Fourth of July long weekend looms large in everyone's plans for the coming days. And next Tuesday, I have my interview with Howard Lumber. I wonder if I should cancel it, but square my shoulders, shaking my head. No. I want to confirm there's a career awaiting me. No matter my decision about this problem, I must know that.

From downstairs, Mother calls me to dinner, and I tuck Tony's photo back between the pages before burying the notebook deep in my bag. Pasting a smile on my face and filled with secrets, I leave my childhood bedroom. It's disquieting how many lies you can hide from the people who know you best.

CHAPTER 5

On Tuesday after the Fourth of July long weekend, I drive north in a new coupe off my father's car lot for my first job interview. Buick has been advertising this model as "suited for Milady's Motoring" and my father encourages me to use the coupe. He hopes folks will get used to seeing women driving on their own, opening sales to the other half of our population.

It should take about three hours to reach the Howard Lumber Company offices, near the Everett port. To avoid rougher roads, I stick to the paved Pacific Highway. As always, I find the route exhilarating. There are shiny roadsters, rusty flivvers, farm equipment, and teams of horses, all moving with purpose to their destinations. The scenery is diverse, offering lush forests, rolling hills, and glimpses of Puget Sound. Since my last trip, new roadside diners and gas stations have popped up, catering to the surge of everyday folks becoming motorists.

Father taught me to drive on my thirteenth birthday, two years before the state officially issues licences, and I was soon an expert, manipulating the clutch, gas, and brake with ease. Now, I proudly pay $1.00 every two years for the little beige motor vehicle operator's licence with my name and details typed onto it. I crave the freedom of driving and beg to test drive every new model Father gets in. And while he's proud, Mother's appalled at the spectacle I become when motoring at twenty miles per hour down the neighbourhood streets, scarf flapping in a most unladylike fashion. It's probably good she hasn't seen me flying along the Pacific Highway auto trail where speeds are even faster.

This light new coupe's smooth clutch is thrilling to drive, distracting me from the flutters in my stomach. My interview is with Mr. Howard himself, at eleven o'clock sharp, and it's a coveted opportunity. Professor Barry recommended me for this position. He's been consulting for the Company on their timber replanting practices in northern Washington. Apparently, Mr. Howard is innovative and uncommonly forward-focused. He runs the kind of outfit I hope to work for, which makes this opportunity particularly enticing.

For weeks I've been thinking about this interview, preparing impressive answers. Professor Barry had been candid when we discussed my employment opportunities, lamenting that I didn't have a family connection into the business, like Thomas does.

"If you manage to find a placement, you'll prove yourself. But getting that first job won't be easy for you." After speaking with Mr. Howard, the professor felt I had a reasonable chance with Howard Lumber. I desperately hope he's right.

As I near Everett's maritime hub, the road becomes a wide gravel thoroughfare. I drive slowly, snaking past every type of wood industry, mesmerized. From train cars, logs dump into the ocean, stored in floating booms until the mills process them into lumber. A smokestack, silo, and water tower rise above the yard of an immense shingle mill. All around me, the acrid smell of smoke combines with the warm, woody scent of cut red cedar. I swallow a laugh as a buzz of excitement surges through me. Belonging to this progress is what I've been chasing, and it brings a shiver of delight to see it up close.

Between the splashes of log dumps, clanging of railcars, and whooshing discharges of steam, a couple of seagulls squawk overhead. The sweet sounds of industry are in harmony with the *Larus argentatus*. The bird's scientific name pops into my mind easily, thanks to another training my father has fostered. Even before we could read, he paid me and Tony a penny for every wildflower, tree, and creature we could correctly identify. He loves nature walks, Latin, and Greek, so on Sundays after church, while Mother took a break from us, we searched for new species. Back at home, we huddled over his prized journals hunting for a matching sketch among the colourful plates, struggling to pronounce the scientific names. Those afternoons with Father, strolling through the woods and chatting out our troubles under the tall timbers, were a cherished ritual that didn't end until I started university.

Now, at 10:45 a.m. I arrive at Howard Lumber, parking the coupe in a gravel lot next to a foreign luxury car whose make I don't recognize. I pull out a pocket mirror and tuck wayward locks back under my bucket hat, pleased by the flush in my cheeks. Then I adjust my stockings, smooth my skirt, and yank down the cuffs of my blouse. Head high, I walk into the front office, hoping I look calmer than I feel.

Inside, a secretary sits at a large roll-top desk, stabbing at a typewriter. When the door thunks closed, she looks up, eyebrows raised.

"Can I help you?"

"I have a meeting with Mr. Howard at eleven o'clock." Behind her is an open room stuffed with women sitting at a dozen desks, each stacked high with overflowing wire baskets. She pushes back her chair and consults the appointment book.

"Miss Roberts?" I nod. "Have a seat." I sit stiffly on the offered wooden bench under the front window. "I'll tell him you're here." She hurries through the workspace, knocking on a door of a glassed office. Inside, a man shouts into a phone receiver and waves his hands. When he ignores the knock, the secretary taps on the glass and mouths something to him, pointing at the clock. Mr. Howard nods, then turns his back, still gesticulating wildly.

For the next hour, I observe the hum of the workplace. In three glassed offices on the right, men hunch over their phones, scribbling notes. They slam out into the open room often, shouting at the women in the middle desks, who scurry for the papers and transform them into something cohesive at their typewriters. The energy is edgy, but everyone has a smile in their eyes, and I yearn to be part of it.

"Gina!" The shout finally comes from the far end of the room. Mr. Howard holds his arm high, fingers beckoning, his rolled-up sleeves flapping. Gina, the secretary, summons me and the room's buzz quiets noticeably as I follow her back. The women peer at me curiously from under lowered lashes, and from inside their glassed offices, the men, too, watch me intently.

"Miss Roberts. A pleasure." Mr. Howard, a mature fellow in his forties, begins to offer his hand, then gestures at a hardback chair. "Please, take a seat." His features are tanned and rugged, with an inquisitive glint in his eyes as he peers down into mine. He closes the door behind me and I sit while he settles into his desk chair across from me. "So, tell me about yourself," he says. I swallow and clear my throat, smiling tightly, telling him I was born and raised in Seattle, and am the younger of two. He knows from Professor Barry that I've just graduated with a Master's in Forestry, but I remind Mr. Howard of that, anyway.

"And thank you for seeing me," I say, my appreciation a little late. This man's time is valuable, and he's doing my professor a great favour with this interview.

"Tell me, Miss Roberts, why should I hire another forester?" I cock my head and look at him, eyes narrowed, reciting my well-rehearsed, passionate speech.

"I've seen the cuts Professor Barry has been working on for you. There are so many things you could do to regenerate the habitat faster, to protect the water, and to prevent fires." I lay out my idea to collect native seeds before cutting, then increase manual replanting, speaking without hesitation as I lean forward. Imagining my concepts put into practice in a real forest quickens my pulse. I'm beaming and a little breathless when I stop.

"You do know we're running a business here, Miss Roberts. A for-profit business? These things you're talking about all cost money. A lot of money." His cheeks twitch as he clenches his jaw, but there's a twinkle in his crinkled eyes.

"The money is an investment, Mr. Howard." My ribs tighten and my smile fades as I lift my chin, shoulders stiffening. Industry often dismisses the sustainable practices we've studied as impractical and academic. I search my inventory of practised responses for a way to backpedal. "If you let me help, you'll be able to harvest again in fifty years." He raises his eyebrows. Clearly, that timeline seems distant to him. I try again, floundering. "Or you can sell the timber stand in ten years, as a healthy young forest." None of this is new to Mr. Howard, and I'm confused by his combative questions. I take one last stab at refuting his challenge. "I've been studying how to get the best survival rates out of replanted seedlings." As I explain the details of my thesis topic, Mr. Howard's attention wanes, and I see my chances at a job trickle away. "I can help make inexpensive changes that will give you a return for years to come. It's the way to the future, Mr. Howard." It's my best argument, and I delivered it well, thanks to countless dry runs. But I'm not sure it's enough.

He leans back in his chair and pulls a pack of cigarettes from his breast pocket, offering them to me, but I wave him off. He lights one for himself and drops the match into a square amber glass ashtray, taking a deep drag. Glaring out across the log booms on the misty Pacific, he sighs.

"Look, Miss Roberts. I appreciate your enthusiasm. You come highly recommended and know your stuff. That's clear." A cold sweat forms between my shoulder blades. His next word will be but. "But... we're not ready for you." There it is — the dreaded b-word. "We need someone the men will respect. Someone who can drive. Wears appropriate attire. I just don't see it working." He takes another drag of his cigarette, ash falling to the wood floor, and I open my mouth to respond, but he holds up a palm, halting my interruption. "I mean, I'm progressive, Miss Roberts. But on the level —" He stands, so I scramble to my feet as well. "— my crew isn't ready to take advice from an academic, much less an academic who's a woman." His voice lowers, hesitating before he hammers the final nail in my dreams' coffin. "Then there's the risk of a looker like you starting a family, quitting on me. The economic odds for investing in you are just... not good. I'm sorry." This time he holds out his hand and I stare at it, adrenaline tingling through my body. Heat rises up my neck, replacing the cold between my shoulders, and my cheeks flush. His last words ring with truth.

"I see," I say after a few seconds, but I don't shake Mr. Howard's hand, staring into his dark eyes. "Would it make any difference if I told you I drove myself here from Seattle today? And that I own more trousers than skirts? Or that I've learned to make myself heard in bull sessions? I have no trouble getting the men to do what I tell them." My chin lifts, fists clenched at my sides. A sad smile flits across his features before Mr. Howard shakes his head.

"No. I'm afraid it's not enough, Miss Roberts. You're a modern thinker. But... well... we're not quite ready for the likes of you." He pushes his hand toward me again and I now take it, shaking it slowly but firmly. "Good luck," he says.

"Sir." I should thank him for his time, but this single word is all I can muster. Then I turn on my shiny black heel, open the office door, and stride down the aisle without letting him see me out.

My head held high, I push through the front door, breathing in the industrial perfume of the air outside. But there's a lump in my throat. I long to be a part of this. With a heavy exhale, I stop next to what I'm sure is Mr. Howard's maroon machine, parked beside my coupe. The cursive script on the grill spells out Hispano Suiza, and I have an urge to rip the silver stork ornament right off the shiny hood. Profits over progress. That's the problem with these old boys. I'll have to make my mark without their permission. But between their prejudice and my pregnancy, doing so seems hopeless.

Chapter 6

On the drive back to Seattle, I fight tears and a queerness in my gut. Low clouds cover the sun and the shadowless terrain reflects my dark mood. I replay each part of my conversation with Mr. Howard, wondering why he agreed to meet when he clearly never intended to hire me. A heaviness expands through my core and I shudder. Maybe he was just curious or owed Professor Barry a favour. But I wonder if he would have hired me if I were a man.

My chest still feels tight as I park outside Millie's. I dread having to share this failure. The challenges in Mr. Howard's explanation loom like a granite wall — a formidable barrier I'll need to breach to enter the male domain. The prospect seems impossibly daunting as I drag myself up the walk. Millie opens the front door before I reach it, takes one look at my expression, and folds me into a long hug. Her chestnut hair smells faintly of lemon and tension leaves me as I melt into my best friend.

"What's happened?" She pushes me away, hands on both my shoulders, examining my face, eyebrows pulling down in concentration. Millie doesn't need words to know something big has gone wrong. The fluttering in my stomach boils over into anger as I push past her onto the front landing's wide plank floors.

"It's not fair!" I snatch off my bucket hat and throw it on the piano, stomping through to the kitchen to pace the chequered linoleum. "Have you got anything to drink?"

"Take it easy. You'll wake the baby." Millie points toward the ceiling, putting a finger to her lips to shush me, and reaches into the cupboard for their liquor prescription. "You know this is meant for teething, to rub on the baby's gums." She winks, pouring a splash of "medicinal whisky" from a small labelled bottle. Even in my agitation I reflect how strange it is that our doctors have become our only legal supplier of alcohol. Millie passes me the bourbon glass, leading me to the back sun parlour, which overlooks the landscaped backyard. "Now. Tell me everything."

With my pulse speeding and hands quivering, I relay the details of the interview with Mr. Howard. Millie listens, inserting all the obligatory sounds of sympathy and understanding. When I get to the part about them not wanting a woman, just as Professor Barry warned, injustice flares inside me, and her eyes widen. She sits against the flowered cushion of the banquette, chewing her lip.

"What?" I know that look. Millie wants to say something, but she's afraid of how I'll react. "Spit it out."

She wets her lips. "I'm really sorry this happened to you. But... I'm not surprised." She runs a hand through her hair and tells me about Leo's recent promotion. "He didn't deserve it. There was another girl who knew the job better. But she was passed up." She purses her mouth, avoiding my eyes. "Leo figures he got the job because she got engaged. And because she's a woman." Millie takes a sip of whisky. "It won't be easy for you out there. The older generation doesn't like women working for any reason, much less in a man's profession. And forestry is a man's world, Eva." Her words hit me hard.

Driving back from Everett, I replayed the positive things Mr. Howard said. I know my stuff and am ahead of my time. But Millie's summary echoes the negatives he listed, and I realize how naïve I've been. Earning a Master's won't earn me a career. Getting a job is outside my control. And I don't like it. Not at all.

My gut feels rock hard with the weight of this realization, then just as quickly, my insides loosen, and I lurch to the kitchen sink before I throw up. Millie is beside me in an instant, rubbing my back and handing me a towel to dry my face. I know another inquiry is coming. She confronted me on the weekend when I felt queasy at the barbecue, and I had admitted pregnancy was possible.

"Have you been to a doctor?" I don't move. "Eva!" Millie's lips pinch together and she slams the drawer. "Listen. This isn't something you can ignore. It won't just go away. For God's sake." She shakes her head, glancing out the window at the children in the backyard, jaw clenched. "Honestly, going off to interviews? When you might have this... this problem to deal with? It's not like you to believe in fairy tales." She blinks, flashing me a look of concerned disbelief.

I lean my elbows on the kitchen counter, tears streaming down my cheeks and my shoulders heaving as the unfairness envelops me. Damn Mr. Howard and his sexist views. Damn that night of liquor and my lapse in judgment. Damn my body for betraying me.

"Oh, honey." Millie pulls me close, patting my trembling back as if I'm a child. "Have you decided what to do?" I slump against her, shuddering, bracing against the inevitable truth that will derail all my careful planning. When my sobbing stops, I step away and crumple into a kitchen chair, laying my head in my arms on the table.

"It's not for sure." My voice is a whisper.

Millie looks at me with raised eyebrows, filling the teakettle as the twins tumble in the back door. "Honey, I'm pretty sure." I sit up, drying my eyes as Millie helps hang their coats. After Eddie and Lizzie each give me a kiss, Millie shoos them into the living room with a snack and turns to me, awaiting my response.

"What... what am I going to do?" I choke out the words, unsure which problem I'm asking about. If I really am with child, I'm in for some upheaval. And if today's interview is any indication, my career dreams might also be pie-in-the-sky thinking.

"Well, first off, you need to stop daydreaming! Go to the doctor." Millie lights the stove. "Apparently, you need a medical declaration to make this real." She thunks the kettle on the burner, mumbling the last sentence under her breath, but it hits me like buckshot.

"And what if I am... am pregnant?" My head droops, the whispered question making me cringe. It's the first time I've said the word pregnant out loud, and I feel my aspirations turn into a tumbleweed.

"Then we figure it out. Together." Millie sits down beside me and puts her hand over mine, but her touch does nothing to ease the rock-hard lump of fear in my stomach.

Two days later I borrow the coupe again, claiming I'm going shopping downtown. Instead, I drive back to Millie's house, where I have an appointment with Miss Weston, a midwife. We've heard she's skilled, kind, and discreet. Millie will claim the visit was for her if anyone sees Miss Weston come by. Already the lies are piling up, and my stomach feels heavy.

While we wait, Millie chatters about the weather and the kids. She needs no response, which is good because my thoughts are a roiling river, rushing and cascading like a waterfall. At exactly ten o'clock, there's a rap from the front hall, and we both freeze. Millie recovers first, answering the door, taking Miss Weston's coat, and making introductions.

"Let's get started, shall we?" Miss Weston is all business after refusing the offer of tea or coffee. I follow her broad backside up the stairs to the guest room, where I sit on the bed, adjusting my skirt, my stomach churning. Her stern demeanour does nothing to ease my anxiety.

"So. When was your last menstrual cycle?" Miss Weston places her brown leather bag on the towels Millie has laid across the comforter. She slides the top lock so the front of the worn case falls open. Time feels like it's slowing and my chest tightens. Metal tools are strapped inside, and glass apothecary bottles tinkle in the silent room. The rushing in my ears increases as I picture how the shiny instruments are used.

"The last week of March," I say after a moment, squirming. She unwinds a tape measure and wraps it around my middle, then jots records with a stubby pencil in a black notebook.

"And the last time you had relations?"

"The fourth of April. It was just once." It's the truth, but there's no reason to say that. My insides quiver and I start to sweat, glancing at the door. I wonder if Miss Weston's steady expression would show surprise if I bolted downstairs.

"And have you been feeling sick? Tired?"

I focus on a knot in the wood floor, shaped like a bunny's head. After another beat, I admit I've been nauseous and throwing up daily for the past two weeks. "I've been tired, of course. But with finals and graduation, that's normal."

Miss Weston's eyes narrow at my rationalization. Then she pushes her palms against her chest, asking whether my breasts are tender. I mimic her probing and wince, finding my bosom sensitive and swollen. My mouth goes dry as I confront another symptom I've been ignoring.

"We'll do an internal exam, to be sure." She motions me toward the bed and I pull down my undergarments, laying as instructed, heels near my bottom. Fighting back tears, I curse my stupidity, wishing I could shrink into the sheets. "You'll feel some pressure. Maybe a little pain." I grind my teeth and close my eyes as Miss Weston examines me. Less than a minute later, she says, "Okay. You can sit up and dress." While I put my stockings on, Miss Weston tells me I'm at least ten weeks pregnant. "The baby will come in early January." Her voice is impossibly calm, her words matter-of-fact. Smoothing my skirt, I stare at her, unable to speak, feeling dizzy and weak. My shoulders slump as the last flicker of hope dims, a dark chill settling in my gut. So it's true. I'm pregnant.

Chapter 7

"This fellow, is he a good man?" Miss Weston breaks the awkward silence, glancing at my bare ring finger. I say nothing, staring at her wide-eyed. "My advice is to marry him, Miss Roberts. As quick as you can."

No! The word echoes over the rush of blood in my ears. Squeezing my eyes closed, I fall onto my side, sagging into the bed, numb to Miss Weston's presence. She packs her bag, snaps it shut, then latches the door with a quiet click. The wooden stairs creak as she descends, followed by the murmur of voices in the foyer. Moments later, the front door thumps closed below. From the next room, the baby wails, the sound echoing my defeat. Miss Weston's question tumbles through my mind. Is the fellow a good man? No, as I've found out, he is decidedly not a good man. Not someone I will go to for help, much less marry.

I moan and curl into a ball, letting my tears flow as Millie moves through the house. She bounds up the stairs to little Flora's increasing howls. After a diaper change, the baby's hiccuping cries settle to a happy gurgle, the rhythmic rasp of the rocking chair on the other side of the wall a soothing lullaby. I wonder if I could do that, if I could be responsible for another human. A thickness fills my throat as shame floods over me again. How could I have been so stupid?

Eventually, Flora finishes nursing with a contented burp. There's a tap on my door and Millie enters, placing the baby next to me on the covers. I sniff, opening my eyes and peering at her tiny features, the sweet scent of powder drifting from her. Millie flops on the bed behind me and wraps an arm over my shoulder. We lay in silence until I croak, "Oh Millie, what am I going to do?"

After a quiet cup of tea, I drive by rote from Millie's, unsure of my next destination. My head pounds and my thoughts distort, like a fun-house mirror, all wobbly and out of proportion. The warm sunshine and darting swallows in the blue sky feel flippant after such horrible news. Fifteen minutes later, I find myself parked on the university campus overlooking Union Bay and Broken Island. On a bluebird day in early May, Thomas had taken me to Sand Point to witness four Douglas World Cruisers leave to attempt the first flights circumnavigating the globe. We had walked back here together, and on that bench, Thomas had proposed. I'm filled with an ache for his quiet presence, calm smile, and easy laugh. He would straighten out my scrambled sentiments. But I bury this craving — being with him is complicated now.

On the car seat beside me lie two small brown books with red canvas spines, left for me by the midwife. One is titled "Prenatal Care", the other "Infant Care". My skin tingles as I flip through the pages. Around me, the campus bustles with jolly students. It's astonishing they can act so normally while my world is crumbling. I toss the books onto the floor of the passenger seat, wrenching the car door open and stomping across the gravel. Pulling my coat tight, I settle into the curved bench slats, gazing over the lake.

My mind wanders back to the night that sparked my current troubles, a brisk moonlit evening in April, with cherry blossoms in full bloom. Thomas and I had a lovely roast duck and beef stroganoff dinner, then moved on to a hazy basement gin mill. Inside, the atmosphere had buzzed with celebration, fuelled not by any special occasion, but by the exhilaration of defying prohibition laws. The bartender recommended a cocktail — a sweet, fiery brown liquid in a coupe glass served with a smouldering rosemary sprig. By the time we left, we had several more, and I felt brilliant, elegant, and carefree.

After I stumbled on the cobblestones on our walk home, Thomas suggested he make me some strong coffee before returning me to my boardinghouse. It would be difficult to hide my warm intoxication from our kind but nice-nelly den mother, Mrs. Murdoch, so I allowed him to lead me up the narrow staircase to his small apartment.

Thomas helped me out of my wool coat, his intense face flushed. He had hung our things, his hands clenching before relaxing by his sides, but hadn't moved toward me. I had met his hazel eyes, a warm thrill tingling every nerve ending. When I ran my palm down his sleeve, squeezing his forearm, I surprised us both with my boldness. Our contact to that point had been as pals, limited to platonic shoves and shoulder bumps.

A slow smile had spread across his features as he tucked a curl behind my ear, accepting my unspoken permission, all thoughts of coffee forgotten. Thomas trailed his fingers, cold from the walk home, down my neck toward my cleavage, his palm resting over my heart. Unable to deny the fluttering in my chest, I had mirrored his movements, placing a quivering hand on his shirt pocket, feeling the pounding rhythm beneath the white linen. It was a moment of carefree bliss.

We explored each other with roaming eyes, until a soft groan broke the silence and Thomas leaned in, his lips sampling the skin of my cheek and neck, leaving moist prints of aching pleasure. The world stood still as I breathed in his scent. It felt natural, exhilarating, and right.

We had stumbled to his bed, just steps away in the tiny apartment, while I fumbled to unbutton his shirt. My trembling fingers drifted over the muscles of his bare chest in a pleasurable fog, and I never wanted it to end. But at that moment, Thomas pulled away, standing stiffly.

"We can't," he'd said, his voice hoarse. "God, I want to, Eva. But we can't. Not like this." Thomas had tucked his shirt, bundled me into my coat, and walked me back to the rooming house, the coffee long forgotten. Inside, a boisterous Friday gathering greeted us, but Thomas hadn't stayed. Barely acknowledging my roommates' pleas to join them, he deposited me on the davenport inside and departed hastily.

I had sat amid the music and laughter in quiet confusion, wondering what I had done to make Thomas turn me down. The rejection hurt and when someone offered me a colourful cocktail, I had accepted, aching to regain my earlier untroubled cheer.

Now, a loud splash and flurry of flapping interrupts my thoughts, as a duck lands, webbed feet skating across the glassy water, leaving a small wake. To my surprise, just thinking of Thomas has my bosom and other parts tingling for his touch. I frown, my mind racing, searching for answers.

I shudder, remembering the rest of that night. The night I met James, a charming tawny-haired alumnus, for the first and last time.

He had handed me a second colourful cocktail and asked why the prettiest lass in the room was alone. Squeezing onto the davenport next to me, he introduced himself over the din of the phonograph, tipping his gaudy trilby at me with a dimpled grin. I had taken the drink and tilted my head to bring him into focus. When he urged me to take him to a quieter spot, I led him out to the garden patio, where we talked about my thesis and sipped on whisky from a flask he pulled from his boot. My elegance and invincibility returned, and when he asked to see my room, I had taken him there.

I should have stopped it, but I said yes. I said yes because Thomas's rejection hurt, and because I felt validated by an older man. But that was fleeting. The next morning, when I squinted around my sunlit room, a dull throb pulsing behind my eyes, James and his showy striped hat were gone. He left an amber trace in a glass by the bedside and a tear in my dress, discarded in a puddle on the carpet. Beneath the cotton covers, my fingers had grazed my unfamiliar nakedness. Outside, birds chirped as the cool fabric rustled and rubbed against my raw nipples. I held my breath, willing the fragmented memories to resurface in the silence.

Closing my eyes, a fleeting image of intertwined limbs and warm skin on mine teased at the edge of my consciousness. I had buried my face in my pillow, where the scent of his cologne lingered and the subtle ache between my thighs bridged gaps in my memory. That week, as I asked my roommates about James, their accounts illustrated a playboy who travelled for work, and when he came to the city, left a trail of broken hearts. With each revelation, a new pang of regret gnawed at me. That night is still a blur, shadows lost in a whisky haze. But the baby inside me now bears witness to it.

I look out across the lake, pushing away the memories and forcing my mind back to good times with Thomas. Our friendship was clear and uncomplicated until we muddled it with courting, and then a proposal and rejection. He was, objectively, my best friend. In class, we've been colleagues for years, partnering and working on projects together through weekends. When we have free time, we find reasons to spend it with each other. If there's good news, it's Thomas I crave to tell. Nothing feels real until I share it with him. When my lovely brother Tony, who survived the Great War, died anyway, it was Thomas who pulled me out of my blackness. When Millie got married and had children, it was Thomas who listened to my tirade against tradition and the suppression of women. So my yearning to debate this pregnancy with Thomas is no surprise. He is my sounding board, my logic, my conscience. Or at least he was.

Everything's changed since that night. It took us weeks to get back to our usual easy banter after our date. And Thomas had ruined things again by bringing me here to propose. I understand he wants more. I felt it too. But he, of all people, should grasp my aversion to marriage. Still, that evening had awakened something powerful and dangerous in me. Nothing threatened my plans to become a successful forester until then. But this all-consuming ache scares me. And if I'm not careful, it could win.

Out on the lake, the duck quacks, its green iridescent head shimmering in the lowering sunlight. More and more in recent days, I've wondered if I should just give in. Tell Thomas I've gotten it wrong, get married, and let him take care of me. He would, even though this child isn't his. But can I ask him to do that?

I shift on the hard wooden bench, leaning my elbows on my knees, holding my head in my hands, and wishing I could turn back the clock. Instead, my thoughts turn to my immediate future. Dealing with Mother and Father this evening, and acting as if nothing has changed, feels impossible. Once again, I curse myself for moving home, which

I only did because my lease at the boarding house was up. As soon as I get a job, I'll leave. My childhood bedroom is a temporary stopover along the way to my glorious life. Although that plan feels decidedly shaky right now.

I sigh, looking skyward. The first timid star emerges on the canvas of muted pastels, transporting me back to Mrs. Murdoch's rooftop. Just blocks away off campus, the girls and I would crawl through the window onto the sloping shingles to sneak a cigarette. We'd watch Seattle's lights twinkle as we gossiped and giggled. And on those rare crisp winter days when the skies dried out, in the distance Mount Rainier would turn into a pink pyramid of snow and rock as the sun set. Now, feeling a need to be surrounded by their familiar, innocent silliness, I decide to call in there. I can't turn back time, but I can pretend, for one last night, none of this is real.

So, instead of facing Mother and Father, I drive the short distance to my old boarding house, where the girls and Mrs. Murdoch greet me with open arms. From the front hall, I phone my parents, telling them I'm staying the night, before joining my former roommates to catch up on their lives. When I finally pull the patchwork quilt over my shoulders, I'm grateful to be alone. An evening of sharing half-truths has exhausted me, and I'm no closer to knowing what to do.

Thomas is the one who can talk me through this mess and I need to decide whether to call him. Whether to tell him this secret. If I do, nothing will ever be the same. But maybe that doesn't matter. Everything has already changed.

By morning, I'm cricked from sleeping on a lumpy trundle bed in the boardinghouse's spare room, but I've decided to talk to Thomas. There are only a few choices left to me. Regardless of which track I run down, I'll need someone to help me execute my decision, and Thomas is the most logical someone. Telling my family is out of the question. Millie is busy with the children and her household. Plus, she's already sentimental about all this.

So it has to be Thomas. Deciding on this action fills me with a sudden lightness. Whatever I've done to him, no matter how he feels right now, he will help me. I'm sure of that.

I wash up in the shared bathroom, but nothing I do can conceal the dark half-moons under my bloodshot eyes. Turning away from the hazy mirror, I unsuccessfully smooth the clothes I slept in, then go to the front hall phone. Pressing the receiver to my ear, I ask for Elliot 9365 and wait until I'm connected with Thomas.

"Hello?" His greeting is abrupt, and businesslike, with murmurs swirling in the background. I bite my lip, imagining him on the fourth floor of his father's downtown office.

"Thomas?" My voice is timid and my stomach quivers. Maybe this is a mistake.

"Eva? Is that you?" He sounds so hopeful that tears flood my eyes, and I sag against the wall, unable to form a response. "Are you there?" I blink, swallow, and stand up straight. We haven't spoken in over two weeks. Thomas and I haven't been apart this long since last summer when he went up to Canada to work for his father. His voice puts a weight in my chest and I'm not sure if my reaction is because I've missed him or because I dread what I need to tell him. "Eva? Are you there?"

"Can I see you today?" I ask when I'm finally able to speak.

"Today? Sure. Of course!" Thomas's voice rises to an eager half-laugh. "Downtown okay?" I say yes, thinking we can go for a walk, but he continues. "Fine. I'll make a six o'clock reservation at the Olympic."

My plan wasn't to sit through an entire meal with Thomas, but I don't have the energy to argue with him — he'll need to eat after work. "Alright then. See you tonight."

"Tonight. And Eva?" The line crackles in my silence. "I'm glad you called. See you soon."

I hang up the receiver without responding, the tension in my shoulders releasing a little. Thomas will make things better. I hate to admit it, but he always does.

CHAPTER 8

When I walk into the Olympic at six o'clock, Thomas is waiting for me in the lobby, leaning against a marble Corinthian column. I stop, taking in the sight of him, and a subtle warmth spreads through me, both comforting and unsettling. With a deep breath, I move to join him. The air in the opulent surroundings is heavy with the scent of polished wood and fine perfume. When he sees me, Thomas beams, and then his eyebrows draw together as he observes the pale tension in my face. But Thomas doesn't pry. Without a word, he offers me the elbow of his pin-striped suit, and I take it. For an instant, he places his hand over mine, squeezing it, gazing at me with such intense care that a lump forms in my throat. I lower my eyes to the terrazzo floor, nudging him toward dinner, and glad that he hasn't tried to greet me with anything more.

We're soon seated in a private high-backed corner booth, and Thomas carries the conversation until we've ordered. He shares office antics and updates on our classmates. When he waits for my input, my answers are clipped syllables, stilted by the distraction of the news I must share in moments. We're both halfway through our dinners when Thomas puts his fork and knife down, dabs his lips with his napkin, and sits back.

"You're not yourself. What's happened? Was it your interview with Howards?" His summer tan brings out the green in his hazel eyes, which are peering at me with such concern that I wince. He thinks the cause of my malaise is as benign as a work-related rejection.

I swallow, but decide it's not yet time to ruin the evening. Instead, I share my experience with Mr. Howard between bites. Thomas leans in, urging the details from me. When I recount the disappointment, his smile weakens, and he nods sadly.

"But you're not surprised," I say with sudden clarity, "that Mr. Howard won't hire me." Thomas picks up his utensils again, concentrating on cutting a thin slice from his perfectly grilled steak. He clears his throat, fumbling for words.

"It's going to be hard... for you to get hired in a position... you deserve." He flashes me a smile that doesn't reach his eyes. "I'm sorry." Thomas's pained expression shows his regret. Not because it's his fault, but because the situation is so unfair. He's offered to put in a word with his father, but I've refused the help. If I'm going to get a job, it needs to be on my own merits. Not because of a favour. Still, his empathy now releases the floodgates. Just like before his proposal made things awkward, I vent my frustrations at the state of the world. And just like before, he makes me feel heard.

"It's good to see you so animated," Thomas says, a moment later with a gentle chuckle, as my tirade trickles to a close. He leans back to let the bow-tied server clear our plates. I swallow hard, knowing my news needs to be shared before we order dessert and coffee. When the server leaves us, we both speak at once.

"Look, Thomas —"

"Eva, I —" Thomas waves his hand across the table, letting me go first. I drop my head, closing my eyes, steeling myself for his reaction.

"I'm pregnant." Without a preamble, I blurt the words that have been tumbling through my mind since yesterday. I can't look up, my stomach clenching and nausea rising. Tears well behind my eyelids and I let them roll down my face, my lips quivering. "And I need help." My last sentence is a whisper. I grip the white linen napkin under the table, rolling and unrolling it, my teeth grinding. My cheeks burn with shame and my insides crumple. I've never felt so small.

Around us, in the dining room, the world continues. Jazz drifts from the piano at the entrance, laughter erupts from a table nearby, and the bartender shakes a dry julep. I flinch when Thomas touches my chin, wiping a tear with his thumb. He forces my head up, and I look at him. He's biting his bottom lip, blinking rapidly, the colour draining from his face. I'm not sure what I see there. Shock, definitely — but also pain and confusion.

Thomas pulls his gaze from mine, his jaw set, signalling for the check from the server behind me.

"Let's get out of here." His voice is thick. I dab the tears from my cheeks, snuffling. Thomas helps me into my coat and leads me through the sparkling lobby, a supportive arm wrapped around my waist, guiding me out onto the cool sidewalk. He steers me down Union Street toward the waterfront. Twice, as we pause to let cars pass on the cobblestones, he starts to speak but cuts himself off. The quiet between us holds a primal tension. When Thomas's stiff stride falters, I look up at him, expecting he'll finally ask who the father is, but he just pinches his lips tight and propels me forward again. I imagine our roles reversed, imagine how I'd feel if Thomas told me he slept with another woman, and a cold jolt runs through me. This curveball must be a kick in the stomach.

Ten minutes later, he settles me onto a bench overlooking the bustle of Elliot Bay. He kneels in front of me, clutching my hands in his, and looks up, pleading.

"Marry me, Eva." I stare down at him, blinking rapidly. This is not a response I expected from him. Bewilderment. Anger. Blame. But not another offer of wedlock. He's completely misread the help I'm asking for. I should have brought my little red notebook. Showing him the table of pros and cons would save me a lengthy explanation.

"I can't marry you!" I try to pull my hands away, but Thomas's grip is firm. Why does he still not understand this? I'm not ready to give up everything and be a wife.

"Why?" Thomas's question is gruff, his voice ragged. "Explain. Are you seeing someone else? Is the... the father... doing the right thing by you?" His eyes are moist, darting, unable to settle on mine.

"No. There's nothing like that. And I haven't seen the fellow since... well... since that... night." I untangle my hand from his, staring at him with a painful lump in my throat. "But getting married isn't the kind of help I'm asking you for." He carves his fingers through his hair, still avoiding my gaze. Then his expression softens, and he sits back on his haunches, looking at me with a determined nod.

"Okay, let's take things step by step. What do you need? How can I help?" His features still reflect puzzled unease, but his voice is now steady.

"Well..." I hesitate, placing a palm on my belly. "One option... one option is getting—"

"No!" Thomas interrupts, pushing away onto his heels, his jaw slack with understanding. He grips the first bench plank now, on either side of my legs, white-knuckled. "No. Not that. I won't help you do that. Not after what happened to Mel." He lurches upright, pacing a patch of dirt. "No back-alley butcher is touching you. No way!" He covers his face with a shaky hand, remembering two years ago, as am I. For weeks, no one knew whether his sweet sister would survive the infection caused by the 'butcher' that ended her pregnancy.

"Then a maternity home. Help me find one. Drive me there. Cover for me until I get back."

"Cover for you? When's the baby due?" he asks, incredulous. When I whisper in January, Thomas's eyes widen again. "Are you delusional? Honestly Eva! How do you expect to keep this from everyone? And for that long? What about Christmas? It's impossible." He turns away, sputtering in disbelief as a mournful steam whistle drifts up from the train tracks.

Thomas shakes his head, gripping his temples between his palms. Shifting restlessly, he gazes over the waterfront. In the chilly silence, the roast duck I had at dinner tumbles in my stomach. I've never seen Thomas so agitated, and it's daunting. When he turns back to me, his tone is softer again.

"You should tell your family. They'll understand. They need to. You can't do this on your own."

"No," I say, shaking my head. "No! I won't tell them. And it can work. We can sort out a cover story. I just need some help. Your help." My voice rises as I draw myself up to full height, wrapping my coat around me and lifting my chin toward him in defiance. We rarely disagree, and his reluctance now is frustrating. Thomas swallows hard, his gaze never leaving mine. He steps closer and tucks a loose strand of hair behind my ear.

"I love you. You know that, right?" His touch and his tone are soft, sending a shiver through me. But this is territory we've covered and I say nothing. "Why not just marry me?"

"Because I want to have a career." I push past him, fighting back tears and focusing on the blinking lights of a ship in the harbour. "Because I want to make a difference in these forests. And do the work I've trained for. Is that too much to ask?" I'm almost shouting as I crumple back onto the bench. The familiar pressure of disappointment makes my heart feel like it's shrinking and I can't help finishing my thought. "It's so easy for you! You study and then just go get a job with your family. Simple. It isn't fair." I sound like a petulant child, and I drop my chin to my chest, eyes wet, ashamed of my outburst. But it isn't fair. That James fellow is out there somewhere, living his life, without a care. And I don't begrudge Thomas his advantages, but mixed in with my happiness for him is a deep envy. My life would be much simpler if, instead of pursuing my passion, I studied commerce and went into the car business with my father. But the thought of spending my days selling shiny machines from a gravel lot makes me shudder.

Thomas is quiet for a while. A steam engine puffs and muffled shouts of dock workers drift from the wharf below. Then he grunts, slumping onto the bench beside me.

"Alright." Thomas puts a hand on my hunched back, rubbing it. "I'll help. In whatever way you want. Alright?" I'm a little surprised he doesn't argue with me more. My tirade isn't entirely true or fair. But I'm glad he's focused on helping me rather than correcting me. Maybe he sees how close I am to becoming unglued. "Just promise me you won't do what Mel did? No back-alley butchers, alright?"

"I promise," I say. "Thank you." His agreement fills me with gratitude and hope. Facing this ordeal without him feels impossible.

He bumps my shoulder with his and says with an exasperated smile, "You sheba's are wearing me out." This coaxes a shaky laugh from me. After his bursts of anger, I'm relieved he's trying to lighten the mood.

Wrapping my arms around Thomas's biceps, I lean my cheek against his shoulder. He drops his face atop my head, as worn out as I am by our debate. We sigh simultaneously, which draws soft chuckles from both of us. What I'm going to do is still unclear. But with Thomas by my side, there will be no more pretending. We'll tackle it like a biology lab, step by step. Together.

Chapter 9

The following Saturday morning, Thomas calls to ask if he can drop by for a visit. At first, I refuse, asking him to tell me his news on the phone. I don't want my parents to get the wrong idea, but Thomas insists he comes by and the urgency in his voice makes me curious, so I finally relent.

"It's a swell day out there. You can take me for a walk around the neighbourhood," I say.

At the stroke of two, Thomas arrives as planned. He greets my parents in the foyer, managing my mother's rapt attention and my father's work questions with ease. They couldn't show more eagerness if they clipped a dog collar around his neck. Cringing and gritting my teeth, I feign ignorance of my parents' attempts to showcase their single daughter. Dragging Thomas outside, we stroll shoulder to shoulder down the tree-lined street toward Volunteer Park and the cemetery.

"How are you feeling?" Thomas looks down at me and a flush heats my cheeks. It's odd to share how my body's reacting to the clusters of cells growing inside it. But he's witnessed my nausea, and I know he won't relent until I give him an answer. So I do.

"Better, actually. The morning sickness is gone. Just tired." I pull a thread from the cuff of my blouse, unable to meet his eyes. "So what's so important you had to drive all the way out here?" I wonder whether Thomas found a maternity home. He said he would do some discreet inquiring. Hopefully, it's good news he wants to deliver in person.

"I'm getting transferred," he says. "To Canada. In a week." I stop mid-stride and turn to face him, as stunned as if he'd told me he's going to China. Instead of helping me, he's running away. "You should come with me." His gaze is unwavering, his words calm. It takes me a moment to process what he's said.

"What? That's crazy!" I gape at him, feeling light-headed. "I thought maybe you'd found a maternity home for me to go to." My voice is a hoarse whisper.

"Oh, Eva." He shakes his head. "That option won't work. How would you explain going away for six months? A trip? A job? I just don't see how you'd be able to keep this quiet. Your parents ask too many questions. You have no money for travel. And if you say you got a job, your father would use it as an excuse for a road trip and come visit you." Thomas's expression is tender and kind, a familiar look that echoes the countless times he's explained difficult concepts at school. My legs are restless and I turn on my heel, looking down at the sidewalk, moving toward the park again. I don't want to hear it, but his logic is sound.

"I'm going back to run the logging camp I worked in last summer. You should come with me." Thomas walks beside me. "Father needs me up there, but I've been refusing to go because I couldn't... wouldn't... leave you behind." Clearing his throat again, he glances at me. "And he was hoping I'd take a wife with me. Wants to test a theory that men with wives and kids will reduce turnover up there. Hard to turn a profit when you're always training greenhorns." Thomas pauses, perhaps realizing he's not selling the place he wants me to uproot to. He forces a smile. "So you see, this arrangement helps my family, too." I stare back, trying to make sense of what he's saying. "Honestly Eva, I've thought it through. If you truly want to hide this mistake, let me marry you." I grimace and shake my head, feeling exhausted. This plan means keeping the baby.

"What exactly would we do? When?" I ask. Focusing on immediate details feels more manageable than contemplating a decision to raise a child.

"We'd get married early next week, at the courthouse. Then travel north the following Monday. No one will suspect anything. Just a sudden transfer pushing up the timeline of our love story. It's a good cover." He speaks in absolutes, glancing my way with every other step.

The past week has been unbearable. All I want to do is escape through unconscious hours, but I've hardly slept. Feeling trapped and lost, I hate who I am right now. I resent Millie for her contentment when she fully deserves it. I buy new clothes to get a brief burst of delight, when I know in a few weeks they won't fit. And I fear the condemned life a child would lead if I abandoned it at a maternity home.

"And the baby? We... keep it?" The question catches in my throat. But if we do this... this... outlandish thing, we need to understand one another. Thomas stops, turning toward me, reaching for both my hands. His hazel eyes hold mine, his eyebrows close together before he responds with a slow nod.

"We raise it. As ours." He squeezes my fingers, his face relaxed. I understand, in that moment, Thomas forgives my blunder and my heart swells.

I've imagined a future married to Thomas, and it's not all bad. Maybe it's a mistake to refuse him. Saying yes to him means I give up a career, at least for now. If I say no again and he transfers, I'll be left here alone. As he pointed out, hiding this baby from my parents on my own will be nearly impossible. The thought of getting caught being dishonest makes my stomach lurch.

We stroll side-by-side, off Prospect Street and into the park. The concourse is hot and the scent of wilted grass and charcoal cookouts wafts from the reservoir area. Boys drop down the steep metal slide and teenagers splash with gleeful shouts in the water. The scene turns my thoughts to the worn photo of my young brother's mischievous grin, frozen in the winter snapshot taken by my father from this very spot. Tony was so proud of his skating ability, even back then. This neighbourhood and this city regularly remind me of Tony's loss. Leaving Seattle might ease that. Tears well, and I avert my gaze.

Nearby, wooden teeter-totters sit abandoned and a group of mothers lean on the fulcrum, gossiping while they watch their young charges. An icy wave washes over me as I imagine myself as one of them. I don't want to be a wife and mother like traditionalist ladies. Again, remorseful fury engulfs me for allowing this to happen.

Ahead of us on the path, a small child in a bonnet drops her mother's hand, pointing a chubby finger at the ground. The girl looks up as we approach.

"Bug!" she says. "Where going?" Glad for the distraction, I hitch my skirt to crouch beside the child.

"It's not a bug. It's an ant." I examine its red and black body. "A thatching ant. *Formica obscuripes*. And its home is probably over in the bushes. They like the forest." The girl takes in this information with wide eyes, her tiny lips forming a solemn O.

"Thatch-ant," she says, crawling on all fours to follow the insect. "Go home." She focuses her full attention on the ant's purposeful gait, and I watch, wondering how old she is. Thomas chuckles from overhead, and I stand, my gaze locked on the girl, imagining her as mine. A year from now, we could have a daughter. Or a son. The thought leaves me breathless.

"Are you sure you don't want to crawl along with her?" He watches the mother rush over and scoop up the child, scolding her for soiling her stockings. When he turns back to me, Thomas takes a deep breath. "I love you. You'll be a great mother." His fingertips skim my jawline, but I spin away, striding from him, my skin tingling.

I still can't say yes. You're supposed to love your husband. And he's just Thomas. My very good friend Thomas. And although we've proven that with enough liquor, our bodies match well, I am not sure I love him. How do you even know?

Thomas catches up and we stroll in a heavy silence until we leave the park and enter the cemetery, passing between two stone entrance pillars. Leading me into the shade under a large fir tree, he leans me against the rough trunk, planting his palms on either side of me. His musky amber cologne fills me as I catch my breath. My fingers ache to touch the stubbled skin of his square jaw and my chest flutters. Is this love? Or just nature's evolutionary forces?

"Look, you stubborn, gorgeous girl. I want to give you a happy life. I think this move to Vancouver Island is the best choice for you. For both of us." His voice cracks with emotion, his eyes bright. Then he takes my hands in his and gets down on one knee in the grass.

"What are you doing?" I glance around uneasily, biting my lip to suppress a smile. This romantic gesture amid our current negotiations feels silly.

"If I convince you to come along as my wife, you'll also need a believable proposal story." Thomas is right. Saying yes means Millie and Mother will ask for every detail. "This is the last time I'll ask," he says, and beams up at me. "Now, will you marry me?"

CHAPTER 10

An icy chill runs through me as I gaze past him, where rows of headstones stand erect. I imagine a carved epitaph: HERE REST EVA'S DREAMS. Wetting my lips, I look down at Thomas, who has pulled a simple gold band, set with a cut diamond, from his pocket. The same ring he offered me two months ago.

"Fine. Yes." I smile and shake my head, laughing. "I mean, yes, of course. Yes!" What choice do I have? How bad can it be?

Thomas slips the ring on my finger and kisses the glinting stone before he stands. He hugs me close, chuckling in my ear. As I breathe in his scent, a sense of lightness fills me. Yet when I examine the glittering stone on my hand, regret floods my thoughts.

Two weeks after our courthouse ceremony, on my last afternoon in Seattle, Millie sits on my bed, her gaze fixed on the faded fabric of my trousers as I fold them into my trunk. She leans in, fingering the rivets on the brass band edging. With every bit of preparation, my departure becomes more concrete. Millie has been a steadfast presence, conveying a medley of emotions — sadness, anticipation, and a subtle hint of envy for my impending adventure.

"I knew Thomas was sweet on you. And I'm so glad he persisted. But I still can't believe you're going," Millie says now, her lips pouting. "And without a proper wedding? It's just so crazy!" I smile, remembering that I used the same word when Thomas suggested this whole thing.

Today her conventional views make me feel appreciative, rather than annoyed. Whatever Millie's flaws, she's always supportive, but maybe that's because she doesn't know the whole truth. Even before I saw the midwife, she asked who fathered the baby. I had been evasive, never giving her a direct answer, which I'm thankful for now. Once we were engaged, I admitted to Millie that Thomas proposed once before and, without any affirmation from me, she's concluded the baby is his. Though it pains me to have a lie between us, I won't be correcting her.

"You know I hate weddings," I say. "A wedding wouldn't have been about me. It would have been about everyone else, anyway." As I embrace life with Thomas, I see more positives, and not having to plan a marriage celebration with Mother is a huge plus.

"But your mother is devastated. Cheated out of a gala." Millie shakes her head in mock sympathy.

"She's just thankful her old-maid daughter finally got hitched!" I chuckle and fold a sweater into the trunk.

"That's true," Millie says, grinning. We both know by the time my mother tells the tale at her country club, she will embellish this union into a prestigious adventure. And she'll forgive me for skipping a ritzy shindig because of Thomas's family's illustrious reputation among Seattle's elite.

My parents had been shocked when Thomas and I returned from our walk in the park engaged. Mother's delight over my new diamond had quickly turned to dismay when Thomas explained his transfer and our accelerated timeline. My father had given me a quizzical look and a knowing glance before offering his congratulations. I wonder whether he's guessed my mistake, but everyone has accepted our cover story, welcoming Thomas into the family with open arms. Mother always hides her emotions well, and while I wouldn't describe her demeanour as happy, she's certainly relieved, and maybe even pleased, that I'm now married.

Millie hands me two pairs of sturdy leather boots, her nose wrinkling. "No one will even know you're a woman if you wear all this rugged stuff up there." But sensible clothes are a necessity. There won't be pavement or cobblestones or lawns where I'm going. And while it's difficult for me to imagine such a place, it's nearly impossible for someone like Millie. She's spent her entire life surrounded by glass and brick, finding nature creepy and dangerous — to be avoided.

"I'm looking forward to the change." Placing a palm absently on my middle, I realize it's true. The logical part of me recognizes the difficulties of isolation. Amid the current attention and bustle, I yearn for a place without demands. "The quiet will be good for me." I beam over at Millie.

"You look good now. Glowing." She tilts her head, teasing. "Babies will do that to you."

"Hush, now!" I put a finger to my lips and shake my head. My mother must not hear this kind of talk.

"No. No, I'm not pregnant," I say in a loud voice, just in case Mother has come upstairs without me noticing. "But I suppose I could be," I glance at the open bedroom door, flashing Millie a mischievous grin, rolling my eyes. She squeals and clutches my forearm, playing along.

"Oh Eva, I hope you are pregnant. You'll love being a mother. It's the best. It really is." Her voice is sticky sweet — she's a terrible actress, but I give her a quick hug, a lump in my throat. I'm going to miss this lovely girl. Our exchange turns my thoughts to Thomas, which puts a fluttery sensation in my chest.

After a frill-free private ceremony at the courthouse last week, we had sat through a stiff dinner with both sets of parents at the Olympic. From the heads of the table, our fathers toasted our union with brief speeches. Mother was silent, a tight-lipped smile plastered to her face as she nodded and hung onto every word the men said. Thomas's mother was upbeat, welcoming me into their family with questions and small talk. She seemed genuinely pleased with the match, and if the absence of a wedding disappointed her, she hid it well. While walking to the restaurant, she confided Thomas has been smitten for some time. "I'm so glad you found each other, dear," she had whispered, squeezing my forearm.

As soon as it was politely possible, Thomas and I excused ourselves to our opulent stateroom up on the twelfth floor. There, Thomas helped me out of my coat and hung it. Then he'd tucked a hair behind my ear and trailed his fingers down my neck until his palm rested on my chest, awakening every nerve ending. I had placed my hand on his shirt pocket with a laugh, replaying our truncated evening from months before.

His heart pounded beneath the crisp cotton as his dark eyes locked on mine, and when he leaned in to kiss my collarbone, it was my groan that broke the silence. Thomas was eager, but gentle and attentive. With my head clear, I committed every detail of his muscled body to memory, wanting fresh memories to replace the hollow of my rotten first time. Each look, each touch, carried both the comfort of our friendship and the excitement of exploration.

Much later, we had lain curled together, spent and complete. Nibbling on room service, we talked long into the night, imagining our future days, months, and years. It was a night I'll always cherish and thinking about it now floods my chest with a pleasurable ache.

"You'll need to write. And come back for Christmas." Millie's voice breaks through my reverie and she sniffs into a handkerchief. I promise to mail letters, sliding the bottom interior tray into the steamer trunk, but I disregard Millie's reference to Christmas. By the holidays, I'll be almost eight months pregnant. Remembering Millie's bulging belly and aching feet at that stage, I'm not certain we'll travel back — it's a long trek. While modesty doesn't concern me, the size of my belly by Christmas will certainly announce that I conceived well before my wedding day.

I sigh, deciding to take the changes day by day. My worries are endless and they'll crush me if I let them take hold. We fold and stack the last of my blouses, sweaters, skirts, and outerwear into the trunk. Then we arrange my stockings, undergarments, and toiletries in the floral fabric-lined sections of the top tray.

"Where is this place again? Near Vancouver?" Millie has never been interested in geography beyond the layout of a department store.

"It's called Camp 2. That's where the house is." Before he left, I had asked Thomas why they only gave the place a number, not a name, but he just shrugged, saying the accountants had numbered the camps. No one else was sentimental enough to rename a temporary workplace. "And it's not 'near' Vancouver. It's 300 miles northwest, on an island. A big island." I say now. Millie has no concept of distances, so I add, "That's ten times as far as from here to Everett." She frowns.

"That'll be a long drive," she says, but I don't correct her. I'll mail a map when I get there, so she can see that there's no way to *drive* from here to Camp 2. My trip will be by rail, steamship, boat, and something Thomas calls a speeder. I've never travelled very far alone, but have visualized each leg of my itinerary. While we initially thought we'd make the trip together, Thomas soon agreed cramming my preparation into a single week was an unnecessary stress. Especially with all the arrangements Mother insisted on before sending me off.

When he returned from his work placement there last summer, Thomas entertained me and our classmates with tales of how rugged the bush camp had been. The stories of mouse-ridden bunkhouses and buzzing outhouses had made us all laugh, not to mention his descriptions of the rough and tumble logging crew, all with colourful nicknames. If he had known he'd be bringing me there, Thomas wouldn't have shared the most sordid details. He left with a promise to prepare a tidy bunkhouse for us, looking relieved to get our new home ready for my arrival.

"There," I say now, slamming the black lid of the trunk and clicking the brass latches closed. I turn the centre lock and thread the key onto the silver chain around my neck for safekeeping. "Give me a hand." We each take a leather handle and wrestle the trunk down the stairs and onto the front porch, lining it up beside its twin and two milk crates of my spruce tree seedling specimens.

The other trunk contains my biology field guides, the two red-spined pregnancy books from the midwife, and our household items. I'm not one of those girls who embroidered doilies and filled a hope chest with linens. So instead of planning my wedding, Mother has taken me shopping to outfit my new home. She bought us enough sheets, pillowcases, towels, tablecloths, and napkins to outfit a four-bedroom house, most of which didn't fit into the trunk. But it gave her a bit of pleasure I couldn't deny.

Now, as we turn to go back inside, a car door slams on the street. Father climbs out of a sparkling emerald green four-door, striding along the walk, beaming.

"How are my favourite young ladies?" He heaves up the front steps, greeting us each with a peck on the cheek. "All set?" His eyes hold mine and my vision blurs. I'm going to miss this man. My protector and champion. I wrap my arms around his middle, leaning my cheek against his wool suit jacket. Father clears his throat and pats my back.

"Let's go have supper, shall we?" His voice sounds falsely bright and his smile quivers as he starts inside.

Dinner is rowdy, with Millie's family stacked around the dining table with us. Leo, Millie's husband, makes jovial conversation with Father, the twins need constant reprimanding, and the baby is fussy. Without these distractions, the gloom of this last meal would have stifled me. Mother barely touches her food, and I push the chicken around my plate, doing my best to smile and join the discussion before the inevitable tearful goodbyes.

Much later, after undressing in my childhood bedroom for the last time, I tuck under the lavender-scented eiderdown, imagining my surroundings a week from now. By then, I'll take my meals at a rough-hewn crew table, in a quiet wilderness, far from this modern world. My stomach knots and my pulse quickens as I consider the commitment I've made. Lifting my chin, I grit my teeth with a slight head shake. I will not let this fail. I've never failed anything. Yet.

Chapter 11

Early the next morning, Father and I drive toward King Street Station, rehashing the twins' anecdotes from the night before with easy chuckles. But once we catch our first glimpse of the city skyline, electric lights twinkling in the dawn, a heavy silence engulfs the cab. We enter downtown, soon passing the grand stone entrance of the Olympic, and a flush fills me as I think of Thomas. By tomorrow night, I'll be with him again. The cobblestones rumble beneath us, and beyond the city's silhouette, the bright pink sunrise tints Elliot Bay a glossy shade of purple. At that moment, I can see why some call this cosmopolitan hub beautiful. Seattle is showing me her best colours today, and I wonder when I'll be back.

As we approach Pioneer Square, a street car jangles, a few early morning passengers hanging off the side. I stare up at the dark fifty-foot totem at the small park's centre, stiffening. The landmark has always made me feel as if something was amiss. Crimson rhododendrons bloom along the wrought-iron fence, and under the park's glass-crowned pergola, a hobo sleeps on a street car bench. Years ago, our class came here on a grade-school field trip, learning the ancient legends the pole depicts. The stack of carved animals is painted with accents of red and blue-green, and I try to recall the lesson. But all I remember is the confusion I felt as our teacher explained the folklore. Even as a child, my logical outlook didn't agree with symbolic allegories.

As we drive by, I look past my father at the curved beak of the totem's bottom raven. I suddenly remember the glowering bird represents parental love and something to do with giving the moon and the stars. Father catches my eye, offering a soft smile and patting my knee before downshifting around the corner. We leave the totem behind, slowing for a delivery wagon, and the horses' hooves clack on the cobblestones as they balk at our car. The driver nods and Father returns an apologetic wave. My throat thickens and I blink back tears. I still can't imagine being away from him.

We're nearing the train station now, and I'm glad for every extra moment with my father as he slows to admire the white terracotta façade of the Smith Tower, looming ahead of us. Recently, a one-armed stunt man parachuted from the top. And years ago, we would detour our family outings to mark the construction progress as the steel-frame skeleton became the tallest building west of the Mississippi. After watching the cranes and high-flying riveters, Tony had dreamed of becoming a steelworker.

On a warm July day, a decade ago, Father had surprised us all with a ride up to the Chinese Room on the building's opening day. We stood in line for over an hour before entering one of the Smith Tower's eight high-speed elevators, the ornate metal gate clanking closed behind us. I had been nervous, taking Tony's hand in the crowded wood-panelled carriage that whisked us skyward. It carried the faint scent of oil, polish, and ladies' perfume, swaying as it pressed into my feet. The uniformed operator ran the mechanical wonder's brass controls while explaining the functions of the cables and lift motors.

My brother had been grinning with excitement, squeezing my fingers as the building's blue mosaic floor numbers flashed by outside the elevator doors, counting up to the 35th. The Chinese Room, with its ornately carved teak ceilings and blackwood furniture, was as stunning as the view. But the visit cured Tony's dream of being an iron worker. His fear of heights had hit him as the city sprawled below us. My chest warms as I remember how he inched along the observation deck, our roles reversed as he gripped my hand for courage. The memory of that day with Tony is like catching a fleeting glimpse of sunlight through rain. I ache to see my brother's smile and feel the tenderness in his teasing just one more time. A glance over at Father's pinched expression confirms he, too, has Tony on his mind.

Now, as the twelve-storey clock tower of King's Station comes into view, I wonder whether I'll miss the reminders this city prompts. It hurts every time Tony's memory surfaces, but I also never want to forget him. His faded photo is still safely tucked inside the last page of my notebook. I glance at the haversack by my feet, vowing to frame the snapshot once I get to my new home.

Father's shiny red Master Six growls as we pull under the huge suspended entrance awning, and I shudder along with the engine as it shuts down, already bracing for this goodbye. We hop out onto the concrete pavement, unloading the luggage to the curb. I drop my haversack to the ground by my trunks and smooth my skirt, then peer down into the wooden milk crates of Sitka seedlings. So far, they look unharmed by the trip, their roots secured in soil-filled soup cans and held upright by the thick wire grid meant to hold half-pint bottles.

I wait for Father to park, wishing I could skip ahead onto the northbound train and avoid another emotional scene. After two days of farewells to friends and family, I'm drained. Each sendoff carries a weight, made heavier by the half-truths I have to keep track of. It's all left me feeling like a worn book, with its pages turned too quickly. I fear this last goodbye with Father will crack my spine. The unspoken lie of my pregnancy drags at my heart like an anchor. I've never lied to him. Maybe I should just come clean about our cover-up. Father would understand. But if I tell him now, he'll be obligated to tell Mother, and she'll be impossible to live with if anything threatens our family's reputation.

When he returns, Father flags down a porter with a luggage cart. We follow him inside and my gaze lingers on the mosaic floor inlay of a compass rose, guiding me north. We stride across the cavernous waiting room toward the ticket counter, our steps clicking on the gleaming terrazzo. Overhead, the vaulted ceilings soar in a sea of decorative plasterwork and ornamental mouldings. A station agent checks my trunks and promises they'll take good care of my "little trees", then slides a ticket over the mahogany counter. I turn to my father, glancing at the clock.

"I should let you get to work," I say. It's hours before the car lot opens, but dragging out this farewell feels unbearable. "I'd like to go to the ladies' waiting room until they board us." I have no desire to spend time there, but Mother had raved about the luxurious room and she'll be glad I went. Father clears his throat, taking off his hat.

"Well..." His eyes shine and he brushes a fingertip against my cheek. To avoid his sad smile, I wrap my arms around his middle. Father hugs me tight as I suppress tears, my cheek crushed against his crisp shirt, breathing in his cologne and tobacco. We stand intertwined and unmoving while the crowd bustles past us. Now is my last chance to come clean, to explain I'm carrying his grandchild, to leave here with a clear conscience.

But before I can say anything, Father leans close, whispering in my ear, "This won't be easy, my girl. But I know you'll do well."

He gently pushes me back to arm's length, hands clamped on my shoulders, eyeing me. I can't read his expression. For just an instant, his gaze drops to my belly before he locks eyes with me again. "And if... if you... or Thomas... need anything, anything at all, you send us a telegram, okay?" He pauses again. "And find yourself a doctor up there, alright? Promise me?" Now I'm certain my father knows I'm pregnant. He wouldn't mention my health otherwise, and it's no surprise he's guessed. Father is always the first to notice subtle changes in me, and I'm filled with a surge of deep appreciation. I give him a small nod before burying my face against his chest again, hugging him hard.

"I promise." The words come out sounding strangled. They're not the confirmation his look is asking for, but I know he saw the silent answer in my expression. This bond I share with Father will be sorely missed. He's a core part of my identity, and I wonder how I'll navigate life without a regular dose of his wisdom. His confidence always gives me courage and makes me feel capable. I sniff and step away. "I'll write. We'll continue our Sunday debates in our letters. They'll take months to finish, but that's okay." My lips twitch, imagining a slow-motion argument, and Father manages a chuckle.

"Write to both of us. This is a difficult time for your mother, too. She's going to miss you terribly." He shuffles his feet, fiddling with his hat, his face tightening. I doubt my absence will affect Mother much. Nothing ever does.

As I hitch my haversack onto my shoulder, I glance up at the clock, and when I turn back to Father, his eyes are wet. He's only cried once, at Tony's service, and I pretend I don't notice.

"So. See you later, okay?" I force a smile, my vision blurring. Father nods, placing his hat on his head, leaning over to kiss my cheek. He winces and swallows hard, then turns away, saying nothing more.

Halfway to the station doors, his heavy-footed walk falters. I expect him to turn and give me a last wave, but he squares his shoulders and continues, leaving the building without looking back.

Blinking away tears, I take a deep breath and head toward the ladies' waiting room. I choose a table in the corner, pulling out two of the heavy oak Craftsman rockers. The seats are richly upholstered and I place my bag on one of them, fingering the tight row of intricately stamped pewter clavos surrounding the soft chocolate-coloured leather. Mother would love these elegant details, and for a heartbeat, I wish she were here. But she would taint the moment with her bitter aftertaste in a jiffy. I sigh and sink into a rocker, leaning my head back to admire the ornate coffered ceiling and more of the glistening electric chandeliers.

The hustle of people has surrounded me for days, and I'm grateful to be alone. Because of our wordless exchange, Father now knows part of the truth. The tight knot of deception in my stomach has loosened, and a thread of excitement finally runs through me. This will be an adventure like no other. Through the tall, two-storey window, I watch the steady stream of passengers milling by outside, hurrying to their office jobs. Anticipation stirs in my belly as I imagine the next leg of my journey. I smile, gently biting my lip. Heading north holds a sparkling appeal.

CHAPTER 12

The ladies' waiting room is quiet, and its stodgy splendour soon bores me. I feel restless and eager to start my journey, so taking my bag, I walk toward the terminal. Observing my fellow travellers with curiosity, I play "Where are they from & what do they do for a living" as I go. Tony and I invented the game when we were teens. It would begin whenever we were bored and in a crowd, by one of us calling out a location and occupation. Then the other would make their guess and we'd argue our positions.

We rarely found out if the candid conclusions we drew about the folks around us were correct, but getting it right was never the point. Our game helped pass the time when waiting for a train or stage show, debating for sport. Father would chuckle and join in, while Mother shushed us, hissing at our poor manners.

The last time we'd played was before Tony volunteered, waiting for one of Chaplin's vaudeville shows at the Grand Theatre. Tony had elbowed me in the ribs, discreetly lifting his chin at a sharply dressed chap and his opulent socialite, putting the game in action.

"San Francisco. Import-export." Tony had a good eye for detail, but I had disagreed immediately.

"No way," I'd said under my breath, countering his assessment. "Look at the chic cut of his lapel. And the swanky fedora. New York. Stockbroker. Definitely." I had enjoyed the banter, unaware it would be our last. When Tony returned from the war, he refused to go to shows, finding all entertainment other than hockey, pointless and shallow. By then, the Grand had been gutted by a terrible fire, anyway. So many everyday things we did in those days hold such significance in the present, immortalized as "last times" with my brother.

Now, in the main waiting room, I pull my mind away from Tony's memory and focus on the game. A bent woman in well-worn widow's weeds shuffles onto a bench, her deeply lined face framed with a black kerchief knotted below her chin. She drops her bundled laundry to the floor, her eyes shifting, anticipating being shooed away. If Tony was here, I'd say, "Yesler Flats. Washerwoman." His thoughtful smile engulfs me again, and I sigh, my steps faltering as I hitch my haversack.

Near the terminal doors, I pass a commotion. A toddler about Eddie's age in a tiny dishevelled suit yanks a toy from a plainly dressed woman crouched by him, who I assume is his governess. She tries to soothe him, but his sharp cries echo off the marble walls, fading only when the heavy doors swing closed behind me and I settle onto a bench outside on the platform.

On the far track, a steam engine puffs, the earthy scent of coal everywhere. Around me voices hum and luggage trolleys bump by rhythmically, but the wailing child has turned my mind to Millie's twins. We visit regularly, but every time I see them, they've grown inches and have a new talent to show me. Now it's going to be months before I cuddle Eddie and Lizzie again, and with an ache in my throat, I wonder whether they'll remember me.

The toddler comes through the doors, draped over the shoulder of his father's tailored pinstripe suit. A torrent of incoherent words still spills from the little boy. The man shoots me a grimace and shrugs, as if to say, "You know how it is. What can I do?" I grin back before looking away. Behind them, a young woman with bobbed hair under a cloche hat follows stiffly. She speaks tersely to the governess, who's weighed down by two large bags. Expensive perfume hangs in the air as they move by. *They're from Broadmoor. A business tycoon and his lavish lady, off on a summer sojourn near the beach with their tantrumy toddler and the help.* I drop my chin to hide my smirk — Tony would like that one.

The family stops in the reserved area of the platform and settles onto a bench. Perching the boy on his knees, the father speaks into his ear. But nothing settles the writhing child, who howls until our train approaches a few minutes later. The grand locomotive chugs past, hissing and clanging. This quiets the toddler, who watches wide-eyed as the train lurches to a stop in billowing clouds of steam. The wood doors creak open, spilling a stream of passengers on their way to downtown jobs.

After taking a last look at the family, I step up into the railcar and shove my bag onto the brass luggage rack above a window seat on the left. Father had reminded me that this side gets the best ocean views on the way north. Outside, the conductor shouts "All aboard!" and we jerk into motion, slowly gathering speed, trundling through the city's backstage.

I lean my forehead against the mahogany window frame, letting the music of the tracks fill me. Soon we're passing the bustling piers behind Pike Place Market, where farmers and fishermen are unloading their wares from tractors and wagons, carting crates inside to their stands. Passing under the overhead footbridge, we enter Seattle's waterfront, where stacks of lumber, cargo ships, and grain silos pass by.

The snippets of industry make me wonder how Thomas is doing this morning. He's anxious about how he'll be received by the crew, coming back to camp as their manager and not a co-worker. These past summers he's worked with the crew because his father believes you can't lead a worker until you understand his role. So Thomas has laboured as a whistlepunk, filer, choker, chaser, faller, and even ran the yarder's steam donkey. Before he left, I pointed out that the crew would likely appreciate his hands-on knowledge, not resent him for his position.

"It's not your fault you were born into the business," I said. "And I imagine the men will be glad to have you, rather than that fellow they call Jello. You complained about him for weeks." Thomas had returned from Camp 2 frustrated by the poor decisions the manager made throughout the summer. He was a smooth talker, who, like the dessert of his nickname, moulded effortlessly to any situation. The men despised both his insincerity and his wobbly moral code, so the name Jello stuck.

"Maybe. Jello doesn't plan and doesn't listen to the crew." Thomas had explained why he agreed with the workers. "The men know what needs to be done and what order to do it in. If he just used the decades of knowledge he's got working for him, the camp might be profitable. As it stands, Father needs to replace him." And now it's Thomas replacing Jello, who's getting transferred to Camp 1 for one last chance. Thomas's uncle spends a lot of time there and the Company hopes Jello's performance will improve with more oversight. From what Thomas has shared, I doubt it'll work. Besides the defects Thomas has listed, the man apparently skips work to go fishing whenever the mood takes him. None of these traits makes him a good leader. I wonder why the Company is extending this fellow so much opportunity — they usually react harshly to infractions. He must be related to someone important. I'll have to ask Thomas when I get up there.

The railcar dims in the shadows of the towering evergreens as we move inland from Elliot Bay. When we emerge on the coast again, the morning sun glints off the endless ocean. Beyond the rocky coastline, tree-covered islands dot Puget Sound and the billowing sails of an occasional sailboat are visible in the distance. I've never been on a boat, and as the train skirts the shore, I imagine the steamship from Vancouver will be equally picturesque.

A clatter from the railcar door, followed by the siren wail of a child, pulls my gaze from the stunning view. A glance up the aisle confirms the cries belong to the little boy from the station. He toddles down the aisle, eyes red, hiccoughing sobs. One chubby hand clings to the finger of his father, while the other schlepps a wooden toy along the carpet. They move slowly toward me. The child making eye contact with every passenger between whimpers, unabashedly sharing his misery.

He pauses when he gets to my seat, and I smile down into his tear-stained face.

"That's a very nice toy you have there," I say to him, pointing at the Jacob's Ladder dragging along the floor. He stops crying to answer me, his expression solemn.

"It bwoken." He holds up the toy, shiny eyes wide. Instead of flopping over one another, the little squares hang limply, one ribbon torn off the wood.

"I see. Will you show me?" I pat my lap, glancing at the boy's father, who's watching us indifferently as the boy piles the toy onto my skirt. "Yes, it's torn right off, hasn't it?" I finger the ribbon, leaning over the square pieces of smooth maple, laying the frayed end of the narrow binding back across the wood.

"I pull it," he says, his voice sad.

"You need glue. To fix it. You need glue. And I have some." The words leave my lips before I think about what I'm offering. There's no reason to involve myself with these people. But it's a long trip and a little distraction can't hurt.

"Weally?" The child's face looks so hopeful that I'm glad I extended my help.

"I think so," I say. "Will you pass down my bag? That one there?" I address the boy's father, pointing to my haversack on the luggage rack. He hands it to me, eyebrows raised, clearly stumped at why a woman, or anyone, would carry glue around in their hand luggage.

"I use mucilage to glue pressed flowers into my field books," I say, shifting in my seat to put my bag beside me and rummage through it. The toddler moves closer, his hands on the toy in my lap, his little body warm against my knees. He watches me carefully as I pull a bell-shaped bottle of LePage from the bag.

"Dat gwue?" he asks.

"Yes. This is glue." I wiggle the angled rubber red tip, clearing dried film from the slot, then tip the brown glass bottle upside down. The thick liquid inside falls in a languid movement.

"Hurry up, gwue. Hurry up!" He taps at the yellow and red label, grinning at me.

"Here. See how sticky it is?" I take his hand and dab a small amount onto his forefinger, with a glance at his father, who's biting his lip to hide a smile. He settles into the empty seat opposite me, leaning his head against the velvet seat back, looking relieved. At least his child is no longer disrupting everyone's journey.

The little boy pinches his thumb and forefinger together, then pulls them apart, the thin strands of honey-like glue fascinating him. He looks up at me, pointing at his toy.

"You can stick it?"

"I can try. Do you think we should try?" The boy nods eagerly, leaning close, still sticking and unsticking his fingers. "Let's lay it out flat first." He helps me arrange the wooden squares on the narrow windowsill over the radiator. I dab glue on the broken piece, lining up the ribbon carefully before pressing it into place. "There," I say.

"Have it now?" The boy reaches for the toy, but I stop him with an upturned palm.

"No, we have to wait for it to dry first." The child's face scrunches, ready to wail again. I scramble for a distraction, remembering a craft I did with Lizzie. "Let's make a paper chain while we wait." I reach into my bag, tearing a few blank pages from my little red notebook. "Have you ever done that? Like this." A few moments later, the tyke is on the floor, the tip of his tongue out, bent over a strip of paper he's scribbling on.

The boy's father has pulled the brim of his fedora down over his face. A narrow silk tie in subdued tones of navy and mocha hangs askew on his rumpled white dress shirt. Feeling my eyes on him, he sits up, pushing at his hat.

"Thank you," he says. "Junior's been inconsolable since he broke that thing. Two-year-olds are exhausting." Shaking his head, he peers down at his son, a mix of pride and weariness lining his expression. "I'm Dr. John Moody." He tips his fedora, then places it on his lap, smiling warmly. So, he's a doctor, not a business tycoon. I can almost feel Tony elbowing me in the ribs as I return the man's smile.

"I'm Miss... Mrs.... Eva Clarke," I say, blushing.

"You're very good with him. Do you have children?" The man is gracious, ignoring the stumble over my new name, eyeing my wedding band.

"No. Not yet," I say, shaking my head.

"Well, they'll be in good hands when you have them." He beams through a yawn, shifting in his seat. "Say, can I leave the young chap with you while I get us some coffee? Do you drink coffee? I could really use a strong cup." Eager to avoid a repeat tantrum, I lean down over Junior and ask him if he wants to stay with me. The boy nods.

"I stay wiff you," he says, handing me a strip of paper, covered in pencil scribbles. Satisfied, I look up at Dr. Moody.

"Cream. And two sugars, please."

"I'll be right back, then." He walks down the aisle in step with the train's lurching rhythm and disappears with a clank through the vestibule door. I loop the strip, forming the first link in the chain and securing the ends with glue. Pressing the paper between my fingers, I gaze out across the glimmering ocean. The peanut-sized bundle of cells inside me is growing into a tiny, tantrumy human of my own. It's comforting that a stranger thinks my child will be in good hands. Turning back to Junior, I smile, imagining how life will change once I meet my baby.

Chapter 13

As Junior's paper chain lengthens, the view from the train grows more picturesque, with the rugged coastline on our left and towering timbers on our right. I long to flee the rail chatter and wander the forest's dank depths.

Dr. Moody returns with the promised coffees, and we spend the time easily until he and his family disembark at Stanwood Station. Tony would have lost half the bet — they were indeed heading to a new vacation home on Camano Island.

"It's a beautiful spot. Junior loves the beach. Spends all day collecting shells and driftwood. And harassing crabs." Dr. Moody smiles down at his son. "We all love it. Even though the island is busier now, since they've replaced the cable ferry with a bridge. Elsie, my wife, is convinced our neighbour is a rumrunner." My eyebrows raise at his scandalous statement, and he laughs easily, shrugging. "Could well be. Who knows? It's a short trek across the strait to Canada, as the crow flies. Maybe she's right."

The train car feels a little lonesome without Dr. Moody's soothing company and Junior's sticky fingers. Inspired by the idea of smugglers, I occupy myself imagining a whisky bottle's trip south across the border, along the intricate waterways of the Pacific outside my window, and into one of Seattle's basement speakeasies.

In Vancouver, I arrive to find the *SS Cardena* behind schedule. The baggage agent walks me through the grand Waterfront Station, a gorgeous new building boasting large columns, archways, and landscape murals. Beyond the station out on the docks, he dumps me and my trunks among the other passengers and piles of northbound cargo, with instructions to sit tight while they offload the ship.

So I wait on the dock perched atop my trunks, fanning myself with a magazine, my travel outfit sticking to me in the July heat, enveloped by Vancouver's bustling city port. The clanging of railcars echoes alongside the shouts of porters shuffling luggage. Wooden carts stacked high with mail sacks, valises, and dry goods rattle by on the worn planks of the wharf, while the briny stench of low tide and rotting fish threatens to bring back my morning sickness. I swallow hard and look up into the clear blue sky where a gull drifts on the summer breeze.

Across the small bay, a yacht club and a military installation front the tall green timber stands of Stanley Park. I yearn to leave the bustle here and walk the trails to the Monkey House and the Big Hollow Tree shown on the map I picked up inside. Thomas and I will need to explore this city the next time we return to Seattle. Below me, a stately blue heron scans the shore for prey, poised motionless. The subtle blue-grey plumage of the *Ardea herodias* ruffles in the breeze. It stands almost as tall as me, and its silhouette reminds me of the pterodactyls in the science fiction book by Conan Doyle, which was my gift to Tony on his last Christmas.

A crash from my right makes me turn away. Tin cans roll across the wharf, toward me and the dock's edge. Two workers in newsboy caps shout, shaking fists over a smashed wooden crate, the *Cardena's* freight lift swinging above it. I hop from my trunk and corral the rolling tins with my feet before they launch onto the barnacle-covered rocks below. Crouching, I collect the lacquered but unlabelled cans into my skirted lap. One worker bounds over and I pass him the cans one by one, my brow furrowed.

"It's salmon." He stacks the shiny tins expertly in his arms, answering my unasked question. "From canneries all up the coast. Whole ship's full of 'em." Standing, I watch the young men wrestle the cans into an open-top box, remembering the salmon bites on the elegant sandwich tray at the Olympic. While Seattle has canneries of its own, it had never occurred to me how far food travels to reach us.

I rise, sighing heavily. Was that hotel luncheon just a month ago? A lifetime of change has happened since my triumphant graduation day. The sun's heat radiates off my trunks and I flop Tony's old canvas military haversack onto one of them, unbuckling the straps and digging for my Thermos. I carefully water each of the forty seedlings in the stacked milk crates by my feet. When the blue vacuum bottle is empty, I stuff the cork back into its glass-lined neck and move the crates to the shady side of the trunks, attempting to keep their roots cool.

Settling in a sliver of shade beside my seedlings, I arrange my skirt over my crossed legs and lean my head against my luggage. My unladylike posture would horrify my mother.

"Fill that up fer ya?" A pair of worn leather boots with mismatched laces stop beside me on the wharf. I shade my eyes, craning to meet the kind eyes of a crinkle-faced man.

"Pardon?" I say. He's older, maybe in his sixties, and I try not to stare at his big ears.

"Yer bottle. Can I fill it fer ya?" His own dented canteen swings empty from a knotted canvas strap. "I'm goin' up that way, anyway."

He juts his chin at the cityscape, and I tilt my head, unsure, as the sun beats down on us. My Thermos could use refilling before getting on the boat, but if this guy runs off with it, I'll be even worse off. "I'm George." He tucks the canteen under his arm and touches the brim of his fedora with thick, crooked fingers. I lift my bag off my lap so I can stand, but he holds out a palm. "Don' ged up. Just watch my stuff." He jabs a thumb toward a scuffed brown suitcase topped with a filthy canvas backpack.

"I'm Eva," I say after a beat, matching his informal introduction, twisting the thin stainless cup onto my Thermos and passing it up to him. If I leave the dock in search of water, someone would have to watch my belongings, and I'd rather lose my water bottle than my luggage right now.

"Nice to meetcha." George takes my bottle and strides toward the city. "Be right back," he says over his shoulder, winking. "And watch my stuff!" He melts into the crowd, his black hat, grey shirt and sturdy wool pants, indistinguishable from the dozens of other working stiffs roaming the dock. I flip the pages of my Time magazine and wonder if I'll ever see my lovely new Thermos again.

⚘

Twenty minutes later, George hands me a full Thermos, and something wrapped in newspaper.

"Cold chicken on rye." He nods down at the sandwich in his hand. "Best bread in town." I'm touched by his thoughtfulness and dig a quarter from my skirt pocket, dumping it into George's palm as I take the food. He peers at the eagle on the coin's silver face before shoving it back at me, shaking his head, refusing payment.

"American, huh?" I nod, unwrapping the sandwich, hoping I don't gag in front of this nice man. I'm hungry, but the smells of the port are still making me queasy.

"Are ya on this boat, too, then?" George bites into his sandwich and motions at the *Cardena*. Again I nod. "You a Clark, then?" He asks through a mouthful, scuffing his boot over a white patch of seagull waste, and watching the dried remnants fall between the wharf boards. I freeze, my sandwich pausing inches from my lips, where the smell of fresh bread makes my mouth water. How could this man know my name?

"Heard the Boss Man's kid and his lady is coming up." George shrugs and answers my unasked question. It takes me a moment to grasp he's referring to Thomas as the kid, which makes me the referenced lady. I blink, my mouth hanging half-open. To hide my surprise, I take a bite of the thick sandwich, stifling a moan, my eyes widening. "Good, right?" George beams a knowing grin, hooking a thumb behind his suspender and thrusting his chin out.

"It's delicious!"

"I can't beat their bread," he says, his tone rueful. "I'm a cook. In camp." He slumps visibly and shakes his head, as if he's disgusted with his lacking ability, but the edges of his blue eyes scrunch. "We're no beans n' bacon outfit, but the bread from these fellas here — well, I can't top it."

"It would be hard to beat. I don't think I've ever had better," I say with a laugh, intrigued by this stocky, big-eared man. Between bites, I learn George is heading back to the same camp as me, where he's been a cook for years. As he speaks, I realize Thomas told us about him, the cook who made the best venison stew, but I had imagined him to be taller and younger. And rougher, somehow. "Do you know my husband, then? Thomas? He worked up in Camp 2 last summer."

"Yes, ma'am. I do." George nods, stuffing the last bit of crust in his mouth, then cocks his head. "Also how I reconnized ya. From the photo he carried around. Of you and yer li'l trees." My brows furrow as George continues. "Ya know, we gots plenty of trees up there, right? Big 'uns. No need to bring yer own." He looks at me with a teasing twinkle in his eyes. "Anyway. Should be boardin' soon." He nods toward the ship, then motions to the saloons bordering the dock area. "The fellas, they all been gettin' likkered up while they wait. Might be a rowdy evening."

I should ask what exactly he means, but I'm still digesting his other news. That Thomas showed his coworkers a snapshot of me last summer. Last summer, months before we started to see each other socially. I know the snapshot. He would have clipped it from the university's alumni journal. I had received a scholarship from their fund and they had taken a photo of me and my "li'l trees", to include with a brief article on my research.

A whistle from the *Cardena* interrupts my thoughts, and a mate is calling us on board. George asks if I need a hand, but I tell him the ship's crew will help. He touches the brim of his fedora with a nod and joins the row of men with worn suitcases shuffling toward the gangplank, while I wait beside my luggage for a deckhand. Thomas warned me a dozen times to make sure my stuff gets on each train and ship. Things get left behind too often.

When my trunks are secured on board, I cross to the wooden ship deck, showing my ticket to a man dressed in a brass-buttoned jacket, and a pipe clamped between yellow teeth. My new name, Mrs. Eva Clark, is neatly printed on the one-way ticket to Alert Bay, and I trace my finger over the letters. It's strange to have one name for a lifetime only to trade it in for someone else's. At least transit fares require me to use my own first name, and not the even more diminishing Mrs. Thomas Clark.

"Where's your husband?" The uniformed man peers over my shoulder, scanning his passenger list for a match.

"He's gone north already," I say. The man grunts, his pipe waggling as he clenches his jaw.

"Your cabin's on this deck, on the starboard side, halfway down the passageway. Keys are on the wall. Should arrive in Alert Bay about this time tomorrow." I nod, realizing I have no idea what the place looks like. But I'll make sure I'm ready to disembark by midday tomorrow. If I miss my port, I could end up on an unwanted Alaskan detour.

"I'm the ship's steward," he says. "If there's any trouble, ma'am, come find me. Or go to the wheelhouse." He points three decks above us. Trouble? But the steward is already punching the tickets of the young family following me.

Hitching the strap of my bag onto my shoulder, I head down the passageway to my cabin, closing the door behind me. The faint scent of furniture polish, cigar smoke, and something musty drifts in the air. On the left, a narrow sleeping bunk hangs from chains at chest height, a metal ladder at one end. Underneath, a tiny desk is secured in one corner with a sturdy wooden chair under it. In the other corner there's a small mirror above a basin, with a chipped enamelled chamber pot tucked below. Straight ahead, the sun streams through a round porthole high on the ship's hull, the bustling city peaking in at me.

I take the key from a hook and hang my bag, then glance in the mirror, tucking stray curls under my bucket hat. After locking the cabin door behind me, I explore the ship. The size and construction of this boat are impressive. It's at least 200 feet long and maybe 40 feet wide.

While lapping the main deck, I find the kitchen, a dining saloon, and a newsstand. I climb steep stairs to a covered walkway encircling the upper deck, where wood-topped metal rails surround the perimeter. Larger berths, with square windows, are arranged on the bow and stern. I sit on a bench near the red and black tilted steam funnel, feeling the steady thud of the engine somewhere below me. The top deck is open to the sky and I gaze past two wooden lifeboats lashed down with cables, to where dark green forests glisten in the summer sun, far across the harbour and up into the north shore's mountains.

I've studied the route the ship will take, an ocean voyage through straits and inlets, always close to land. The briny breeze caresses my damp skin, and the sun warms me. A contented eagerness vibrates my insides. What an adventure I'm on! A deep blast from the steam whistle startles me, and I find a spot along the front rail for our departure.

On the main level, passengers pack the pointed bow and the open side rails, some waving their caps at loved ones on the dock below. The men who stand near me are about my age, their thin shirts taut across thick chests. All of them are ruggedly fit. But unlike the gaiety of the crowd on the bow, these fellows have hands stuffed in pockets, their chins drooping and shoulders hunched.

Locking eyes with me, the tallest young man wipes his face with a red handkerchief. A wide scar on his left eyebrow gives him an ominous look and, without breaking eye contact, he takes a swig from a flask. His glassy scowl hardens my stomach and I shift my gaze to a small tug assisting the *Cardena* out into the harbour. Still sensing Red Handkerchief's liquor-glazed glare on my back, I make my way down the staircase, moving to the port rail away from the man, feeling unsettled.

The ship rumbles and creaks as it slowly gains speed. Below me, along the shore, I catch glimpses of cars and buggies glinting on the road encircling Stanley Park. The shore slides closer and closer until we reach the First Narrows, where a few people wave at us from beside the semaphore station.

As the ship glides out into Burrard Inlet, there's a scuffle from the staircase where Red Handkerchief is stumbling my way. I turn away, twisting my wedding band, wondering what to do. Swallowing hard, I feel rattled enough to go find George. As much as I'd like to think I can take care of myself, I've also learned to heed my instincts. And right now, my gut is telling me to get help.

As I move along the deck, I glance back once, but Red Handkerchief isn't there. I cringe a little. Maybe I'm being silly. But I could use a glass of water anyway, so I head to the dining saloon. George is lined up at the bar, laughing with two men. Hesitating in the doorway, I realize I'm the sole woman present and that's enough to make me leave.

But when I turn, I crash into someone, our bodies colliding with a solid thud. I raise my gaze. Red Handkerchief's flinty eyes squint down at me. He smells of yesterday's whisky and unwashed laundry. When he lurches to one side, he jostles another man who spills half his beer. Then Red Handkerchief reaches for my arm, but he gets a fistful of my chest pocket instead, his scarred eyebrow lifting in surprise. I stifle a shriek, pushing off him and scrambling backward.

And suddenly there's chaos. Beer Boy grabs Red Handkerchief by his shoulders, righting his lolling head long enough to punch him in the face. In seconds, a sprawling brawl surrounds me. I flatten myself against the saloon wall, glancing over my shoulder, looking for the doorway. A young red-faced man snags a chair, swinging it overhead and aiming for a shorter man's chest just as someone grips my waist. I whirl around, palm raised to slap the culprit, but it's George's enormous hand that catches my wrist in mid-air.

"Easy there, Boss." His words are a low grunt as he tucks me under his arm, guiding me through the turmoil.

"Oh, my goodness!" Outside on the deck, my voice is shaky and breathless. "Thank you!" I look up at George, who's peering into the dining saloon, chuckling.

"See yer causin' a ruckus already, eh?" He rocks back on his heels, hitching his thumbs into his pockets. "Won't be gettin' me a beer now. Nope. Captain'll shut down the bar for sure." George watches the brawl with interest, flinching at the sound of breaking glass.

"Maybe I should go to my cabin?" I wonder if I can survive the next day and a half in that tiny room. But being among the drunken workers doesn't seem smart. I bite my lip as two ship's constables push past us into the dining hall, their billy clubs held high.

"Well shoot. That ain't gonna make things any better." George shakes his head as one constable cold cocks a man from behind, drawing a roar from the surrounding men. "Yep. Not good. Let's getcha outta here." He escorts me along the starboard rail, toward my bunk. As the din of the brawl fades behind us, George pauses, pointing out across the glimmering ocean, toward a pair of pointed peaks in the distance. "The Lions." He stands still, both hands on the rail, his voice filled with awe. "View from up there must be mighty fine."

"It would be. But the view from down here is pretty spectacular, too," I say. We stand side by side in silence and I feel nature settling my soul until a crash from the dining hall spurs us along. Outside my room, I thank George and apologize.

"I'm sorry. I didn't mean to start anything. I really didn't." But George laughs, his bushy eyebrows waggling.

"Those fellas were itchin' for a fight. It woulda started some way, with or withoutcha." He suggests I stay in my cabin until morning and tells me to lock up. "I'll bring ya some supper when things settle down." And with that promise, he strides away. I latch my door and lean my back against it, wondering what I've gotten myself into.

CHAPTER 14

Early the next morning, I snuggle the covers under my chin. Dust dances in the single beam of warm orange sunlight entering my bunk through the porthole. The ship rocks gently and the engine's thrum vibrates around me through the creaking wood. Beyond my cabin door, the passageway is now quiet.

Late last night, George had brought me dinner and recommended I stay put.

"It's turned into a right brawl-a-thon. Saw a table go overboard. And a toilet." He grinned at my shocked expression and handed over a steaming bowl of stew. "Yep, tore the John clear off the floorboards." George had chuckled, shaking his head. "The whole crowd turned on them coppers. Using their clubs for no good, they were. Captain's gone an' locked 'em up fer their own good. Only way to keep 'em safe."

George reported that even with the bar closed, most of the passengers were still getting rowdier, finishing whatever liquor they had smuggled aboard. He had glanced around my room, jutting his chin at the sturdy chair tucked under the sleeping bunk.

"Best shove that against your door for the night." I had set the bowl of stew on the edge of the basin, then hugged my arms around my middle, glimpsing my wide-eyed stare in the mirror. I had tried to rearrange my expression, to appear as if this were commonplace advice, but George had seen my concern. "Look, they're good lads, but whisky sours the best of 'em. This dust-up will settle by mornin'. You'll be fine in here 'til then." Nodding, I had promised to stay in my berth and locked the door behind him, wedging the chair back under the doorknob as George had instructed.

Throughout the evening, bodies thumped and boot steps thundered along the corridor outside. As I was getting changed, a man's fists pounded on the door. His slurred shouts accused someone named Tommy of locking him out. I didn't answer, not wanting to draw attention to myself. After a few moments, he tromped away, swearing, and I eventually fell into a fitful sleep. The ship docked twice overnight, the clanking of cargo waking me both times.

Now, as the morning light brightens the room's shadows, my stomach growls. Despite my restless night, I throw back the covers, eager to leave the room's dank air and explore. The thin metal rungs of the slippery ladder bite my feet through my wool socks as I carefully clamber down from the bunk. After pulling my toiletries from my bag, I drag the chair from under the doorknob and perch on it, marvelling at the clever design of the cabinetry below the bed. I rinse my toothbrush with water from a white pitcher. It's held in place by a circle and slot cut in the rimmed shelf's wood, to receive its rounded bottom and handle. The wash water runs into an enamel bowl, which is similarly secured against the ship's movement, needed when the seas are much rougher than now. I strip off my cotton nightdress, scrubbing my body, neck, and face with a soapy washcloth. Shivering, I dry off with a hand towel and pull on yesterday's clothes again.

I peer at my reflection in the tiny mirror, working my curls into a thick braid and tucking loose strands behind my ears. Nothing about my face or body reveals I'm pregnant, and I let myself push it from my mind. With my morning routine complete, I empty the washbasin and the chamber pot into the metal bucket under the desk.

After unlocking the cabin door, I cautiously peek out into the dim passageway. Except for the ship's rhythmic creaks, it's quiet and there's no one in sight as I carry the pail carefully to the back of the ship. A season of men's caulk boots has roughened the walkway's wooden floor, and even in the morning breeze, the stench of fresh vomit greets me in several places. Men. Despite being steps away from the entire ocean, they still yack in a corner instead of overboard.

When I open the door to the head, I see George wasn't fibbing. The porcelain water closet is gone, with just a couple of rusty spikes and splintered wood surrounding the rank hole. I hold my breath, emptying my bucket of wash water with a wrinkled nose.

It's only once my pail is empty that I finally take in the scenery. I'm alone at the back deck's wooden rail, staring after the bubbling white trail the slow-moving ship leaves in the glassy ocean. The sun is low and reflects a bright gold patch. At the horizon, a deep crimson bronze tints the sky, somehow blending to a dark blue above me. Wisps of marine cloud hover in shades of pink. I squint into the rising sun, its warm early morning hue gilding everything with gold dust.

Taking a deep breath, I cleanse the ship's foul smells from my lungs with the cool morning air. A bald eagle leaves its perch with a keening squawk and dives, flapping back to shore with a squirming fish silhouetted below it. America's bird, the *Haliaeetus leucocephalus* with a silver salmon. Near a patch of bull kelp, the adorable face of an otter, clasping its fluffy big-eyed pup, gazes up at me. The mother otter eyes the ship with a protective glare, then strokes the pup's head. *Enhydra lutris* comforting her young among the seaweed. In the distance, two cargo ships mimic the *Cardena's* near stationary pace, and I wonder what the captains are waiting for.

My stomach growls again, urging me toward the dining room. But as I turn, a queer quiver nudges my bladder. I stop in my tracks. There it is again. Like a herring swimming around my gut.

I drop the metal bucket to the deck with a clatter, then grip the rail, my knuckles whitening. There's the flutter again! My heart races and I gasp, realizing what it must be. It's just a light touch, a flicker. The quickening. How stunning! A tiny elbow or foot draws a soft path across my insides, as the new life inside me kicks about. I straighten, pushing my palms against my abdomen, over the strange sensation, but the movement is imperceptible from the outside. A wide smile spreads over my face and a warmth floods over me, my skin tingling with the urge to share this wonder, and my amazement, with someone.

As I glance about, George strides around the corner, puffing on his pipe.

"There ya are, Boss!" He halts, touching the rim of his hat and pulling on one of his thick earlobes. "You okay?" When I nod, his gaze moves from my beaming face to the hands on my belly. A flash of understanding crosses his features before he looks away and comments on the "beaut of a sunrise". Like the otters in the kelp bed, so much of *Homo sapien* communication is non-verbal. I'm positive George has just guessed my secret, but he faces the ocean, gripping the rail, asking nothing. Which is just as well. I like George and would hate to lie to him right now. His respect for my privacy eliminates that decision. I ache to share this miraculous moment, but restrain myself. Sharing now is not part of our cover story.

"Should be headin' past Ripple Rock shortly. Captain's waitin' fer slack. Yer fella tell ya 'bout them narrows?"

"He did. Is that why we're not moving?" I step next to George, who nods, peering up the starboard side of the ship.

I'm glad to hear our captain is patient. Thomas's last trip back through Seymour Narrows was delayed due to headwinds. Their captain had navigated the channel in a lower tide. And though the crew downplayed it, Thomas felt sure they had a close call in the whitewater wake over Ripple Rock.

"Let's watch from the bow." He picks up my bucket and leads the way. We lean against the ship's front rail and the deck beneath us shudders as the engines engage. From inside my skirt pocket, I press on my belly, wanting to feel the movement inside me again. But the first concrete evidence that I'm indeed pregnant doesn't return.

The *SS Cardena* leaves her holding pattern, surging forward, and when she turns starboard, George points ahead to our right.

"See there? Where the water humps up? We gotta stay left of them underwater rocks." Up ahead, the channel narrows and the water swirls, looking more like a river than the ocean. "A vile stretch of water, this is. Shipwrecked plenty." George shakes his head, his pipe clenched between his teeth, tendrils of fragrant tobacco smoke drifting at me. To our left, the towering dark green forest closes in as the captain positions us to navigate the scant safe waters.

As the bow moves into the narrows, the strong tidal currents tug on the ship, pulling it toward the rocks, then pitching it back toward shore. It feels as if the *Cardena* is on ice, slipping and sliding in the chaotic eddies. Below us water rushes past, spray splashing up the hull, but beside us, the rugged rocks and trees seem to move in slow motion, inching past. The massive ship lurches once more, the deck shifting and creaking, until finally we steam out of the turbulent water, where the engines growl, shifting lower.

George and I stand side by side at the rail as the sky brightens. Ahead of us, the inlet widens, rich green island silhouettes jutting from the ocean. In the distance, the marine mist pulls the colour from the trees, softening them to shades of sage, and beyond that, the land melts into the hazy horizon like a dream.

The breeze tugs at my curls, and a seagull drifts by, flying low beside the ship. With my palm pressed over the new life inside me, among this ethereal wilderness, things feel perfect. Beside me, the rhythmic puff of George's pipe stops, and I glance over at him. He's smiling at me with twinkling eyes and picks up my bucket, suggesting we go find the breakfast buffet. I follow the old camp cook toward the kitchen, wishing I was sharing this moment with Thomas.

Chapter 15

At the dining saloon's buffet, I make healthy choices, consuming nutritionally optimal ratios for the baby. The baby. Huh. It's the first time I've thought of the growing mass of molecules inside as anything other than 'it' or a 'mistake'. But feeling the fetus kick ended my ambivalence. She needs protein and vitamins to develop properly. Or he... Nope. She feels like a she.

George tells stories of his time in logging camps while we eat, and when I'm finished, I take my coat and a magazine to the upper deck. The mid-morning sun warms me and I sit, alternating between reading and watching the coast stream by. The view is stunning. Rocky island outcrops brim with gnarled *Thuja plicata* cedar trees. A pod of glistening white-sided dolphins plays near the bow, and later, the giant tail of a grey whale slips under water below the smoky mist of its blowhole. The life under the calm surface of the sea fascinates me, and I imagine the expanse of nature's colourful ecosystems below us. When the words on the page begin to blur, I tuck my feet onto the bench and make a pillow with my coat, laying my head down for a nap in the sun.

I wake with a start when the ship blows its signature whistle of one long, two short, and one long blast. The sun is now straight overhead, and the engine's thrum deepens as we slow into a port of call. We enter an inlet, the forest closing in. Below me, the *Cardena* dwarfs Port Neville's small pier, which mills with people. The steamship's weekly arrival is evidently a big event in this tiny isolated community. And rightly so. Without rail or road access, the vessel supplies the essentials for survival along this coast. Food, equipment, tools, and mail.

Once the men push a rolling wooden staircase against the *Cardena's* gunwale, the ship's purser is the first one off. He walks down the steps with a tray of chocolates and magazines from the newsstand strapped over his shoulders like a carnival worker. Children and dogs wrap around his legs and the residents crowd close, eyeing his offers and straining to glimpse the newspaper headlines. Cargo is lifted off, one man boards as a passenger, and a half an hour later we're on our way, the whistle sounding our departure.

Down in the dining saloon, I buy a bowl of soup and a hard-boiled egg for lunch, plus a sandwich for later. The mate behind the counter confirms Alert Bay is our next stop in less than an hour, so I go back to my cabin and pack up my things.

Out on the main bow deck, I find George on the starboard rail, his filthy backpack slung over one shoulder, tobacco smoke drifting from his pipe. My heart beats with anticipation and I twist my new wedding band as we wait for our destination to come into view. Thomas has told me that from the camp, the closest grocery store and medical care are in Alert Bay. When George points into the distance, I see plumes of smoke rising from an island against the cloudless, brilliant blue sky. A dozen fellows line up with us, all workers toting backpacks and telling jokes amid good-natured shoving. As the steamship chugs closer, the fidgeting increases and voices rise.

Alert Bay is built along the shore of a small island, with trees towering behind the row of buildings. The settlement's south end features a pier with a ramp leading to a floating dock, where tall piles tether tugs, cedar canoes, and fishing boats. Beyond it, a series of totems, with wide paddle-shaped painted wings, line a white fence. Pointing, I nudge George.

"Graveyard," he says. My eyes linger on the colourful carvings, reminded of Pioneer Square.

Past the burial ground, shanties on stilts perch above the high tide line of the gravel shore. Between the shacks, stacks of driftwood litter the beach along a wooden boardwalk, where the entire community seems to scurry toward the largest pier in the bay as the *Cardena* docks. Once the gangway is secured, I'm directed to disembark first. With the eyes of a few dozen locals on me, my cheeks burn as I step onto the wharf's wood planks, moving aside to wait for my trunks. A child of about four pulls away from her mother and squats at my feet. She runs a finger over the toe of my new shoes.

"Shiny," she says. "You got boots?" The little girl stands, her hands planted on the hips of her blue cotton frock, as I furrow my eyebrows. "You need boots, Mrs. Eva. For camp." I look at her wide-eyed. How could she know my name? By now, the girl's mother has joined us, taking the child's hand before speaking softly.

"I'm Mrs. Roy Bowden." She rubs her palm down the front of her skirt and holds out a hand. "Grace."

Flustered, I stare at her, unmoving. She drops her hand, giving me a nod instead, her brown eyes meeting mine with a friendly smile. "Mrs. Thomas Clark," I say, nodding back. "Eva. But you already know that." I'm still confused as I study her freckled face and don't smile back, waiting for an explanation.

"She needs boots, Momma." The girl tugs on Grace's skirt, peering up at her mother with a worried frown.

"This is Daisy." Grace tucks a strand of blond hair behind an ear and turns her daughter around by the shoulders. "Say a proper hello Daisy." When the girl curtsies clumsily in her boots, I stifle a smile, saying I'm pleased to meet her.

"I'm four." She stands up straight, tucking in a thumb before shoving four fingers at me. Her wide blue eyes are so serious, I soften and grin, first at her, then at Grace, already liking them. Throughout my trip, I've been careful who I connect with, fearing a needy stranger might latch on. But now, in this wilderness of endless trees and ocean, I temper my aloofness and turn to chat with Grace and Daisy. A clunk on the wharf beside me pulls my gaze from my new friends. A deckhand delivers my trunks and seedling crates stacked high on a hand truck. When he asks for instructions on where to put them, I twist my ring again, glancing about, unsure. My journey has two more legs organized by the Company, a steamboat and a rail speeder, but I realize with a tightening chest I was told no other details. I have no idea where or when to find that transport.

"She's with us," Grace says to the deckhand, pointing to the other end of the wharf, where George and the other fellows from the ship are already tossing their gear on board a tug. She takes in my furrowed brow and continues. "My husband's the foreman in camp. He and Thomas sent us to look out for you."

My shoulders relax as the deckhand looks for confirmation. When I nod, he wheels my trunks toward the *Prosperity*. The tug is much smaller than the *Cardena*, maybe sixty feet long. Her gunwales sit low in the water and two bright white life boats perch atop a covered area next to the wheelhouse.

Daisy runs ahead after George, and Grace walks beside me, my solid heels clacking on the dock. I'm offered a respectful hand to climb over the side rail by one of George's pals, while Grace is greeted on board with friendly waves and hiya's. The captain and first mate watch us from the back windows of the second-floor wheelhouse, but no one takes tickets or checks names.

"There's benches inside." Grace points to a small door under the covered area. "But we can find a spot on the bow. If you're okay with being outside." When I nod, she points me toward the narrow side deck. Grace stops to chat with a worker on the stern, so I shuffle to the front without her, feeling the eyes of the workers on me.

Daisy's footsteps pitter-patter on the wooden deck as she sprints to greet each of the men. Her enthusiasm is contagious and everyone returns her smiles and waves. Soon, a tall young man hoists her onto his shoulders, eliciting a delighted giggle from Daisy. When he turns toward us, I recognize the scarred eyebrow and swollen black eye with a start. It's Red Handkerchief. I haven't seen him since the bar brawl. Just my luck that this is his port, too. He lowers his head and shuffles across the narrow deck, removing his newsboy cap as he approaches.

"William Barlow, ma'am. Billy. An' I'm real sorry, ma'am. 'Bout what... happened..." One thick, calloused fist wraps tight around Daisy's tiny stocking-clad ankle, while his other hand clenches his hat over his heart. "I hope... I hope you wasn't hurt." He's staring at his feet now, his voice shaky.

"Let's go, Billy!" Daisy drums her fists on the man's head and kicks her heels. Billy peers at me through curly bangs, moving only his eyes. His drooping chin trembles and there's no trace of the vicious gleam I saw in his gaze last night on the ship. It's hard to believe this is the same person, the contrast giving credence to some of the temperance movement's claims. But Grace clearly trusts him with Daisy, so after an unblinking pause, I respond, my words firm.

"Thank you, Mr. Barlow. No harm done." Billy lets out a long breath, letting his head fall back.

"Hey!" Daisy giggles, Billy's hair tickling her rosy cheeks.

"Thank you, ma'am." Billy's eyes close as he exhales a shaky laugh and a slow smile fills his face. As he bounces Daisy away, she squeals. I lean against the bow, watching a seagull on a driftwood log pecking at a purple starfish. The *Pisaster ochraceus*'s soft appendages are no match for the *Larus argentatus*'s sharp yellow beak. George sidles up beside me as the greedy gull grapples with its unwieldy prey.

"Told Billy he better make good with the Boss's lady." George crosses his arms. "He do okay?" I shrug, unsure how to respond. "Kid's been through the wringer." George sighs and shakes his head. "No excuse. But..." He trails off, glancing across to the mainland's coastal mountains, then retreats to join his buddies.

As George moves away, I bristle, unsettled by the respect I receive solely because of my husband's status. Another piece of the old me, the independent, capable Eva who graduated top of her class, is disappearing like hummingbird wings in sunlight. The person I've worked so hard to become is blurring. I cringe at my uncharitable thoughts. These people could just ignore me or, worse, make things harder. But instead, everyone is kind and welcoming. Maybe it's time I open my heart to them, just a little.

CHAPTER 16

When Grace joins me on the bow, she hops onto a stack of crates, then helps me up, too. She kicks her heels, keeping an eye on Daisy, whose shrieking laugh cuts the warm evening air like a seagull's screech as Billy roughhouses with her. Workers light cigarettes and lean against the outer deck's rails, squinting into the sunlight.

"You got boots with you?" When I tell her yes, Grace explains that I really should change into them. Even though it's the driest month of the year, once we're off the tug and docks, she promises there will be mud. "And Daisy won't forgive you if you ruin those shiny shoes of yours." Grace gives me a rueful grin, wondering out loud how Daisy will fare in life, having such expensive taste already. I chuckle just as the boat whistle signals our cast off.

Grace points out Camp 1, directly across the strait, less than two miles away. There's a cluster of buildings and a couple of structures jutting into the water. The tug steams over the glassy ocean and it won't be long before we dock again.

"I should find my things and put on those boots then," I say, hopping down to the deck and excusing myself from Grace. I wrap my coat around me, the breeze flapping it open as I walk along the narrow side deck to the stern, where the freight and luggage are piled.

Thankfully, my trunks are accessible, set in the deck's corner. I fish out the keys hanging from my neck and soon have one unlocked. But I hesitate before lifting the lid, feeling curious eyes on me.

When Grace appears beside me again, asking if she can help, I give her a sheepish look.

"Would you mind blocking the view? From the fellows?" I nod toward a group of workers, pretending not to watch me. "My unmentionables are packed right on top." I purse my lips and shrug, sharing the last part in a hushed tone, feeling unprepared again. Grace just laughs and spreads her coat wide, hands in pockets, shielding me from the men's prying glances. She faces me, chattering on about Camp 2, while I lift out the upper trunk trays. Mother's lavender linen spray fills my next breath, and a tightness clamps my chest. My mother's clipped goodbye, with a trace of her Austrian accent, echoes in my head now. Blinking quickly, my fingers dig for the sturdy boots Millie referred to as macho. I find them near the bottom and pull them out, saying, "Jackpot!"

When Grace sees my well-loved footwear, she nods in approval. The creased leather of the scuffed boots tells a story of hours spent on rugged terrain. The tilt of Grace's blond head makes me think she was expecting them to be stiff and unworn, bound to create blisters. I lace up, then tuck my shiny shoes in with the rest of my belongings, snapping the trunk's lid shut again.

We return to the bow for a better view of Camp 1. Grace points to a long, timber-pile breakwater jutting over 800 feet into the shallows. She tells me it was built to calm the turbulence of the booming grounds where the Nimpkish River meets the ocean's tides on our far right. Close to the river mouth, a steam train piled high with logs is parked on another structure. The timber is massive, much of it well over six feet in diameter. I count fifteen railcars and as we chug closer, five of the cars tilt. Men shout and steel clangs as cables tighten through blocks at the top of poles leaning over the track. Soon, the railcars dump with an enormous splash, the logs dunking under and bobbing to the surface like corks.

The resulting wave hits the bow of the *Prosperity*, sea spray misting my face.

"'Nuther splash, Mrs. Eva. Big splash!" Daisy sits in Billy's arms, clapping her hands in anticipation, pointing at the workers hooking up the winch. The scent of freshly cut timber envelops us and the logs roll off the bunks with another clang. In this section, one car holds just a single cedar log, its diameter as wide as the rails. The next five loads of timber hit the water, causing a swell, and Daisy squeals in delight and points, mumbling, "Uh oh. Jack pole. Tommy not like dat." Some logs come up crisscrossed instead of floating flat on the surface.

Grace leans in, explaining that Tommy is one of the boom crew, and this jack poling is difficult to resolve. "One end of the log gets stuck in the ocean floor and it's almost impossible to free up by hand. It's dangerous work." Grace looks like she's about to say more, but after a glance at Daisy, she turns away, silent. I'll have to ask Thomas what happened out here.

Our tug is now inside the breakwater and the log dump, steaming up to a short pier near the shore in between them. Grace points out the coal bunker and the new stiff leg crane for unloading freight. Deckhands throw thick ropes, yelling greetings to their cronies, and the *Prosperity* is soon tied up. After we unload, we wait, watching the freight and our luggage get man-handled off the deck. Most of the workers travel light, grabbing worn suitcases as they're thumped onto the wharf, then walking to the gravel road toward a cluster of buildings.

Straight ahead is a big white house. The sole two-storey building boasts a prime view of the booming grounds, and I guess that Thomas's uncle lives there. Definitely management housing. I've never met the man, but have heard he's the brawn to Thomas's father's brains.

To our left, an angled row of smaller cabins, propped on stilts, line the shore along the curving gravel road. Workers from these bunkhouses wander toward a large, flat building where they queue by an open door next to a huge triangle dinner bell.

One of the dock workers heaves a big-wheeled hand truck toward shore with my luggage, George's suitcase, and crates of Grace's groceries stacked high. The thunk-thunk of wheels on dock boards echos my quickening heartbeat, and I fall in behind Billy, who has Daisy on his shoulders again. As promised, the dirt road running parallel to the rail track is both dusty and muddy, coating my boots with muck in the first few steps. I'm glad Grace made me take Daisy's advice.

The dock worker picks a safe route for the cart, chatting with George about the dinner menu. As we reach the cookhouse, the men in the lineup eye me curiously, shouting greetings at the others. A young worker is walking up the queue, collecting coins into a coffee can, and scribbling in a leather-bound notepad with a stubby pencil. As George and Billy approach, the man bounds over.

"You fellas want in?" He raises his eyebrows, pencil ready to take notes, but George shakes his head gruffly and Billy's eyes dart my way. Grace, too, is giving me an uncomfortable look. There's something they're hoping I won't understand.

"Come on, boys! Easy money," the younger man says. George steps chin-to-chin with him and growls something I can't make out. The coffee can man backs off with a slow whistle, saying, "Well now, don't flip yer wig there, Cookie!"

Unable to suppress my curiosity, I ask Grace what's going on. She shakes her head, looking at the ground. I lean over and grip her arm.

"Tell me, Grace. What's he talking about?" She holds my gaze for a moment, then lets out a breath and quietly explains they're betting on how long I'll last here. I stiffen, as heat creeps up my neck and into my cheeks. But anger also boils in my stomach. I stare down the line of men. A few of the older fellows give me a respectful nod, but most won't meet my eyes.

"What's the longest?" I stand tall, my voice steadier than I feel. The coffee can bookie scans his ledger with a smirk.

"Thirty-four days, ma'am." My eyebrows furrow. "An' that's only cuz it's summertime." I shake my head. Unbelievable! They're betting against me. In days. Not even in weeks or months. Now the crowd looks on with interest, my reaction sure to be the talk of their dinner tonight. Keeping my expression neutral, I lift my chin, digging into my skirt pocket. Then I pull a crisp dollar bill from my money clip and hold it over the can, doing a calculation.

"Today's the first of August. Five months, three with thirty-one days..." The bookie waits, puzzled. "So... 153 days," I say, dropping the money and ignoring the murmur rising from the crew. "I'll collect my winnings on the first day of 1925." Wide-eyed and shaking his head, the bookie solemnly adds my bet to his list. I peer down at the names and quit dates listed above mine, glaring over the bookie's shoulder to address the lineup of men, all of them sure that I'll be a goner by autumn. "Betting against me won't pay, gentlemen. I promise you that." I turn on my heel and push past the dock worker who's loading our belongings onto what can only be the speeder. Hoisting my skirt, I climb in without a backward glance. Then I collapse onto my luggage, leaning my head back against the rough wood interior wall, my heart pounding. I run my fingers over the steamer trunk's row of brass tacks.

Although it was shiny and new when I left Seattle, its first journey into this wilderness has already dented one metal corner. I know just how it feels.

CHAPTER 17

The speeder is a minimalist wooden box built over the frame of a single railroad car. The inside of the contraption is warm from the sun, smelling of sawdust and motor oil. I'm sitting on my steamer trunk beside the door opening, head slumped against the sidewall. Across from me, there's a row of four windows, all of them cracked, with a long bench below. At the front of this rickety passenger car are two rudimentary stick controls, next to a wood bump-out that I assume separates the engine from the interior.

Breathing heavily, I watch my muddy footprints dry into the dust on the filthy plank floor. I hate being the centre of attention. My face and neck still feel impossibly hot and I stand to wrestle off my coat. Through the cracked glass behind me, I see Camp 1's cook saunter up to the group I just bolted from. Dressed in a long white apron and a floppy chef's hat, he hands Grace and Billy each a wrapped packet, while he and George exchange a hard look. His expression softens when Daisy shouts for hers, and he drops something from his big hand into her tiny open palm. The cook squeezes her calf, winking, then stiffens as a tall young man emerges from the last bunkhouse.

The newcomer wears a tailored pinstripe suit and a striped trilby low over his brow. He ambles toward the coffee can man, looking like he's heading for a hotelier's five-course meal rather than a camp cookhouse. The jovial mood melts into uneasy murmurs. Jaws clench under grizzled beards and the younger men hold wide stances with their chests thrust out, rolling their eyes behind the man's back.

"What's the wager?" the suit asks loudly. The coffee can man bites the inside of his cheek, refusing to answer. "Come on then. What are we at?" Cook nods slightly when the coffee can man glances at him, so he answers.

"A dollar," the younger man says. The suit whistles between his teeth in response.

"Is that a fact?" Shifting his hat off his forehead, he turns, eyebrows raised, facing me for the first time. "Put me down for five, then." He reaches inside his suit, pulling a crisp note from a billfold, his eyes locking on mine through the speeder's window. I gasp in recognition as an uncontrollable shudder sweeps through my body. I haven't seen him in four months, and he's the reason I'm here now. The man in the gaudy trilby, just twenty feet away, is unmistakably James, the father of the child inside of me.

My legs weaken under me, and I collapse onto the bench. I roll my coat into a ball on my lap and lean over it, my mind racing. The speeder's floor swirls into a hazy brown and a roaring tide rushes through my head. It's impossible. I must be mistaken, must be seeing things. The air feels thick and the pulsating beats of my startled heart drown out the voices. It can't be.

When Billy lifts Daisy into the speeder, the blurred edges of my vision sharpen again, and I steady her as she crawls onto the bench.

Daisy chatters beside me while the men heave the freight on board. When Grace sits across from us, she raises a brow.

"You okay? You're pale as a ghost."

"Just a little hot," I say, nodding. "Who is that man?" My voice is low and surprisingly steady. She glares out the door.

"The suit? That's James. The men call him Jello. Thomas must have told you about him." I nod again, my thoughts tumbling. Could the James that ruined my life also be the foreman Thomas is replacing? It's inconceivable.

Billy jumps inside, flips down a small seat on hinges, and pulls a striped engineer's hat from a hook near the controls onto his curls.

"This here cap turns me into a proper railway man." His eyes twinkle at his own joke as he fiddles with the choke. "That Jello put in a fiver on you. Did you see that? He's got more money than brains, that one." He chuckles, shaking his head and clearing his throat. "No offence, ma'am." Billy turns back to the control.

Maybe I'm muddled, in a fog, seeing things because the baby is on my mind. If it is James out there, I should confront him. Stand up and introduce myself as Thomas's wife. See if he recognizes me. Or not. Thoughts tumble through my mind like leaves in the breeze.

When the speeder's gas engine finally fires, it sounds just like one of my father's Buicks, sputtering at first, then purring like a bunny getting its head scratched. George recognizes the motor's rumble as the signal to step inside. He's the last to board and directs me to the seat behind the newly minted engineer, where the views are best. I slide over, keeping my head below the window, and Daisy follows, kneeling next to me, her tiny fingers gripping the bottom windowsill and her nose pressed to the glass.

"Jello's comin', Momma." And a moment later, when he leaps onto the first step of the speeder and leans inside, there's no doubt. Jello is James. He scans the rocking speeder, his eyes finding mine.

"Nice to see you again, Mrs. Clark. Good to have another pretty lass up here." My heart races as his voice echoes through the air. So he does recognize me. And knows who I am. I tilt my head and force a polite smile, trying to mask my unease, unable to find my voice. James looks around the rail car, a charming grin on his face. "You folks have a safe trip now." His gaze flickers back to me. "Be seeing you around." He tips his trilby before stepping down and out of sight.

The speeder is silent for a long moment. I keep my eyes on the floor, hiding my trembling hands under my coat, where the flutter of a tiny foot grazes the inside of my belly.

"Do you know him?" Grace asks. I force another smile, hoping I'm hiding my distress.

"No. No, I don't."

"He seemed to know you, though." Grace persists, and all eyes are on me for a response.

"I ran into him once. At a house party. In Seattle. I... I'm surprised to see him here. That's all. He never said he worked in forestry." My voice sounds shrill, but the answer satisfies my new friends.

"All set, then?" George asks. Everyone nods, so Billy ratchets a creaky lever, engaging a rusty drive chain. The reluctant wheels move us first along the shore's open flats, then around a bend into the shadows of thick forest, on rails that incline steadily. The motor groans with the increased load, but soon we're moving at a pace that feels a little unsafe.

When, a few minutes later, we slow and stop, I'm glad. Billy hops out to throw a heavy manual switch, moving us past the intersection down the right-hand track. He disembarks again to heave the railway switch back, before urging the jouncing car to a suicidal speed. The cool forest air wraps around us, carrying the earthy scent of the moss-covered floor. Thick trunks of rough fir rush by and sunlight dapples the drooping ferns. The rail cuts uphill, in gentle curves, our bodies lurching against each other and the walls, but my fellow passengers are undeterred by our perilous pace.

Bouncing along with the railcar's beat, Grace opens the packet the cook gave her and offers me half her sandwich. I refuse it, taking out the one I bought on the *SS Cardena*, hoping the activity of eating will distract me from the unexpected reunion with my past. Beside me, Daisy plunks on her bottom and unwraps a white saltwater taffy, her gift from the cook. Gold evening light streams in through the window behind Grace, dust specks dancing between us.

Daisy's chubby fingers untwist the jostling wax paper wrapper, her concentration fully on the morsel inside. Grace watches her daughter from beyond the swirling sunbeam, her face soft, eyes filled with pride and love. My mother never gave me that look. Not even close. Although I've seen it on Father's face. He enjoyed us as children, while Mother found us noisy and messy.

"It's mint!" Daisy holds up the candy between grimy fingers, her chest thrust out, her lips pursed. She studies the taffy and looks around the speeder at each of us. "Share?" she asks. I shake my head, smiling, and the rest of the group does too. Daisy sags against the vibrating sidewall. Her instinct is to share, but her pure relief at not having to softens my face into a smile as she takes a bite of the candy, a wisp of pulled sugar sticking to her chin.

We've been in the rattling speeder for over half an hour when the grade goes downhill again. My rump is sore from the rhythmic clunking, but my belly is full and I let my eyelids droop, wondering if I'll ever look at my child the way Grace does hers, without regret or shame. I've been able to suppress those feelings, but seeing James again has shattered the fragile peace I've built these past few weeks.

I startle awake in motionless silence. The speeder is parked, the chugging engine shut down, and Daisy scrambles from the bench using my skirt for balance, her fists pounding my knee.

"We're home, Mrs. Eva!" Home indeed. I move to the open door, my pulse pounding as I squint at Thomas's silhouette in the evening sunlight. The wind ruffles his thick, dark hair, and behind him, the lake water sparkles. He peers into the shadows of the speeder, unable to contain a grin. Striding close, he grasps my waist and lifts me out of the railcar, swinging me to the chunky track ballast. His eyes are wide and glowing as he tucks a curl into my hat, cupping my cheek with his palm.

"How was your journey? How are you feeling?" His brows draw together as he glances at my middle.

"Bumpy. Good. Exhausted." Without thinking, I nuzzle my face into his rough palm, savouring his touch. Just being near Thomas soothes some of the churning anxiety my encounters at Camp 1 caused. "It's good to see you."

Daisy is already scampering along the main track, away from the spur where the speeder is parked. Grace yells after her to be careful, laughing and shaking her head as Daisy stumbles on the gravel path and disappears beside one of the middle buildings. Billy follows Grace, both of their arms loaded with groceries and supplies.

Beside us, George is loading crates onto a large-wheeled wagon. Thomas says a few words to him before he turns back to me.

"Your seedlings make the journey alright?"

"I think so," I say, nodding. "It was pretty hot in Vancouver, but George got me water." As my thoughts shift to my work, a slow warmth fills my chest, but it's quickly replaced by an ache in my throat. Without a job, my new ideas about manual replanting won't be tested for a long time.

"Let me take you to the cabin. The fellows will bring your things over." Thomas offers me his elbow and leads me along the track. The evening is a perfect temperature, with a strong breeze off the lake kicking up my skirt and swirling dust devils on the rail ballast and gravel ahead of us. He guides me to the first building and stops at the front door, squinting at me.

"What is it?" I ask.

"Well, I was going to carry you over the threshold." He awaits my reaction, the corners of his mouth twitching and eyebrows raised. The day's stresses melt away at his mischievous look.

"Oh, fine!" Laughing, I shift my bag out of the way and throw an arm around his neck, letting him sweep me into his arms. Thomas leans in and kisses me for the first time since he left.

"Welcome home, my love." His hair smells of wood smoke, and he presses his lips to mine with such tenderness that my heart flutters. Kissing him back, I'm filled with an urge to tell him the truth. I should be honest with my husband. My husband. This man becoming a father to my child. Husband. Father. Both words roll around my brain. If the facts about me and James and this baby came out — the thought makes me shudder.

Thomas pulls back, his gaze locked on mine, sensing the shift in my mood. But he just climbs carefully into the cabin, where I hop out of his arms, dropping my bag against the spindles of a hardback chair.

"What do you think?" Thomas stands motionless, studying in my reaction.

"You're not sure I'll make it here, are you?" The doubt on his tight face is easy to read.

"I wasn't even sure you'd show up today." He tries to laugh, but his voice comes out gruff as he shoves his hands in his pockets, rocking onto his heels. "And I'm really glad you did." His eyes follow me as I take a quick inventory of the one-room cabin.

The window above the kitchen basin floods the room with light, and I run my palms along the smooth wood countertop, staring over-top the rail tracks, and across the vast lake to the towering forest-covered mountains.

"It's lovely. A million dollar view." I turn back to Thomas with a smile. "Could use a woman's touch, though, huh?" He laughs, relaxing, and I say, "Lucky for us, Mother packed more frills than we'll ever use." The room's only fabric is a wool four-point blanket on the bed. Sitting, I run a hand over its thick stripes in Queen Anne's colours, then notice a milk bottle brimming with fireweed and salal on the bedside table.

The crunch of gravel outside announces the delivery of my trunks, which Thomas and two workers haul into the cabin, dropping them onto the plank floor. When the men leave, Thomas offers to fetch a meal from the cookhouse. But I shake my head, still fingering the ferns tucked around the arrangement of *Chamaenerion angustifolium* and *Gaultheria shallon*.

"No. I'm ready for bed." This afternoon's events and yesterday's restless night make my bones feel leaden, and the urge to lie down overcomes me. "Did you do this?" I point at the flowers, looking up at Thomas. He nods.

"Thought you'd like a taste of the flora around here." A shy, radiant smile lights his face and my throat tightens with emotion as I imagine him picking flowers with me in mind. He steps close, cupping my cheek again. "I'll let you get settled then. Be back shortly. Just gonna do a quick round of the camp."

A few minutes later, I'm curled under the wool blanket in my nightdress. The coil springs creak as I roll onto my side, the encounter with James flashing through my mind. It's unbelievable. There's only one human I never want to see again... and he's here, at the end of the earth. What an absurd coincidence.

My stomach churns, and the room feels small as I contemplate my options. If Thomas knew James had fathered this child, it would complicate his relationship with James even more. From what I gather, James is already upset about being replaced by a complete greenhorn. And James doesn't know I'm pregnant. Yet. He just knows we shared a night. Once.

A chill snakes down my spine and a weight clamps around my heart as I squeeze my eyes shut. The bunkhouse is quiet, except for the faint lull of waves lapping against the beach somewhere below me. My body weighs heavily on the mattress ticking, but sleep doesn't come. Some time later, across the water, the sun slips behind the mountain, dimming the room and leaving me in grey shadows.

I flinch awake when Thomas returns and quietly latches the front door. Beyond the window, stars now sparkle. When Thomas spoons me from behind and wraps an arm over me, I stiffen. His presence still feels foreign. But I soon relax into him as his rough hand skims the length of my body, then rests on my tight belly. I'll have to tell him about the baby movement I felt. Exhausted, I close my eyes, breathing in the fresh air of my new home, wondering if this simple place can get any more complicated.

CHAPTER 18

When I wake up the next morning, Thomas is gone and the bed sheets beside me are cold. The clear sky is a dark blue, but brightening. I fold a pillow under my head and pull the soft covers under my chin, watching the shade gently shift as the night pushes away. Inside, the rhythmic tick of Thomas's silver-faced alarm clock accentuates the silence. With the wind gone, the lake is quiet, but in the woods behind me, a squirrel chatters and a bird whistles cheerfully. A robin, maybe? I listen to the repeating, flute-like notes. Yes, definitely a *Turdus migratorius*.

Then nature's sounds are drowned out by the crunch of footsteps and laughing voices outside. Workers stream by on their way out onto the lake and the rail, their canvas hats bobbing past the cabin's window. My stomach tightens with envy at their purpose, as I wonder what I'm supposed to do here all day.

Suddenly restless, I throw off the covers and open my trunk, picking heavy cotton trousers and a short-sleeved blouse. My wool socks catch on the rough-hewn floor planks, so I dig out my slippers and pad over to the corner away from the bare window, where I'm the least visible while dressing. I'll have to hang the curtains today. The baby's soft kick at my bladder reminds me to find a bathroom and breakfast.

On the counter is a note scrawled in Thomas's neat handwriting.

Good morning! Go see George at the cookhouse for breakfast. I'll check in at lunchtime. T.

His simple message makes me think of the old Thomas, the one who was just my friend, whose loyal interest in me felt easy, and I smile. Outside the front door, I sit on the step and lace my boots, watching a black garter snake bask motionless on the warm stones. Standing, I breathe in the sweet scent of summer, startling the *Thamnophis sirtalis*, which slithers under the bunkhouse. From my left, the work crew's shouts and clangs drift across the bay. The clatter gets louder until empty railcars come into view, the steam of the engine trailing a path above the forest until its black body also exits the trees.

I walk away from the action and find the outhouse across from our cabin. If I leave the door open, which I don't, it has a stunning view of the lake and mountains. There's no crepe finish toilet paper here. Instead, a stack of old catalogues is piled neatly in the corner. To distract myself from the stench that is equally stunning, I flip through last winter's Spencer's catalogue, stopping on a page on how to order hockey tube skates to match your boot size. I tear out a sheet depicting hockey sticks, priced from twenty-five cents for a boy's to a dollar for a goalkeeper's, and wipe. This defiant anti-hockey act makes me think of Tony, and a grin tugs at the corners of my mouth before a pang of sorrow tightens my chest.

When I step outside, I breathe again, filling my lungs with the honeyed aroma of sun-kissed foliage. My stomach growls as I latch the outhouse door, then walk down to the shore to wash my hands before heading in for breakfast.

The cookhouse here is much smaller than the one at Camp 1, but the same triangle dinner bell hangs next to the entrance, and inside the smell of bacon and coffee makes my mouth water.

"Well, there you are!" George grins, waving long tongs. "Have a seat." But instead of sitting, I lean against the dimpled sheet metal counter separating his kitchen from the four sturdy sawbuck tables in the dining hall. "Over easy okay?" he asks. I nod, famished, as he moves with practised ease around the compact workspace.

Behind him along the far wall, pitchers and pots dangle overhead from railway spikes hammered into the support beams. Firewood is stacked as high as the counter, and on the main burner of the large woodstove, a pot of chili simmers. Beside the pot, my eggs fry, and when they're ready, George flips them in the air. He pours me a mug of steaming coffee from a huge dented percolator, disappearing for a moment behind towels draped on the drying rack above the stove.

He comes out of the kitchen, motioning me to the table, and I slide onto a heavy half-log bench. George passes me a muffin on a tin plate, placing the coffee in front of me on the smooth oilcloth table covering.

"Mug up, Boss," he says, with a teasing smile. I sniff the brew cautiously. A few days ago, the aroma set off my morning sickness. Thankfully, that stage seems to have passed and I inhale the thick scent of my first camp coffee. It's bitter and burnt, but heavenly. George watches with satisfaction as my eyelids flutter closed and I sigh, cupping my hands around the hot mug. He strides back into the kitchen, clattering plates and pans.

I tear open the muffin, laden with huckleberries, and spread it with butter. As I finish the last bite, George slides a plate of eggs, bacon, and fresh bread in front of me.

"This all looks delicious. Thank you." And it is. Especially the bread, and I scold George for suggesting that his baking isn't as good as the Vancouver port's famous sandwich spot. "Your bread is better, George. It really is." His chest puffs out a little and he can't hide his smile as he wipes down the counter, but then he stops, crossing his arms and looking stern.

"Tomorrow, though, it's six o'clock if you wanna eat, Boss. No more custom meals." I blink at his harsh words, as he plunks a stoneware crock beside a huge dented bowl.

"I'm sorry. I didn't know." But George waves me off, softening, so I ask him when his day starts.

"Well, I'm in here at four. Bakin' bread and preppin' breakfast. The fellas come in at five o'clock, family and office staff at six. Then dishes and lunch prep. More baking for supper." He takes the lid off the crock and pours a fruity smelling batter into the bowl. Before covering it again, he stirs flour and water into the remaining batter.

"Sourdough starter." George replies to my unasked question. "Gotta feed it every day. Started it here last year — just lake water and flour." He tucks the stoneware crock back under the counter, continuing his monologue about his daily routine.

"'Bout this time of day, I make more bread and cookies or cake. Then fix the lunch. More dishes and supper prep. Supper at five and six o'clock." He adds water and flour to the dented bowl, stirring with a flattened wood stick before dumping it onto the floured counter.

"If everyone eats quick, I get to bed by eight or nine." He kneads the sourdough, pushing and folding it deftly, adding flour with a dash of his hand when it sticks.

"That's a long day, George." My eyes widen, mesmerized by the flipping dough.

"An' I don' get Sundays off, like the fellas."

"I couldn't do it." Logging is a tough occupation, but I hadn't considered the work needed to keep everyone fed. And I'm in awe of George's commitment and sixteen-hour days.

"Aw, ya could, if ya had to." George shoots me a grin, a twinkle in his eye as he cuts the lump into four pieces, shaping round loaves with just a few pulls of his big hands. After he slices the tops and lays a towel over the dough, he wipes the bowl clean. When he starts to grate carrots, I push away from the table and excuse myself.

"Thanks again. See you at lunch." George waves and shouts a good-bye from the woodstove door, where he shoves a piece of firewood inside, frowning and muttering.

Outside, the morning is bright, and the wind has started a ripple on the sparkling lake. Thomas and two workers huddle near the cook-house, across the tracks, stretching a paper scroll between them. Plans for the new shingle mill, probably.

Beyond our cabin, the workers at the reload haul logs from the water. The equipment, which I've only ever seen in textbooks, is big, loud, and dirty. A groaning Empire engine hoists cable on a loading boom, dragging dripping timbers up out of the lake, and swinging them overtop the empty railcars. When the steam locie revs to move the train forward, I'm jolted from my reverie. I've been standing in the sun, watching the work, for at least half an hour. Reluctantly, I turn to the cabin — I should get something productive done before I see Thomas at lunch.

Inside, I flip open the steamer trunk of Mother's carefully selected linens and take an inventory, resenting that this is the task I'm relegated to. But, I've vowed to make the best of this situation. So making Thomas's life a little brighter, while he earns a living to support me, is a fair trade. I'll just have to keep my mind engaged. I wonder whether Thomas will share his work with me. Until now, we've collaborated well, to the point of competition. We're close to equals academically, and working with each other pushed us to do better in our studies. But now, proper work, paid work, might make him less willing to share.

I tackle the curtains first, climbing on a chair to hang the lace netting from the rough cast-iron pipe nailed above the window. Mother had agonized over whether the Philadelphia or New York fabrics would suit best, while the decorator at Frederick & Nelson presented her with endless samples. I had worked hard to hide my impatience, nodding and murmuring my approval of each of Mother's tedious decisions.

Standing back now, the fine spun fabric veils the view and provides privacy, while still letting in most of the bright sunlight. It's perfect. The heavy brocade curtains, which I pull out next, are another story. Rich burgundy silk is woven with a raised silver pattern, oozing an air of deluded elegance in this rough cabin. I lay the material back in the trunk, unable to imagine its purpose out here in the wilderness.

The rest of the trunk is packed with Egyptian cotton sheets, a stack of linen tea towels, and a collection of woven dish rags. First, I remake our bed, tucking the sheets over the tufted mattress's stained ticking with military precision, then spreading the wool blanket back overtop. I tug until the red, green, yellow, and indigo stripes are perfectly parallel to the steel tube headboard. Since George runs the only kitchen in this camp, the cooking linens are useless and get stacked back in the trunk. I'm a housewife without a kitchen. How ironic.

By eleven o'clock I pull the lace curtains closed and lay across the crisp sheets, breathing in the lavender scent of home, as the sunlight warms my body. My thoughts drift to the career I hoped to build, the methods of manual seedling replanting I aspired to prove profitable.

My days here won't be as I imagined life after university. I'm surrounded by the forest I crave, but instead of implementing new ideas,

I'm hiding a stupid pregnancy. An ache fills the back of my throat as I curl my body around a pillow, sobbing softly until I fade into sleep.

Chapter 19

When I wake up, the sun hangs high over the mountain peak across the lake, and I squint into the brightness. I cross the rough floor to the counter and find another note from Thomas, propped against a tin bowl.

"Didn't have the heart to wake you for lunch. Feed the little bump some of George's chili. See you at dinner. T."

Out on the front step, I devour the rich, meaty broth, my spoon scraping the bowl clean. I'm glad Thomas didn't wake me. There's no benefit in him seeing my sadness, and I couldn't have hidden it.

In the thicket to my right, on a papery salmonberry stem, a hummingbird perches, its iridescent orange-red throat patch flashing in the sunlight. A breeze shakes the branch and the tiny bird emits a high-pitched warning chirp. Then the *Selasphorus rufus* turns toward me, taking flight and hovering so close I can hear the low hum of its wings. After it flits away, Daisy appears from around the cabin.

"Hi! Lookit." She greets me like an old friend, then thrusts her palms into my face, above the chili bowl. Together we watch a fuzzy caterpillar work its way across her grubby hands, wriggling its orange and black banded body until it finds the edge and Daisy flips her palm over to let it do another lap.

"That's a banded woolly worm. *Pyrrharctia isabella*. It lived all winter as a caterpillar, and soon it'll spin a cocoon and pupate into a big white moth, able to fly around." Daisy considers this with wide eyes, brushing the woolly worm's long white bristles with a gentle finger. Without warning, she dumps it into a patch of grass by my feet, where it curls into a fuzzy ball.

"There. Pretty Isabella grow into a flutterby now." She wipes her palms together and puts a hand on my thigh, looking up at me with a measured expression. "You don't look bad, Mrs. Eva." She tilts her head and scrunches her nose.

"No?" Baffled by where her little brain is headed, it's all I can think to say. This has nothing to do with caterpillars.

"No. But you is here cuz you got in trouble." She nods solemnly. "So you must be bad if you gots in trouble." My eyebrows raise as I piece together her meaning, but I stifle a laugh.

"Oh? Who says so?" I have a guess, but I'll let her confirm it.

"My daddy. He says you gots in trouble. And that you and Mr. Thomas had rifles at your wedding." Daisy turns her blue eyes up at me, frowning. "Why you have shooting at your wedding, Mrs. Eva? I gotta know." Her face scrunches even more. "When Momma's friend Josie gots married, I be very quiet and throw flowers. Then I ate cake. Lots of cake." She smiles and nods, running her tongue over her lips at the memory. "But no guns." She shakes her head, puzzled.

I feel the urge to be honest with Daisy, to explain the term shotgun wedding and exactly how women get themselves in trouble. But I decide against it. Given Daisy's eloquent rewording of adult conversations just now, being honest here can only cause more problems. Instead, I distract her through her stomach.

"What kind of cake did you have at Josie's wedding? I had chocolate." This isn't strictly the truth, since we didn't have a wedding. But I did enjoy a delectable slice of ganache tart at the Olympic the night of our marriage. Daisy chatters on, and I wonder what we could do to kill the afternoon. Then I have an idea.

"Can you give me a tour of the camp?" I ask, and Daisy stands a little taller.

"Yep. I know all the things! Come wiff me." And she grabs my hand, pulling me off the step and across the landing. "This is one outhouse. For pee and poop." I nod solemnly. "Waaay over there, 'hind George's cookhouse, is 'nother outhouse. Better bwing George dat bowl, Mrs. Eva." She points at the chili dish I'm still holding. "Let's go there first." Daisy tugs me toward the building at the far end of camp. "Maybe they gots cookies."

A sweet caramel scent greets us outside the cookhouse. Daisy stops under the forged metal dinner bell, pointing at the single piece of steel, bent into a triangle, hanging from a thick leather cord.

"Billy bangs with this —" she says, pointing to the clangour hooked on a nail in the siding, "— on that, and makes a big noise. Means hurry up, food ready!" Her sing-song words make me smile as she stands on tiptoe to turn the doorknob, heaving the heavy door open. She scampers in shouting, "Hiya George! Hiya Edith!" Daisy disappears into the kitchen before I even step inside.

When my eyes adjust to the dimness, I walk to the counter. Edith, a stout woman in her sixties, wearing an apron dusted with flour, leans down to give Daisy a cookie. Salt and pepper streaks weave through her wiry hair, bundled into a bun on the top of her head. When her wrinkled face clears the countertop, her eyes crinkle into a smile.

"Can I offer you one, Mrs. Clark? Chocolate chip." Her words are raspy, but her welcoming tone makes me nod without hesitation. With a veined hand, she slides the cookie plate across the counter. "They're delicious. Ol' Coot's recipe." She jabs a nicotine-stained finger at George, who's banging a sheet tray into the wood stove, grumbling about the fire.

I take a bite of the cookie, the buttery crunch oozing with generous chunks of dark chocolate, still warm from the oven.

"It's delicious," I say. Daisy gobbles hers, with little-girl fierceness, concentrating hard to not drop any, and I smile at the older woman.

"I'm Edith. Edith Campbell." She nods, stretching across the workspace, wiping crumbs from the counter. Her white sleeves are rolled past her elbows, and lines of burns, old and new, pock her forearms. "I'm the cookee. With an e-e. Not an i-e." She chuckles at herself. "Help George with 'bout everythin'."

"Nice to meet you," I say. She brushes her hands on her apron again before turning to a bowl of raw potatoes, her knife creating curls of peel that spiral in a heap with impressive speed. George and Edith move around each other in the tight kitchen with unspoken understanding, passing ingredients and utensils back and forth. When Daisy licks the last trace of chocolate from her fingers, I reach toward her.

"Come along, Daisy. These two have work to do." She places her sticky hand in mine as I pull open the door. "And thank you for the cookies!"

Daisy echoes my words over her shoulder, "Thank you, Edith!"

Back out in the sunshine, Daisy scampers ahead, leading me to the row of bunkhouses. I count nine buildings, and all except one face the gravel landing. Each is railcar-sized, with a cedar shake roof and board and batten siding. Wooden steps lead to identical front doors, their painted numbers the only thing differentiating each from the others.

Daisy crouches to pick up a barkless stick and points it at number seven. "That's Billy's. You know Billy. He's the bull cook. But he don't cook, he do chores. Like chopping wood." She points to a large round with an axe stuck in it, beside the cookhouse. "So why do they call him that, Mrs. Eva? I gotta know!" Her puzzled gaze looks up at me, and I shrug.

"In some places, bull cooks start the day by feeding livestock. So they sort of cook for the cows. But you're right, Daisy, it's an odd term." Her brows stay furrowed, but she moves on undeterred.

"Daddy says Billy gets demons inside. From rotgut. What's rotgut? I gotta know!" This time, I tell Daisy that it's a type of drink. Her eyes narrow, my answer not making sense to her, as she walks to the next building.

"An' this, is Edith. Her crazy Ken got killed by a mainline." Daisy runs her hand across her throat and sticks her tongue out to the side, lolling her head. She giggles as I clasp a hand over my mouth, horrified. "And she put 'im on the train in a wooden box and he never came back. The Company said Edith go home, but she said no way so now she works for George, the ol' coot." Daisy leans over to poke a large muddy-brown banana slug. Its slimy tail collects tiny pebbles and pine needles and an iridescent liquid crystal trail tracks its meandering route.

"*Ariolimax columbianus*," I say, and Daisy frowns.

"No. 'Nana slug," she says, correcting me, before flicking it under building five and pointing her stick at the bunkhouse.

"An' this one, this is George. He's been here always and is the best cook in all the camps and we're very lucky to have the ol' coot." Daisy giggles again. Grace would likely ask her not to call George that, but

I'm not the parent here. I lay a palm over the top of my trousers, feeling a kick. I'll have plenty of time to make child-rearing choices when our own little person joins us. "Daddy says George is goofy for Edith. What does goofy mean, Mrs. Eva? I gotta know!" Is it wise to tell this wordy child? Probably not, but I refuse to lie. Or to be evasive.

"It means George likes Edith."

"Maybe." Daisy tilts her head and shrugs. "But they're always yelling at each other and throwing towels. Bein' goofy must mean fightin'. That's what I think." Daisy kicks a piece of driftwood, revealing a pill bug. She crouches, picking up the squirming insect between her thumb and index finger. It promptly rolls into a little grey-brown ball.

"Wood bug." She thrusts her palm toward me.

"*Armadillidium vulgare*. It's not a bug. It's a soil-dwelling crustacean." Daisy narrows her eyes at the big words.

"Armadillo —" Daisy struggles to say it, then laughs, and drops the critter to the ground. "You talk funny, Mrs. Eva. It's a rollie pollie wood bug. That's what I think." She stands and pulls me toward the next bunkhouse.

"This is Donkey Donny an' Crank. They run the train and are pretty good for a couple of Yanks."

"And what are Yanks, Daisy?" The connections her mind makes are fascinating, and I can't resist asking.

"Well..." She kicks the gravel and cocks her head. "I suppose Yanks are fellas who help the train pull." She motions, as if yanking on a tug-of-war rope, and I grin.

I learn that Tetley and Paul live in the next cabin. They run the reload and if they're not more careful sprinting along the booms, one of them is for sure gonna drown any day now. In the neighbouring bunkhouse, two brothers, Grinder and Slim, make their home.

Daisy admits they're not smart, but they're strong and friendly. Useful flunkies to have around.

We're back at my cabin, the clanks and shouts of the reload louder here, and Daisy points to the building tucked into the trees close to the rail spur, explaining it's a guest bunk. I consider what to do next when Daisy tugs on my arm, pulling toward camp.

"Let's go to my house! Come see Momma. She'll give us tea and snacks. Daddy's at work. He's the boss, you know. Well, Mr. Thomas is the boss, but my daddy does all the work. Come on!" We turn and see Thomas approaching, the smirk on his face confirming he heard Daisy's last declaration.

"Well hello, Daisy. Are you showing Eva around?" She nods her head solemnly, wide blue eyes gazing up at Thomas until he crouches. "Thank you." He holds out a hand and Daisy shakes it with a serious look. "It's hard to move to a place without friends, so I'm glad you're being a friend to Eva." He peers at me over Daisy's blond curls and winks from under his dark bangs.

"We're going for tea now with Momma. And snacks."

"Snacks are great! But I'd like to take Eva for a walk. Would it be okay if she came back to see you later?"

Their serious conversation fills me with a sense of calm, and for the first time, I picture being a family with Thomas. He's good with children.

"I guess." Daisy lowers her chin, her shoulders drooping, but answers the question in the way the grown-ups expect her to. Thomas ruffles her hair, stands, and offers me his elbow.

"Thank you for the tour, Daisy. It was fun. I'll see you at dinner, okay?" She mumbles her agreement and scampers toward cabin eight, shouting for Grace. Turning to Thomas, I say, "You'll need to explain everyone's nicknames. I'm intrigued." He laughs, shaking his head, as I continue. "It's a bit early for you to be off, isn't it?"

"I'm worried about you." The way he tilts his head and holds my gaze confirms he noticed, when he came home for lunch, that I cried myself to sleep. We know each other so well. There's no use in pretending, so I just smile ruefully and change the subject.

"I felt the baby kick. On the steamship yesterday." Goodness, was that only yesterday? Thomas's face lights up and he bends to kiss my waist, whispering something into my belly. When he straightens, he fiddles with his shirtsleeves before wrapping his arms around me.

"I love you. And I'm going to love this baby." He pulls back, tucking a strand of hair behind my ear and cupping my cheek with his hand. "I just want you to be happy here."

"I know. But I miss having a project, a purpose." Leaning against his palm, I look into his eyes, realizing this truth. "And I'm just not sure what that is anymore. I'll figure it out." Thomas's lips form a tight line, then he nods and leads me toward our cabin. Without the distraction of Daisy's chatter, the ache returns to my throat. If Thomas's love was enough to give me purpose, I would thrive up here. But I'll need a meaningful pursuit to sustain me if I'm going to collect on my one-dollar bet on New Year's Day.

CHAPTER 20

The next day, after breakfast, I wander down to the river behind the cookhouse. With five long hours to kill before lunch, I perch on a driftwood log, picking at the bark and wondering how I'll survive the day. The river murmurs lazily over cobbles and around old stumps, its banks lush with greenery. Nootka rose, red-twig dogwood, and Pacific ninebark bushes flank the water, with tufted hairgrass rustling along the damp shoreline in the morning breeze. Midstream, atop an old silvery cedar blowdown, moss and ferns grow. On the far bank, yellow pond lilies dot the surface.

A distant shout and metallic clunks from my left break into nature's scene. Across the river's headwater, a series of logs are chained together, and far beyond it chugs a steamboat. It tows a raft-like log boom from one of the Company's other camps on the lake. Voices drift across the water as the men from the boat and our camp work to lash the precious timber to the piles inside our booming grounds. The reload crew will load these logs onto railcars and haul them to Camp 1, where they'll be dumped in the Pacific for transport to market.

When the steamboat blasts a whistle and chugs south again, I stand, rubbing my aching rump before scrambling up the gravel riverbank. The scent of baking bread and the rhythmic thunk of wood chopping greets me behind the cookhouse. I round the corner and lurch to a stop as a piece of firewood tumbles toward my feet. Billy faces away from me, burying his axe into another twelve-inch round and heaving it from the ground onto the chopping block. He pries the shiny silver blade from the wood, spinning the round until its level and steady, then stands wide, swinging the axe over his head easily. The muscles of his bare shoulders ripple beneath glistening tan skin. With a few more blows, he whacks the round into six even pieces.

Billy drops the heavy axe head onto the chopping block and sniffs, digging for a handkerchief. He wipes the sweat from his brow and blows his nose, freezing when he turns in my direction, seeing me for the first time.

"Morning, Billy," I say, smiling. "Going to be a hot one today."

"Yes, ma'am." He blinks his red-rimmed eyes, turning away and clearing his throat. His sharp movements mimic those of Tony's when he was upset and my breath catches. Growing up, I always wanted to remove my brother's suffering, while being keenly aware of my inability to do so. Instead, I'd sit with him, or work beside him on whatever punishment he was given, silently showing my camaraderie.

Now, as my gaze refocuses, it feels wrong to just walk away from this boy, who's clearly troubled by something. So, I stoop to pick up a split piece of fir, stacking it under the overhang built along the cookhouse wall. I try to match Billy's rhythm, but he's taller and stronger. We work side by side without a word. When the last of the chopped wood is piled, I break the silence.

"I'd like to try that," I say, nodding toward the chopping block. Billy frowns, and his gaze drops to my mid-section before he clears his throat again.

"Dunno, ma'am." He holds my gaze. "Not so sure the boss would like that."

"I just need... I need something useful to do." My voice shakes a little and my shoulders slump. It seems everyone here knows my secret. Whether it's my pregnancy or something else that makes Billy treat me like I'm fragile, it's frustrating. I need to do something more than walk and sit. Billy straightens, pointing to a black tool mounted to the wall of the cookhouse.

"You can prob'ly use the kindling splitter." He raises the tool's arm, placing a piece of wood against one notch in the stepped cast iron. When he presses the two-foot-long sharpened arm against the chunk, it splits. Billy repositions the wood onto progressively higher notches to maintain leverage as the cut advances. After just a few strokes, he drops the kindling into a wooden crate and holds out the remaining wood to me. "Give 'er a go." I struggle at first, but with a few tips from Billy, I'm soon reaching for another chunk, grinning. "Good goin', ma'am!" His excited tone again reminds me of Tony. At least my presence seems to have distracted Billy from whatever was upsetting him when I arrived.

"Thank you. And for goodness' sake, Billy, call me Eva."

"Sure, ma'am. I will, ma'am." He grins, pulling his shirt off the woodpile, striding off to his next chore. I smile after him, envying the purpose in his gait.

I cut kindling until lunch, then return to the bunkhouse after taking my meal with the others. A short while later, Thomas brings home a metal tube of drawings.

"I could use your help on something." He unrolls the prints onto the table and weighs them down with a couple of empty mugs. "These are maps of our setting, showing all the timber we aim to harvest in the next five years." Thomas explains the planned sequencing, and the biggest challenge he's contemplating with management. "See this section here? It's more than half our current cut. But to log it, we need to get across this ravine." He circles an area south of camp with his finger. "We need to find a route that lets us build the railroad within safe grade tolerances. And minimizes the size of the bridge."

I spend the afternoon poring over the maps and sketching elevations on graph paper. After dinner, Thomas sits with me as I ask countless questions about the work. When he finally insists we go to bed, it's well past dark. I'm still filled with unanswered queries when we tuck under the covers and he gently blows out the lantern. As the rafters disappear into shadow, ideas swirl through my head. Thomas rolls to his side, placing a palm on my hip.

"Tomorrow we're topping a spar. I'll take you out to the setting. It's something to see." I nod, reaching to squeeze his hand, eager to observe the active work site. "I love you, Eva," he whispers, kissing my fingers.

Thomas is soon snoring, but sleep eludes me for hours. The night is quiet except for the scurrying of deer mice across the floorboards. The *Peromyscus maniculatus'* tiny claws create a delicate percussion as they scurry around the bunkhouse, a hypnotic accompaniment to the familiar energy of a challenge vibrating inside me.

Thomas knows me well. I thrive when tested by complex projects, and this bridge work will require intricate calculations, knowledge of materials, and an understanding of the local terrain. It's not strictly forestry work, but my math skills were the best in our class, and my drafting is decent. Plus, where the new rail line is placed will affect our harvest's impact on the habitat. When I finally drift into sleep, there's a smile on my face. Maybe this is the perfect way to exert quiet influence over the Company's ways. The only improvement would be a monetary recognition for my contributions.

Thomas comes by after breakfast and we head out to the setting to-gether. Tall, uncut timber borders the railbed on both sides for the first part of the hike. In the damp morning shade, the no-see-ums feast on every inch of uncovered skin, leaving itchy red welts on my arms and calves.

An hour later, when the grade levels, we emerge from the forest onto a logged plateau. In the distance, the train track ends next to a single remaining fir tree with a large white X carved into the bark at its vast base. Donkey Don and Crank are talking to Roy beside the steam donkey parked nearby. Thomas explains they already removed the limbs up to the 170-foot mark, and today Roy will top the fir, leaving only the sturdy trunk. Then the crew will rig it with pulleys and cables, as the central point of our high-lead logging system. With the help of the steam donkey, the spar tree will act like a crane, dragging logs to the train track, and loading them onto cars. It stands like a lone soldier on a battlefield, its bottle brush branches a salute to the fallen comrades surrounding it.

Beyond the spar, at the edge of the clear-cut, the crew is falling a tree. A pile of fresh, pinkish-yellow wood chunks lay below an under-cut wide enough for five men. Up on springboards, notched into the trunk, Grinder and Slim jerk a misery whip back and forth above the root collar. Standing between them, Billy oils the saw and taps a wedge into the kerf. We watch from a distance, the blade biting deeper with each stroke.

When the tree finally leans, Billy yells a warning, and the men scramble away. The giant fir creaks and lets out a thunderous crack.

It falls in a whooshing silence and crashes through the underbrush, snapping twigs. The ground under my feet trembles as the thick trunk bends and whips up once with surprising flexibility, and then settles into the clearing. Grinder and Slim give a loud hoot, grabbing their bucking saws, and start removing limbs while Billy moves their gear to the next tree.

Thomas climbs onto a log, pulling me up after him. We traverse the toppled tree trunks crisscrossing the setting, high above the thick underbrush. At the south edge of the clearing, atop a small knoll, he hoists me onto an enormous red cedar stump. The ancient giant's heart is hollow, full of fluffy rust-coloured decay. I crouch, fingering the dark redwood tree rings, counting over 600, and estimate the rumpled edges of the stump measure twelve feet across.

"They're so old and huge, when you see them up close. Way bigger than they look from a distance," I say. As he pulls me upright, Thomas grins at my wide-eyed amazement.

"And we have hundreds of acres of these monsters." Thomas points south, the vista below breathtaking. "You're looking at half the lake. It's almost fourteen miles long in all." The valley spreads out below us. Steep slopes of pristine, green forest surround the mile-wide, glistening, black body of water. He turns, pointing toward our camp on the right, nestled at the headwaters, hidden from our view by trees and terrain. "And the only way to get any of this timber out to the Pacific and to market is through our camp's reload. Over the past ten years, we bought up all this land." He waves his arm across the north end of the lake. "Our competitors can buy timber rights up and down this lake. But they'll have no easy way to get their logs out to market." Thomas grins at his family's cleverness. "We've got a lifetime of work out here, Eva. A lifetime." I'm filled with awe at the vastness of our task. And apprehension for the destruction we will cause.

There's a shout from our left, where Roy is waving his hat at us from the base of the spar tree.

"Looks like they're ready for the main event." We nip along the felled trees, hopping down onto the railbed near the rumbling steam donkey. Thomas shows me the big metal machine proudly, explaining over the noise how it will yard timber and load railcars once they rig the spar tree with block and tackle.

Beside us, Roy perches on the sloping moss at the base of the tree, tucking in the tongue of his tall leather caulks. With one hand, he hooks both laces back and forth up the boot's brass studs, tying them with practised speed. He wraps the padded leather straps of steel climbing spurs around his calves, tugging on the buckles and yanking them to position until he's satisfied.

His footsteps clank as he next buckles a heavy leather waist belt. Roy whips the end of the thick climbing rope around the trunk, threading it through the spliced end loop and leaning back to check the length before knotting it once. He kicks his spurs into the chunky bark, standing upright along the tree, his arms wide on the rope. After lifting his hat at me with a grin, he starts his climb.

I stare up into the blue sky where the fir's top sways gently, hundreds of feet above us. My insides quiver and I twist my wedding band, thinking of Grace and Daisy. When we talked about a high rigger's skill at university, there was never anyone's husband or father tied to the danger.

Beside us, Donkey Don and Crank run the steam donkey along the track, safely away from the spar. Thomas takes my hand, and we follow the chugging engine until it's parked and shut off. Without the mechanical clatter, the rhythmic thunk of Roy's spurs drifts down to us. About halfway, he pauses, adjusting the length of the rope to the smaller tree diameter. Then he flips the rope up and takes four vertical steps before repeating the sequence. I shut my eyes tight, but can't stop my imagination from creating a vivid scene of Roy crashing to the ground. I shudder, a feeling of powerlessness urging me to flee.

But the crew is in a festive mood as we gather on a cedar log. Donkey Don and Crank punch one another in the arm, Thomas lights his pipe, and Billy chews tobacco, gazing awestruck up the spar. Shaking my head, I wonder if these men share ignorance or bravado.

Billy's gaze holds mine, recognizing my fear.

"It ain' dangerous. Not for the likes o' Roy." He spits into the salal, his tone earnest. "He's the only one up there, an' he don' make mistakes." Billy's logic does nothing to loosen the knot in my throat. But the pride in the group around me convinces me to stay. To watch closely. Being here today will let me reminisce with them in the future.

Overhead, Roy's axe flails on a tag line below him. When he disappears into the upper branches, he pulls it up, and after a few crisp chops, a large limb tumbles to the ground. Roy steps down into view, his axe hitting the trunk with a cracking cadence, the bite of an undercut widening against the August sky.

The razor-sharp blade thwacks just inches from the single rope that's supporting Roy. I turn away, pulling open my haversack and pouring a steaming cup of chamomile tea, its floral notes failing to soothe me today. I pull strips of *Thuja plicata* bark from the log under me and begin weaving it into a primitive basket as a distraction.

Finally, a crack and a holler drag my gaze skyward. The pointy green top of the fir tree falls away, but my eyes don't leave Roy. He waves his hat like a cowboy, whooping, as the trunk kicks, whipping him back and forth. The men beside me laugh and cheer along with him. When the tree steadies, Roy clambers onto the sloping stump, waving again and kicking his heels against the thick bark of the now branchless fir, almost 200 feet in the air.

"What is he...?" My voice shudders, the words drying up mid-sentence.

"He'll be rolling a smoke. He's got the best view in the valley." Thomas stands tall, his chest thrust out. I shake my head, keenly aware that while Roy sits atop the tree trunk, there's nothing securing him from a fatal fall.

I look away, taking a sip of tea, and weaving another round of my cedar bark basket, my stomach still churning. Roy's showy stunt is the most dangerous part of what he's done today. It's so unnecessary. And so typical of these men. My jaw clenches. It's selfish for a family man like Roy to take additional risk. I force a hard smile, feeling nervy.

A few moments later, Roy threads himself around the tree, and bounds down the trunk, losing his hat in the flurry. He hits the base of the fir, grinning, and even silent Slim claps him on the shoulder. The crew basks in the accomplishment until Roy catches Thomas's eye.

"Well then, boys — let's get this thing rigged up now!" With a toothy-white smile, Roy delegates to the crew, unstrapping his climbing gear. Donkey Don jogs along the track, coaxing the steam engine to life and Crank follows, unwinding a coil of hemp rope.

Thomas and I sit trackside as Roy turns to Billy.

"You up for setting the rigger's block today?" Billy glances at the topped spar tree, accepting the challenge with wide-eyed eagerness. He hungrily eyes the chance to hang the six-inch sheave at the very top. From it, they'll hoist the larger full-size rigging into position.

As Billy straps on Roy's unfamiliar climbing gear, the knot returns to my stomach.

"I think I'll head back now." Thomas nods, so I pack my haversack and trek to camp, scratching at the *Ceratopogonidae* bites on my arms while considering all I've witnessed. Today, the men showed astounding grit, alarming egos, and a distressing sense of invincibility. But these qualities also turn our profits. Like the forest itself, the business of logging is a delicate, complex web. And it'll take some getting used to.

Chapter 21

For the next week summer rain drenches camp, a welcome respite from the heat. The perfectly timed storm gives me a reason to retreat indoors as I grapple with the engineering problems of the setting's ravine. The work provides me with a sense of control I haven't felt since university. I sketch endless cross-sections and elevations, sharing them with an attentive Thomas in the evenings. Not only am I searching for a suitable railway route across the ravine, I'm also considering ways to minimize the impact of our work on the flora and fauna. Although our education is similar, Thomas is more business-focused. We often debate how to accomplish what's best for the land while controlling costs. And since our hike out to the setting, I've been considering how to experiment with my manual replanting. Once the logs are pulled from around the spar tree, the barren slope surrounding would be a perfect location to evaluate my theories.

My stomach growls, and a glance at the clock confirms it's nearing noon. Lunchtime is quickly becoming the favourite part of my day, with the grub and banter never failing to lighten my mood. Outside, the rain patters on the rooftop as I pull up the hood of my oilskin. Between our place and the guest house, the crew builds stairs for two new bunkhouses, housing for the Chinese sawmill workers Thomas has hired. I sidestep puddles and gaze over the water. In just a week, the lake level surged over a foot due to runoff from surrounding terrain. Mist softens the tree-covered mountains encircling our camp, cloaking everything in a ghostly haze.

By the cookhouse entrance, hidden by rainwater cascading from the eaves, a worker smokes a cigar. I nod a greeting as I reach for the door handle, but the man swiftly blocks my way. When I look up, my stomach heaves. The figure isn't one of the camp workers. It's James.

❧

I jerk my hand back, retreating into the rain. For the last two weeks, although he's just a train ride away, I've been able to dismiss James's existence. But here towers all six feet of him, squinting down at me with raised eyebrows.

"Mrs. Clark." His head tilts to one side, and a slow smile builds as he lazily drawls out the syllables of my married name. "I didn't mean to startle you. How are you settling in?" He looks amused and curious. "Let's get you out of this monsoon."

James steps toward the door, waving me over, but I stand motionless, the heavy rain pelting my shoulders and dripping from my hood. His presence rekindles the bitter regret that smoulders in me whenever I recall sharing my bed with this playboy. A man who, after finishing with me, pursued the affections of my boardinghouse roommates. No one here can know how much his presence rattles me, and the scientist in me is curious about the man who shares my baby's blood. So I shrug, staring up at James's dark silhouette, and let him lead me inside. Feigning a cordial relationship might maintain the equilibrium.

For once, the warmth of the cookhouse doesn't calm me. George and Edith's greetings are muted when they recognize James, their features tightening as they bustle around the kitchen without their typical chatter. I shake my oilskin in the corner and hang it before taking my usual place, facing the kitchen. James slides onto the bench opposite me. Thomas's spot.

"So. What brings you up to Camp 2, then?" I choke out the words politely, suppressing an urge to spit.

"Working," he says, chuckling, but his eyes squint with intensity. "I hear you've been meddling in our business." My brow furrows as I wonder what he's referring to. Has Thomas told him I'm helping with the bridge design? Or maybe he remembers my thesis work from our evening chat on Mrs. Murdoch's garden patio, so many months ago. James tucks a napkin into his collar. "If I recall, you're all about reducing harm and manual replanting. You know we're here to harvest timber, not to protect the bugs and bunnies, right?" His tone is light, but his words prompt a familiar anger in me. My work placements during university showed me that most timber barons care little for the newfangled techniques we foresters spout. Industry views are short-sighted. Since none of these men are going to benefit directly from the second-growth harvest, it's understandable that they pay no attention to repairing and replanting. I feel a compulsion to fight that viewpoint whenever I hear it.

"Replanting the land will increase long-term profits." My voice rises over the thrum of the rain. "And it keeps sediment out of streams, preserving spawning grounds. You should care about that. You like to play hooky to fish, don't you?" As soon as the words are out of my mouth, I regret them. Calling out Jello's poor work ethic in a group is not a good way to remain unobtrusive, but to my surprise, James laughs.

"Just as intense now as in Seattle." He holds my gaze, but I look away, heat flushing through my body as I examine a tear in the oilcloth table covering. Someone squeezes my shoulder and I flinch, glancing up. It's Thomas, grinning as he steps over the bench to sit beside me.

"What's intense?" Thomas joins the conversation, leaning across at James with an open expression. Holding my breath, I twist my wedding ring. I should have asked James not to tell Thomas we know each other. I should have been humble and kind instead of sharp and angry. If James implies he and I have a history, Thomas will figure out the truth. And it would raze him.

"Oh, we were just discussing the pace up here in the wild compared to the noise and bustle of Seattle." James winks at me. "Seattle is intense." Thomas senses a deflection and his brows narrow as he presses his lips together, looking down at me. Nodding, I swallow and force a smile, relief that James hasn't exposed the truth flooding me. When Thomas turns back to James, I let out a deliberately quiet exhale.

As Edith serves steaming bowls of rich grouse noodle soup and crusty sourdough, my attention drifts from Thomas and James's discussion. I can't ignore the disruption James could unleash, undermining Thomas's credibility, especially with the gossip-prone crew. If it came out that the Boss's wife played around with Jello... well, that would be a spark in a powder keg, the gabble echoing through every corner of the Company.

A shudder runs through me as I slather a bread chunk with butter, then dip it in my soup. James catches my eye and winks again, leaving me puzzled. His expression is inscrutable. I wonder what I would do in his shoes. A man whose wife he shared a bed with has demoted and replaced him. It's straight out of a dime novel. For now, I resolve to be friendly and helpful when James is around. Getting to know him can't hurt, and it'll give me hints about our baby's traits. Beside me,

Thomas pushes back his tin bowl, taking my hand under the table. I lean a cheek against his thick upper arm as he threads his fingers into mine, smiling up into his hazel eyes. The truth might still come out, but I vow to shelter Thomas from it as long as I can.

Chapter 22

Two days later, the sunshine returns, turning the camp vegetation lush and vibrant. But instead of the expected after-rain freshness, an orange haze fills the mid-August day. Somewhere in the province, acres of forest are ablaze, tainting the air with an acrid tasting smokiness. Grateful the burning is far away, Grace and I prepare for a shopping trip to Alert Bay. The Company provides monthly transport for women living near and far. There are families south of us at Camp 6 along Kinman Creek and at Camps 3 and 5 at the lake inlet. These camps have water access only, so the women catch a ride on a supervisor's thirty-foot steamboat at sunrise, which chugs into the reload at Camp 2 after breakfast.

Billy ushers us all aboard the speeder, waggling his scarred eyebrow with a grin, dubbing this the Powder Puff Express. Grace, Daisy, and I pile in with another six women, and everyone is in high spirits as I'm introduced to them all. The ride has a festive air, with home remedies and gossip exchanged, the chatter hardly ceasing when we transfer from speeder to steamboat at Camp 1. I savour the wildness and beauty of the view during this second crossing of the Broughton Strait. Seagulls fly low alongside us, their dance against the smoky skies mirrored in the glassy water. Beneath me, the boat rumbles and the salt breeze pulls at my hat.

An hour and a half after we get on the speeder, we dock in Alert Bay. Grace leads us onto the wide wooden boardwalk which fronts the small town. We meander our way toward the shops at a vacation's pace, in contrast to the hurried strides of residents, all with somewhere to be.

A young girl runs by, maybe five years old, and stops when her puppy cuddles Daisy. The mutt is brown and black, wriggling in floppy-eared delight as Daisy crouches to pet his tummy. The girl stares at us with inky eyes, biting the inside of her nutmeg cheek. On this summer morning she is dressed just like Daisy, in a simple cotton dress, thin wool knee socks, worn leather shoes, and a modern scratch-finish felt hat. She backs away from us, almost stepping off the boardwalk and into the tall grass, twisting the end of one long black braid around a finger.

"What's your dog's name?" I ask, smiling and wondering whether she understands me.

"His name is Wokwabas." The girl responds softly in perfect English. Daisy tries to repeat the name, giggling, and the girl's round features crack into a laugh and she nods. We wander toward the shops, the puppy and the girls scampering behind us, along the narrow walkway, here flanked on both sides by buildings. On the ocean side, small houses on piles are surrounded by tumbled driftwood and punctuated by tall timber electric poles. Larger buildings line the upper side, some with log porches. Dominating the view is a line of totems, guarding the largest building with their ferocious beauty. Set against today's murky orange skies, they look otherworldly.

A stout woman in a bohemian smock and black headband stands at an easel, painting the scene in bold, vibrant brushstrokes. I'm mesmerized by the abstract shapes on her canvas and by the craft of the totems themselves. Among the stylized carvings, I spot a bear, raven, eagle, whale, sun, and perhaps an otter. I yearn to learn about the carvers and the stories the totem poles tell.

"Come on, Eva. Leave the tiger-bird. We're goin' shopping." I grin at Daisy's apt description of the menacing figure atop the tallest pole as she yanks at my hand. Catching the eye of the painter, I smile, but she scowls, arching a thick brow and turning away.

We catch up to Grace in front of a nondescript building near the cannery. There's no sign or display window like the city stores, but the door glass states "Alert Bay General Store" in ornate letters, and a bell tinkles as we enter. Inside, we both take a dented wire basket. The floors creak as we explore the shelves, crammed floor to ceiling full of everything from tools to toys to canned goods to linens. The organization is eclectic, nothing like Seattle's Bon Marché. Tennis racquets lean against rifles, and pen knives stack on peanut brittle. As I wander the narrow aisles, the scents of spice and sweets and moth balls blend into a dizzying perfume, overpowering the forest fire's smoke from outside.

My shopping list is short. First, I browse the craft section, picking out a soft four-ply fingering yarn. Among the limited colour options, I settle on a neutral silver grey, piling twenty one-ounce skeins into my basket. It isn't ideal for a layette, but next to the knitting needles, I find rolls of silky taffeta ribbon. I pick out the pink, white, and sky-blue decoration to liven up my knitted creations. Then, as an afterthought, I also take a two-ounce skein of sport weight in a bright cardinal red.

Unable to find the elastic or bathing suits, I wait at the till behind a plump woman buying a four-pound tin of raspberry jam. When she's finished, the clerk smiles at my inquiry, pointing to a stack of swimwear and walking me to a bin of sewing sundries in the third aisle.

I thank her, and tuck a spool of white half-inch garter elastic under my arm before moving back to the stacks of bathing suits.

The worsted wool swim garments come in two colours: navy with white trim or brown with tan trim. The blue is stunning, but I soon find that everyone else must prefer it too, with only the smallest and largest sizes remaining. I settle for the brown and select one from the stack a size larger than my usual to accommodate my expanding belly and chest, then I refold the remaining suits before taking my selections to the front.

"What are you making with that yarn?" Grace falls in line behind me, eyeing my purchases. Without thinking, I glance at my waist and shrug, turning away. Adding a one-pound box of bull's-eye mints, Thomas's favourites, to my pile, I wonder if it's wise to confide in Grace. I've longed to discuss the baby with someone other than Thomas, but it's too early if we want to maintain our ruse, which is a little stupid. We aren't fooling anyone in this community. Even Daisy knows we had a shotgun wedding, for goodness' sake.

"A layette. For our baby." I roll my shoulders back, smiling and standing tall.

"There!" Grace raises her eyebrows and in a loud conspiratorial whisper says, "Isn't it better with the secret out? I'm due in December. You?" My eyes widen and I grin at Grace, who's laughing and patting her own belly. I had no idea Grace was also pregnant. How did I miss that? Shows how wrapped up in myself I've been. Her cheer makes me glad I chose honesty.

"Congratulations!" I say, and tell Grace our baby is expected in early January. Then I turn to the clerk who is unrolling my spools, cutting yardage of garter elastic and each ribbon colour. She rings up my purchases and when I hand over two five-dollar bills, her eyes widen a little. Most of their customers run credit from company pay checks, but Thomas warned me he hasn't organized that yet. I take my change, tucking the shinplasters into my coin purse and stacking my wares into my brother's worn haversack.

As Grace pays, I leave the store, buckling the bag's straps and running an involuntary palm softly over Tony's faded stencilled name, as I've done hundreds of times now. The ache of missing my stupid older brother hits me with a dull thud, and I wonder if I'd be up here if Tony was still alive. He would have protected me and helped me sort out what to do about James and Thomas.

When the store door tinkles and clunks behind me, I'm jerked back to the present. The sun glows in a reddish ball, the smoke thicker now, our shadows eerie in the apocalyptic light. Daisy runs over, pulling on my skirt.

"I got candy fish, I got candy fish!" She shoves a fist toward me and opens her chubby hand, revealing the prized possession.

"Oh, thank you." I smile, reaching down as if to take a sticky candy. In a flash, Daisy clamps her fingers over the fish, twisting away. Then she turns back, realizing she should share, slowly opening her hand again and wrinkling her brow. I reassure her quickly, saying, "I'm joking, Daisy-girl. I have my own candy. Thank you." I hold up my bag and shake it, the bulls-eye mints rattling inside. Daisy lets out a jittery laugh in relief, and I tousle her hair, looking over at Grace, who's doing a poor job of suppressing a smile at her daughter's transparency.

Grace asks if I've seen a doctor here yet, and when I shake my head she says, "Then you'd best come with me to see the doc, too. He won't mind you don't have an appointment." Grace links elbows with me, pulling me off the boardwalk and onto a gravel path. In the hazy orange sunlight, we stroll out to the Catholic hospital beside the burial ground, our companionable conversation crowding out thoughts of Tony, Thomas, and James. At least for now.

Chapter 23

On a crisp September morning, I walk the ridge along a trail I've been building beside the lake. Rains doused the distant forest fires and the skies are now clear. I'm settling into a daily routine, beginning each day by having breakfast with Grace and Daisy. Sometimes, after getting the crew going, Thomas joins us. And most days, Edith and George sit for a chat, which is always entertaining.

After breakfast, Thomas goes to work and I go for a walk, breaking trail toward the inaccessible section of the setting where the bridge will go. But oh, how I have had to fight for this simple pleasure! I asked the doctor during our Alert Bay trip a few weeks ago, and he agreed walking is healthy for me, and for the baby. With the Doc's endorsement, Thomas finally allowed me to scout farther afield, but only after he taught me how to shoot.

That first week in camp, even after I started working on the bridge and setting plans, I had been stir-crazy. There were chores to do, of course. Scrubbing our laundry down by the lake, lugging water behind the cookhouse for my seedlings, and my daily kindling cutting all gave me a bit of exercise. I swim in the frigid lake every day, too, but my ache to explore never stops. Thomas was concerned about me wandering the wilderness alone. It's no different from our school days in Washington, but men with pregnant wives are overly protective. It's sweet. And annoying.

So Thomas took me out behind camp, showed me how to load the rifle's magazine through the loading port, line up a target, and fire. After a couple of days, I had a very tender shoulder and raw knuckles from getting pinched in the lever action, but I could hit three tin cans off a stump at 100 yards. This satisfied Thomas — he figured I could kill a cougar or bear if they were bold enough to cross paths with me.

Now, I'm a mile from home, on a narrow hiking path built by me, with a Winchester 30/30 slung across my back and a machete in my hand. My trail heads south, beyond the rail spur and the little finger of land that gives shelter to the booming grounds. This rocky point is a gorgeous spot overlooking the lake, well-used by the men for evening fires and drinking.

For days now, I've trekked past the point, cutting a route along the lakeshore's varied terrain. It starts in the forest, close to the shore. I marked my way with my newly purchased red yarn, and when I was happy with my layout, hacked through the walls of dark green salal with a machete. In the next section, tall rocky cliffs sit about fifty feet above the cobbly beach. I scrounged some old rope from camp and tied it to a tree above the steep, blocky climb. On the cliff top, some areas are easy walking, on heather and crunchy moss. In other spots, underbrush needed clearing.

Today, the forty-minute walk along the trail is brilliant. I hike barefoot, as has become my habit, savouring the intimate connection to the temperature and texture of the earth. Sun dapples the path, shining streaks of light through the thick red cedar and Douglas fir canopy. *Thuja plicata* and *Pseudotsuga menziesii* — the trees' Latin names roll absently through my mind. I love to stand at the base of these great giants, my feet sinking into the cool spongy forest floor, and my palms gripping their rough bark. Staring skyward, their trunks rise like spears, joining the tops of neighbouring trees to form a receding green halo.

Huckleberries have ripened along the path. I pick the translucent red fruits without stopping, savouring the sour bursts, until I reach my favourite spot, a little out of breath. Here, nature has provided the *Vaccinium parvifolium* with ideal growing conditions — a small sunny clearing where a stream burbles into the lake under an old, moss-covered nurse log. The dense huckleberry bushes grow the length of the log, the rotting timber's nutrients feeding the branches of smooth, oval leaves stretching high overhead toward the sunshine. Today, there are more ripe berries than I can eat. On the walk back, I could pick enough for George to bake one of his meringue puff pies. My mouth waters at the thought of his desserts.

After wrestling the rifle's leather strap off my shoulder, I lean the walnut stock of the gun against an old blowdown close to shore, checking the hammer isn't cocked, like I practised. Imagining all the ways things could go wrong with a loaded chamber makes me uneasy, but as Thomas says, you don't pack around an unloaded gun. May as well carry a stick.

I wrench my gaze from the rifle and stretch, pushing my palms into my tender lower back and lifting my eyes. Above me, in the branches of a spruce, the cones have ripened. Their soft, light green flesh is now hardened to a rich golden brown, with opened scales revealing their thin, papery seed wings.

The tree's trunk diameter is about two and a half feet, making it somewhere between sixty and a hundred syears old. Perfect seed-bearing age — for a tree. I'll harvest some, I decide, and clamber onto an ancient stump so I can reach the branches. Then I twist off a few dozen of the Sitka spruce cones, dropping them into the pillowcase I carry in my backpack, the first seed specimens I've harvested.

Back on the ground, I sit in the prickly heather, leaning against a mossy log, and scribble notes into my field book. Next to the date, I log details about the tree and the cones. Tonight, I'll spread the cones on our countertop, drying them until they open enough to shake the seeds out. Lost in thought, I tie the top of the pillowcase, and with unhurried, relaxed movements, I tuck my pencil and notebook away. A familiar warmth spreads through me in anticipation of this new experiment.

Letting out a deep, gratifying sigh, I finally take in the view across the lake, which is stunning. The morning water is almost glassy, patches of ripples dancing out toward the middle, where soft gusts whirl. A dark spot bobs about fifty feet from me and after a minute, it dives under, confirming it's not a dead head. It resurfaces even closer to shore, the enormous eyes of a seal staring at me, and I grin. They are saltwater mammals, but follow salmon upriver and survive easily in the lake's freshwater. The seal plays near the shore, and I lean back, stretching out my legs and running a palm over my growing stomach.

I'm into my fifth month, and can no longer hide the pregnancy. Today I'm wearing one of Thomas's flannel shirts, and I unbutton it, letting the warm sunshine glint off my tight belly skin. My trousers stay up with a pair of suspenders I clip under my shirt, plus I've added a loop of garter elastic between the button and buttonhole, so that helps too. At home, I wear my skirts above the bump, but in the bush, dresses are a hazard, so I was keen to adapt my trousers.

A breeze rustles the huckleberry bushes behind me, and a twig snaps farther back along the trail. I take a deep breath of the sweet forest scents, taking in the calm nature sounds around me. The squirrel's chirp, the fly's buzz, and the seagull's cry.

I squint down the length of my changing body. My breasts are obnoxiously huge, like a movie star's. They're tender and achy and make Thomas look at me with a special hunger. I'll be glad when my chest shrinks back to its normal, unassuming size. My navel sticks out now, and often the baby punches from inside my belly, as if trying to escape through my skin.

Drawing another contented breath, I watch the seal dive under again and scan the sparkling surface for its reappearance, but it's gone. *Phoca vitulina* can stay underwater and swim six miles, so it's not surprising that it doesn't come up near here. Another crunch from the trail behind me, close now, startles me to jerk the flannel shirt around my bare middle.

The birds and squirrels are suddenly silent, and from my slouched position I crane my neck to look beyond the log, nervous about who would have followed me out here. Buttoning my shirt, I scan the path, but it curves and only a ten-foot section is visible from here. My chest tightens and my breathing speeds up. No one should be here during shift hours. I consider this *my* trail. The fellows have walked it on their days off, but they should all be at the landing right now.

Kneeling, I keep my gaze near the rustling, groping for the rifle. The city-girl in me considers humans first, but it must be an animal. A bear maybe. Or a cougar. My fingers connect with the round nickel steel barrel and I pull it toward me silently, eyes glued to the path. With the gun across the log, I push off and struggle to my feet. I'm off balance these days, my centre of gravity changing day-to-day.

The scuffling along the trail gets louder. I hesitate for a moment before pumping the lever action and raising the rifle butt to my shoulder, training the sights low on the path, both eyes open, just like Thomas taught me. My heart races. Aiming at tin cans during target practice didn't knot my stomach or loosen my bladder. The post wobbles in the v-notch sight as the crashing in the brush grows. My finger moves from the guard, ready to squeeze the cold metal trigger, and I take another steadying breath.

Chapter 24

With a deafening crunch, a shiny boot, and a pleated trouser round the corner. I gasp, ripping my finger off the trigger, raising the barrel skyward. My gaze meets James's wide eyes.

"Whoa there!" He flings his hands over his head and lets out a low whistle, the bellows of the camera around his neck jostling against his chest. "Well now. Look at this barefoot diva. Aren't you a ruggedly handsome vision?" His drawling words are inappropriate in any setting. The gleam in his eye, and our isolation, heighten my discomfort.

I half-cock the rifle before dropping it carefully by my side. My loss of equilibrium now has nothing to do with the child growing inside me.

"What are you doing here?" I sit heavily, catching my breath. James has lowered his hands, palms down, like he's trying to settle a rabid dog. Gripping the camera, he directs the round Kodak lens at me, peering into the viewfinder. He twists a knob, presses the push-pin, and the shutter clicks. I stare at him, my surprise a motionless pose.

"Nice shot!" James looks up, beaming, and winds the film before continuing. "I just wanted to see the trail. Heard about it at breakfast this morning." He cocks an eyebrow at me. "The men watch you closely, you know, wondering when you'll crack and which of us will win that coffee can wager." Strange that James sat his meal with the workers. I wasn't aware he was here today, and I feel suddenly guilty that I'm alone with him. And angry that he's reminding me I'm the subject of their childish bet.

My last run-in with James a couple of weeks ago had created tension. Thomas had gone off with him after lunch, and on that evening had pushed back, insisting James had valid concerns about the cost of my setting design. It marked our first real argument, ending with me storming to bed, wondering aloud how Thomas could give credence to such a selfish cad.

And now I'm by myself with this wretched man, his eyes again roaming me top to bottom, the glint in them making me regret I put the rifle down.

"You should go." But James takes a step closer, pulling a handkerchief from his pocket. He removes his hat and wipes his forehead, the scent of shaving cream and whisky vapours drifting on the breeze. The distinct mix of musk and alcohol sends my pulse racing, and transports me back five months. Heat rises along my neck and into my cheeks. I back up in quick, jerky steps, stumbling to my knees on the uneven ground.

In a single stride, James is beside me, one hand on his Kodak, the other grabbing my elbow and pulling me upright.

"I'm fine." I try to wriggle free, but his grip is firm until I'm standing in front of him, our waistlines almost touching. Twisting away, I wonder what to do. There's nowhere to go from here. James is blocking the trail, and the rocky beach is too rough for a quick getaway, especially in my condition. I am trapped at a dead end.

"Why are you here?" I ask again, turning to James, trying to assess his intentions. He's unbothered by the inappropriateness. Silently, he drops my arm, stooping to pick up his hat. He sighs heavily, his brows gathering above glazed eyes.

"You…" He stops, turning toward the shore. "You are… all of what… Thomas described, Eva." He pauses, running a hand through his hair. "Do you…? Last summer… I…" With a slight headshake, his slurred words lose power. Above us, a gust rustles the huckleberry bushes, and James gazes across the lake. I stand stock-still behind him, my mouth dry, every nerve jangling, but glad that he's keeping his distance.

Finally, James recovers himself enough to string together a coherent sentence. "If you ever need anything, Eva… anything. I'm here… to help." He clears his throat, puts his hat on, and touches the brim. "I'll leave you to it. Take care of yourself." And with that, James walks back along the trail, the thick brush enveloping him after a few strides. I watch the spot where he disappeared until the forest sounds return. When I'm sure he's gone, I slump next to the stream, shaking my head and feeling repulsed, wondering what that was all about. I mull over James's fragmented words, but they're nonsensical. For a moment there, it sounded like an apology was coming, but that's silly to expect. At least he didn't mention my pregnancy. Everyone here is aware of it now, and I still don't trust myself to react neutrally when it comes up with James. I'll need to plan my response carefully.

My encounter with James leaves my mouth parched. Leaning on a large boulder by the stream, I scoop a drink of cold water, examining my reflection in the swirling back eddy. My hair is a puffy mess, escaping in the breeze from under a blue silk scarf, a birthday gift from

Millie. I *am* the ruggedly handsome sight which James declared a few moments ago.

A quiet chuckle escapes me. Positive thoughts about my looks aren't a usual experience. I've always been the clever one, indifferent to my appearance, but this pregnancy agrees with me. They say women glow when they're with child, and Thomas says I seem to have sunshine bottled up inside me. It's strange that I radiate wellness and still feel so rudderless.

The slow water curls behind the boulder and my reflection in the stream rumples. I lean over, re-rolling my hair in the scarf and tying the silk ends neatly above my left ear. As I sit back on my haunches, there's a glint from beneath the surface. A golden spark of sunlight refracts for just an instant, and I almost ignore it, then move forward again until the sheen repeats. Something is down there. A pea-sized lump of yellow set against the stream's murky bottom.

Kneeling, I roll up one sleeve and reach into the cold water. The view distorts as the current runs past, so I pause until the yellow fleck reappears. Moving slowly, so I don't disturb the sandy bottom, I find the fleck and pinch it between my thumb and forefinger. I lift it out of the frigid water and drop it into my dry palm, gazing at it in stunned disbelief.

It's gold. A little nugget of gold. It can be nothing else.

CHAPTER 25

My breath catches as I stare at the little metal blob. It's almost round, with a dimpled surface of darker spots, and about the size of a large huckleberry. No one is around, but I glance over my shoulder anyway, before tucking the nugget into my trouser pocket. I kneel closer to the edge of the stream, staring into the water, tilting my head to search for any other glinting flecks, but I see no more like it.

I spend the next two hours moving upstream, scooping handfuls of sandy gravel from the water. With my fingertips, I rub each palmful, but find nothing else that looks like gold. The morning warms, and the sunshine heats my back. When I get to a small waterfall, I settle onto a mossy stump in the shade and I grope for the nugget's lump in my pocket against my upper thigh.

Stories of gold fever roll through my brain. Father was in his early twenties when the *SS Portland* docked in Seattle, loaded with dozens of rich miners returning from Alaska with over two tons of gold. If it wasn't for his burgeoning relationship with Mother, Father too would have raced north to seek his fortune. Instead, he acted as a bicycle agent for an Indianapolis manufacturer, and benefitted from the riches others brought south. In 1900, after the first automobile drove through Seattle, Father knew his future was in car sales. He still says selling was never easier than the years after the gold rush.

The Klondike's gold helped grow Seattle and lift Father's generation out of the depression, but it had a horrific impact on the environment. Photos of soil erosion and water contamination in our forestry textbooks are a stark contrast to the greenery around me and the crystal clear stream bed I'm drinking from.

As the sun nears its apex, I stroll back to camp and into the cookhouse for lunch. I'm still deep in thought when Thomas leans in to kiss my cheek, climbing onto the bench beside me.

"How was your morning?" he asks and I smile at him, pausing just a heartbeat before responding.

"Uneventful. But beautiful." These half-truths slip from my tongue too easily. I glance across the table at James, who watches me with a pinched expression. His presence fills me with the compulsion to flee, overshadowed only by the excitement of my discovery. When it's clear that I'm not sharing our trail-side encounter, James drops his chin imperceptibly in relief. Thomas would not be happy to know James followed me today, and James seems to realize the inappropriateness now. Maybe today's unrevealed rendezvous can help keep the first one between us from surfacing.

"You're not overdoing it in this heat, I hope." Thomas's eyebrows furrow and he squeezes my hand gently, glancing at my belly. I just shake my head, blowing on a spoonful of the rich pork and beans Edith plunks in front of us.

"I'm good, Thomas. Really." I reach under the table and rub his thigh reassuringly, pondering the thrill of my gold secret.

The next morning when George and Edith join us for breakfast, I smile at them as I smear butter on a pancake.

"These are great, as always." Taking a bite, I chew and ask casually, "Has there ever been any gold fever around here?" Last night I pored over the Grand Trunk Pacific Railway map Thomas has in our cabin, finding two intriguing place names just a hundred miles southeast, where the Gold River flows from Gold Lake out to the Pacific in Muchalat Arm. That river and lake must have earned their golden labels somehow. But George shakes his head.

"Ain't no one found nothing close by." He slurps some coffee. "Did hear of a hit 'bout fifty miles from here? Outta Esperanza Inlet." He looks over at Edith, raising his brows. "When was that? Three summers ago?" Edith nods.

"We lost a few young fellas to that find. But nuthin' come of it." She slices a fluffy triangle off her pancake with the side of her fork, then stabs it, circling the plate to mop up syrup. "Some o' them runned off bootleggin' after. Grinder and Slim, they went out, an' came back a few months later. Could ask them." She eyes me over her coffee cup. "Why you askin' 'bout gold, anyway?"

"Oh, I was looking at the railroad map last night. Just noticed those places called Gold River and Gold Lake. Made me curious, I guess." I can lay a good line when I need to.

"The only thing gold them boys come back with was that Scotch broom I gots planted behind my place." Edith laughs at her own joke, and I smile, recalling the profuse golden-yellow blooms of the *Cytisus scoparius* thriving behind her bunkhouse.

"Well, when you find gold, Eva, you be sure to tell us," James says from across the table, watching me closely, his sharp eyes squinting. He's the only one who knows exactly where I was yesterday. But I just grin.

"How am I going to find gold? It's just a silly question," I say. This time it's Thomas who shoots me a glance, head tilted. He knows I don't ask silly questions. Thankfully, the conversation breaks off into smaller groups and Thomas leaves his suspicion unspoken until we're alone that evening.

❧

"What's all this about gold, then?" He hangs his hat on a hook and sits on a stool near the door, pulling off his boots and rubbing his toes. Shrugging, I rock gently in our new upholstered glider. After my first visit to the doctor in Alert Bay with Grace, I wrote my parents the news of my "suspected" pregnancy. My father had shipped this gift all the way from Vancouver, congratulating us. He had also urged me to come home and take my confinement in the city, which I declined in my last correspondence.

"It's nothing. I was just curious. And I hope we never find gold here," I say. Thomas nods, remembering what we learned at university about the Klondike.

"It would mess up our timber business, that's for sure. Men would quit in a heartbeat for a chance to strike it rich." Thomas crosses the room, stopping the glider's motion to peck me on the lips. Then, kneeling on the rough floor, he nods at the pleats of my bulging wool skirt. "How's the baby bump doing?"

"Seems good. Take a listen." He hesitates before placing an ear on my belly, face turned toward me, closing his eyes in contented exhaustion. I drop my knitting beside the chair and run my fingers through his hair. "She's kicking and poking at my bladder all the time. See!?" As if on cue, the baby nudges Thomas in the cheek and his eyes widen. He grins up at me with a slow, disbelieving shake of his head.

"Amazing. You're both amazing." He lifts the hem of my skirt, running a rough palm up my calf and onto my thigh, the caress making my skin tingle. Still on his knees, Thomas nods at the knitting piled on the floor. "Say, when are you going to make *me* a sweater?"

I laugh, shaking my head. "Probably never. You're way too big! I'm having enough trouble with this little thing." Glancing down at the frustrating pile of silvery-grey yarn, I sigh. Before Thomas came in today, I spent a quarter hour fixing a dropped stitch. "At least when I have to rework a row on this project, it's only a few inches at a time. Babies are so tiny."

"Well, I won't hold my breath for a sweater then." Thomas shrugs and squeezes my thigh, leaning forward to kiss the baby bump again. "I can't wait to meet her." My heart fills. This active little person growing inside me will rely on Thomas and me to care for her. A warmth tingles my chest.

That night, as Thomas helps me to bed and spoons his warm body along my back, I'm filled with a deep sense of belonging. Of things being right. Even if I'm not being completely honest with my husband.

⚶

Every day for the next two weeks, I head out to my trail, rain or shine. I clear underbrush from the path, and harvest more spruce cones, working just enough to make my bush hours seem plausible. In truth, I'm searching for gold.

Alone in the woods, a sense of belonging washes over me. I love this place. The smells of nature, the sounds of the forest, the connection to the land. Autumn is creeping in, the serrated margins of the salmonberry leaves turning colour and the dull blue-black salal berries dropping into fuzzy mush. Most of the tiny hummingbirds Daisy and I love to watch have left, migrating south to Mexico. I'm learning the seasonal heartbeats of this habitat and loving it.

My first days here I'd spent curled up in the cabin, pining for home. I missed visiting Millie and the kids, and even Sunday dinners with Mother and Father. Craving the creature comforts, I longed for a warm bath and a toilet without buzzing insects. But mostly I had missed the freedom of hopping in a car and going wherever I fancied. In this tiny camp, with only a dozen other humans, I felt trapped.

Now, leaning on an old cedar tree by my little gold creek, basking in the sun, I am whole. This land brings a tranquillity to my being that I hadn't known was absent. Nature and her amazing offerings have always attracted me. Among these gifts, away from city distractions, I find peace, frequently humming and laughing. My love for this place, the baby, and even Thomas, softens the deep disappointment of not working. Maybe it's the hormones, but I feel willing to move forward.

I sit up, peering upstream, where the creek burbles over a large boulder, into a small waterfall. This is where I'll look next. So far, there's been no hint of more gold. The nugget that reached the stream's mouth is one-of-a-kind, but maybe I've been looking in the wrong places.

Yesterday, I finally ran into Grinder, one brother who went to explore the Esperanza Inlet gold strike a few years back. As we walked the short distance to the cookhouse on Sunday, I had casually asked him about it. Grinder was enthusiastic about his experience, although he had nothing to show for it now.

"I loved it. It was nice out there, nicest place I've been. Green and steep." Then the young man laughs wryly. "And claustrophobic. I always wanted to leave." Grinder recounted his dreams of riches, and his scrambled information was not very useful. Except one sentence. "One day, I got tired of mining the river, and I went fishin' instead. And would you believe the gold hangs out in the same pools and eddies as the fish do?" Grinder shook his head and shrugged, grinning widely as he settled onto a cookhouse bench beside his brother.

The location of my original nugget, behind a boulder's swirling back eddy, gives meaning to Grinder's words, making today's search feel less aimless and more calculated. Until now, I've worked my way upstream, scooping random samples of stream gravel into a tin plate I took from the cookhouse. I swirl the plate, like I've read about, washing away the lighter granules, hoping to reveal the telltale yellow of gold, but so far, I've seen nothing.

These last two weeks have helped me understand the gold fever that infected men and drove them to endure horrible conditions on their quest to the Klondike. Each morning, I wake up energized, ready to hit the trail, confident that today will be the day I discover a massive gold deposit. But it would cause chaos if I did, so part of me also hopes I never find more.

I peer into the pool below the small waterfall, taking off my boots and socks, then roll up my pant legs. The stream is only five or six feet across, but under the waterfall, it widens. Not wanting to fall, I grab a walking stick to keep my balance in the frigid water flowing past my calves. As I shuffle closer to the waterfall, the crashing splashes block out all other sounds, and I step deeper, the pool now above my knees.

A glowing rainbow forms in the waterfall's mist, where a ray of sun-shine breaks through the tree canopy. I watch, mesmerized, thinking. The gravel at the fall base is my target, but the pool there is deep. So deep that if I bend down to grab a sample, my belly will get soaked. Either I bring back a ladle or a shovel, or I strip to my unmentionables and submerge to take a handful.

On this warm, late summer day, the wind building on the lake doesn't reach me among the tall trees upstream. Since my encounter with James out here, I have seen no one on my trail. And so, ten minutes later, I'm perched on the mossy bank of the stream, wet and tingling. My white lace brassiere trickles cold water down my back and my thin cotton bloomers stick to my thighs. Droplets speckle my tight, smooth belly skin, gleaming in the sunlight. And on my quivering knees sits a tin plate with four dime-sized glinting gold nuggets in it.

Chapter 26

A couple of weeks later, James returns to camp. He and Thomas have found an amiable work rhythm, and during breakfast, James suggests the three of us go fishing over the lunch hour.

"The pinks are running. We oughta be able to get George a good haul." James fishes the lakes, streams, and ocean, often when he should be working, so it's no surprise he's the first to know the run is in. Thomas nods rapidly, rubbing his hands together and they both turn to me, expecting agreement. James is the last person I want to spend time with. He glances at Thomas before directing his words at me. "Or are you too busy working? Babying your pine cones and little trees." Thomas's smile wavers, and I appreciate the silent support.

I've been collecting spruce cones from dozens of trees, adding different seed strains to my collection daily, while planning a manual replanting program for the spring. Thomas says the Company's reaction to my experiment has been mixed, and with James's jab, it's clear he's heard this, too. Although I'd rather be chasing gold than fishing, I remind myself of my commitment to befriend James.

"Sounds like fun. Where and when?" I say, feigning enthusiasm. They decide to meet me at noon on the far side of the point. I nod tightly, the men discussing bait and gear while we finish our meal.

My foul mood persists on my walk to my gold stream, resentment toward James festering. I'm also frustrated with Thomas for taking his side without my input. I curse them, jaw clenched.

Once I'm sitting by the waterfall, catching my breath, the forest's sounds and smells soothe me, the tension in my spine drifting off in the breeze. I've been adding to my gold stash almost every day, discovering where the stream hides the flecks and small nuggets. True to Grinder's advice, the eddies below rock outcrops have shown continued success. But I still haven't told anyone about this discovery, not even Thomas.

Today I find just a few specks and pack up early, giving myself ample time to walk back. After stashing my tin panning plate behind a mossy stump, I carefully tuck the gold inside a small leather coin pouch, low in my skirt pocket.

The late September day is clear. I'm breathless and sweaty when I get to the rocky point where the others will join me soon. During another Powder Puff run to Alert Bay last week, Grace and I saw Dr. Adams again. I've gained nineteen pounds and feel bigger every day. But even with my changing figure, I never miss my daily dunk in the lake. My wristwatch confirms it's only 11:30 a.m., leaving plenty of time to change, swim, and dry off before the men arrive at noon.

A few minutes later, I wade into the crystal clear lake, following a winding strip of sand among the cobbles. The frigid water creeps up my body and I gasp as it reaches the tight skin of my belly. To the south, the first snowfall dusts Pinder Peak. Goosebumps cover my arms, and I scoop handfuls of icy water over my shoulders and curls. Then, gulping in air, I dive under.

The lake always invigorates me, and the weightlessness is a comfort. I feel free and fit, unencumbered by the extra load of my growing baby. With gentle strokes, I move through the water and flip over. My belly breaks the surface as I float on my back. Wispy white clouds stretch across the azure sky, my breath echoing in my ears as a bald eagle drifts near the treetops. The *Haliaeetus leucocephalus* glides lower until its thick yellow talons splash into the water a hundred yards away. It grips one of the same pinks I'm here to catch, the salmon writhing as the graceful bird disappears into a treetop.

I reach my toes back down to the sandy lake bottom, wading into the shallows, then pull out my soap from between my breasts beneath the bathing suit. Facing the sparkling lake, I roll the bar of Palmolive in my hands, rubbing the creamy lather into my skin, over the ugly brown wool of my swimsuit, and finally into my hair. I place the slippery green soap on a rock before returning to the deep water to rinse, a trail of bubbles floating around me.

When I turn, my eye catches a glint on the shore. It's James, standing at the edge of the underbrush in wide-hipped khaki breeches, his camera at his chest. My towel and clothes are draped over a driftwood log twenty feet away. The sooner I get to them, the less of me James will see. But he's already picking his way over the cobbles, fishing poles in hand. He's early. And where's Thomas?

With gritted teeth, I stride to my things, drying my face and legs off quickly. I cross my arms and hang the towel over my front in a fruitless attempt to hide my figure. Water drips into my eyes as I look up. James stands a few feet away, head tilted and lips pursed, sunlight glinting off his smoked glass spectacles.

"You..." His words trail off, his brows narrowing as he clears his throat. "You're..." Again, his voice fades and my stomach knots as a smirk cuts across his face. "I see now why Thomas got you out of the city in such a hurry. You would be causing some tongue-wagging back home." He leers at the outline of my belly under the tiny towel. A cold tremor ripples my body and I grab my clothes, rolling them into a bundle under my arm.

"If you'll excuse me, I'm going to get dressed." I hiss the words and spin away, marching across the beach, my toughened bare feet hardly feeling the rough rocks. When I reach the dense salal thicket, my heart is pounding. Just like everyone else here, James is savvy enough to see I'm more than three months pregnant. The difference is, through the Company, he has a connection to Thomas's family. Our lies would disappoint Thomas's mother, in particular. Bitterness tightens in my chest again.

Worse than that, having James aware of our timeline falsehoods brings him one step closer to the other truth — that I'm carrying his child. A chill runs through me and my limbs shake as I pull off my towel, imagining how Thomas would take the news. One stupid choice has led to so many problems. I dry off, buttoning my blouse and wool skirt over my underthings, then struggle to buckle my watch strap as a heavy resentment trembles through me.

When I return to the beach, Thomas has arrived and is laughing at something James has said, a broad grin lighting his face when he sees me. As I arrange my own features into a bright smile, a fierce protectiveness surges through me. I never want to hurt this man.

He takes my hand and kisses me on the cheek, oblivious to my turmoil. "There you are! Ready to do some fishing?" he says. I nod, following the men up the beach to a couple of large rocks they insist are perfect casting spots. James places the Kodak on a boulder, dropping his wicker creel on the ground beside it. He hands each of us a bamboo cane rod, showing us how to thread the silk line from the brass reel through the rod's guides.

Even though I'm new to fishing, I effortlessly keep up with the men, my small fingers an advantage on the delicate gear. When James pulls a rosewood box from his vest and opens it to show his collection of salmon flies, I gasp.

"They're beautiful!" And they are. Each hook is tied with coloured thread, feathers, and fur. Individual works of art. "Where do you get these?" Curiosity fills me and I pay close attention as James ties the red-bodied fly I pick to my line.

"Most of them I tie myself." He beams, rocking onto his toes. His skill and genuine pride surprise me. I hadn't thought this man could create anything so elegantly handsome. Maybe there's more to him than everyone says.

When we all have our gear ready, James gives me a quick casting lesson. After a few tries and with the afternoon breeze behind me, I soon get the fly out past the rocks.

Thomas and James spread out along the beach on either side of me. After a few tranquil moments of casting and reeling, there's a sharp tug on my rod and I squeal with delight as line peels off the drum. The men shout advice about setting the hook and palming the reel and letting it run, none of which I find useful. Laughing, I fight the fish, my fingers slipping off the domed ivorine handle twice, until I finally clamp both hands on the reel and walk backward, dragging the splashing salmon onto the rocky beach.

The pink is about twenty inches long and leaves a glistening trail of slimy silver scales as it flops madly on the cobbles. I put down my rod and grab the line, holding the bouncing fish out proudly.

"Unique technique. But nice job!" Thomas shouts his congratulations, grinning as he reels in his own catch. "I'll come help in a minute."

An hour later, Thomas and I sit side by side in a sandy spot, leaning against a barkless driftwood log. At the lake's edge, James rinses his pocket knife, wiping it on his pants before folding the blade into the staghorn handle. The creel at his feet brims with gutted and scaled *On-*

corhynchus gorbuscha. I lean a cheek against Thomas's cotton sleeve, pulling in a deep, contented breath, soaking in our success.

"Did you have fun?" Thomas weaves his thick fingers through mine, running his other palm up my arm.

"I did. Very much." I squeeze his hand, surprised at the energy fishing ignites in me, so similar to my hunger for gold. But I can't tell Thomas that.

"Look at those arm muscles." Thomas pauses on my flexed biceps, grinning down at me, his touch making me tingle. "Camp work is making you strong."

"It is," I say, wishing I could share that it's the shovelling, not just the chores that are sculpting my slim frame. But instead, I change tack. "I wonder how George and Edith will cook the fish." As we pack up the gear and walk back, the three of us share our favourite fish recipes. Outside our place, we stop and I turn to James, smiling genuinely.

"Thank you. That was really fun." I take my hand from Thomas's and offer it to James, who shakes it slowly, ducking his head.

"You're welcome. We'll do it again." I watch the men stroll toward the office before I go inside our bunkhouse. After changing into clean clothes and hiding my gold pouch low in my trunk, I grab the bridge plans. A vase of fresh wildflowers sits beside them, and I pause before moving them out of the way, a warmth spreading through my chest. Thomas must have picked the arrangement for me before fishing. To-day, we witnessed another side of James, a tolerable side. I'm still afraid he'll expose my indiscretion, but hopefully, our fishing adventures will produce some goodwill.

Unrolling the drawings, I decide there's no point in worrying whether James will piece together the truth. When the baby comes in January, anyone who can count will know we lied. But with a grandchild in their arms, I'll bet another dollar that none of our parents will bring it up. I just hope the child resembles Thomas in some way.

Chapter 27

Summer continues to creep into autumn at Camp 2. It's subtler than in Seattle, where the fiery foliage of fall maples dots the landscape. Here among the rainforest evergreens, the change is muted. Cedar branches turn rusty, ferns wither to a bronze brown, salmonberry leaves grow crimson, the Scotch broom's hairy black seed pods crack open, and the last of the dark blue salal berries drop off. With the changing season comes the rain.

Today a downpour batters the roof, finding its way inside in two spots, where I've placed buckets to catch the drips. We had rain in Seattle. It's even known as the rainiest city in America, but it never rained like this. Water pours off our gutterless cabin, etching a deep line beside the foundation, and splashing mud high onto the siding. The gravel path outside our door is a murky puddle, spilling over the bank near the cookhouse, taking muck and rocks with it. The lake dances with heavy silver drops, a persistent roaring percussion.

I'm struggling to reach past my belly to tie my boots when Thomas bursts in, slamming the door behind him, water streaming off his oilskin.

"I brought breakfast. George worked his magic with those chanterelles you picked." He tips the rain off his hat, placing a dented aluminum lunch box on the counter next to rows of drying spruce cones. "You don't want to go out there right now." I kick off the half-laced boot and let Thomas haul me to my feet.

"Thanks. You going back?" The scent of bacon escapes from the container and I can already feel the heartburn it'll cause, but I open the lid eagerly, scooping the steaming mushroom scramble onto a slice of George's fresh sourdough. Thomas nods.

"I'm glad we poured the footings for the mill last week. Got the boys digging drainage trenches around the footprint now." Thomas grins, settling his hat on his head. "Always easier to dig a ditch when there's water to show you how it flows." He steps in to kiss me, but I hold up a palm.

"You're soaked and I'm freezing. Stay away." Thomas laughs, brushing his fingers across my belly instead, then nods toward the wood stove.

"You might have to keep that going for the day. Think you can handle that?" I snort, rolling my eyes, and he laughs again as he stomps out the door. Through the window, I watch him pull up his collar and hustle back to work, a steady calm embracing me. The rain and mist hang in a pale-grey gauze, concealing the opposite shore. Though I'll miss the morning cookhouse gossip, I'm thankful there's no reason for me to go outside.

As I finish the last bites of my breakfast, the fire crackles, warming the cozy room, and filling it with the sweet, woodsy aroma of my drying spruce cones. I lick the fork and return it to the lunchbox before placing both hands on my back, arching with a groan. Every day, a new ache tests my body. I roll my head and stretch my neck, wondering how I'll manage another three months of getting fatter.

With a sigh, I lean over my cone collection to examine the rows of specimens, their sample numbers printed neatly on thick paper scavenged from grocery packaging. I collected the oldest and driest ones the day I pulled the rifle on James, almost a month ago. Now, tapping the open cone scales makes the papery seed wings drop out.

Deciding these samples are ready for seed removal, I place the row of cones in a napkin, then gather up the four corners and shake them about. When I unfold the fabric and lift out the emptied cones, a pile of gossamer, creamy gold, teardrop-shaped samaras, like a collection of fairy wings, line Mother's Egyptian cotton napkin. I pinch one, rolling the dark nub at the point between my fingers until just the tree seed remains. It's tiny, less than an eighth of an inch, and I marvel that this glossy black speck will, if properly nurtured, grow into a towering 300-foot conifer.

I twist and roll the seeds inside the napkin until the wings loosen. Then, blowing away the papery bits, I pour the remaining seeds into folded paper packets. After harvesting seeds from three other rows of dry cones, I update my field book and label all the envelopes.

Outside, a gust of wind blows sheets of rain against the window as I stack the seed packets into a pile. Rain rattles the rafters and I wonder if this downpour will reveal more treasure in my little gold stream. With a quiet smile, I shuffle to my steamer trunks stacked one atop the other beside the bed. After lifting the lid, I reach under Mother's expensive linens to pull out my leather pouch and a dented green Lucky Strike tin.

The tobacco tin was one of my father's, a keepsake I brought up here, filled with bobby pins, hair ribbons, and a bit of jewellery. Now, those items have a home by our tiny mirror, and it holds my gold instead. It's almost full, and heavier than you'd expect. I pinch a nugget, twisting it in the dull light, considering the buttery yellow piece of Earth's history.

Keeping this secret from Thomas, from everyone, still makes me second-guess myself, but if the camp workers find out there's gold just a short hike from here, they'd abandon their work and start mining. The frenzy would forever change Thomas's business and destroy the landscape I love.

But why am I not telling Thomas? That question is harder to answer. I trust him. That much I'm sure of. Talking through this with him would be helpful. Like me, he values protecting the land, but he's also a loyal employee in the family business. If he felt there was a commercial argument for mining, he'd feel obligated to pursue it. So here I am, holding almost a thousand dollars in precious metal with no one to share it with.

I drop the nugget back into the tin and snap the lid shut, the big red bull's-eye on the green tin fading out of focus. Shaking my head, I tuck the heavy bundle under the linens, close the trunk, and neatly replace the napkin and books on top.

Shuffling to my glider, I pull my knitting onto my lap, leaning back as the expected heartburn spreads its heat at the base of my throat. I rock gently, decreasing a stitch to shape the underarm of a tiny grey sweater.

A sharp pain hovers near my rib cage, and I push on my belly. "What do you think, little one? Don't I deserve some wealth of my own? Just in case?" But the child inside me doesn't respond, not even with its usual kick to my bladder. But for now, I'm keeping this gold to myself.

A few evenings later, Thomas comes home with a newspaper.

"Looks like they made it." He points to a headline dated two weeks ago, declaring 'First Around the World'. I read with interest the adventures of the four Douglas airplanes that Thomas and I watched lift off from Sand Point so many months before. It was the day of his first proposal, marking the start of an awkward period between us. I'm sure Thomas remembers it now, too.

He stands behind me, reading over my shoulder and filling his pipe. Leaning down, he kisses my cheek, laying a palm on my belly.

"I'm really glad you're here with me."

"Mmm." I close my eyes in agreement, inhaling the earthy aroma of his dry tobacco and the musky scent of unwashed clothing. It's another piece of camp life I wasn't prepared for — the cooler weather has reduced everyone's bathing and laundry frequency. Thomas pulls out a chair and sits beside me, debating the bridge variations I've been drafting. Our deliberation is productive but tiring, so I'm glad when he changes the subject.

"See this slope here?" He asks, pointing to the map of our current work area. "There's a buck up there. I've been up there with the boys, seen him every day." His eyes sparkle and his grin is wide. "A gorgeous little three-point. Will you come hunting with me tomorrow? Try an' bag him?" My mouth goes dry and I twist my wedding band in the lantern light.

"I don't know. I... it's a long walk." I rub the back of my neck. The idea of killing a beautiful creature unnerves me.

"Let's get to the spot before dusk. And we can take Daisy with us. She's a good little hiker." Thomas takes a deep breath, placing a hand on my forearm. "Come, do this with me." His voice is soft, and it melts my hesitation.

"Okay," I say. Thomas tightens his grip in response, then releases me, turning back to the maps, humming.

The next afternoon Daisy, Thomas, and I trudge up the mainline on our quest for a buck. Thomas has our rifle slung over his shoulder, and I carry my knapsack with a water canteen and snacks. Thomas and I adjust our stride to hit each railroad tie, while Daisy scampers ahead of us, dragging a stick along one steel track. For the first quarter mile, I'm on edge, worried she'll trip on the rough, sharp-edged ballast. But Daisy soon proves she's more sure-footed than I give her credit for.

Following the morning's rain, the sun is now out, a refreshing change from the hazy grey. I take a deep breath of the crisp air, so different from Seattle's offensive autumn odours of rot, smoke, and mildew.

Soon we approach the first cut block where the strong, clean, piney-fresh scent of sawn Douglas fir envelops us. The citrusy notes of the *Pseudotsuga menziesii* remind me of Christmas as I follow behind Thomas. His wool red-checked mackinaw matches the red of Daisy's blanket-cloth coat and tam. Their bright tints stand out against the dark browns and greens of the forest, like thimbleberries in summer. When the *Rubus parviflorus* ripens next season, I'll have a child of my own.

Thomas quickens his step to catch up to Daisy, touching her shoulder and putting a finger to his lips. She halts and turns to look at him, blue eyes wide. Thomas crouches beside her, placing his big hands over her temples and turning her head to point up into the cut block while whispering in her ear. Daisy scrunches her eyes and nods suddenly, grinning and wriggling with glee. She puts a finger to her lips and settles her bottom onto the far steel track, nodding in response to

Thomas's next command. With their cheeks flushed and eyes shining, the two could be father and daughter. Time slows and blood rushes in my ears, as I wonder if my baby will look anything like Thomas. Maybe I should just tell him about James.

Thomas waves me over, so I creep along the railroad ties to stand beside him, following his gaze uphill. Finally, I see the camouflaged shape just a hundred yards up the steep side slope. The three-point buck sits regally amid the dark green salal, its creamy grey coat blending into the silver blowdown it's perched on. The *Odocoileus hemionus* senses our presence, turning its black nose and four-foot antler crown toward us. Thomas silently holds out the gun, offering me the shot, but I shake my head, no. He's watched it for days now and led us right to it. This shot is his.

I glance at Daisy, who's still sitting obediently, hands clamped over her ears. Thomas raises the rifle to his shoulder, never taking his eyes off the buck. Before he finds his mark, the deer hops up onto sturdy legs, turning away and flashing its ashen rump and black-tipped tail toward us. At that moment, it's an impossible shot. It bounds off the blowdown and into the salal, then steps to face us. Then, head high, its white throat patch offers a gleaming target.

The shot rings out, echoing across the valley as the deer falls into the thick brush. After a single spastic hoof kick, stillness blankets the forest.

"Got him!" Thomas lets out a hoot and turns to us with a wide grin, unloading the gun. "Dropped him cold."

My heart pounds as the metallic tang of gunpowder fills my throat. I move to comfort Daisy, but she doesn't need reassurance. She bounds to her feet and bounces from foot to foot.

"You got 'im, Thomas! You got 'im!" Thomas swings her up into his arms and she sits tall, craning toward the deer. "I don't see it! Where is it? I gotta know!"

"Oh, he's there, Daisy-girl. But we'll wait a few minutes before we go up." He explains animals can be dangerous if approached too soon. Daisy nods and listens, still peering into the brush. In the golden glow of dusk, their long shadow dances across the railbed, linked as one. I place a hand on the growing shelf of my stomach, my chest tightening, imagining this child.

After a few minutes, Thomas decides it's safe, so we scramble up the slope, sinking into salal and bronze decaying ferns. The deer is lying on its side, glassy eyes facing us, its antlers tangled in a huckleberry bush. Thomas sets Daisy on a nearby stump, poking the animal's belly with the barrel of the rifle.

"Always be sure it's dead before you get too close." He hands me the gun, glancing all around us. "And keep an eye out for bears and cougars. The scent travels a long way." Thomas kneels next to the deer, gently stroking its hide. He bows his head and murmurs something we can't hear before gripping the rack and lifting its nose high, grinning at us. His tenderness toward his kill and proud smile, combined with the threat of carnivores, put butterflies in my tummy.

For the next half hour, Daisy and I watch Thomas work in the waning light. After dragging the deer down onto the railbed, he splays it on its back, underbelly facing up. Then he takes off his mackinaw, rolls his shirtsleeves, and unsnaps the leather sheath of his buck knife. Thomas crouches beside the deer to gut it, explaining each step.

"You start down here to make sure you don't contaminate the meat with bowel contents. Poop makes the meat bad." He explains with a wink at Daisy, who giggles. I wince as he cuts around the anus, deep into the deer, to free the cone, and up beside the scrotum beneath the hide. "And this" — he raps the carcass with the blade of his knife — "is the pelvic bone." He slices deeper, exposing dark red meat and white bone, and I catch the coppery scent of fresh blood. Daisy and I stand over Thomas, mesmerized. I've learned the anatomy of animals from textbooks but never observed it up close. In the city, our protein came wrapped in brown butcher paper, making us oblivious to its source or the creature's shape.

Next, Thomas finds the buck's sternum and runs his knife down the belly, just under the hide, to the bare pelvic bone.

"Now I'm ready to cut into it... careful not to nick the stomach." He returns to the sternum and cuts carefully through the muscle and the buck's belly slides open, steam rising from the jiggling iridescent white entrails. "There."

Thomas stands, stretching his arms overhead and rolling his neck. Then asks me for the small bone saw in our backpack, which I place into his bloodied palm.

"This part is hard work." Thomas pushes a lock of his dark hair off his sweat-beaded forehead with the back of his hand, leaving a trace of blood on his face. I'm passing Daisy a snack of dried apricots when a rustle from the underbrush makes me reach for the rifle on my back. But the flapping is just a ruffed grouse, cocking its mottled grey-brown plumage at me and scrambling back into its hideaway. My heart pounds as I watch the *Bonasa umbellus* disappear, then scan the block for predators. Thomas's grunts and the hollow rasp of the bone saw fill the surrounding dusk. So far, no bears or cougars have caught a whiff of our kill. When the pelvis is cut out, he moves to the sternum, sawing up through it from belly to throat and cracking it wide to get at the oesophagus, windpipe, and diaphragm.

"There. Now all these guts are just loose." He grabs the steaming innards and rolls them free of the carcass, cutting the liver and kidneys out of the jiggling mess, and placing them on a clean rock. Then Thomas pulls up on the heart, fingering the blood vessel tendrils crisscrossing the tapered organ's smooth surface.

"No wonder he dropped like a brick." Turning the heart to one side, he shows us the bullet hole that extinguished this majestic animal's life so permanently. "Glad you didn't suffer. Thank you, little fellow." Thomas directs his soft words at the buck as he sets the heart down, then pulls the guts across the ballast until they tumble over the steep bank.

"Now, watch this trick." Thomas hums as he works in the fading light. First, he cracks the front legs of the deer, breaking it at the knee joint and cutting the hoof free of the tendon. Thomas walks behind the buck and cuts a slot through each hock. While Daisy and I watch, a little perplexed, he threads the front hoofs through each back hock. The floppy shin bones lock in place crosswise like a barb, looping the front and back legs together.

"You'll need to help me with the next part. I'm going to carry it like a backpack." He crouches at the edge of the railbed, washing his hands and the buck knife in a puddle, before devouring the trail mix I offer him, then taking a long swill from the water canteen. "We should get going. It'll be dark in an hour." I nod, tucking our snacks away and wrapping the still-warm liver and kidney in the cheese cloth we brought.

Thomas flops himself onto the underside of the deer, threading his hands through the makeshift buck straps he's just created with the deer's legs. He pushes up onto his haunches and rolls forward, the buck's head lolling.

"Hold on!" I say, grabbing the antlers before they hit the back of his head. "Okay. Go ahead now." Thomas lurches upright and I carry the weight of the deer's skull until he's standing, then pass him the antler to grip with one hand.

"It's hugging you." Daisy laughs and skips a circle around Thomas. "It's funny."

"How does it feel?" I try to stifle a giggle because it looks like the deer is randy for Thomas.

"More comfortable than you'd think." Thomas wiggles his hips and grins, the buck's antlers lolling some more.

"You're definitely having a bath before you come to bed tonight," I say, twisting my face in disgust, and we all chuckle.

We walk back to camp in the dimming golden light, Daisy chattering comfortably. Thomas huffs along at a steady pace, his chin held high, a swagger in his step. I grin, taking a satisfied breath. I'm proud of him too. Edith and George will grumble about the butchering, but it will thrill everyone to have fresh meat for the next few days.

Even after our long days' adventure, my limbs feel light and energized. Warmth radiates through me as I walk between Thomas and Daisy, our hands linked as the sky transforms into a deep, inky canvas, the stars glistening like precious gold flecks. The serene twilight urges me to unload my secrets on Thomas. But with truth comes upheaval, and it's taken me all summer to reach this place of tranquillity. A little more procrastination won't do any harm.

CHAPTER 28

The next morning, after George feeds us a breakfast of venison liver, fried onions, and lake-water sourdough, Daisy and I sneak behind the cookhouse to check on our deer. Thomas and Billy hauled it up into a tall tree last night, and it now hangs high by splayed hind legs. Daisy crouches beside a small pool of blood, pulling a stick through the thickening crimson and painting an uneven star in the frosty grass.

Above us, a blood drop traces the buck's leathery black nose, and as I stare into its glassy eyes, I'm filled with awe at the cycle of life. We can't ignore it in this place like we do in the city. Up here, all around us, there's life and death, birth and decay. I run a palm over my belly before reaching for Daisy's hand, leading her back to Grace's place before heading out on my trail.

This morning is crisp, with frost lacing the windows and foliage. I've abandoned my barefoot hikes, forced to wear boots again. With satisfying crunches, I stomp the ice crystals rimming the puddles in abstract art. The sun, low in the sky, slowly thaws the earth, as it plays with the clouds of my condensed breath.

Behind me, the thud of hammers echo. Thomas's crew is making good progress on the mill construction, with the timber supports and heavy plank floor now installed. On this sturdy foundation, the simple square structure of the mill is taking shape. Large timber posts and beams edge the perimeter of the main work area, topped with ship's knees to maximize headroom. Thomas expects the milling equipment to arrive sometime next week. Once it's in position and installed, they'll add the cladding to the existing skeleton to enclose it. Today, the men are starting on the roof trusses, straddling large beams and shouting at one another between hammer whacks.

In front of me, Tetley is barking directions as Grinder and Slim fumble with a heavy cable under a railcar, loaded with thick-barked fir. Their breath hangs around their heads and a haze rises from the landing and the boom, making the bay look like a watercolour painting. The boom sticks, shackled to piles, encircle the hundreds of floating logs ready for loading.

Despite some recent challenges, all this noisy activity is evidence of the Company's robust business position. Just yesterday, Thomas got word from Seattle about the thriving market conditions. Besides steady local orders, the Japanese demand for our west coast timber remains high as they rebuild in the aftermath of the Great Kanto Earthquake a few years ago.

I trudge past the reload, waving at the workers with a mittened hand. My pace is slower than ever, and I now always bring the walking stick George carved for me. Despite being strong and fit, my balance changes every day, and relying on the third point of contact with the uneven ground has saved me multiple times. At the trampled trail entrance, I gaze back toward camp. Daily, I pause here, away from the camp's bustle, and reflect on things big and small.

Today, I'm grateful Thomas is in good spirits. He's fulfilled by his job and being recognized for it. Since replacing James, profits have been up. By joining the men in the physical work, Thomas gained their respect. And this month we'll complete the bridge plans and rail layout we've worked on together. We're an effective pair of logical thinkers. Our joint efforts develop the most efficient sequences for the many tasks in logging. I take a cleansing breath of crisp autumn air and continue, singing softly.

Standing at the lake's edge, I gaze across the misty surface, a hand on my quiet belly. The baby has been less active this week. I last felt strong kicks on Friday, the day Thomas found out about the customs delay on the sawmill equipment. We spent the evening huddled over the plans, debating which parts of the building they could still erect without restricting access for the biggest pieces of machinery. That night, as we pored over the drawings, the little one interrupted our work often, pushing against my bladder and belly, making us both laugh at the distraction. But in recent days, the baby's activity has dimmed.

Now, somewhere in the lake's haze, a loon hoots, searching for its mate. A dull ache spreads across my lower half, as the Gavia immer's call darts a flicker of unease through me. I shuffle my boots wider, shifting my weight and tilting my pelvis to release some tension.

But today the move doesn't work, and the ache below my belly tightens. I clench my jaw, leaning forward, and grip the walking stick. My breath swirls around my face and I frown, baffled. The pain mounts and I'm unable to stifle a groan as I close my eyes, gulping for air. Slowly, the wave subsides, leaving a smaller stabbing cramp in my lower abdomen. I straighten, pulling on my belly with one gloved palm, glancing around to see if anyone witnessed my weakened state. My intent today was to track my gold farther upstream, planning new areas to search when the weather warms up, but maybe I should head back to camp.

Shortly after the first twinge, another wave grips me. Under my hand, my belly muscles tighten. My insides feel clamped in a vise. It could be those practice contractions I read about in the birthing pamphlet. Again, riding through the gouging pain without collapsing requires my full concentration. There's no choice now. I must return to camp. A cold sweat slides down the back of my neck as fear fills me. I want Thomas.

Stumbling up the short path from the shore to the reload, my heartbeat races. On any other day, this walk takes me less than five minutes. In my current state, it feels like forever. Another piercing cramp blocks everything else out, forcing me to pause, and I try to recall if the baby kicked at all since last Friday.

I lean over, panting, a mittened hand on my walking stick, the other on the smooth bark of a red cedar tree, dread spreading through me. The little one has been worryingly inactive all week. A piercing ache tightens around my belly and my vision blurs. Then my heart lurches as wetness trickles down the inside of my leg. With a moan, I stagger the last few steps into the reload clearing.

What looked peaceful and idyllic just moments ago now seems remote and treacherous. From here, when the weather's good, it's a bumpy two-hour trip to the hospital, where the doctor's presence is uncertain — he could be in any local community. Whatever's happening to my body must be bad for the baby. Based on the pamphlet's description, this feels like labour. But it's far too early! Three months too early.

Swallowing hard, I stumble along the rough gravel as another knifelike cramp splits me in half, this time sinking me to my knees where I land on all fours. This position, with my belly hanging from my spine, eases the agony. I bow my head and take deep breaths, finding a pattern in the contractions. This one will end soon.

Through the haze of pain, I register shouts and a bustling commotion. Gravel crunches beside me, and Tetley crouches, his hand landing next to mine. I bring his big dirty fingernails, round as quarters, into focus. As another wave of pain hits me, I register half his pinkie finger is missing; the stump wrapped in dirty gauze. I clamp my eyes shut. Another worker injury I didn't hear about.

When Tetley's other hand touches the small of my back, I flinch and force my gaze on him. He contorts until his hat touches the icy earth, peering up at me with concern etched across his face, his dark eyes blinking rapidly.

"Let it pass. We'll help ya back." His gruff voice is soft, and he forces a tight smile, squeezing my shoulder gently. Tetley retreats and barks orders in a clipped tone. "You, gimme a hand. You, fetch Thomas." Thomas!

Thomas went to Camp 1 this morning. But I'm too weak to form the words. They'll figure it out.

CHAPTER 29

Slim's running footsteps fade away as I emerge from the pain again. Tetley and Paul haul me up by my shoulders, slinging my arms over their necks. When I stumble, the pair share a glance. Without a word, they hoist me into a sitting carry all the way to our cabin. Inside, the men try to settle me on a wooden chair, but I can't sit. It hurts. Everything hurts.

"Floor," I say through gritted teeth, just as another wave hits.

"We'll get the women." Tetley nods with a frown as they slump me onto all fours, then leave me alone. I wonder at this. Grace has given birth once, to Daisy, and Edith doesn't even have children. How much help can the women possibly be?

But another bolt rips through my insides, interrupting my musing. I lean forward again, panting, unable to suppress a moan as more warm liquid leaks onto the floor between my legs. Everything feels hot and clammy, and my heart pounds in my chest when Grace bursts through the door, bringing with her a cooling gust of autumn air.

"Oh, Eva!" She squats beside me. Her rosy cheeks are bright on her pale face, and her features soften when her gaze drops to the crimson stain blooming on my skirt. She places a hand on mine. "It'll be alright." Her tight smile, wrinkled brow, and furtive glances at the door worry me even more. She has the look of a caged animal. "Phew, it's warm in here."

Grace bustles about, talking like she's visiting for coffee, not like someone who's just seen half my insides leaking out. She hangs her coat and helps me out of mine. Edith is coming, she tells me, once she gets Daisy over to George's. Grace chatters calmly, filling the kettle from the pitcher and placing it on the wood stove. Finally, my harsh breaths settle as the contraction ends. Almost immediately, another hits and I suck in my breath.

"Oh God." My words come out choked. I drop my head, looking past my knees where blood is dripping onto the rough floor. That'll be a task to clean up. The pain increases, like a knife cutting from my pelvis to my ribs. The image of Thomas's buck flashes through my mind as another moan escapes me. I close my eyes, colours blazing across my inner lids. Oh God, make this stop. Save my baby. Bring Thomas home. Help me!

I rock forward and backward, agony lacing every nerve as I try to soothe the writhing presence inside me. My wrists and knees grind into the floor with my weight. The skin over my belly stretches like an overinflated balloon. And with every breath, my lower half feels as if a red-hot steel tree wedge is splitting me in two.

Another burst of cool air envelops me, but I barely notice as more fireworks crack inside my eyelids. Then a crooning surfaces in my consciousness. It's Edith. Assuring me everything will be fine. This is all normal. Women have done this for millennia, and I'll be no different. Her tobacco-roughened voice asks if I feel like I need to push.

"I feel like I need to go... to the outhouse." My gasped answer makes Edith laugh.

"That's it then, girl. You're ready to push. Dunno why them doctors ain' more clear about that." Edith and Grace bustle around me, laying an old picnic blanket on the cabin floor first, then a couple of sheets and pillows. They wrestle me to my back and I moan as another fiery poker pierces me and subsides for a second.

I lean my head against a pillow, staring up at the rafters. A dusty spider web glows in the low sunlight, erupting into a sparkling haze as the next contraction hits. Grace and Edith kneel on either side of me, moving my heels close to my bottom, each firmly gripping a hand.

"Push now!" Edith grunts the command, lifting my shoulders a little, forcing my chin to my chest. And I push. At least I think I do. It's like nothing I've experienced, using muscles I didn't know I had. A shredding pain sears for an instant, and with a wet thud, the fiery ache subsides. Edith moves from my side, disappearing behind the barrier of my skirt, stretched between my knees. Grace holds onto me tighter, stroking the top of my hand with her thumb.

Silence settles over the room. I wait for another cramp, and when it comes, Grace instructs me to push once more. Edith tugs on something as wetness slips out of me, and again I remember the steam rising from the jiggling iridescent white entrails of yesterday's buck.

"Good girl." Edith peers over my skirt, her face unreadable. "You're all done now." Panting, I let my soaked head drop onto the pillow, the metallic scent of blood filling my lungs. Above me on the ceiling, the glimmering spider web quivers, shaking in an invisible draft below the tar paper.

"Can I see?" My whispered words echo through the stillness. Grace grips my fingers, mouth open, her expression stricken. I strain, peering over my soft belly, but can't see past my skirt. Edith places a hand on my knee, and shakes her head, every part of her face sagging, as she looks into my eyes.

Oh God. No. No. A gut-wrenching wail fills the room, an animal cry. It's only when I try to breathe that I realize the primal, anguished sound is coming from me.

The next hours pass in a fog, yet the smallest details imprint on my memory. Specifics like Edith's croon. "Four times I pushed out l'il ones what never took a breath," she says, helping me out of my drenched clothes and dressing me like a child. She props me in the rocking chair and lays a cool towel on my brow, turning me to face the window, then brushes my hair. "Four times. Three girls and a boy." Her strokes pause, as she stares across the glassy water, but she sighs and carries on. I didn't know Edith had lost so much, so many times. Her hard edges sharpen at that moment.

Behind us, Grace cleans, bundling my crimson-stained clothing and sheets. "I'll be back in a flash." Through the window, we watch her walk away, both arms wrapped around linens. Tetley runs up to her, hopeful eyebrows raised. Grace faces him, chin quivering, and shakes her head once. Tetley slumps and he pulls off his toque, gripping it to his chest. He looks toward our cabin before trudging back to the reload. I shiver.

Edith takes the woollen point blanket off the bed and wraps it around my shoulders. She keeps brushing my hair. The rhythmic pull is a soulful massage. My lungs feel so heavy, it amazes me I'm still breathing. All this can't be possible, feels unreal. What will I tell Thomas? Oh, Thomas!

When Grace returns, Edith puts down the hairbrush and joins her behind me. They murmur words I can't hear, as I rock, rock, rock. I glance over my shoulder and they're both bent over a tiny bundle on our bed. My baby. My unbreathing baby. Did I have a daughter? Or a son? I realize with a jolt that I don't even know. Why have I not asked?

"What... what is it?" My mouth is pasty, and my voice croaks.

In two quick steps, Grace is gripping my fingers. "What's that?" she asks, crouching next to me, her other hand on my thigh. I clear my throat and lick dry lips.

"What is it?" My words echo around the room.

"Oh, Eva. It's a girl, honey. A tiny little girl." Grace's eyes are wide and shiny. She nods, almost imperceptibly at Edith, who shuffles over and places the weightless bundle on my lap. I pull my hand from Grace's, grasping the rocker's armrests. Staring at the motionless heap, a wave of fear and sorrow crashes over me, and I fight the urge to run away, to escape into the forest and leave behind the unbearable reality of the past two hours.

My baby girl is swaddled in a lace blanket. Her dark eyes are open, and her tiny, glassy-eyed stare pierces my heart. She's beautiful. I release my grip on the armrests and rub a fleck of white from her pale purple lips. Her mouth is open, just enough to show the glint of her gums. My trembling thumb looks huge next to her miniature features. I lift the bundle gently, tucking her into the crook of my arm before unfolding the knitted cotton. Grace has dressed her. Not in the layette I spent hours knitting but in a much smaller, vaguely familiar, light-green outfit. I run my fingertips down the side of my little girl, then pull out her hand. Her tiny, tiny hand. Perfectly formed.

I stretch out her fingers, fragile as matchsticks, and rub my thumb over her flawless, paper-thin fingernails. Needing to see more, I unwind the blanket and caress her bootie, realizing with a start why I recognize it — the outfit belongs to Daisy's doll. I exhale and untie the bootie's twisted bow knot with one hand. Why? Why has this happened to me? To us? With a soft tug, the bootie slips off, revealing the translucent blue skin of my baby's impeccable little foot. I hold it in my palm, stroking it, my tears falling freely.

The sun's last rays glimmer across the lake when Thomas finally bolts past the window and slams inside. The golden evening light fills the doorway, his shadow stretching over the still-damp floor. When he locks eyes with me, his face contorts into an expression I've never seen. Without taking his boots off, he falters over, his gaze running the length of me, hesitating at the bundle on my lap. He stands beside the rocker, then lays a palm on my cheek, turning me toward him, and kisses the top of my head gently.

"Eva. Oh. Eva. I'm sorry. So sorry I wasn't here." His forehead leans on mine and the sadness in his gruff voice starts my tears again. "Are you okay?" I peer into his dark eyes, inches away, blinking rapidly, my mind blank. A tear beads the inside corner of Thomas's eye as his lids flutter closed. He grips the back of my neck, leaning heavily on me for just an instant before he rolls his shoulders and straightens, clearing his throat. Then, kneeling on the rough floor, he nods at my lap.

"Can I meet her?" His gentle voice is gruff and tortured. My shattered heart dissolves as Thomas strokes a thumb down the baby's nose and bends to kiss her forehead. I bury my hands in his hair, a grief-choked wail ripping from me. He wraps his arms around me and I collapse into him, strangled sobs filling the room again. We rock, our bodies forming a trembling tent over the inert bundle on my lap.

When my cries diminish into wheezing breaths, Thomas finally pulls away, his eyes red and vacant. "Have you named her?"

All afternoon, as I rocked by the window, my mind had been blank, my heart numb, and limbs heavy. Now, sharing it with Thomas makes it all real. This tiny creature derailed my life plans, but in the past months, everything I've done has been to nurture, protect, and prepare for her. I've imagined our cheery family picnicking at the point next spring, a blanket spread on the beach for the baby. And my parents' beaming delight as our a tiny toddler tumbles across their manicured lawn. Millie's kids cuddling my child, sharing trucks and dolls and rattles. Daisy patiently coaxing my girl to take her first steps. An imagined future, snuffed out by the breathless bundle in my lap.

"Her name is Ruby," I say, and put my hand over his. I don't know where the name came from, but it's perfect for her. My tiny gem of a baby, who couldn't take her first breath.

There's a soft knock on the door. Thomas struggles to his feet, his movements lacking strength, then shuffles across the room. The entire camp crew stands outside.

"Our condolences." It's Tetley who speaks, gripping his toque to his chest, sad eyes glancing past Thomas to look at me. The rest of the men nod and murmur in quiet agreement. Tetley lowers his voice and asks Thomas something I can't hear. Thomas freezes and his eyes widen. Then he shoots me a frown before coming back to me.

"The boys wanna know where you'd like to bury her." My ears ring and I go completely still. Bury her? Oh God. Shuddering, I imagine her alone in the dirt. No. No! I stand, spinning away from Thomas and the men, shielding Ruby from them with my body, jostling her up and down. Which is silly. It's me who needs settling, not Ruby.

My trembling lips part and I take a deep breath. Of course, we need to bury her. I just hadn't thought about it. Not yet. And if we must bury her, she'll rest in the most beautiful place I know.

"By the lake, on the point." I look down at Ruby as I speak, my voice a hoarse whisper. "To the left of my trail. Under the big cedar." Thomas puts an arm around me, pulling the blanket off to hold Ruby's hand, just as I did. We're motionless, a splintered family portrait. Then Thomas clears his throat and pulls away, turning back to his men.

CHAPTER 30

The rain thrums on the roof of the cabin. Thomas rolls off the bed, shuffles to the counter, then strikes a match and lifts the thumb lever with a metallic clatter to light the kerosene lantern. I used to roll over and chat as he stoked the fire and dressed. Before Ruby. But for the past three weeks, each morning I've kept my eyes closed and my breath steady, feigning sleep. There's nothing he can say to make me feel better. Nothing anyone can do to lift the heaviness in my soul.

We had buried Ruby that same evening as the rain started. The entire camp, except Roy, who stayed with Daisy, followed us in silence down to the point. Thomas propped me up, his arm wrapped around my shoulder, and Grace held my hand as she stood next to me. George and Edith each said a brief prayer, brimming with kind words I can't quite recall.

But other vivid snippets of that day revisit me. The spicy sweet scent of red cedar as I bundled Ruby into the tiny makeshift casket. Mother's rich burgundy silk brocade curtains, cut into straps to lower the vibrant, copper-tinged wood into the ground. The hollow thud of dirt clumping against the cedar box.

My most lucid memory is of the dank smell of turned earth wafting from the massive grave, so much larger than our precious bundle.

When I commented on this the next morning, Thomas had nodded. The men dug the pit wide so it could be deep enough. Deep enough… so the animals didn't catch her scent and dig her up.

I shudder and my breath catches as the crushing thought returns, like it does every dawn. Ruby is buried beneath the soggy soil, alone in the rain. Rain that hasn't stopped since that terrible day.

Thomas says everyone in camp is grumpy. Fist fights break out almost daily and he's trying to bolster the men's spirits, but the Novembers here are harsh. The deluge blows in relenting sheets, and the temperature drops to near zero, making work outside ridiculously unpleasant. Thomas has asked for my help finalizing changes to the bridge plans, but I can't focus, preferring to burrow under the covers right after I eat the dinners he brings me.

Now, Thomas grunts quietly as he pulls on his boots, then shrugs into his oilskin slicker and hat. He latches the door softly behind him and I roll over to watch his silhouette pass the window in the early morning dimness. He leaves the lantern on for me like I've asked him to. Alone, I can no longer bear the dark. I roll the down comforter under my chin and stare at the ceiling.

I know I should do more and try harder. My limbs feel as heavy as boom chains, and I have no reason to get up. Not just yet. The weather is miserable and there's nobody I want to see. Grace has been lovely, but honestly, her growing belly reminds me of the future we lost. Edith is kind, delivering breakfast and lunch with a few brusque encouraging words every day, even though I hardly eat or talk. In the days after Ruby, she also brought cool compresses, cabbage leaves, and advice to help suppress my milk supply. But she's busy with her work and each minute Edith stays with me, she has to make up somehow by working faster.

Thomas has done what he can to bring me back from the darkness. The morning after, he stayed home, helping me pack away the layette. As I folded the knitted outfits and blankets, he crawled across the bed, kneeling behind me and wrapping his arms around my shaking shoulders. Silent tears fell on the bonnet clenched in my fist, the bonnet Ruby would never wear.

"We'll find a way through this. We'll have our family. We will," he had said, kissing my tear-stained cheek, as his eyes locked on mine, urging me to focus on the good still to come. "It just wasn't meant to be this time." He had gathered me in his arms and held me in his lap with my face under his stubbled chin, but when my insides stirred, aching for more of him, I had pulled away, staring across the lake.

We haven't been intimate in months. At first, it was because Thomas worried about hurting the baby. Then, after Ruby, the doctor vaguely stated I should let my body 'recover' before trying again. The pain of losing a child, even one you never knew, is now stunningly clear to me.

The day Thomas helped me pack away the layette, I had dug the carefully crafted pieces from the trunk again. Flopped across the bed, I had clutched the tiny garments to my chest, and fingered the stitches, crafted with so much innocent hope. Then I moved to the rocking chair, where I sat hunched over in the dim cabin, rhythmically ripping out each carefully crafted piece, until they lay in a tangled heap of yarn at my feet.

The pile of kinked wool mirrored the mess of emotions in me. My body still flushes with hot anger, my lungs constrict with anguish, and an icy heaviness fills my core when the shock of it all returns. But now, most days, I'm numb, wishing for a comfort that doesn't exist.

On that first day, as the pile of yarn grew, so did the ache in my chest. Each unravelling thread tore away a piece of my heart, the heart that broke with Ruby's stillbirth. It's odd — something initially unwanted, causing so much pain with its loss. I won't risk repeating this agony. I can't. So I've been pushing Thomas, and everyone else, away.

An hour later, when Edith pounds against the door, a tin plate loaded with my breakfast, I'm still curled under the covers. She usually brings a hot water bottle and offers some kind words while she sits for a moment beside me, sharing the morning gossip, and stroking my hair. Today though, Edith clomps across the room muttering under her breath.

"Three weeks be 'bout 'nough now, Mrs. Eva." She plunks the plate on the counter by the lantern before stomping over to glare down at me. "It's shit. It's awful. But ya gotta get the gumption to get movin'. Now." With that word, she pulls the cover off the bed, rolling it into a clump against her thick chest. I stare up at her, dazed, the frigid cabin air nipping at my bare toes. "Ya ain't the only one with problems. Grace needs carin' for." She throws the bundled comforter into the corner of the room, wrinkling her nose. "Ya should wash, too." Before I can ask about Grace, she turns on her heel and stalks away. "An' ya better bring me that plate when ya comes for lunch." Just like that, Edith slams the front door so hard the fork clatters. The days of sympathetic meal deliveries have apparently ended.

I lie, uncovered, on the mattress, staring at the closed door. A shudder shakes me as the even colder air from outside hits the ruffled neckline of my nainsook nightgown, springing me into action. I jump off the bed, snatching the comforter from the corner, then hurl it back onto the sheets with a growl.

The sound surprises me, and I cover my mouth, whirling around to check if anyone heard. Which is stupid because there's no one to hear me. Nothing but the mice and spiders. *Peromyscus maniculatus* and

Pholcus phalangioides, my brain reflexively echoes, but today I find no comfort, no calmness, in my scientific name fixation.

My heart pounds and my breath rasps as I spin around the cabin, fists clenched at my side. I need to get out of here. Away from this godforsaken place, to where I'm distracted from this heaviness by people and things to do. Somewhere I can get into a car and go for a drive. Somewhere I can blend into a crowd. Somewhere I can go buy a decent pair of shoes without waiting six weeks for Spencer's to mess up my mail order!

With another guttural groan, I pound my fists on the countertop until they ache. Then, just as suddenly, the fire leaves me and I collapse back into bed, yanking the comforter around me, and I sob, my thoughts racing. That's it. I'll write to my parents. I've avoided it so far, but they need to know we lost the baby, and that they won't be grandparents. Knowing everyone down in Seattle still imagines me pregnant has been soothing. It's not quite real until I pen it onto a sheet of airmail stationery. As if Ruby's existence in their world means she's not truly gone. I shove the pillow over my mouth and scream again.

Ten minutes later, I've scrubbed myself from top to bottom, dressed in a blue-striped flannelette overblouse and trousers, layered over my favourite wool vest and drawers. The mirror reflects a pale, blotchy face with red-rimmed eyes. But I'm clean. And hungry, I realize with a start. The breakfast Edith brought is cold, but still delicious. At the table, my shoulders relax as I finger Thomas's winter arrangement of evergreen boughs, salal, pine cones, and snowberry branches. He's never stopped filling that vase and bringing me the outdoors. I push aside the greenery and the ignored bridge plans, spooning bites of cold pancake into my mouth, then write letters to Seattle.

CHAPTER 31

When I settle into my spot at the cookhouse table for lunch, everyone greets me as if I haven't been absent. No one mentions my weeks of self-imposed confinement. No one talks about our dead baby. Edith and George serve the meal, as they do every day, with sarcasm and love. And for this routine, I am thankful.

Daisy crawls on the bench beside me to show me her doll's new clothes. The table talk hushes as everyone registers the outfit needed replacing because they buried my Ruby in the doll's other dress. But when I exclaim at the frock's prettiness, the sidelong glances avert, and the chatter in the cookhouse resumes.

See? I'm not falling apart. I can come for lunch and remember my loss without crumpling into a vale of tears. The camp residents are relieved they don't have to be on tenterhooks with me, which I don't want either.

"I've missed you, Daisy-girl." I wrap an arm around her and kiss the top of her lemon-scented head, thankful for the unflinching routine this child models for me. It's only then I register Grace's empty seat, remembering Edith's words from this morning. "Where's your momma?"

"She sick." Daisy looks at me with wide blue eyes. "Mr. Doctor told her to stay in bed. Why he do dat, Eva? I gotta know!" I glance across at Edith, who shrugs and raises her eyebrows, conveying it's my turn to step up. Giving her a nod, I tell Daisy we'll go visit her momma as soon as we're finished here.

Once the plates are cleared, Edith gives me a lunch pail for Grace. Daisy hops off the bench and uses both hands to push open the heavy cookhouse door. The rain dances across murky puddles on the gravel path, which she stomps through before I can stop her. Taking a deep breath, I feel some of the heaviness leave my limbs for the first time in weeks.

"You'll get all wet!" I call after her as she splashes, running ahead and jumping into another puddle with two feet. My laugh surprises me — I haven't made that sound since before Ruby.

"Already wet." Daisy doesn't look at me as she replies, just stomps into the next lagoon, giggling with glee as the muddy brown water sloshes her leg. She runs up the steps to her cabin, stretching for the doorknob. "Eva's here, Momma!" Daisy drops her jacket on the floor and plops onto her bottom to struggle out of her soaked boots.

I close the door behind me, hang Daisy's jacket, then shake off my oilskin hood and cape before turning to face Grace.

"How was lunch?" She speaks first, pulling a wet cloth off her forehead as she struggles to sit up in bed.

"Edith's famous venison chili. You'll like it." The lunch pail clunks on the counter and I pull off the hot metal lid, the meaty aroma wafting through the stuffy cabin. Grace arranges the towel I toss over her quilt and looks up with a weary grin.

"That's not what I meant." She reaches her hand toward me, and I move to take it, a lump forming in the back of my throat. Grace's features soften as she gives me a pained look, her gaze holding mine as she squeezes my fingers.

"Everyone was good. They made it easier," I say. Grace nods at my description with a small smile.

"Well, you look like you've been through the wringer. But I'm really glad to see you." Her lighthearted honesty makes me laugh as I fetch her lunch. "It smells delicious," Grace says, sniffing the chili with a contented sigh when I place it on her lap, below the unmistakable bulge of her belly. For a moment, I can hardly breathe. Reminders of Ruby are everywhere. Then I force a settling breath and straighten.

"How are you?" I look at Grace closely as she takes her first bites. The hand holding her spoon is puffy, the skin pulled taut and her wedding band half-hidden by her finger's swollen flesh.

"Not so good." Grace frowns, the spoon quivering. "My hands and feet are all swollen. My head hurts, and I'm always dizzy." She motions to a crumpled heap next to me on the bed, where a pair of Roy's wool socks lay discarded beside a wooden darning egg. "And my eyes... I can't even do the mending." Her voice cracks as she shakes her head, biting her lip, and my stomach churns when she explains how her vision has changed.

"What did Dr. Adams say?" During lunch, I had pieced together that the doctor had also seen Grace the day he came to see me. After we lost Ruby, I had refused the journey to the hospital in Alert Bay, so Thomas had called for the doctor, who made the trek out three days later.

"He says rest." Grace shakes her head again and shrugs her shoulders. "Stay in bed. But I don't know how I can." She trails off as her gaze darts around the dishevelled cabin before it locks on Daisy. "There's so much to do. It's not fair to Roy. Or Daisy." Silent tears roll down Grace's cheeks and she pushes away the lunch pail, leaning back on her pillows heavily, her eyes closing. I twist my wedding band, wishing I came sooner. This is why Grace hasn't come for days. Thomas and Edith had both mentioned she wasn't well, but it hadn't occurred to me it could be something serious. I cringe at my selfishness.

On the floor, Daisy finally rolls out of her wet knickers, pops upright, and runs to the bed, gripping the quilt to wriggle herself up. She snuggles under Grace's arm and peers at her mother.

"When you gonna be better, Momma? I gotta know!"

"Soon, Daisy-love. Soon." Grace smiles tightly and pulls her daughter close.

My heart beats again as I watch them. Helping Grace and her family is something I can do. Something I can make better. Pulling in a deep breath, I swing the lunch pail off the bed before Daisy spills it, and turn away quickly before the others see my tears.

Staring out over the rippled lake, I settle on a few things. No more slumping under the covers, hiding from the world. It's unfair Ruby died, but I can't change it. What I can change is Grace's outcome. I'm going to help her protect her unborn child. If the doctor has prescribed bed rest for my friend's health, I will make sure she follows his instructions. Grace and her family need someone. And it may as well be me.

"I'll help." I walk to the bed, where Daisy throws her arms around my neck. "We'll manage. Right, Daisy-girl?" Hoisting her to my hip, I rub noses with the child as she giggles, then I pat Grace's puffy hand. I'll just have to rewrite my letters home. My exodus from Camp 2 is going to wait a little longer. At least until Grace has her baby.

Thomas enters the cookhouse that evening, chuckling with Roy, returning from a day up in the setting. He stops mid-stride when he spots me crouched in the corner, buttoning Daisy's jacket. His smile widens as he approaches me by the coat hooks. Daisy pulls away, running to her father, who swings her up into a hug. A lump fills my throat and my vision blurs as Roy tickles his daughter. I take a breath before standing next to Thomas. He swallows, his chin dipping slightly as he too witnesses Roy's joy with Daisy. Then Thomas squeezes my hand and puts a palm on my cheek.

"It's good to see you up and out. You've been to see Grace? How is she?" I frown at our hands, telling Thomas that I'll fill him in later, and shrug into my coat before turning to Roy.

"I'll take Daisy home and bring Grace her meal." I hold out the supper pail. Roy thanks me and Thomas nods, tromping over to the cookhouse counter.

"Hey Edith, I'll take my grub to go please!" Thomas winks at Edith, who returns his smile with a conspiratorial nod, and I wonder what secret they're keeping.

After I deliver Grace's food and drop Daisy off, Thomas meets me outside, swinging his supper pail. He offers me his elbow for the short walk home and I thread my arm through his. The rain has finally stopped, leaving a damp world behind. A half-moon sits low over the lake, casting blue-tinged shadows across the surface. I take a big breath and lean my head against Thomas's shoulder.

"Thank you," I say.

"For what?"

"For getting Edith to kick me in the pants." I smile up at Thomas, who chuckles. "It was you, wasn't it? You asked her to show me some tough love this morning?" His eyes shine as he leans down to kiss my forehead.

"I was worried about you. Still am." He stops, stepping in front of me, his eyebrows drawing together. "So I asked Edith what to do. And she said, with my permission, she'd try a l'il somethin'.'"

"That she did," I say, shaking my head with a smile.

"She insisted she didn't want to lose the cash she bet on you," Thomas says, grinning, "but I know she did it because she cares."

I chuckle, recalling Edith's concise ultimatum to Thomas and say, "It's hard to tell whether her crusty motivational speech was out of care or frustration, but I guess it doesn't matter."

He grins and puts a hand on each of my shoulders, gently holding me at arm's length, with his lower lip caught between his teeth. I meet his dark gaze and look away. Although he and Edith were right to propel me forward, I should feel manipulated. But I just feel a comfortable warmth fill my chest.

I face Thomas, whose strong eye contact sends a sweet tremor pulsing through my veins. He wants me to say I'm okay now, but I can't give him that. Not yet. I got out of bed today. And I probably will tomorrow, because Grace and Daisy need me. Beyond that, I'm unsure, so I change the subject.

"Tell me about work." I take his arm, nudging him toward the cabin. "What's left to do on the mill? Have you made progress on the new setting?" Thomas's animated chatter carries us home. The mill is almost operational, and he's been out on the setting twice this week.

Inside our cabin, Thomas is still talking as we unlace our boots and sit at the table. Pointing to our maps, he says our chosen route to the new bridge location has proven wise, with track being laid faster than expected despite the weather.

"We should finalize those structural plans." Thomas's eyes glow and his eager words fill the room. As I follow the path of Thomas's finger on the map, part of me wants to retreat and crawl into bed. My silence worries Thomas, who lays his hand over mine. "When you're ready." I nod but gently withdraw my hand. My brain feels foggy, unprepared for complicated calculations. There's a dense mist clouding my thoughts, a haze that refuses to lift, obscuring the path ahead and leaving things blurred and uncertain.

Today, my community rallied around me and showed me ways I can contribute in return. But the bridge drawings, once an exciting challenge, feel daunting. Ruby's loss brought my world to a standstill, and today has marked the beginning of its slow rotation once more. Though my heart still aches, that's a start. I'll get to the bridge plans. When I'm ready. And if this fog lifts.

CHAPTER 32

The next morning, I shrug into my coat and pull on a toque, grabbing the three letters to Seattle off the table on my way to breakfast. At Grace's, I pick up Daisy and she scampers ahead to the cookhouse, full of childish energy. Once inside, I place my envelopes in the mail basket. Billy will deliver them to Camp 1, where the fellows take them across the strait to Alert Bay's postmaster.

I settle in beside Daisy on the bench, with an ache in my throat, responding to her distractedly as we eat our breakfast. Last night, instead of working on the bridge drawings, I had rewritten the letters home, excluding any plans for me to flee from the north island. The two notes to our parents are short and to the point, chronicling Ruby's wrenching loss, the status of Thomas's work, and our shared hopes for the future. They paint a more positive picture than I feel.

The letter to Millie is candid, spilling my grief, jealousy of Grace, and uncertainty about my marriage across the page in long, winding sentences. To my distant friend, I admit yearning for a career, for meaningful work, and for recognition. My aspirations don't fit with staying here, where there's no proper role for me. Yet there are parts of camp life I love.

I push back my empty plate and wrap both palms around my coffee, elbows on the table, finding comfort in the dark liquid's warm familiarity. But before I can take another invigorating sip, Daisy interrupts my musings with a tug on my sleeve.

"Come on, Eva! Let's go see the sawmill. How it work? I gotta know!" Her bubbly babble and glowing eyes make me smile, challenging my resolve to give up on having children of my own. But they can hurt you so much!

As I follow Daisy to the new mill building, I run a palm over my now-flat belly. Since motherhood isn't in my future, getting a job is once again a possibility. Like a *Crocus sativus* blossoming in spring, the idea has sprouted, and it propels me forward. Starting a career would mean returning to the city, where options for women exist. Maybe I could get a government position. Not until Grace has her baby, of course. And what about Thomas? Leaving wouldn't be fair. Then my chin drops to my chest.

Even considering such a move fills me with guilt, as if my longing for a career played a part in Ruby's loss. Did I will her away somehow? There must be a good reason she didn't join our world. Life is so complex, it's not surprising some of nature's creations don't survive. Ruby had appeared perfect, and we'll never know what caused her to be stillborn. That's just life. And death.

Now, on our way to the mill, my lips tremble, and I press them together as we check in on my seedling collection, stacked side-by-side in milk crates near the cookhouse wood pile. The original specimens I brought from Seattle are still thriving, and in the three months I've been here, Daisy and I have scavenged dozens of old tin cans from George's garbage pile. We filled them all with soil, ready for planting my locally harvested seeds.

"No bugs an' no rot, right Eva?" Daisy crouches, lifting a Sitka spruce's soft green new growth, looking for signs of pests and disease like I taught her.

"That's right, Daisy. You're taking good care of them." I smile as she lifts a tin can with both hands, weighing it for water content.

"An' they don't need water... still heavy!" She plunks the seedling to the ground, stands, and nudges one of the empty tin cans with her toe before peering up at me. "When we gonna plant seeds, Eva? You said soon a very long time ago." She pats my thigh impatiently and her wide-eyed stare pulls a laugh from me.

"How's tomorrow? Can you wait that long?" Since Ruby, I haven't given my experiment any thought. Now, prompted by Daisy's eagerness, I feel an urge to nurture those tiny spruce seeds, abandoned on my bunkhouse countertop, into trees.

"Yep. We'll do it tomorrow," she says, turning toward the mill. "Now let's go!"

At the sawmill, I help Daisy pull open the door. We have the entire morning free, and I'm determined to let her set the pace of our day. Sharing Daisy's cheer should distract me from my confused thoughts.

Just inside, Daisy crouches over an earwig, flipping it over with a stick. The *Forficula auricularia* wriggles its pincers and antennae until it's upright again, then disappears into a crack between the bright pinkish-white planks of the new mill's fir floors. Daisy shoves her stick into the gap after the insect, her tongue poking out the side of her mouth in concentration, her current speed firmly in neutral.

I've always hated seeing children rushed, so I step past her and wander through the new sawmill. My slow footsteps echo around the silent space, now fully enclosed with board and batten siding and window panes high on each wall. I run a finger along the smooth steel of the futuristic-looking machinery, fingering the cold, shiny tubes, dials, and riveted metal pressure vessels. Soon this place will squeal with spinning blades covered in cedar dust. Thomas says it's almost ready to fire up. They're only waiting for a critical piece to connect the steam turbine generator to the electric motor. The circular saw will be operational in a few weeks, and after that, Daisy and I won't be welcome in here.

The morning is frosty and my breath freezes to the door's glass pane until the view of the lake disappears. I walk out onto the small deck and gulp the crisp autumn air, just as a loon makes a call to its mate. A chill traces my spine and I wrap my coat tighter. That mournful hoot will forever remind me of Ruby, of those peaceful moments when I stood at the lake's edge, gazing across the misty surface, a hand on my swollen belly, just before I lost her. Funny how our brains connect emotions to sounds and smells. Taking a few deep breaths, I shake off the memories, focusing instead on the newly built structure.

On my left, an arching trestle ramps from the water to the shingle mill entrance. Raw cedar blocks go in on the lakeside and get processed inside. Then, stacks of sawn shingles exit on the rail side, where the bundles get loaded on flatcars, sending them to market by train and scow. I lay a hand against my breastbone, enamoured by the automation and technology. Every house in Seattle incorporates these building materials, but their origin never crossed my mind.

Seattle. I imagine the route my letters home will follow and wonder if I am making a mistake by staying here. Why am I delaying my inevitable exodus?

"Eva? Go now?" Daisy scrambles up beside me. She grabs two spindles of the guardrail and sticks her cheeks between them, watching her breath drift lazily in the calm morning. My heart softens.

"Sure, Daisy. Let's go now. To the waterfall?" Daisy nods and scampers back through the mill and camp to my place. Grabbing the 30/30 and my haversack of snacks, I decide there's no reason to rush my plans. Seattle will wait for me. Frowning, I twist my wedding band, biting the inside of my cheek as I follow Daisy. If I leave, the sparkle will drain from Thomas's dark eyes. He would be so hurt. As we move along the trail and the hush of the forest surrounds me, my soul settles. My indecision baffles me. One moment I yearn to flee, and in the next moment I feel at home. What a mess.

An hour later, Daisy and I settle onto a couple of smooth boulders below the waterfall, unpacking our snacks in the dappled sunlight. It's been a month since I last came here, the day before Ruby. Her loss has quashed my interest in most things, including finding more gold and working on my seedling experiments. It's bewildering to have life dismantling my plans every time I get moving in a firm direction.

I consider searching for nuggets, but quickly dismiss the thought. Maybe it was a bad idea to bring Daisy here at all. If she sees gold, there's no way she'd be able to keep the secret. But Daisy is oblivious to my concerns, perching quietly on a rock, carefully eating shelled almonds and sultana raisins in alternating order.

"I like to eat one. And then a other one." She looks up at me as if she was explaining a special trick. "Tastes gooder that way." She smiles, popping another nut into her mouth, crunching it loudly, her lips parted. The snacks came in a care package my parents sent last week, and I can almost hear Mother scolding Daisy to chew quietly.

I reach past the 30/30, into Tony's haversack, and pull out a crumpled catalogue page from my bag. Daisy munches as I explain how to light a fire.

"First, you crumple the paper. Then, you put small sticks on the paper." I pile the materials in the damp moss next to the stream, then tear out a match, folding the matchbook over, and pinching the match head against the striking surface. When I pull, it ignites with a sizzle, the sharp sulphur scent reminding me suddenly of my father smoking. "See. Light the paper... and it goes!" Pushing away thoughts of my family and Seattle, I blow on the flames to start our small campfire, showing Daisy how to add larger twigs as the pages burns.

"I see dat?" Daisy points to the colourful matchbook, an ad for Wrigley's spearmint gum printed across it in bright white, green, and red. I hand it to her and she opens it carefully, folding the cardboard back to examine the comic strip of a pharmacist printed on the inside, under the remaining matches.

The dank scent of damp moss mixes with smoke, tingling in my nasal passages as I suck in a contented breath. I open my Thermos, its pristine red paint now scratched from daily use. The mint tea steams as I pour, and I blow on it before handing a cup to Daisy.

"Careful. It's still hot." She wrinkles her nose at me before placing the matchbook on a rock beside her, balancing the steaming liquid on her knees.

"Smells yummy." She leans her face over it, gripping the metal cup with both palms, and takes a careful sip. "See. Not too hot." Daisy flinches as she swallows the hot tea.

Stubborn girl. I raise my eyebrows but stay silent, slipping off my boulder and lying down in a mossy patch, rolling the haversack under my head. Daisy passes the cup back to me, then crouches by the stream, throwing salal leaves in and watching the little leaf boats float away toward the lake. She peers over her shoulder at me. "Go up there? Throw boats?" Daisy points upstream, asking permission to climb to the top of the five-foot waterfall.

"Sure, Daisy. Stay where I can see you, though." Through half-shuttered eyes, I watch her scramble up the steep moss-covered embankment, intertwined with plenty of tree root footholds. Very safe, as far as nature's climbs go.

At the top, Daisy puts her hands on her hips, then waves and says something. I can't hear her words over the burbling water, but I wave and smile, my chest filled with contentment. She settles onto her bottom, her short legs dangling over the edge as she picks at the thick stair-step moss, chucking clumps and watching the *Hylocomium splendens* disappear into the base of the falls below her. Daisy has endless energy for throwing things. A grin stretches my cheeks and I close my eyes, contemplating seed planting, more relaxed than I've been in weeks.

I'm startled awake by the chirp of a Stellar's jay. The *Cyanocitta stelleri's* sharp chook-chook-chook call echoes through the woods. I sit up, twist around, and yell for Daisy, but she's nowhere. Lurching to my feet, I wipe my hands on my trousers, calling out again. The sooty-blue jay flaps toward the vacant ledge above the waterfall, and the only answer to my anxious cries is the bird shouting. I must have dozed for a while. The fire is burnt out, a ring of barely warm black ash. Clouds now block out the sun, so I can't gauge the time. I shiver, my fists clenching and unclenching. Dammit.

I stride past my haversack, along the path to the lake shore, sure Daisy has just gone to throw rocks. But when I reach the beach, there's still no sign of her. A cold sweat runs down the middle of my back now, and between quick, shallow breaths, I call her name louder and louder. My gaze darts from the dense forest to the deserted beach, then out across the endless stretch of inky lake water. My stomach churns. Dammit. I need to find her. How much of a head start does she have?

Retracing my steps up to the waterfall, I keep shouting for Daisy, pausing along the path to listen for a reply, but only forest sounds answer my call. Where is she? I scramble to the top of the waterfall. Kneeling, I place one palm over the bare spots in the thick moss, as if I'd be able to feel her there, where I last saw her. The ground is damp and cold. My other hand presses against my chest so hard it hurts. No, no, no. This isn't happening.

I scream Daisy's name again, my pitch and volume elevating. Down at our picnic spot, I sling my bag over one shoulder, grab the rifle, and start along the trail to camp. Every minute matters. If I can't find her myself, I need to get help. I jog around the first bend, still shouting for Daisy.

Then I see her. Just off the path, huddled on her haunches next to a rotting log, her arms around her head and her face buried in her knees.

"Daisy!" I rush over to her, tension releasing, but she glares up at me. "Are you okay? Where did you go?"

"A squirrel ask me to follow him. So I runned here. Then... I couldn't find you," she says, her eyes wide. Her little face pinches in anger, and I reach toward her. "You lost me! Just like you lost your baby." I freeze, my hand recoiling. "I don't like you!" Daisy's voice rises to a high-pitched wail, and she turns her head away in a huff.

My legs buckle and I slump to the ground beside the child, trying to decipher her comments. My eyes close and my head falls against the crumbling cedar. Pulling my coat tight, my breath slows and my heart rate returns to normal. Gratitude for finding Daisy fills me, but she needs reassurance. And I need to unravel another one of her misunderstandings.

I take a deep breath, my mind searching for the right words. "Daisy, I'm sorry I let you get lost. I was so worried about you... So scared. I fell asleep... and I'm sorry."

"But you supposed to take care of me. Like you supposed to take care of your baby." Daisy looks up at me, her eyes red from crying.

"Oh, sweetie." Daisy, with little-girl logic, thinks I misplaced my baby. She doesn't understand that Ruby was stillborn. My chest tightens, and I curse the twists of the English language. Then I reach out and pull Daisy into a hug, holding her close. "I love you, Daisy. You're a great friend." I realize with a start that this is true.

She snuggles into my embrace, her little body warm against mine. We sit there for a few moments, wrapped up together, before I clear my throat. Maybe Grace should have let Daisy see Ruby's burial after all.

"Now. About my baby..." Hesitating, I wonder how best to clarify. "I... our baby isn't lost, Daisy. We know exactly where she is." I explain in a soft voice that our baby died, and that when a baby dies before it's born, we call it losing a baby. Daisy frowns, puckering her lips.

"But if she's not alive, where is she then? I gotta know!" Her fear and anger from a moment ago are replaced with curiosity. I smile gently, glad she's no longer upset.

"Come on. Let's go back to camp and get warmed up. We can make some hot cocoa and snuggle you under a quilt with your momma. Then I want to talk to you about planting our tree seeds." I stand and take Daisy's hand. "And on the way back, I'll show you where baby Ruby is now." Hand in hand, we traipse toward home, and I wonder how much of today's adventure we should share with Grace.

CHAPTER 33

Back at camp, Daisy beelines for home. Our ruckus rouses Grace from a nap and she squints at us from under twisted sheets. Daisy wriggles out of her knit leggings, then dumps her coat and tam on the floor before hauling herself onto the bed, chattering the whole while. Grace struggles upright, stroking Daisy's hair, listening to tales of our morning. Daisy starts with the earwig on the mill floor and shares a long description of our snack by the waterfall. When she skips past the part about getting lost, the tightness in my chest loosens. It's dishonest to omit my blunder, but Grace has enough to worry about without doubting my childcare abilities. Then Daisy explains our visit to Ruby's grave.

"Did you know Eva's baby isn't lost, Momma? She's just dead. Her name is Ruby, and she's buried under the ground by the lake." My fingers clutch the flannelette lining of Daisy's coat in mid-air as my body stiffens again. I lean a palm against the wall, my eyes closing, and a painful longing to hold Ruby tingles through every extremity before Daisy's voice brings me back. "An' me and Eva are gonna plant tree seeds, Momma. It's part of a sper-ment. I'm a good helper. Can we make cocoa now? Eva said we can have cocoa. Eva!" I hang the coat, pasting on a smile before I turn.

"Sure, Daisy. Let's make that cocoa." Grace stops stroking Daisy's hair and looks over at me with apologetic eyes. Daisy pushes her mother's puffy hand away and twists to face her.

"Our baby's not gonna be dead, is it, Momma?" Grace and I lock eyes now, and we both glance at Grace's swollen fingers, silently acknowledging the very real risk of another tiny grave being needed.

"I hope not, sweetie." Grace recovers her voice first, patting Daisy's cheek. "If I do all the things the doctor says, our baby should be okay." I hear an accusation in those words, but that's not what Grace means. All the most current papers recommend the moderate exercise and movement I did during my pregnancy. It's an old-fashioned notion that pregnant women are invalids. Except, of course, in cases like Grace's. Pre-eclampsia is a serious, known condition. And Grace should definitely follow the doctor's advice to stay in bed. Our situations are not comparable.

"George came by looking for you," Grace says, changing the subject. I raise my eyebrows, wondering what he might want. "Edith is down with a flu, so he's hoping you can give him a hand." I wonder if the whole camp is trying to make me feel useful, but I shake it off. The idea of Edith with influenza makes my blood run cold. That illness has brought our family so much grief, and I glance at Tony's old haversack, remembering my brother's last days. His blue skin, wracking cough, and frail body. It was a terrible decline to witness in someone so young and strong. Our Edith may be stubborn, but she's not young. A tendril of dread wraps my heart as I push away the thoughts.

"I'll go see him. And Edith. As soon as I'm done here." I add powdered milk to the pot on the woodstove, stirring. "You gonna help me, Daisy-girl?" Grace gives me a grateful look and flops her head onto the pillow as Daisy slides off the bed. She pushes a chair over to the counter, where I give her the tin of Fry's and a spoon.

"Let's pry off this lid. And find me the sugar." Daisy's little tongue sticks out the side of her mouth, as it always does when she concentrates, and I grip the tin to avoid a mess.

"There! See... I did it!" Daisy looks around triumphantly as the round lid rolls off the counter. She hops down to retrieve it, then pulls a bag of sugar off the bottom shelf.

"I don't think we need the whole bag, Daisy. But we can fill the sugar bowl." By the time Daisy has filled the white porcelain bowl, there's sugar on the counter and floor. While the milk heats, we mix the cocoa and a bit of water into a paste.

"Here Daisy... smooth out all the lumps. That's it!" Smiling up at me, she can't resist the bittersweet scent of chocolate. I mop the sugar mess, pretending not to notice as she sticks her finger into the paste and licks it.

"Oh! Yucky!" Daisy's face contorts with wide-eyed distaste. "Why it so bad, Eva? I gotta know!" Grace chuckles and I smile as I explain to Daisy that we'll add sugar to make it taste good.

By now the milk is hot, its sweet aroma filling the bunkhouse. I bring the pan over, reminding Daisy to be careful, then fill three mugs. Daisy divides the cocoa paste and adds sugar, stirring each steaming beverage, sloshing chocolate milk all over the countertop.

Once Grace and Daisy are settled with their hot drinks and a picture book, I excuse myself, promising to return in the morning to plant tree seeds. In the cookhouse across the way, George is behind the counter and when I ask if I can help, he nods once.

"Sure, Boss. Check on Edith, will ya?" His eyebrows draw together and his voice deepens. "She never showed up. An' won' let none of us men inside..." George's words trail off.

"Of course, I will. Anything else I can help with here?" George touches his temple and glances around the kitchen. I follow his gaze to a bucket of unpeeled potatoes, an empty bread bowl, and a full leg of venison. Dinner prep has not started. "I'll come back as soon as I can." George's glazed look makes me giggle, and I can't help teasing him a little. "For someone who's always telling Edith how much she's doing wrong, you sure seem to miss her." But the laugh catches in my throat when I meet his eyes. He rubs the back of his neck without a hint of humour. He's really worried about her. With a gentle touch, I squeeze his bicep, softening my tone. "I'm sure she's fine, George. I'll go see her now." He grunts and offers me a wave of thanks as I hurry along the gravel path to Edith's place.

There's no smoke rising from her chimney. I knock gently and push the door open, peeking inside. A small lantern on the bedside table casts a soft glow in the dim room. Edith lies on the bed, covered in blankets, her eyes closed. I take a step closer. She's pale and still hasn't acknowledged my entry.

"Edith? It's Eva. George asked me to check on you. Are you okay?" I glance around the barren room, my words soft, not wanting to startle her. In all the months I've lived here, she's never invited me into her home, and I look around curiously.

Her eyes flutter open, and she bites her lip, blinking rapidly. "Eva? What're ya doin' here?"

"We're worried about you. How are you feeling?" I ask.

Edith tries to sit up, but she grimaces and collapses onto her pillow.

"I'm not so good, Mrs. Eva. I jus' got a bad flu or somethin'." I nod, pushing down the urge to flee when she utters that ominous f-word: flu. Her unfocused eyes mirror the feverish delirium in my late brother's last gaze, and I swallow the lump in my throat.

"It's freezing in here. Aren't you cold?" Edith just moans from under her covers, so I pull open the woodstove, then place a few crumpled newspaper pages into the fluffy white soot. While stacking the red cedar kindling on top, I tell Edith about my morning with Daisy. All except the part where I lost her.

The fire catches easily with the first match I strike. After the flames devour the kindling, I add firewood, blow at the base, adjust the damper, and hold the door ajar. That's when I notice the yarn, and my grip on the unlatched handle tightens. In the corner behind the stove, hang a dozen carefully wound hanks of silver grey. My eyes narrow and my heart pounds with confusion, but I'd recognize the neutral colour and soft fingering weight anywhere. It's my layette wool, the wool I frantically ripped out the day after we buried Ruby. I last saw it piled in a kinked and tangled heap on my floor and assumed Thomas hid it away. But it looks like Edith took it.

A sharp crack from inside the stove jolts my gaze from the yarn. I latch the door, ignoring the tightness in my chest, and resume my monologue.

"There, that should warm this place. I'll go find Thomas now and have him fetch Dr. Adams. We'll have you better in no time." As I silently calculate how many hours — no, days — it will take to get the doctor here, a cold lump knots my stomach. The longer I'm here, the more concerned I am about Edith. She hasn't made a single sarcastic comment.

The fire pops inside the stove as I place the back of my hand on Edith's forehead. She's running a fever. Her face is ashen and her breath is shallow and rapid, as if she's just run up the stairs. As I turn to leave the sour-smelling room, Edith's weak voice calls out. "Don' bother with the doc. Not yet. I don' wan' no fuss." I pause, turning toward her.

"You're sick. Let us help you."

"I jus' need'n rest," she says. "You'll see."

I sigh and nod, saying, "Okay." An argument with Edith serves no purpose, so I just pour her a cup of water, placing it within reach on her bedside table. When I ask her if she wants anything else, she only shakes her head feebly, pulling her covers over her quivering shoulders.

After promising to return in a few hours, I hurry back to the cookhouse, the jittery feeling in my belly building. I'll talk to Thomas when he comes to dinner. Calling for the doctor isn't Edith's decision to make. We may need to do it to protect the health of the whole community. I scrub my hands in the cookhouse sink, another uneasy chill running through me.

CHAPTER 34

Back at the cookhouse, I slip Edith's apron over my head. As I take the first russet from the pile of potatoes, George plops sourdough from the bread bowl onto the countertop and asks about Edith.

"Sure looks like the flu," I say. The fruity sweet scent of the dough reminds me of Edith's dank room, and I shudder. George hears the fear in my voice, and looks up, eyebrows raised, so I feel the need to explain. "I lost my brother, Tony, to the Spanish flu. The bugger made it all the way back from the Great War. And then died at home. In the influenza outbreak." I barely keep my voice even as the paring knife trembles. Turning the potato in my hands, I try to run the blade just under the skin like Edith had done.

George only nods, cutting the loose dough into three pieces on the floured counter.

"We lost good people in that fight," he says, stretching and folding the first loaf. I nod, thinking of the classmates and friends who never returned. Moving here has reduced the reminders, and I rarely imagine their demises like I did back in Seattle. Late at night, when sleep wouldn't come, my active imagination would paint scenes so horrific I would break into a sweat, staring at the ceiling.

But I don't share any of this. George's stories flow only after great pauses, so I remain silent, ineptly adding to my stack of very thick potato peels.

"I was away three years." George flips the dough over, sprinkling the loose white mound with flour, then spinning and pushing it into a tight round. "Saw too many fellas... lose." He shakes his head, sliding the sourdough onto a baking sheet with his bench scraper before starting on the second loaf.

"Only thing dragging us through was family. An' then for alotta fellas, when they got back, the fight'n didn' stop. Like your Tony." He kicks his chin out at me. "Not right that he go down by flu. Not after all he done for his country." George is spinning and patting the sourdough so hard I'm afraid he'll smash all the bubbles out of it. "And so many fellas thought they were fight'n for somethin'... someone... only when they got back, it wasn' how they 'membered." I wonder what George is referring to, but again only nod and concentrate on keeping the paring knife from drawing blood.

It's only after George has shaped the third loaf and draped damp towels over the baking sheet that he continues. "Billy an' I used to gill net up here. Before the war, we fished t'gether. An' then we left t'gether, same ship, joined the 102nd Battalion outta Comox. Military liked us working stiffs. Grunts made good soldiers." His unfocused gaze looks through me, his movements halting. "Billy's treasure was a photo of his girl. She was one of them level-lying Lehto girls." George's nose wrinkles in distaste. "An' Billy was young. No more'n eighteen. Head over heels for her. She was a pretty thing, livin' up in Sointula."

George's gaze returns to the present and he raises his eyebrows at my pile of peels, shaking his head, fists on his hips. "Geez Boss. We gonna be havin' a hash for breakfast, I guess." Tingling sweeps the back of my neck until even my ears feel hot, and I grin at him ruefully.

"It's harder than it looks — I'll never be as good as Edith at this," I say. George grows still when I mention his cookee. He nods, his face softening with concern.

"Come to think, Billy's girl... she looked a lot like you. Prob'ly why he lost his marbles back on the ship." He pauses as we both recall the bar brawl on the *SS Cardena*. After a moment, George continues. "But when he came back, she'd married another fella. Told Billy they'd bin too young to mean anythin'. Some good fightin' did for Billy. The whole thing with the girl wrecked what was left of his soul after the war." George slams a huge wood cutting board onto the counter, then hoists a sack of onions next to it, taking a cleaver to the first onion with alarming speed, a neck vein bulging.

"I'm so sorry about Billy. I've heard bits and pieces, mostly from Daisy, which didn't make a lot of sense." My pile of potatoes is only half peeled, yet George is almost through dicing the dozen onions he's butchering. "Thanks for telling me." My kinship with George grows as we work side by side, the pungent aroma of raw onion filling the cookhouse. Our sniffling joins the rhythmic clatter of George's cleaver, as the volatile compounds wafting around us prickle our eyes and tickle our nasal passages.

I'm suddenly transported back to an evening with Thomas, long before the night I made my bad choice. He'd cooked spaghetti sauce at my boardinghouse and we'd all laughed through our onion tears at some story Thomas was reciting. My roommates had loved him, and thought him handsome and clever. And after they found out we weren't courting, every one of them had flirted shamelessly with him whenever he came to study. It had been so distracting that I begged him to move our homework sessions to the campus library.

Now, I yearn to go back, to decipher why my roommate's banter made my chest burn and my fists clench. If only I could have allowed my relationship with Thomas to develop naturally without this forced union. If only my reputation hadn't needed rescuing. If only.

"What?" I say now, looking up from my work, realizing George has asked me something.

"Watch what yer doin' there." He points at the potato I'm holding, spiralled to half its size, way past the peel. "Yer mind's halfway to London. What's botherin' ya?" And with that, I clunk the paring knife down on the counter.

"Can I tell you something, George?" He shrugs his assent as he lifts a huge cast iron Dutch oven by its bale handle, swinging it easily onto the wood stove. "Thomas and I… we got married to hide my pregnancy," I say, a thickness in my throat.

"By golly, Boss. Ya don' say?" He bulges his eyes out, covering his gaping mouth with a palm, and stares at me squarely. He looks so ridiculous, feigning shock, with his big ears wiggling, that I burst out laughing, breaking up the knot in my stomach.

And for the first time, I share my deepest uncertainties with another human. George listens like he talks, with chasms between words, and I fill the voids with my troubles. As he browns the sizzling venison in hot bacon fat, I tell him I still ache to work and do the research I trained for. Now, without the baby, I am free to choose. The cookhouse fills with the aroma of the searing meat and the clatter of George's utensils.

My voice lowers to a whisper as I confess my darkest thought. "Do you think I somehow caused Ruby's stillbirth? Did I wish her away by wanting something different?"

"Now look here, Boss." George shakes his head, draining the brown pieces of venison and tossing them into a dented metal bowl before moving closer. "Ya din' cause nothin'." He clears his throat, patting my shoulder. "Ya scared the piss outta all of us. My Rita dun died two days after she lost one o' our l'il ones." His eyes flutter closed, his features softening at the mention of his wife. Then he steps back to the stove. "You's still here. An' none o' it is yer fault."

My eyes prickle with tears at the affection in George's gruff voice. I gaze at my hands, the paring knife frozen over another potato. Untying the apron, I pull it off over my head and twist it into a pretzel as I continue.

"It's just... I'm... I'm very fond of Thomas, but I'm not so sure I love him. I mean... how do you know? Isn't love supposed to be exciting? Thomas is so... comfortable. It's all so confusing."

Now George glares at me with raised eyebrows. "Boss, you got somethin' real good there." He bangs the ladle against the rim of the pot, giving me a look of baffled frustration. "That boy worships you. In all the best ways."

My feet itch for movement, so I shuffle to the cookhouse's dining room, throwing the pretzeled apron onto the counter between us. I lean on my elbows, chin dropping into my palms as I stare through the hazy kitchen. The venison is finished, a steaming pile of browned stew meat settled in the dented metal bowl beside the cast-iron Dutch oven. Facing me from across the counter, George's thick hands grip either side of the cutting board loaded with diced onions. His gaze locks with mine, his lips parting and eyebrows raising, as if he wants to speak. But he turns, dumping the load into the waiting pan.

Again, we're silent. George stirs the crackling onions, their symphony accompanying our thoughts. A meaty caramel scent soon drifts from the pan, taking me back once again to that spaghetti night with Thomas. Life was so much simpler then.

"I wonder if I would've fallen in love with Thomas. If we had a chance at doing it the normal way, unrushed."

"What difference does it make?" George asks. I look up, startled. I hadn't meant to say that out loud. "He loves ya. And I see ya love him. What difference does it make, how you gots here, Boss?"

Tears blur my vision. George's assessment might be true, but the city still beckons me. Pushing away from the counter, I wipe my hands on my thighs, then turn away. I've shared enough, and there's work to do. Grace and her baby need me, as does Edith. And I promised Daisy we'd plant seeds. Seattle can wait a little longer. I just hope confiding in George doesn't backfire on me.

CHAPTER 35

The next morning Edith is worse. When I enter her bunkhouse, the air is stale and even though the room is freezing, her forehead glistens with perspiration. I give Thomas, who stands in the doorway, a quick shake of my head. He nods and rushes away to send for the doctor.

"How are you today, Edith?" She moans and writhes under her light blue sheets, a dark circle of sweat around her. With a wet washcloth, I gently wipe her face, shoulders and arms, just like the nurses did for my ill brother. I shiver, trying to keep my voice upbeat as I share with Edith my adventures in the kitchen. The rhythm of the cool cotton soothes her, but she doesn't crack a smile or a sarcastic retort in response to my stories. Not a good sign. A tightness knots my gut.

Continuing the sponge bath in silence now, I think of Tony. I miss my brother. He was a silly half-grown fellow when he left for the Great War. Too young. He thought himself noble, with no idea of the horrors he'd see, having lived a sheltered life of privilege in the city. He came back changed. A hard, hollow shell of the boy he had been. None of us could reach him.

Tony and I had had a special bond, communicating without words. A glance or a gesture used to send us into hysterics, but war killed that joy. The jovial brother I had once known was gone. Forever.

The winter after his return from the war, the Stanley Cup playoffs were the one thing that piqued his interest. So our family became Seattle Metropolitan fans. I'd never listened to a sportscast before in my life, but every night the Mets played, our family would gather around the shiny black 5-tube radio's loudspeaker in the living room, hoping for news that would spark a smile on Tony's gaunt face.

Thank goodness the Mets did well, winning the Pacific Coast finals, and playing for the Cup against the Montreal Canadiens. Tony's joy returned when it was announced that the teams from opposite coasts would play all games at the Seattle Arena. On ticket sale day, he joined hundreds of other hockey fans in a line that wrapped around the block, waiting for the box office to open. Tony and a friend were rewarded for their patience with standing-room tickets to game two.

But he came home from that game dejected, after a loss to the Canadiens. Then, despite feeling sick two days later, Tony caught the details of the Mets trouncing the Canadiens in game three. By game five, Tony was in the hospital with a fever of 106, and health officials had cancelled the Stanley Cup finals because of the influenza outbreak.

Tony's flu led to pneumonia, and he died a week later, on the same day as Montreal's star defenceman, "Bad Joe" Hall. Two vibrant young men, with their whole lives ahead of them, were taken by the Spanish flu in adjacent hospital rooms.

Now, I shudder again, moving to the top of the bed, the sound of Tony's last laboured breaths suddenly filling my ears. I tuck the damp sheets around Edith, deciding I'll change them after her fever breaks. *If her fever breaks.* My hand on her forehead confirms she's still too hot, but her breath, although quick and shallow, has none of the crackle Tony's had down in Seattle. I hope that's a good sign.

The wooden chair scrapes across the plank floor of the bunkhouse as I settle next to Edith. A worn, dark-green novel lies on her bedside table and I crack the cloth-bound spine, turning to the title page. *Anne's House of Dreams*. I finger the typeset, inhaling the faint vanilla scent of paper and ink. Although there's a bookmark a few chapters in, I read aloud from the beginning. Edith's eyes flutter lightly at my voice, but soon her breath slows as she fades to sleep and I'm enveloped in the world of Green Gables.

As I start the fourth chapter, Edith wakes up, rolling over with a groan. She looks at me and I help her sip some water. Then she leans back on her damp feather pillow, staring with a bright-eyed look.

"Well. Don' stop there. Read." Edith's voice croaks and she coughs, her whole body convulsing. Turning back to the pages obediently, I read the story of Anne's wedding day. I push through the middle of the chapter, where the description of Anne and Gilbert's love haunts me:

> *"They belonged to each other; and, no matter what life might hold for them, it could never alter that. Their happiness was in each other's keeping and both were unafraid."*

When I get to the next chapter, I flip the page back, silently re-reading the passage. Edith, who had closed her eyes as I read, looks up at me.

"Well? What are ya mullin' over now?" Her head tilts, eyebrows raised, and I'm again surprised at how observant the older woman is. I consider whether I should confess my doubts to Edith too. I'm already regretting my honesty with George. The more I talk, the bigger the chance someone tells Thomas about my uncertainty, but I yearn for a woman's perspective. I've thought about confiding in Grace, too, and would value her view, but talking about anything sensitive within Daisy's earshot is just too risky. It's bound to get retold by the child in a garbled mess at some inopportune time, wreaking havoc and causing harm. I love that girl, but she is not a secret keeper.

Edith's face softens, her steady eye contact a comfort, and again I wonder what her story is. She shared a little on the night of Ruby's death, as did Daisy during my first day's camp tour. That's how I know a severed mainline killed Edith's husband. When I had asked Thomas how true Daisy's tale about Edith shipping Ken off in a box was, he said it hadn't happened quite like that. Edith believed leaving with the casket for the graveyard in Alert Bay would result in the Company shipping her out during her absence. Thomas had chuckled, admitting she might have been right. The Company had no cause to allow non-workers to stay in their camps.

I look at this frail woman beside me, my heart filling with admiration for the resilience she's shown out here.

"Tell me about your marriage." It's an impertinent request and there's no reason she should comply. My cheeks burn as the silence lengthens between us, her sharp eyes boring into me.

Edith clears her throat, shifting her gaze to the rafters above her.

"My Ken was... well... he done the best he knew how, I guess." She turns back to me. "Our stories aren't so different." Her eyebrows draw in and she hesitates, giving a clenched half-smile. I stay silent. Like George's words, Edith's flow at a pace of their own. Finally, she continues, her voice soft. "I met Ken at a dance in Kelowna. My girlfriend an' I had snuck into the city, each of us tellin' our parents we'd be stayin' at the others farm. We was barely sixteen. Ken was a handsome lad. Tall. An' strong from workin' on the railway. He was lookin' for a good time that Saturday, an' we had it together." Edith glances over at me with a knowing look and I laugh softly at what goes unsaid, feeling a blush creep into my cheeks again. I'm so glad she's alert and talking, but can't imagine this sarcastic firestorm as an innocent teenager. "Well, I had a great summer with him. Every Saturday night, he'd pick me up an' take me dancin' or out for a burger." Her eyes sparkle now as she recalls their exploits. My father would have murdered the boy — or me — before letting us go off together when I was that age.

"What did your parents think of Ken? Did they like him?"

"Well, shit. If my pa had ever been sober 'nough to notice I was gone Saturdays, he mighta had somethin' to say." Her nostrils flare and her expression tightens. "An' my mama, she died when I was five." This part Edith shares matter-of-factly, shrugging lightly and again inspecting the ceiling, lost in memories. When she eventually speaks, her voice is soft. "By September I knew I was with child, an' Ken did the right thing an' married me." She gives me a wry smile, wetting her lips. "Turns out we wasn't a great match. He had a temper. An' I had a mouth on me." We exchange smiles.

"But I needed him. More'n I liked to admit. My pa... well, he coulda kilt Ken when he found out I was knocked up." She shakes her head. "I ain't seen my pa since. Heard he died a few years back." She shrugs halfheartedly. I stare at her wide-eyed, unable to imagine a life without my father in it.

"Anyway, our marriage worked best when Ken stayed away in camp. An' that suited me fine, too. Not much of a people person." She mutters the last bit. "But the posting for this job, they was givin' preference to fellas with wives — thought it made them more stable or somethin'." Edith gives a wry snort. "Might be true of some lads. But not my Ken. Still, we came up here and I jus' kinda fell in love with the woods. An' the mountains. Ne'er seen so much green. It suits me."

"And your baby?" I'm almost certain she miscarried, given the words she had for me when Ruby was stillborn.

"Ah, child. That was a bad time. Me an' Ken had some argument. He lunged at me, an' I fell down the stairs. Didn' come round for a while, then there's Ken all white as a ghost, an' me with the biggest cramp in my belly." Her head shakes slowly. "I lost that baby. An' was ne'er able to birth a live one." She offers a small smile through a faraway pained look and continues. "But he ne'er laid a hand on me again. So that's somethin'." I nod, squeezing Edith's gnarled fingers, an ache in my throat as I glance across at the silver grey wool still hanging by her stove. She follows my gaze, then pulls her hand away and stares back at me, pressing a fist to her mouth.

"I tells ya all this... so's you understan' how good you's got it." Her breath is heaving now, and another cough rattles her chest. I pass her a handkerchief. "That Thomas of yours, he's a good 'un." Exhaling, she wipes her lips, flicking a tired finger toward the hanging hanks of yarn. "That there, I wet-blocked it... straightened it for ya, so's you can make somethin' good of it." She directs a piercing stare at me. "An' Eva, I knows you wanna change the world. But you's oughtta know you're already doin' that. Jus' by bein' up here." Her head turns to one side and her eyes flutter closed.

I slump against the hard-backed chair, the sound of Edith's quick, shallow breaths filling the room. Part of me wants to prod her awake and debate my move to the city, but she needs her rest. Sharing her story has already taken too much energy. Getting her thoughts on my life plans can wait until another time.

After pushing back my chair, I cross the room to the stove, fingering the hanging wool. Edith's kindness unsettles me. Yesterday, when I saw this yarn hanging in the dim corner, I assumed she had taken it without my permission, hiding it from me. Instead, she has spent precious time winding, soaking, and stretching the hanks. For me.

Still gripping the soft wool in my fist, I watch my friend's fitful sleep and take a deep, shaky breath. Maybe she's right. Maybe I can make some good of all this.

CHAPTER 36

The next day, George and I are prepping dinner when a familiar clang, sputter, and squeal reaches us from the landing. It's Billy, parking the speeder and hopefully bringing the doctor. Spinning to George, I raise my brows and he responds to my silent question with a grunt and wave of his hand. I throw my apron onto the counter and grab my coat, wrapping it tight against the early November chill. My breath sparkles in the sunlight and brown alder leaves crunch underfoot as I stride to the reload. Thomas has already greeted Dr. Adams, a tall man with a booming voice and bushy eyebrows. The two men walk toward me briskly, the doc's words audible to the whole camp.

I lead the way to Edith's bunkhouse, knocking on the door before entering alone.

"You decent? The doctor's here for you." Edith isn't pleased, grumbling loud curses and flexing her fingers into the blanket under her chin, but I return to the open door and usher the doctor and Thomas inside.

"I told ya's I don' need no help jus' yet." We all ignore her protests, and Dr. Adams pulls a second chair next to the bed, plunking his heavy medical bag on it. "Waste o' money, that's what." Edith grumbles, pulling herself to a seated position with jerky movements. The doctor removes the screw top from the vulcanite case of his glass thermometer and silences Edith by sticking it under her tongue. When he unwinds a stethoscope, Thomas turns to look out the window and I help Edith unbutton the front of her nightgown. With her collar loosened, Dr. Adams places the cold chest piece on her back, and she flinches. His thick black brows draw together and his head tilts in concentration as he asks her to take four deep breaths.

"Well, your lungs don't sound too bad, Mrs. Campbell." Dr. Adams slings the stethoscope around his neck and pulls the thermometer from her mouth. Rolling it between his fingers, he squints at the numbers that the mercury registers. "But you're definitely running a fever. You been using the milk and cinnamon?" Edith had me concoct the remedy this morning, and he gestures to the remains in a pot on the woodstove. She crosses her arms across her chest and nods, daring him to comment on a cure for influenza she's very sure of.

Dr. Adam prescribes continued bed rest, plenty of fluids, and hands me a glass vial of pills. When I ask whether Edith has influenza, he shrugs.

"Can't be sure. But it certainly could be, with her fever, cough, and achiness." He points to the container in my hand, and I pull the cork stopper to peer at the small white tablets inside. "That high-dose aspirin is our most modern flu treatment since the pandemic. Make sure Edith takes it. Four tablets every four hours."

"I'll stay in bed an' drink the liquids, but I won' be takin' none o' yer new-fangled pills." The doctor chuckles, unperturbed by Edith's harsh refusal. He shrugs, opening his mouth to say something more, but he's interrupted by a single forceful thump on the door, seconds before it slams open.

Roy fills the doorway, bracing himself on the frame, panting, his face ashen. With wide eyes, he gapes at us as a gust of frigid air sweeps through the bunkhouse.

"You gotta come quick! It's Grace! She's all muddled — says the baby's coming." He spots the doctor's kit and steps across the room, slamming the black leather handles together, and wrenching the battered bag off the chair. "You done here? Come on!" Roy's fear is palpable, and everyone springs to action. Everyone except me. While Dr. Adams and Thomas hustle into their coats, my feet are suddenly rooted to the floor, my pulse racing in my ears. Thomas frowns, and with a slight head shake, motions me to follow.

"You go ahead, Thomas," I say, taking a deep breath and trying to steady my voice, which comes out a noticeable octave higher. "I'll be right there. I need to get Edith settled." This is a lie. We all know she doesn't need settling. A silent look of concern flashes between Thomas and Edith. When she gives him an almost imperceptible nod, Thomas squeezes my arm, then turns to follow the doctor and Roy, gently closing the door to the bunkhouse behind him.

"Come. Sit." Edith motions at the chair, buttoning her white flannelette nightgown until the tucked yoke collar brushes her chin. But I can't move, thoughts whirling through my head. It's too early. For Grace's baby. It's too early. No. No! We can't lose another one. It's too early for this baby!

Dizziness hits, and I slump into the chair next to Edith as my legs weaken. Images of tiny blue fingers and baby-sized coffins flash through my mind, as I gulp breaths of air. I can't bear this. Not again.

"Easy now. Steady." Edith reaches over and strokes my hand, speaking to me in a tone usually reserved for calming children.

"I'm not ready." My voice lowers to a whisper. After a long moment, Edith squeezes my cold, trembling hand in hers.

"You can do this, Eva. Grace needs ya. Go now. Go on." A soft, encouraging smile crosses her reddened face. "I can't go, so you gotta." She winks, squeezes my hand again, and juts her chin at the door. "Go be me."

There is no way I'm going to be helpful at this birth. I'm not as strong as Edith. I... I just can't. As I pull my fingers away, I wrap my arms around my middle and rock slightly in the chair.

I've avoided thinking about the birth of Grace's baby. Since reading about pre-eclampsia in the pregnancy pamphlet I brought from Seattle, I haven't imagined a positive outcome for either Grace or her baby. And it terrifies me. At least the doctor is here. That's a lucky break.

"Go! Yer friend needs ya." Edith's tone is sharp now, and when I meet her gaze, she's scowling. "Buck up, girl. Go. Keep 'er calm. Slow 'er down. That's her best chance." I nod, not at all sure what she means, or how I'm supposed to accomplish it. But something in her words gets me moving to the door, pulling my coat around me. "And Eva?" I turn back to Edith, whose eyes are narrow and filled with an intense focus. "Watch that Doc. Keep 'im outta the liquor." I step into the chilly afternoon and rush along the gravel lane to Grace's bunkhouse.

CHAPTER 37

T he next day, a Monday, is Armistice Day and Thanksgiving. Canadian Thanksgiving, Thomas and I clarify when speaking with the local crew. We've debated how, and when, to celebrate the holiday, since the American date isn't until the end of November. Thomas finally said, "When in Rome, do as the Romans," and declared we'd go with the local date. The crew will work a half day today, so the men, most of whom fought in the war, can honour their fallen friends and then celebrate with a special meal this evening.

But Daisy overshadows all thoughts of Thanksgiving, becoming the star of the cookhouse. I scoop pancake batter into uneven rounds, watching from the griddle, as Roy perches her on a stool by the counter, giving her a view of both the kitchen and the dining room. Instead of sitting normally, Daisy crawls up and plants her tiny bottom on the countertop, her feet swinging over the top of the stool.

"So." George plunks a stack of pancakes beside Daisy, and she claps her hands in childish delight. "You gots yourself a li'l brother. Tell us."

"Well... Momma was talking funny. Before the doctor came." She folds a pancake in half and takes a big bite from the middle, then unfolds it, peering into the kitchen through the hole she made. "I spy you, Eva!" She giggles and turns back to her audience in the cookhouse.

"Momma was wild and talking funny. Like you is sometimes, Billy. When you get the rotgut." Someone guffaws and the men stare into their plates to hide their amusement. I bite my lip to stifle a smile as Daisy continues. "Daddy had to go. But I was quiet as a mouse and got to stay." She sits tall, holding her shoulders back, and puts a finger to her lips.

Before I arrived, the men had been ushered out of Grace's bunkhouse, and none of us had noticed Daisy, huddled in the corner by the coats, until Grace stopped flailing.

Now, I flip the row of pancakes, focusing on their shades of brown, wondering if I can bear reliving the chaos, and heart-wrenching beauty, of last night. I glance toward the cookhouse door, aching to make a getaway. I could say I need to check on Edith. From across the room, Thomas holds my gaze, his brow furrowed in concern. I pull in a deep breath, propped up by his care, as Daisy continues.

"Doctor gives Momma some little pricks, and she got sooo sleepy." I shudder at the memory. The doctor enlisted my help to have Grace swallow a sedative. While that little pill had helped, he also administered morphine at intervals with a hypodermic needle. I'm not sure which was worse: the wild-eyed accusations echoing through the sticky room before the narcotics calmed Grace, or her glazed gaze and slack jaw after.

"That big loud doctor was purty scared last night." Daisy nods as she takes another bite of her breakfast. "He was grumbling and mumbling and walking circles 'round the house, all the time." This was true. Dr. Adams had been as restless as Grace, replacing the damp cloth on her forehead, checking her blood pressure cuff every few minutes, and examining her often to assess whether she was any closer to delivery. Because of Edith's warning, I watched the doc closely, but never saw him drink. Maybe the work distracted him, or maybe he didn't have his flask with him. I had prepared myself to steal and hide his liquor, and I'm glad it wasn't necessary. Last night was stressful enough without that confrontation.

"Then I played rock-paper-scissors with Eva for a long, long time. I won all the games. That was my favourite part." That was also true. We played for hours, and she delighted at the attention she got, all to pass the miserable minutes. Now, with some difficulty, Daisy contorts her little fist into the rock, paper, and scissor shapes for the crew. "We had fun way, way, way past my bedtime."

Last night, the doctor and I were grateful for Daisy's ceaseless chatter. We let her stay up past midnight, a welcome distraction from the gloom. Early on, Dr. Adams had shared that Grace was in real danger. Although I didn't want to hear about it, he had explained in hushed tones he was subscribing to a Russian doctor's new method of sedating the patient. With this modern treatment, he hoped to prevent the deadly pregnancy-related seizures of eclampsia in Grace by managing *her* health first. Once the eclampsia was under control, the delivery of the baby was secondary, using whatever medical assistance was required.

"And? You have a little brother now?" George delivers tin plates of food to the crew and looks up at Daisy with raised eyebrows. "Get to the punchline, girl!" The men around the table chuckle as they fill their stomachs, enjoying this morning's unusual entertainment.

"I do! I do have a new li'l brother. I won the rock game with lots of papers, an' when it was so, so dark out, he just came out... poof!" Daisy puffs her chest out, her eyes gleaming with pride and nods her chubby little chin. "All slippery, like a fish! But not cold like a fish. And then he made a sound, like a kitten." She purses her lips and makes a small, mewing noise.

My heart skips a beat at Daisy's words. Thank goodness baby Roy wasn't cold like a fish. The doctor had used forceps to help the birth along. Grace had been conscious, but slow and sedated. I'm not sure how much my encouragement to push helped, but Dr. Adams was satisfied and grateful that she ended up dilated enough to deliver. The result surpassed our hopes.

At Daisy's announcement of her healthy baby brother, everyone raises their mugs of coffee to toast Roy, Grace, and their new addition. Daisy stuffs half the pancake in her mouth, chewing loudly, cheeks puffed, and turns to me as I flip the last of the pancakes onto the platter.

"We gonna pwant those seeds today, Eva? Can we? Pwease! You said tomorrow so, so many days ago!" Her words come out muffled as Roy stands beside her, ignoring her poor manners. A grin creases his fatigue-lined face, and despite the knot in my gut, I smile back at them.

"Sure, Daisy. We'll find some time today." Leave it to Daisy to remember my broken promise to do the planting and keep me moving on to the next thing. Behind me, George lifts the giant percolator from the wood stove.

"Sounds like you done good last night." He squeezes my shoulder, and I close my eyes briefly at George's clumsy attempt at comfort. He seems to understand how painful it was for me. Then Thomas is beside me, offering a small smile. His pained look mirrors mine and he places a comforting hand on my back. Thomas, who let me collapse into him last night. Who kissed the tears on my cheek and held me until I drifted into a fitful sleep.

"I'm just so relieved it all worked out." My words are soft but rich with understanding, and both men nod. This is the truth. We're all thankful they've had a good outcome. Last night, Grace had held Roy

Junior in her lap, Daisy snuggled under one arm. Roy had stood next to his little family, thumbs hooked into his belt loops, a toothy grin plastered on his haggard face. Grace had glowed with radiant love, even if she didn't remember how baby Roy came into the world.

Now, as George preps a pumpkin pie and the men shuffle off to their shifts, I wonder if obliterating my memories of Ruby's birth would be easier. I envy the untainted joy others can feel for Grace. But then I frown. No. Those images are the only keepsakes I have of Ruby now. Her tiny blue features are etched into my soul. Though I wish she were still here, painful memories are better than no memories. My pain only exists because of my love for her.

Grief is born of love, after all.

CHAPTER 38

A month later, on a dark morning in mid-December, we awake to a world dusted with snow. Thomas kisses my cheek before leaving for breakfast, and I put down the *Green Gables* book as he tucks a wild curl behind my ear.

"I'll see you at dinner." He trails a finger toward my open collar and his gaze lingers on my chest, then he catches my eye, smirking. "Have a good day." I hit his thigh with Edith's book as Thomas strides away, chuckling. Waves of grief still blindside me, but less often every week. There's a playfulness growing between us since Edith kicked me out of my blue funk, and his suggestive grin and tingling touch make be shiver. Nursing Edith, helping Grace, tending my seeds and seedlings, and finalizing the bridge plans have given me a contented focus. By the end of each day, I'm watching the luminous dial of our black-faced alarm clock, eager for Thomas's return. Our evenings are now filled with lighthearted teasing and bursts of laughter.

I pull the covers under my chin again, cracking the spine of the book, letting myself finish the chapter snuggled in our cozy bed before braving the cold of the cabin. I had read most of this Anne story to Edith as she recovered from her flu, a guilty pleasure that took me away from helping George. But he hadn't minded, his greatest concern being the health of his beloved Edith. Once her sarcasm returned, we knew reading to her was an indulgent luxury that had to end. In typical Edith fashion, she had reclaimed her cookhouse well before her energy was fully restored, shooing me off to help Grace and her kids.

Even though she hadn't yet finished it herself, she had generously lent me the book. I frown, wondering if there's another reason she didn't keep it. Her eyes seem to bother her, especially when the light is dim. I resolve to ask about her health this morning, and not let her deflect with lighthearted joking. While Edith still isn't as fiery as before her illness, the spark between her and George is now obvious, at least to me. When I had asked Thomas whether he thought they were more than friends, he'd just flexed his eyebrows and tilted his head with a chuckle.

"That would be something, now, wouldn't it?"

When I finish the chapter, I clap the book cover closed, placing it on our bedside table next to my photo of Tony. I sling a thick wool cardigan over my nightdress and stoke the fire back to life. A glance at the clock tells me I better hurry and dress to make the second breakfast seating. The days are short now, the clang of Billy's dinner bell sounding out into the darkness for both breakfast and dinner.

Dawn's first light paints the horizon in shades of soft pink and gold as I step outside, my breath forming fleeting puffs. The glow from each bunkhouse window falls onto the glittering snow and Camp 2's morning activities are scribed into the crunchy white crystals. Footprints leave every dwelling, marking trails from their front steps to the privies and the cookhouse. A footprint web, I think with a chuckle, hurrying across the landing to the outhouse, leaving a trail of my own. With the door open, I take in the waterfront view.

The lake below me is unfrozen, the daybreak's pastel hues turning it into a shimmering canvas. In this mild coastal climate, even the old-timers have never seen this vast water body freeze. Beyond the booming grounds, swimming ducks cut V's across the reflection. All around me, the pristine dusting of white muffles the usual cookhouse clamour. I sit longer than I need to, a sense of reverence washing over me. Then a frigid gust on my butt cheeks brings me to my senses, and I rip a page of spice jars from the catalogue to wipe.

My boots crunch softly on the freshly fallen snow, and I stop to finger the crystal-covered branch of a small Sitka spruce. Every detail of the *Picea sitchensis* sits in crisp relief this morning. The sharp, flat needles on woody stubs, sticking out all around the twig, like a bottle brush. The crinkled, toothy scale edges of the cones, with their reliable Fibonacci spirals. Again, a deep peace envelops me. Gulping cold air into my lungs, I turn my back on the camp and gaze at the raw beauty around me.

The spell is broken as the rowdy line of men trudges across the landing to the reload behind me, lunch pails swinging at their sides. The snow evidently is enough to paint some magic onto Camp 2, but not enough to keep the crew from working today. I return their waves of greeting and tromp to the cookhouse.

When I slide onto the bench beside Grace, George brings me my breakfast. And a letter. I push away the steaming plate of scrambled eggs and flip over the envelope. My name is written in my mother's flowery script. Mother's. Not Father's. My fork hangs in midair. Mother has never written to me. I stare at the navy blue five-cent stamps where two faces of Teddy Roosevelt stare back. Under the US Post Office Department's wavy cancellation stamp, I notice the President's ties are crooked. The postmark is dated November 30, 1924. My mother mailed this over two weeks ago.

The surrounding voices recede as I slide my knife under the top flap. With trembling hands, I smooth the thin letter paper onto the oilcloth table covering, skimming my mother's words quickly. Your father collapsed after church... Taken to hospital... Heart condition... Bed rest... Weak... Come home, Eva.

"What is it?" Grace asks, and I look up. In the hushed cookhouse, everyone's eyes are on me. George stands behind the counter and Edith grips his bicep, their faces tight. I feel my face crumple, unable to speak. Tears spill onto my cheeks and I close my eyes, trying to regain my composure.

"It's my father." I sniff, and George pats Edith's hand, his features softening. Grace's jaw drops and she covers her mouth, which pulls a sharp laugh from me as I understand her assumption. "He hasn't died." This is an eccentricity of living so remotely. News of all kinds comes by mail. Mostly good. But sometimes awful. We all worry whenever an envelope gets torn open. Everyone here has witnessed a tiny piece of paper change someone's life. "But he's not well. It's his heart." Grace reaches for my hand, squeezing it gently. But I only want one thing, one person.

"I need to find Thomas." I push my untouched breakfast plate away and climb off the heavy half-log bench, but Grace stops me.

"They've all gone to the setting this morning. You won't find him in camp." She touches the small of my back, guiding me into my seat. "Eat something. You need it. Then we can talk." Reluctantly, I settle at the table, George's meal tasting bland as paper to me today. Another monkey wrench in my plans, coming at a time when I'm finally connecting with this place... and Thomas.

Chapter 39

Just a few days after the bad-news letter from my mother, another envelope arrives, addressed in my father's blocky handwriting. He says he feels much better; still a little breathless, but back to work at the car lot part-time. I needn't rush home on his account, although everyone would love to see me.

Sagging into my rocker in the bunkhouse, I reread this good news, tears welling behind my eyelids. My father has been healthy my whole life, missing work only once, a few summers ago when he'd had the mumps. So after my mother's first letter last week, Thomas and I arranged for me to rush down to Seattle. I've never entertained my parents' mortality — the inevitable reality that one day, they will no longer be here. It feels surreal. It's unsettling to imagine my father as anything but the healthy man I left behind.

Since that second letter, I've bounced through my days' chores, beaming. Instead of travelling to Seattle on my own, Thomas and I have both booked tickets home the day after Boxing Day. My father's health scare has highlighted the preciousness of time. After five months away, we're excited to see our family and friends in the city. If the travel goes as planned, we'll arrive in time to spend New Year's Eve with them.

Now, it's Christmas Day and in the crisp early afternoon air, I trudge across the slushy landing to the cookhouse. While I'm looking forward to tonight's Camp Dinner, it's my first holiday away from my family. My belly knots and a wave of homesickness hits me as I calculate the days until Thomas and I arrive home. In less than a week, we'll see them all.

Down in Seattle, my mother's shiny cherrywood dining room table will be laden with crisp linens in napkin rings of silver-cast poinsettias. The glistening flatware, set with rigid symmetry: three knives on the right, three forks on the left, and dessert utensils one inch above the gilded edge of the bone china service plates. Stemware, a bread plate, a menu, and a place card. My mother has always replicated every detail of a formal tablescape, from a *Ladies' Home Journal* article she clipped and still keeps with the chest of Christmas decorations. And since last year, a gleaming chandelier, with shimmering electric light bulbs, illuminates the whole composition from above.

Instead of the fragile beauty of her crisp linens, I'll spend tonight at a rustic table decorated with conifer cones, the meal served on tin plates, and lit by kerosene lanterns.

For days, George and Edith have been preparing dressings and sides, desserts and drinks. Grace and I have helped with the menial tasks they trust us with, like stringing beans and peeling potatoes. They're planning a special menu and won't tell anyone many details. But there's more fruit and chocolate in the ice box than we've had since I arrived in the summer.

Stomping the wet snow from my boots, I pull open the heavy door. The rich scents of fresh-cut balsam fir and frying onions drift over me as I hang my jacket. Daisy and Grace are already back inside the cookhouse, having left baby Roy in their bunkhouse for his afternoon nap. Daisy is kneeling on a bench, her torso flopped on the table, gluing decorative paper chains. Her tiny tongue licks the side of her upper lip as she carefully cuts the coloured pages of last summer's Eaton catalogue, then glues the strips into chains with a flour and water paste Edith made for her.

"Those look lovely. Where are we going to hang them?" I ask, peering over Daisy's shoulder as I return the shouted greetings from the kitchen with a smile and wave. Daisy points above the countertop.

"Up there. From that post to that post to that post. It'll be beee-ooot—ful!" I grin at her and nod my agreement. Grace clips greenery and arranges it on the burgundy silk table runner I sewed with the rest of my mother's heavy brocade curtains. The room looks magically festive.

A few days ago, the workers hauled a nice *Abies balsamea* inside, fussing with it in the far corner until it was perfectly positioned. Everyone in camp has added decorations from their collections, so the tree has an eclectic feel. The only constant is the thirty-six yards of silver tinsel James brought on his last trip up. He had delivered holiday cheer to all the camps around the lake. Grace and I felt enchanted that he chose something to beautify our Christmas tree, but the men found greater pleasure in the crate of Canadian Club he'd left.

Thomas and I have no Christmas ornaments of our own to contribute, so I used some of the silver grey wool Edith straightened to knit a tiny stocking ornament. Thomas had raised his eyebrows when I told him what I was doing, his dark eyes narrowing as he touched my cheek. But he hadn't tried to stop me, understanding my need to create a lasting symbol of Ruby's memory.

Now, standing by the tree, I flip over the knitted ornament, running my thumb over the "Ruby 1924" inscription I'd embroidered there. My heart aches for her, but the pain is less sharp today than on that terrible day two and a half months ago. This tiny stocking represents another step in my healing and brings a small smile to my face now. It's my baby's first Christmas, even if she's only with me in spirit. I put two fingers to my lips, kiss them, and touch the stocking again. When I turn to decorate the tables, Grace is standing motionless, watching me and biting a quivering lip. She drags her gaze from mine and I swiftly put an arm around her shoulder.

"It's alright. We're alright. You need to savour your blessings, not feel sad for us." Tears glisten in her eyes and she gulps back a sob, burying her forehead against my neck. I wonder if Grace ever thinks about that first trip to Alert Bay, when we confessed our pregnancies to one another under smoky skies, both so innocent and excited.

We stand together, two mothers, with such achingly different outcomes. Today my heart feels full, grateful to have this warm and boisterous place to distract me, even if torrents of sadness hit me once in a while. Healing will take time and distraction helps.

When Grace pulls away, we work together to decorate the rest of the tables, then hang Daisy's paper chain as she directs us in a bossy voice, her hands on her hips, feet spread wide. When our pint-sized foreman is finally satisfied with the position of the chains, Grace says she needs to go check on baby Roy. I raise my eyebrows at Daisy.

"Wanna go have a snowball fight?" She squeals and claps in anticipation, sliding off the bench and running to bundle into her winter gear. Daisy scrambles away, her blond curls bouncing, and I can't help but imagine what Ruby's hair colour might have been.

A pang of longing grips my chest, squeezing the air from my lungs. I take a deep breath, bracing myself against the familiar wave of grief, and waiting for the tingling dread in my chest to fade away, as it always does.

Chapter 40

The remnants of our Christmas feast are stacked high on the cookhouse counter. Tetley sits tall on a sawbuck table, shoved to the room's edge, with a fiddle tucked under his chin and his toe tapping on the half-log bench. A raucous rendition of "Jingle Bells" fills the room. Edith and George polka around the makeshift dance floor, while Donkey Donny and Crank entertain Daisy with a lively version of the Charleston. She mimics them, heels kicking and arms swinging, her head thrown back in laughter.

Thomas had spent time at each dinner table, celebrating and chatting with the workers. It's a rare opportunity when, with the help of James's whisky, the bush hierarchy melts away, replaced by the relaxed camaraderie of the holidays. Now, across the room by the counter, our foreman and bull cook, Roy and Billy, stand arm in arm. With animated gestures, Thomas tells a story that elicits raucous laughter from them, their joy clear in every hearty chuckle. He has earned the respect and admiration of his crew.

Watching my husband effortlessly command the room, my ribs squeeze tight at the unfairness. I ache to be acknowledged for my abilities, not just for being the boss's wife. Unlike Thomas's natural ease, I had stiffly worked the room as my mother had taught me. It was exhausting, but with deliberate effort, I drew even the quiet ones into laughing conversations. Amid the festivities, I steer clear of Grace and James. With Grace, all I see is the healthy baby nestled in her arms. And James... well, James in a whisky fog is best avoided.

With each sip of wine, more frustration festers inside me. I stand alone, avoiding all of them, the drink amplifying my roiling emotions — the defeat of my stolen career, the despair for my lost child, and the disgust over my biggest mistake. Forcing a strained smile, I stumble into the kitchen to pour more wine. When it sloshes to the floor, Thomas appears beside me.

"Whoa, there," he says, turning me to face him. "You wanna go?" I nod, his silent understanding a comfort in the chaos. Thomas puts an arm around me, guiding me to the coat hooks, and announces our departure with a wide grin. The crew raises their glasses to us in farewell.

Outside, the night is crisp and relief washes over me, grateful to escape the gathering. The day's frozen slush crunches under our feet as Thomas and I walk home. Behind us, Tetley's fiddle music restarts, and the crew's foot stomping flows out into the otherwise hushed darkness. I grip Thomas's elbow, unsteady on the icy gravel in my overshoes.

"That was a nice night," he says, pulling me upright with a concerned look as I stumble. "Did you enjoy yourself?" Thomas peers down at me. Silently, I reflect on the evening. The fantastic food, the joyful fiddle music, and warm companionship — they all had their moments. But enjoyment isn't tonight's strongest emotion. Homesick. Resentment. Desperate. These words describe my feelings more accurately.

"Yes," I say. "It was a nice night." Thomas opens the bunkhouse door and helps me up the stairs, where I slump against the wall.

He hangs my coat, then crouches to unbuckle and pull off my wet overshoes. He guides me to my rocking chair without removing my openwork pumps. The room swirls, and I lean my head back, closing my eyes and taking a deep breath.

"What's this?" Thomas asks. From my coat pocket, he pulls out a small present, wrapped in red tissue paper and a silver silk ribbon. I drop my chin to my chest as Thomas lights a lantern and flips over the tag.

"To Eva, our barefoot diva. Merry Christmas… James?" Thomas's voice is unsteady as he reads the words, faltering toward me. "What is this?" He squats on his haunches and plunks the present on my lap, blinking rapidly, the scent of his tobacco and whisky enveloping me. I give a slight headshake, my chest tightening, but say nothing. "Eva? What have you done?" Thomas's eyes are wide, his tone deepening.

"Nothing! I've done nothing wrong." My protest dissolves into a sob, the anguish and disappointment of the past six months flooding to the surface.

I consider whether I can be innocent, when shame and guilt haunt me. Shame for what brought me here, for needing Thomas to rescue me. Guilt for not protecting Ruby, and for questioning my feelings for this man crouched before me.

My betrayals have never been actions. Just thoughts. But I suppose those count. Thoughts are where the deception begins. I let the present fall onto the floor beside the rocking chair and Thomas glares at it before turning back to me.

"Why did he give this to you?" He blinks slowly, going completely still. When I don't answer, Thomas stands abruptly, jerking away. "Is there… are you… is there something between you?" His eyes go wild for a moment before he stomps to the window, fists on the counter, shoulders hunched. His voice shakes through clenched teeth.

"No!" My unsettled soul has nothing to do with James, but it makes sense Thomas might think that.

"Then what? Eva?" Thomas turns, leaning against the counter, rubbing the base of his neck. A spark lights in my belly and my pulse races. My words ricochet across the room, unleashed by wine and frustration.

"I'm sad, Thomas. And lonely. And disappointed." I study my lap, clasping and unclasping my hands. "This..." I look around the rugged bunkhouse, seeing only its defects. "This isn't what I planned for my life." He crumples with every word, his shoulders stooping. "You know this." I say the last words gently, a caress. And Thomas nods, just once, his face crestfallen as he clears his throat.

"I do. But I thought... I hoped... you were finding your way." Without thinking, I reach toward him, my heart aching. But Thomas balks, crossing his arms over his chest. "What have you been doing with James?" I drop my hand back into my lap, picking at a hangnail.

"Nothing. I've only talked to him a few times." Then I emit a muffled chuckle, looking up. "And I pulled a rifle on him the first month I was here. Out on the trail." Thomas blinks rapidly. I never told him about that encounter, afraid he'd reconsider my hiking alone. At the time, I couldn't risk the truth because my freedom was too important. Clearly, James hadn't told him either.

I hold Thomas's gaze now, wanting him to be sure of my honesty. "And since the day we caught those pinks down at the point, I've spent two afternoons with him. Fly-fishing. That's it. He's been teaching me and Daisy to cast... Since Ruby... it's been a distraction. That's all." Reaching my fingertips out to Thomas again, I lean my head against the rocking chair, my eyes never leaving him. "It's not important." I can read his thoughts as they flit across his rugged features. His mouth fell open at the rifle comment, and that surprise fades to a thin relieved smile as he absorbs there's nothing untoward between James and I. Then, as his whisky-blurred brain processes James has spent time with me, his jaw clenches with jealousy. Finally, his lips purse in distrust, but I'm not sure if it's of James or me.

"You gotta watch that James. He's..." Thomas steps toward me now, squeezing my hand and dropping to his knees in front of me. "He's not always a nice fellow." His face softens with concern.

"I know," I say, and Thomas's eyes narrow briefly. For a chilled heartbeat, I wonder if he suspects James was Ruby's father. But now is not the time to address that, so I continue. "I didn't want to cause another rift between you two." Thomas has been annoyed by James's passive work ethic for months, and knowing James skipped out to fish would have grated Thomas.

He looks as if he's going to say more, but after holding my gaze for a moment, Thomas lowers his ear onto my belly, like he did when Ruby was inside me. "We should have a child, Eva. When can we... try... try again?" His words crack, and his shoulders tremble. With tears trickling down my face, I stroke Thomas's hair, his smooth-shaven cheek, and his lips, shushing him softly and rocking a little. Together, we sit in a liquored haze, each yearning for the things beyond our reach.

A ruckus outside interrupts our sad reflection, then the door bursts open, and a blast of frigid air sweeps in. James tilts against the frame, his hair tousled and his suit jacket askew. He blinks at us, fumbling with his hat, mouth agape.

Thomas springs to his feet and strides across the room, propelling James down the stairs before closing the door behind them. The last thing I see is James's clouded gaze on me.

With a long, dejected sigh, I reach to loosen my shiny black leather pumps. Kicking them off, I flex my toes and rotate my feet. City shoes are no match for work boots in comfort. I imagine tromping into the Olympic Hotel in my well-worn leather boots, the sound of clicking caulks echoing on the terrazzo. Picturing Mother's horrified expression makes me giggle.

Standing, I roll my neck, then pick up my shoes and James's dented present. I place my pumps neatly under our hanging outerwear, sliding the still-wrapped gift back into my coat pocket. I should have told Thomas about my fishing sessions sooner, but there was just no good reason to. On each of those evenings, Thomas had brought work issues home that we'd debated long into the night. When he finally asked about my day, it was an afterthought. And pointless to get into.

Now, as I turn to undress, Thomas returns, letting in another gulp of icy December air. Our eyes lock across the bunkhouse.

"What did he want?" I ask, moving to the bed.

"Nothing." Thomas pulls at the thin, round laces of his polished Oxford shoes and kicks them over near mine. "He's drunk. Thought he was at the guest bunk." He drops his gaze as he says the last sentence, running a hand through his hair, his words trailing off. I nod, opening the back neck clasp of my red silk dress. Thomas stands rigidly, hands stuffed in his pockets, his eyes exploring me as I place a foot on the bed. I hitch the hem of the dropped waistline dress to expose my garter clips, releasing the silk stockings and peeling them off slowly. When I finally turn and gesture for help with the snaps down my back, he hesitates and moves close behind me.

I drop my chin, trapped in the dress until he unbuttons me. The room is hushed, the crackle and occasional popping from the fire in the woodstove punctuating our breaths. A moment passes. Thomas yanks at his necktie and loosens his collar before pushing my curls aside. His thick fingers struggle with the tiny snaps in the dim light, brushing my warm skin as he releases each one. When the beaded red silk slides open to the small of my back, he leans his forehead onto the nape of my neck.

"Jesus, Eva... you're... I just..." His breath tickles and a delightful shiver dances down my spine. "I want you to be happy." His words are soft, tortured. I slump back against him and he wraps his arms around my middle, his chin on my shoulder now, his hardness pressing into my tailbone.

I wonder what it means to be happy. The unrest I felt earlier this evening has faded. Thomas's presence calms me, as it has for years. But happiness is complicated by everything else.

"I love you," he whispers in my ear, and a throbbing tingle runs through me as I shift in his arms. Thomas slips the dress off my shoulders, turning me to face him as it falls to the floor. I stand barefoot in my white satin slip as he leans me back, my nipples tight against my brassiere. But I place both palms on Thomas's chest, pushing him away gently. My chin drops as I release a long exhale. I can't... can't let myself enjoy... anything.

Thomas sucks in his breath, recognizing my silent refusal. He touches my face with the back of his hand, trailing it down my cheek and across my breast, making me shudder. Then he lifts me into his arms easily, kissing the top of my head. He stares past the bed and out across the moonlit lake, holding me tight for a moment. Sighing, he tucks me under the covers before undressing.

When Thomas slides between the cold cotton sheets, he spoons me. I feel his heat and hardness, his desire clear, but he just cradles an arm over my waist.

"Please be careful." His voice is low as he skims his palm across my stomach protectively. He doesn't need to say James's name. Thomas rolls away, pulling the covers tight, leaving me wondering why it feels like my heart is shrinking. Sleep envelops me long before I gain any clarity.

CHAPTER 41

The next morning, I roll out of bed as soon as I'm awake, packing my trunk for tomorrow's trip south. Thomas does the same, our conversation limited to practical matters, neither of us mentioning last night's words.

After breakfast, I take Daisy on an adventure to give Grace a break. Roy Junior is seven weeks old, and he's been a difficult baby, exhausting Grace and causing Daisy to wrinkle her nose anytime someone asks her how she likes her new brother. "He's loud an' stinky. That's what I think," is Daisy's usual response.

Snow has dusted camp again and our trail stretches through the forest ahead of us, a pristine ribbon of white. I enjoy stomping fresh tracks almost as much as Daisy. We spend the morning trudging out to the waterfall, where we eat our sandwiches and sip on hot chamomile tea. Daisy flings salal boats and handfuls of glittering snow from the top of the falls, reminding me of the day I fell asleep out here and lost her. She's a delightfully curious and imaginative child, even if she causes us occasional heartaches.

The sun warms me through my thick winter coat as I watch her now, and I cross my arms, careful not to let myself doze off. My wrist presses against my pocket, pushing James's gift into my belly, and I wonder if I should open it, or just throw it away. There were no tracks in the snow outside the guest bunk this morning and none of the men were at breakfast. No doubt everyone is still recovering from their over-indulgences last night. Boxing Day is a rare day off, after all.

With a gloved hand, I pull the box from my pocket, letting the silver silk ribbon glint in the sunlight. It could be a deck of playing cards — it's about the right size. The base of my neck tingles. I need to know what it is. Daisy chants "Hickory Dickory Dock", marching up and down the waterfall crest, gleefully hitting snow off the bushes with a long stick, paying no attention to me.

Pulling off my mittens, I shift so my body shields the gift from Daisy's view, then slide the ribbon off. Inside the tissue paper are a photograph and a polished wooden box. I flip over the print and gasp. It's me, on the lake shore, my pregnant belly in sharp focus. I squeeze my eyes shut, swaying slightly. James must have taken the photo the day we caught the pinks.

The girl in the image stands barefoot amid large boulders. She looks serene, her hand cupping the base of her protruding belly, blissfully unaware of the wrenching loss that's just weeks away.

When my heart stops pounding, I lay the photo on my lap, prying at the box. It's held closed by two small magnets recessed into the edge of the wood, and the case's tiny brass hinges unfold easily. Lined up neatly inside are colourful rows of tied flies, their hooks stuck into the padded, white velvet interior.

Again my breath catches and I lay one hand on my breastbone, fingering the delicate feathers, fur, and thread with the other. Some flies are entomologically correct, tied to mimic insects, such as the Ephemeroptera, a dry mayfly pattern we practised casting with. Others are made to attract fish, like the winged wet-fly called the Professor, crafted with a peacock herl body, black hackle, and mottled brown turkey feather wings. The thoughtfulness of this gift makes me dizzy. It's hours of delicate work, which James did for me.

Then I snap the box shut, my mouth dry. I fold the tissue paper around all of it, stuffing the present deep into my pocket. The photo and the flies are beautiful mementos, but I wonder what it means. It could be James's attempt at saying sorry. But I replay how close he stood at our last fishing lesson, and how he leered at me last night. This gift doesn't feel like an apology for the past, but more like an offer for a future. I'm suddenly overheated, aching to return to camp and be alone with my thoughts. With jerky movements, I stuff the lunch wrappers and Thermos into my pack, cinching the tie closed with a hard tug, and I call for Daisy.

"Let's head home, Daisy-girl!" She waves her stick at me from the waterfall, holding her arms out wide as if she's hugging the forest. "Come on." I motion her over until she skips and slides toward me down the steep embankment, her upturned face bright as she crashes into my legs, wrapping my knees in a quick embrace, before scampering back along our footprints on the snowy trail.

We pause at Ruby's grave, Daisy drawing hearts in the snow with a mittened hand, chattering at the ground as if she were talking to a friend.

"You cold under there, baby Ruby? Maybe a little, huh? That's what I think! I gots a new dolly for Christmas. Do you like dollies? You do. That's what I think." I watch the scene with a full heart, love and sadness huddling together in my tight chest. As we leave, I brush my lips with one snow-dusted mitten and plant the kiss atop the white cross marking my baby's spot. My eyes flutter closed as I ache for this lost Christmas, and all those yet to come.

Back in camp, Daisy dashes over the railway track and beelines it for the cookhouse, where she'll beg for a sample of whatever Edith is baking this afternoon. I follow, ducking behind the building to check on my seeds and seedlings.

We stacked the tins along the back wall, beyond the woodpile, for the winter. It's a sheltered spot, protected from the wind, but with plenty of diffuse light. Direct sunshine can cause daytime thawing and refreezing at night, which I've read can harm the young trees. We also mulched the tops and filled the gaps between the tins with pine needles. This should insulate the tender roots and mimic natural growing conditions for the seeds.

Mouse tracks weave through the seedlings in the fresh snow. The heart-shaped footprints, connected by the imprint of a dragging tail, paint a path atop the tins from the woodpile to a fallen log. So far, the creature seems uninterested in my plants, but I'll have to monitor it.

I poke the soil under the blanket of snow with a stick of kindling. It seems to give way, like always. I shrug to myself. The tins might be colder than the ground elsewhere in the forest. Maybe I could use our thermometer to record the temperatures. I squat on my haunches, deep in thought, drumming the kindling against my knee.

When Daisy and I planted the seeds, we buried them at different heights to replicate the natural stratification encountered in the wild. If I measure the soil temperature at each elevation, I might find a correlation between germination and temperatures. The seeds also need a period of cold to break dormancy, but extreme or prolonged freezing can damage seeds and seedlings. It's complicated.

I sigh, wondering if any of my charges will sprout in the spring. The conditions required for seed growth are overwhelming. And it's awe aspiring to think that they can become trees. Nature already does a pretty good job without our interference.

A clatter and a yelp from within the cookhouse returns me to the present. I hope it isn't an unsupervised Daisy causing the ruckus. Standing, I toss the kindling and wipe my palms together before pulling open the back door to the kitchen.

Inside, Edith stands over the washbasin, wrapping a wet cloth over her wrist. Loaves of sourdough and a sheet pan lay scattered at her feet. She glances up at me, her lips in a tight line, then peers at her arm where a burn blister is forming.

"Another good 'un," she grumbles, fingering the collection of burns on her forearm.

"What happened?" I ask, looking around for Daisy. But Edith is alone in the room. "Can I help you bandage that?"

"Naw, but thanks." Edith throws the wet cloth into the basin, and gingerly pats her arm dry with her apron. "Bare is better. Easier to keep clean."

I grab a towel and salvage the bread loaves, tossing them onto the counter. "The men will never know," I say with a wink, and Edith grins as I slide the sheet pan beside the stove. "Has Daisy been in here?"

When Edith shakes her head, I frown, a sliver of worry creasing my brow. How long since I saw her? Fifteen, twenty minutes? Maybe Daisy went home. I leave the cookhouse, crossing over to Grace's, but Daisy isn't there either. My stomach quivers as I stride to check my place, but it, too, is empty.

As I step back outside, contemplating where to look next, the guest bunk door opens. James gazes out over the lake, filling the doorway, then steps down, glancing my way. He settles on the front stoop, rolling tobacco with practised ease. His eyes hold mine as he runs the edge of the paper along his tongue.

"Morning." His words are raspy and he clears his throat. Striking a match, he cups his hands around the cigarette.

"Morning." The sight of him flushes my cheeks with heat. "Have you seen Daisy?" I ask as I approach and avert my eyes, remembering the box in my pocket, unsure what to do. He shakes his head, then speaks again when I'm closer, his words mingling with a cloud of exhaled smoke.

"I apologize… for my… interruption last night," James says.

I nod with a tight smile, and I glance toward camp. "I should go… go find her." But then I decide I can't ignore his gifts. "Um… the flies… the photo… are beautiful." Better to have this discussion now, in private, than in front of others. Or Thomas.

James clears his throat. He blinks rapidly, scraping a hand through his tousled hair. "Is it alright…? The photo…?" His forehead wrinkles as he glances at me with bloodshot eyes. Out in the forest, the image of my pregnant self had only brought memories of Ruby — not the whisky-soaked night that created her. It's odd how a mind can parse the precious from the haunting. Like unravelling the fragile strands of a tapestry, and keeping only the golden threads.

"No. It's fine. Lovely," I say after a beat. "It's the only photo I have… of… of that time. Thank you." This much, at least, is true. No one else up here has a camera.

"Maybe I can show you where to use those flies. In the spring." He hesitates. "Do you have them?" Again, I nod and look over my shoulder for Daisy. I really should find her. But wherever she's wandered off to, she'll be fine for another minute. Peeling off a mitten, I unwrap the tissue paper, stepping toward James, holding the box between us.

He opens the lid, running a fingertip over the flies. He snags one, pulling it free of the padding, then drops the small, black pattern into my palm. "This one... I named after you. I call it the Charcoal Diva." He leans in, pointing at the silver thread spiralling up the shank. "It's a variation of an old spider pattern. Lots of black hackle and a bit of silver decoration." James takes a drag of his cigarette and quirks an eyebrow. "Just like you."

His teasing unbalances me, and I fight the desire to flee, pinching the fly between my fingernails. "How do you fish it?" I ask. His workmanship is exquisite, the hook a layered piece of art, but I can't imagine it attracting a bite.

"It's a wet fly," James says. "So you can drift it below the surface in a stream. Or twitch it through the water in a lake." He shrugs. "Should work, but I haven't tried it yet."

I smile, shaking my head at his bright-eyed anticipation. My gaze shifts from James's clean hands to his stubbled chin, inches from mine. The heady scent of smoke and yesterday's whisky drifts from him, making my stomach churn, and I step back, dropping the hook into his palm. A prickling crawls along the nape of my neck, urging me to escape.

Just then, a shout makes me whirl around. Thomas runs our way, Daisy draped over one shoulder, her face buried in his collar. He falters, his mouth dropping open, as he takes in the intimate scene between James and me. In the distance, beside the cookhouse, a column of black smoke rises.

Without a word, I bolt toward Thomas, reaching up to take Daisy from him.

"What is it? What's happened?" I ask. Thomas glares past me at James and glances at Daisy, his eyebrows furrowing as he leans near my ear.

"She's fine. But there's a fire inside the mill." His voice is low, his words clipped. "It's bad. Can you take her?"

A chill runs through me. Fires are dreaded out here. Wide-eyed, I clutch Daisy close, absently patting her hair as she nuzzles into my chin. Behind Thomas, Tetley hammers his fists on doors, shouting. Men emerge from their bunkhouses, stomping into their boots, and sprinting toward the sawmill. "I gotta go. George saw Daisy go into the mill and went in after her. I'm not sure he knows she's out. He might still be in there looking for her." Thomas shakes his head as he spins away, his jaw clenched, a visible pulse throbbing in his temple. Before I can utter a word, he's already fleeing, his red-checked mackinaw flapping, as the plume of smoke grows overhead.

Oh God. Please protect them all. With Daisy whimpering in my arms, I stand frozen on the landing, unsure of my next move. James touches my shoulder, startling me. He stands close, his face ashen and fear reflecting in his eyes. Shouts echo across the camp and orange flames flicker above the brush close to the cookhouse.

"Take her into your place. Stay with her. I'll find Grace and let her know." I nod, still speechless. James jogs away, his gaze fixated on the blazing mill.

Keeping a hand on Daisy's head, shielding her from the horror, I peer past the outhouse and across the trestle. My legs weaken and I gasp at the scene. From an open window of the mill, flames belch, already devouring the structure. Alive and hungry, the fire roars eerily in the breeze. Chunks of debris rain down into the lake with sizzling splashes, distorting the shimmering reflection of the inferno. Around us, bits of ash drift by peacefully, landing in dark speckles on the snow.

The men scramble to set up the water pump on the railway, their silhouettes dwarfed by the towering flames. Above us, the plume of black smoke spreads, blotting out the sunlight, and casting a hazy grey pall over the once-bright day. The mill, built atop pilings over the lake, offers limited access for the men to fight the raging blaze. Saving it looks hopeless.

Dread seizes me as flames leap to the shingle bundles stacked neatly on the railway cars parked in the siding next to the mill. The shingles begin to burn, days of work crackling and sparking. When a bush near the cookhouse catches fire, I realize the fire might spread to other buildings. Somehow that hadn't occurred to me until now.

"Oww. Eva!" Daisy wriggles in my arms, her discomfort interrupting my thoughts.

"Sorry, Daisy." I loosen my grip on her, slowly backing until the outhouse shields our view of the unfolding disaster, then drop her to the ground. "Let's go inside, huh?" My voice stumbles, high-pitched and fragmented. A wave of foreboding and the acrid taste of smoke chokes my breath. I take her hand, stumbling toward our bunkhouse, pulling her away from the fire's glow.

I lift Daisy up the steps ahead of me and she turns, shoving a fist near my face. In her palm is a matchbook. A cold heaviness expands through my core as I recognize it from our last picnic. And then, a deafening explosion reverberates through the camp.

Chapter 42

The concussive boom sucks the air from my chest and rattles the windows, the rumble of the explosion echoing across the valley. I bound up the steps to kneel beside Daisy. Through the open front door, we gaze in horror at an immense cloud of grey-black smoke billowing from the mill. As the roaring fades, small chunks of hot debris fall, sizzling in the snow and shaking dust from the rafters.

When the shower of coals stops, I rush outside, stepping away until I can see onto the roof. Dark circles of melted snow reveal the shingles around each chunk, but to my relief, the snow on the bunkhouses cools the hot shrapnel before there's any risk of fires starting.

"Big boom," Daisy says, leaning against the doorjamb at the top of the stairs, swinging one boot across the sill. "What's happening, Eva? I gotta know!" She gazes at the scene, her eyebrows furrowed and lips pursed in that way she has when she doesn't understand something.

The sound of my heartbeat thrashes in my ears. When I last saw Thomas and the others, they were scrambling with the water pump along the main track, between the rail siding and the cookhouse, next to the explosion. They were... Thomas was... right there. Terror cements a sharp icicle in my gut and I close my eyes. My pulse races and bile rises in my throat. Daisy yanks on my hand and I take a deep, slow breath. No point imagining the worst. Thomas… and the crew will be fine. They have to be.

Moments before, I had been determined to protect Daisy from the devastation. But now, I'm desperate to check on everyone. "Let's go, Daisy-girl. We'll find out what's happening." My voice sounds foreign, shaky and shrill.

I force my feet toward the other end of camp, glancing through the trees at the flaming mill, then quicken my pace until Daisy stumbles beside me. Slowing, I haul her upright. A few steps later she pulls away, running to Grace, who's rushing from her bunkhouse with baby Roy bundled in blankets on her shoulder. We gather next to the cookhouse, just as Edith emerges, wrapping a shawl around her thick chest. The three of us line up shoulder to shoulder without a word, staring wide-eyed across the tracks at the destruction, while Daisy clings to Grace's leg.

The thick smoke shifts and two men come into view, lifting and lowering the manual pump to maintain a meager flow of water from the hose. Behind them, the fire rages, a monstrous, roaring beast consuming the sawmill. Billy mans the nozzle, aiming the scant stream through the window, which has no effect on the growling inferno.

I try to count the workers, but their hazy movements make it impossible. The silhouettes at the water pump and hoses aren't the men we're searching for. George, Thomas, and Roy are nowhere to be seen. Spiralling sparks and embers fill the sky, and even with the flames warming my face, a frosty shiver coils in my chest. Where are they?

My hands shake as I grasp Edith's arm, my terror building as I watch the men fight the blaze. The state-of-the-art sawmill's roof, which Thomas proudly completed just a few months ago, collapses in a burst of cracking timber and surging flames. The ground beneath us vibrates with the force of it, as if the earth itself is trembling in fear.

An image from last night flashes in my mind's eye — Thomas's powerful hands struggling with my dress, then caressing my face, and lifting me into bed. Now, those same hands might be lying lifeless beneath charred beams. I force the thoughts away, leaning my head on Edith's shoulder. My stomach clenches, and I pray, something I rarely do.

Edith's lips tremble and she holds her hands over her heart, fingers interlocked so tightly her knuckles are white. Her head shakes in disbelief and my thoughts turn to George. Surely he got out of the mill before the explosion. He isn't careless. But he'd do anything to save Daisy if she was in danger. I bite my lip, then glance at Grace.

Her face is ashen, eyes bulging. She jiggles the baby, unable to stand still, her mouth hanging open. But as the smoke shifts, she glimpses Roy on the beach carrying buckets, and gasps in relief. Grace sinks to her knees and grips Daisy in a fierce hug, smiling through tears, her gaze trailing her husband.

Edith avoids my eyes and rubs her hands down the front of her apron, scanning the scene. She's searching for George, the same way I'm looking for Thomas, but neither of us sees our men. There's a loud crack, and we watch in stunned silence as the pilings under the sawmill collapse, and the main floor tilts, folding into the water. The powerful splash generates a ring of whitewater that spreads from the smouldering mill through to the booming grounds. I choke on the burst of hot, acrid ashes rushing past. Then strange hisses and metallic clanks fill the air as the precious milling equipment submerges below the murky surface.

The men on the pump pause, removing their caps to mop their brows. They watch a cloud of white steam join the thick black smoke as the lake extinguishes most of the fire. Through the haze, a rowboat's outline is visible beyond the last ruined remnants jutting from the water. I squint. It could be Thomas, rowing through the debris. A jolt of hope sparks in me. It looks like Thomas. But I can't be sure.

A shout from our right pulls my gaze from the lake. Next to the sawmill, fire licks up into the dead branches of a looming alder. A gust pushes the flames across the tracks, toward the cookhouse. Amid more shouts, the crew drags the water pump over. They drench the ground, walls, and roofs, shifting their focus to protecting the camp from the remaining spot fires.

I join the bucket brigade near the river, glancing out at the lake with every scoop, looking for Thomas and George, but I still haven't seen either. It takes another fifteen minutes to douse the last flames. By then, we're all drenched in lake water and sweat. My chest heaves and my arms feel limp from the exertion. I leave the exhausted crew, surveying the eerily charred landscape along the riverbank as I rejoin Grace and Edith.

For a long while, we all stare out over the mill's blackened bones, as if our wordless vigil could somehow reverse the destruction.

Finally, Grace breaks the silence. "I can't believe this! It's all gone. Just gone. And so fast!"

"It's jus' stuff," Edith says, her eyes locking on mine. "I'd feel better knowin' everyone made it. Have ya seen our George yet? Or Thomas?"

I shake my head. "I might have seen Thomas earlier. Out in the rowboat. But I'm not sure. No one saw where he went." And I don't want to verbalize my fear about George. My guess is Thomas went out on the water because he's looking for George. Which can't be good. Between the blazing inferno, the building collapse, and the frigid waters, if George was in the mill for the explosion, his survival would be a miracle.

Grace's hand flies to her mouth in horror as she realizes for the first time that not everyone is accounted for. She reaches over to hug me, baby Roy between us. "Oh honey, you're soaked. And shivering. Go home. Get changed," she says to me. "I'm sure Thomas and George are fine." Her words hold no comfort, but I nod. I am freezing.

Head hanging, I walk back to our bunkhouse, wishing I could go back and change the past few hours. Thoughts tumble through my head like a kaleidoscope, and I nearly step on a brightly coloured matchbook. It's a vivid accusation, dropped in the gravel right where Daisy stumbled earlier. I stoop to pick it up, and with trembling fingers, I unfold the Wrigley's spearmint ad from the striking strip.

The comic inside confirms what I already know — these are the matches I used that day Daisy got lost. The day I showed her how to make a fire, step-by-step. With a lump in my throat, I squeeze my eyes shut. I should never have shown Daisy how to use matches. And today, I should have been watching her.

CHAPTER 43

After slipping into dry clothes, I head back to the cookhouse, eager for news of Thomas. And George. The crew skipped lunch while they battled the blaze, so I help Edith heat soup and slice bread for sandwiches. As we prepare the meal, I keep glancing through the back window of the cookhouse, hoping to see the missing men.

Soon the crew shuffles in, heads hanging and feet dragging. Charcoal streaks their pants, patches of raw flesh showing through singed and torn shirts. The acrid scent of smoke, sweat, and burnt hair overpowers the cooking smells as they slump onto the benches. I scan the ash-streaked faces, my hands trembling and an ache lodging in my throat. Thomas and George aren't among them.

The door opens again and I whirl around. But it's just James, in vibrant, full colour, amid the monochrome crew. His clean face and bright white collared shirt speak volumes — he hadn't fought the fire. Otherwise, he, too, would be covered in shades of grimy grey.

His gaze runs a prickling over my scalp and I squirm, staring down at the cracked cutting board, avoiding his eyes. Before I can consider the bitter tang in my mouth, Thomas and Roy enter through the back door. Tears well behind my eyelids as I slump against the counter, relief weakening my knees. I step toward Thomas, craving the comfort of a hug, but he goes straight to Edith, who is stirring the chicken soup on the wood stove. With his cap clutched in blistered hands, Thomas looks into Edith's pale, wrinkled face.

"It's George... he never came out. We couldn't get to him, Edith. And we... haven't found him... yet." His voice is hoarse, and he coughs, clearing his throat. Edith sways, the long-handled ladle in her hand hovering, and lets out a strangled sob. Thomas wraps a brawny arm around her waist, guiding her to a stool as she buckles. Beside me, Grace buries her face in Roy's chest, and I sink to the floor, sliding down the log cabin's wall. Just this morning, George had handed me my coffee with a wink, saying, "Mug up, Boss!". It feels impossible that he's just... gone.

"Ya sure?" Edith's eyes widen, staring at Thomas. He swallows, nodding once.

"We even went out in the rowboat. I... there's no way..." He shakes his head, his words trailing off as he lays a palm on Edith's back. "I'm so sorry."

"No! No. Not that ol' coot." Our strong, stubborn Edith shakes her head slowly as she sags against the wall, her milky blue eyes filling with tears. She brings a quivering palm over her lips and her chest caves in, her spine curling over like one of Daisy's wood bugs. But rolling into a protective ball won't shield Edith from the weight of this pain.

When Thomas finally looks down at me, his gaze is distant. He lets out a long, low sigh, gently pulling the ladle from Edith's clenched grip and passing it over to me.

"Let's get the men fed." He jabs his chin toward the crew in the other room, who sit in bewildered stillness, eyes averted from Edith's pain. I nod, stumbling to my feet. Without offering me any reassurance, Thomas shuffles to the dining room. He has a quiet exchange with each worker, clasping their shoulders and praising their efforts.

My heart fills as I watch my exhausted husband give encouragement to his forlorn crew. The enormity of Thomas's responsibility hits me and I wonder at his strength to lead these men. I blink back tears, turning to the kitchen.

Our proud, big-eared, kindhearted George is gone, and it might be my fault, but we need to eat. Edith sits motionless on her stool while Grace and I methodically fill soup bowls and cut sandwiches. Working in the kitchen reminds me of the day I spent helping George, weeks ago, when Edith was sick. Oh George, you're scaring the piss outta us! Come on back. But wishing for him to walk in, after the force of the explosion, is fanciful hope.

The cookhouse is eerily quiet. Lively chatter usually accompanies the clattering silverware, but today those sounds are hushed, the gloom punctuated only by ragged coughs and throat clearing. Then Daisy spills her soup, crying as the hot liquid covers her pants. Roy springs up and again the crew jumps into action, pulling the drenched clothing off her, and cooling her reddened thighs with cold cloths. They cajole Daisy with funny looks and peek-a-boo until she's laughing through her tears.

These hard men carry such softness. Like the towering cedars, their rugged bark conceals the tender heartwood hidden within. Billy sits back down in front of his meal, his glazed gaze squinting past me, his scarred eyebrow lifting as he shakes his head in disbelief. None of us are ready to accept today's losses.

In the kitchen, I eat standing next to Edith, who won't leave but refuses food. My appetite is non-existent, but we all need sustenance, so I force down a few mouthfuls. Edith rocks a little, rubbing her breastbone, sometimes squeezing her eyes shut. When the mealtime sounds diminish, I pat her thigh and say I'll be back once I clear the tables. Her stare floats past me, as if she's chasing a memory. I catch

Grace's eye and she shakes her head with a deep sigh, stacking dishes by the sink. Nothing we do provides comfort.

As I clean up, Thomas follows James outside, neither of them casting a backward glance. My stomach hardens more, imagining their exchange. But I concentrate on the work at hand.

Even with the tables cleared, the men linger, comparing their injuries, unsure what to do next. They were lucky. We all were. The explosion had pushed out toward the lake. Had it struck the camp and cookhouse, we'd be mourning more than one lost life. Amid today's devastation, the blast's direction is a small blessing.

Thomas returns, dropping a company-issued first aid kit on a table, and hustles out without speaking. Grace tends to the crew's injuries, patching up their minor burns and scrapes. One by one, the workers leave the cookhouse sporting bright white bandages, their furrowed brows flitting to the dazed Edith.

Meanwhile, I heat water, pack up the leftovers, clean the counters, and hoist the pot to the edge of the sink. The routine chores soothe the lump in my stomach a little. But the same thought tumbles endlessly through my brain — I should have been watching Daisy. As I start on the dishes, Grace clunks the first aid kit on the counter.

"Are you alright here on your own? I should go feed the baby," she says. Wringing out a dishcloth, I look at her furrowed brow. She leans over to squeeze my arm and I collapse into her shoulder, stifling a sob, my wet hands hanging at my sides. She hugs me, shushing me like a child. "There, there." I've craved physical contact since I heard the news of our missing George, and now I wish it was Thomas, not Grace, holding me.

"I'm... so... sorry." My words come out in gulps between suppressed sobs. Grace shakes her head.

"We're all sorry, Eva. It's terrible." Grace doesn't know Daisy might have started the fire, and as I look into my friend's delicate eyes, I don't have the heart to tell her.

"I'm sorry, Grace. I'm fine. I didn't mean to... You go." I pull back, rubbing away tears with George's borrowed apron. "Go be with your kids." Grace nods, gives my arm another squeeze, and squats in front of Edith, saying a few soft words I can't hear over the rushing in my head.

When the cookhouse door shuts behind Grace, a cold draft runs through the room, and the air stills, soap-scented steam rising from the sink. Despite my protests, Edith lurches to her feet and shuffles over, pulling dish towels from the rack above the woodstove, then settles herself by the drying stand. We work side-by-side, washing the lunch dishes in the too-quiet cookhouse, our faces pale and eyes red.

"I dunno what I'm gonna do now." When Edith finally speaks, the stack of dishes is half gone and her words catch in her throat. I stare back at her, biting my lip. "They's gonna need to get 'nother cook. An' ain't no one else gonna want me as their help." Edith keeps turning and wiping the spoon she's drying, fear darting across her lined face. "Where am I gonna go? I dunno what I'm gonna do," she says again, her lips trembling. I drop another stack of bowls into the wash water and turn toward her.

"Oh, Edith! You'll always have a place here." I pick up the dish-cloth, swishing out a bowl, knowing I'm overstepping my place. The Company might very well send Edith away. I rinse a handful of cutlery, promising I'll do everything possible to keep her here. Edith doesn't respond, just dries and puts away dishes.

We work in silence, and my mind wanders. All day, I've tried to recall that morning with Daisy at the lake, but the details won't return. I remember Daisy munching on nuts as she watched me light the fire, and how she carefully examined the matchbook. But after that, it's a blur. The terror of losing her, followed by the relief of finding her again, are my only clear memories. Daisy must have pocketed the matches while I was asleep.

"I should have been watching her." The words blurt out before I can stop them, but I can't keep another secret. Not from Edith, so I explain, moving mugs into the wash water. "It might have been Daisy who set the fire. In the mill today. She had my matches, Edith! I should have been watching her." The weight of the day hits me. George's disappearance, Thomas's distance, and James's advances. With me amid all of it. I drop the coffee cup I'm washing into the sink and grip the edge of the counter, then my legs buckle and I crumple to the floor again. With my back against a sack of flour, I pull my knees up to my chest and wrap my arms around them, sobbing uncontrollably.

Edith groans softly as she folds her old body to sit next to me. She puts an arm over my shoulders and leans her wrinkled brow into my neck, the scent of tobacco and liniment drifting across me.

"It was an accident, child. Just an accident. Don' talk like that. An' even if it was Daisy, ain't no one gonna blame that l'il girl. Or you." But as we snuffle in the quiet cookhouse, I silently disagree with Edith.

Once Edith and I finish the cookhouse chores, I walk her home. Inside, she shuffles to the bed, staring down at a wooden soup ladle on her side table as she presses a palm over her mouth.

"Ah. The ol' coot... he... he made this for me." Her voice cracks as she sags onto the bed, gripping the spoon in her lap. "For Christmas. We never done gifts before. I... I can't..." She shakes her head, strands of her wiry silver hair dancing around her crinkled face, and releases a strangled sob.

"Oh Edith, it's beautiful." I perch next to her, putting an arm across her shoulders. She fingers the cedar spoon's handle with her trembling, weathered thumb, tracing the twisted love knot George carved. We sit in silence, eyes filled with tears, too numb to move.

Edith leans forward, pulling a silver flask from under the mattress. She sloshes whisky into the white enamel mug on her bedside table and offers it to me. I start to shake my head, then shrug, taking the cup.

"To George." Edith clanks her flask against my mug and takes a long swig, clutching the ladle to her thick chest.

"To George," I say. His name catches in my throat and when I choke on a sip of the fiery liquid, I can almost hear George chuckle at my inexperience. I set down the unfinished mug, urging Edith to tuck in. She obeys, curling up on the bed fully clothed, squeezing her eyes shut, the gift from George still clenched in her fist. I pull the covers over her, my chest tightening. She looks like a child, crawling into herself. All this misery. Oh, how I wish I could change things.

After tending her fire, I leave Edith's place, feeling hollowed out. Craving a moment alone, I take a detour to the river, scrambling down the gravel bank to the shoreline. Acrid smoke still hangs in the air, and across the river the thicket of leafless, golden salmonberry stems glow in contrast to the bright grey trunks of alder. The December mist wraps each branch and leaf in a gauzy veil until it drips. To my left, where the silhouette of the sawmill should be, blackened piling stumps still smoulder above the water, glowing in the fading light.

Crouching on my haunches, I close my eyes, running my fingers through the frigid gravel, letting nature soothe me. Amid the stillness, the river gurgles and droplets fall. I rock gently, pushing away thoughts by honing in on a distant staccato birdcall, perhaps a *Troglodytes pacificus*. The wren sings a sweet series of tumbling, trilling notes, its complex phrases strung together and muffled in the fog.

Angry voices above me jerk me to the present. Atop the bank, Billy is shouting, his slurred, angry words undecipherable. Someone responds in a taunting tone, Billy shouts back, and then Thomas's sharp voice joins the altercation. I stand, creeping up the riverbank, until the back of the cookhouse comes into view through the charred bushes. Thomas stands behind Billy, gripping him by both arms as Billy squirms, lunging toward James.

"Lemme at 'im! He's jus' a slack-jawed bean counter. Good for nothin'." Billy spits in James's direction, his voice dripping with contempt.

"Leave it!" Thomas growls the words from between clenched teeth, hauling Billy away from James. They stumble, grunting as they fall to the ground near the woodpile. Billy lands on his stomach and Thomas puts a knee into the small of his back. Still gripping Billy's arms, Thomas leans over him, speaking into his ear, shaking him when Billy writhes beneath him. James stands back, a smirk on his lips, cigarette smoke curling around the brim of his striped trilby.

A moment later, Billy goes limp, the fight leaving him. Thomas pats him on the shoulder, still talking softly, but moves off him and stands, offering a hand. Billy lets Thomas help him up, then wipes the wood chips from his shirt, eyes downcast. James steps forward, flicking his cigarette butt at Billy, who jerks his head up, his fists clenching at his side, charging at James. But Thomas grabs Billy, spinning him toward the bunkhouses.

"Get on now, Billy. Go home!" Thomas stands tall, feet wide, shoving him.

Billy staggers, glaring over his shoulder. "Just a dirty rat in a suit," he mutters, but continues toward camp. Thomas watches Billy leave and turns back to James, scowling.

"I want you outta here. First thing." Thomas glares at James, his jaw tight.

"Your grunt labour oughta know their place," James says with a shrug, his tone snide.

"Maybe so. But we need them. All of them." Thomas steps close, his nostrils flaring. "I want you gone. Before you and your liquor stir things up any more." The men stand chest to chest, James an inch taller, but Thomas more solid by far. Working alongside his crew has broadened Thomas's chest and thickened his forearms. My pulse quickens as the two men stand chin to chin, still unaware I'm watching.

For a moment, it looks like they might brawl. I consider revealing myself, but something keeps me silent and rooted. Thomas, still covered in soot, holds his elbows wide, his chin high, the fingers below his torn work shirt flexing. James's stance is loose but guarded in his spotless suit and bright white shirt. They glare at one another as I hold my breath. But James steps back, his face twisting into a bemused smile.

"Oh, I see... This isn't about the men, is it? It's about our barefoot diva." James lets out a quick, disgusted snort, his eyes a harsh squint. "You know, she's not as devoted as you might think..." My throat closes. A flicker of uncertainty dances across Thomas's face before he draws in a slow, steady breath.

"I don't have time for this. You're gone. First thing." Thomas's words are controlled and careful as he jabs his index finger into James's tie. "Gone." He turns, stalking toward the office. Blood pounds in my chest and I feel a surge of protectiveness for Thomas. He's responsible for so much, and today's events add more complications to his load.

Watching Thomas leave, James pulls a soft leather tobacco pouch from his inside pocket, twenty feet from the bushes where I'm crouched. My calves ache as he rolls and lights a glowing cigarette, and I'm glad when he tips his trilby to the back of his head and follows Thomas's route back into camp.

A moment later, I stand, shaking the stiffness from my legs and brushing twigs from my skirt with trembling hands. James's words jumble in my mind, and I glance around as if the answers might be hiding in the trees. Then I press my lips together. The men will need dinner. Once that's done, I can think about what comes next. We're supposed to leave for Seattle in the morning, but Thomas won't go, not now. He won't leave his crew in turmoil. I know that much about him.

With a sigh, I shuffle to the cookhouse, my ribs tightening as I pull open the heavy door. In the water behind me, the sawmill carcass smoulders. It ignites a longing for simpler times back home, when optimism outweighed doubt and my world felt secure, not gruelling.

CHAPTER 44

While baby Roy naps, Grace and I bake George's sourdough and make another batch of sandwiches. We don't have the skill to cook a proper meal for the whole camp, but to our surprise, Li Wei from the sawmill crew joins us to help. He pulls beef from the cooler and scrounges some root vegetables, tasking us with peeling, chopping, and slicing.

When supper time rolls around, Li puts our largest cast-iron skillet on an extra-hot fire, frying the aromatic thinly sliced beef, cabbage, carrots, and onions with some grated ginger and garlic. Once the sizzling ingredients fill the cookhouse with their sweet, meaty aroma, Li seasons the pan with soy sauce from his own imported stash.

Billy comes through the kitchen, looking at his watch, and we give him the nod. He goes to the dinner bell, but when it's still silent after a few minutes, I wipe my hands on my apron and join him on the porch. With furrowed brows, Billy stares at the heavy iron triangle, the clangour clenched in his fist.

"It's time, Billy," I say softly, putting a hand on his solid shoulder.

"It don' feel right... to bang this thing... not without George." Billy swallows.

"I know. But he'd be pissed if we didn't keep going." I place my hand over Billy's thick, trembling fingers, lifting the clangour, and together we call the crew to supper. The toll echoes through camp, and standing next to Billy brings memories of my brother. I miss the strength Tony gave me. My eyes prickle with tears, aching for a noisy dinner at Millie's, Father's adoring smile, and even my mother's admonitions. As the men's footsteps stomp up the stairs to dinner, I push my homesickness aside, feeling George urge me to 'mug up'.

Li creates an exotic meal, but given the day's events, praise is sparse. Thomas and James both eat their food silently at opposite ends of the table. Everyone sops up the mouth-watering stir fry sauce with chunks of George's last sourdough loaves. When he's finished, Thomas slides out of his seat. In the kitchen, he confers briefly with Li while the crew eats in silence. Then Thomas leaves and his men follow. Today should have been a holiday, but they're unwilling to remain idle while the boss isn't. James goes out last, without a word or a glance in my direction.

With the dinner served, the cookhouse grows quiet once more. Li stays behind, telling us Thomas has agreed to let him do George's work for now. "No mill. No job, no mo'. But I cook. I do clean." Li says, beaming. So Grace and I leave him to fill George's shoes.

Back at the bunkhouse, I pull my Lucky Strike tin from between Mother's fancy linens, and hide the gold deep in my trunk. In the city, I might have to explain the source of my secret fortune to cash in. It'll be fine if I'm careful, though — I won't risk starting a gold rush up here. I may not need it, but taking the gold with me soothes the breath that catches in my chest whenever I think about my future.

When Thomas finally returns to our bunkhouse, it's been dark for hours, and by then I'm determined to make the trip home, as planned, in the morning. When I ask how he's doing, he doesn't answer, pulling off his boots and hanging his jacket in silence. He's been with Roy, planning the next steps. I imagine they need to notify the authorities, and file incident reports for the Company. Since the mill is gone, the entire work plan must be rearranged to keep the camp going.

"Li Wei's pretty good in the kitchen, isn't he?" In the stillness of our cabin, I try another tack, willing Thomas to say something, anything. Since he handed me Daisy before the disaster, he hasn't spoken to me except to bark the command to feed the men their meal.

Now, my comment about Li's cooking elicits a curt nod from him, but he continues to undress in silence, his posture stooped and shoulders hunched. He looks exhausted, his thoughts elsewhere. As he drapes his pants over a chair, Thomas's gaze falls on my trunk, now snapped closed and wrapped with a luggage belt, and he stiffens.

"You're still going down to see your parents?" His question is thick with resignation. I nod. "You know I can't leave, right? Not now, with all this going on."

I nod again. "I know. But I need... I need to see my parents... my father," I say.

In the lantern light, Thomas shakes his head — in disbelief or disgust — I can't tell. Then he sits on the edge of the bed, his forearms taut, fists on his knees, and glares at my luggage.

"You're going for good." This time, his words are a statement, not a question. Thomas can't possibly know that I packed my sandals and swimsuit, but somehow he senses I don't plan to be back for spring. His duty to the company requires him to stay, but I can't wait any longer. I feel a compulsion to flee, to run away, to hide where my guilt and confusion don't hit me so often.

"For a while... a month, maybe two... I don't know. I need to go, Thomas. Need to get out of here." He says nothing, but sucks in a breath. "Everything here reminds me of bad things. Ruby..." My daughter's name slides off my tongue in a whisper. "And now this...

with George." I choke on our lost friend's name as I sit on the edge of the bed, hands wrapped around my middle, gripping my nightshirt and undergarments. "I need to see my family. You never know when time's going to run out..." Tears well behind my eyelids as my words trail off. Thomas exhales.

So much hovers unsaid between us. The bed covers form an impassible gulf as we sit back to back on this dark December night. Just six months ago, we were eager university graduates, strolling to our convocation ceremony with a gaggle of laughing colleagues, excited by our prospects. In what feels like a heartbeat, a torrent of change has swept over us. Changes we can never undo.

"You know, there's nothing between James and me." I surprise myself by saying the words. Since witnessing their argument at the woodpile, I've ached to reassure Thomas. "I need you to know that." James has distracted me, but I haven't been unfaithful. And I have no desire to be.

Thomas folds himself under his side of the covers and faces me as I crawl into bed. "He'd like there to be. Any fool can see that." Thomas's eyes are bright, then he rolls onto his back, his jaw clenched. "Like I said, be careful around that one. He's... not a worthy fellow."

Thomas doesn't need to tell me that — I'm quite aware. Does he suspect the truth, especially now with James's hint? The question hangs between us. I try to forget that painful night, but my thoughts circle back to the mess I've made of my life.

Today, a moment of distraction may have caused a dear friend's death. I wonder if Grace knows it could have been Daisy who started that fire. She won't forgive me, and she shouldn't. I might have let her daughter do something disastrous. And if it was Daisy, I hope she never realizes her part in George being gone. That child deserves to keep her innocence. My chest feels heavy and I can barely breathe. My preoccupation could have a lifelong impact on that little girl. I should have been watching her.

"I'm sorry." Rolling to my back, I whisper the weak apology at the ceiling, sliding a hand across the mattress toward Thomas, but stopping before I touch him. "I'm so sorry." Tears slide down my cheeks and I close my eyes. I need to leave. It's only when the mice start their nightly adventures, and tiny claws scurry across the floorboards, that I realize Thomas hasn't asked me to stay.

CHAPTER 45

Rain hammers the camp the next morning as Thomas and Billy haul my heavy trunks to the rail siding where the speeder is parked. I feign surprise when James arrives and loads his own luggage. The men nod at one another with a forced civility, the tension from yesterday's brawl still hanging thick. But I ignore their glares.

When my belongings are stacked inside, Billy holds a lantern to guide our way up the step. I hesitate, turning toward Thomas beside the open door. His face is tight, his eyes dull.

"I'm sorry." The words are barely audible over the din of the raindrops. My guilt feels bottomless. Guilt about Ruby. Daisy. And George. And now disappointing Thomas, my best friend, for so many years. My eyes close, a weight forming in my chest. I'm giving up, losing the wager I placed on myself, admitting defeat by leaving. When I open my eyes, I manage a weak, pensive smile. "We'll write." Thomas nods, clearing his throat and flipping the collar of his oilskin. We'll need to write and figure out what we're doing with our lives from now on. I haven't thought beyond today's escape, but there are decisions to make. In time.

Gazing across the lake, I remember the first time I saw this view, with Thomas silhouetted in the golden evening light. We had started with so much hope and optimism. The rain thrums on the dark water and I shudder, wondering where George is and if he'll ever be found. I climb into the speeder with a sigh, taking a seat away from James.

Billy coaxes the reluctant gas engine to life, and its sputtering signals the beginning of my journey home. As the speeder clatters along the tracks, my thoughts turn to my friends. I didn't say goodbye. Grace and Edith both know Thomas and I are supposed to leave today, but they'll expect me to stay until Thomas can go, too. I lean my temple against the speeder's cold metal wall, wishing once again that I could back up the clock about eight months. Boy, would I play things out differently. I wouldn't let the night with James happen, so I needn't marry Thomas, nor would I follow him to this gorgeous but godforsaken place. So many things I'd change.

The rhythmic clattering of the tracks covers my sigh, and I try to picture my future. But that makes a knot tighten in my stomach. Leaving is the right choice, even if I'm unclear about what I'll do in Seattle. Celebrate the new year with Millie... and then... what? The thought of searching for work hardens my tangled gut. That interview with Mr. Howard and subsequent rejection, coupled with my observations of the men and the Company, have made me realize that getting gainful employment with my Master's degree will be a challenge. I was naïve to think schooling and good grades would get me a job.

When the speeder slows and winds down the incline to Camp 1, I cast my thoughts back to my first view of this shore. That sunny summer day, men lined up, passing around a dented coffee can, betting against my endurance. And now, I'm leaving mere days before winning the wager. I won't make it to 1925 up here after all.

Dawn breaks into the bleak day, but the gloomy rain clouds shackle us to darkness. James offers me his arm to dismount, but I refuse, using the railcar's metal handrail. I do, however, let the men lug my trunks over the potholed, muddy road to the dock. Instead of the tug, today a small boat will ferry us across to Alert Bay. The captain nods at James and murmurs his condolences about George.

I wonder how these men already know. Thomas must have sent someone to report the sawmill fire. The Company needs to know, I suppose. Needs to notify the next of kin pencilled on George's cream-coloured employment card. There are rules, procedures, for such things.

Muttering a thank you to their kind words, I shiver. The city's anonymity beckons. Here, it feels like everyone silently blames me for what happened. Which is ridiculous. Even if Daisy's fire-starting story got out, no one would know I should have been watching her.

Allowing wives and children in our camp had been a controversial policy change supported by Thomas and his father, that has been attracting stable family men, rounding out the typical camp roughness. If it becomes known a child might have caused this fire, the Company could rescind those progressive policies. I'm suddenly sure that Thomas will omit Daisy's part in the sawmill fire. It's easy enough to claim the blaze's source is unknown.

My thoughts are still roiling when I settle into the boat's tiny wheelhouse. It's standing room only in the crowded cabin, tobacco and sweat permeating the dank space. The rain drums on the roof and splatters against the windshield as we chug across Broughton Strait. Tendrils of water streak the glass as the wind surges, whipping up waves and forcing the small boat to a slow pace, white water splashing over the bow with each wave. I wedge myself into the corner to keep my balance, preventing any accidental contact with James or the Captain. The crossing feels endless, the roller's rhythm lulling me into an active, jostled trance. I focus on the splattering raindrops and force my mind to find shapes in the swirls, soothing my tumbling thoughts.

When we arrive at the dock in Alert Bay, the men wrestle my trunks onto a trolley and rattle over to the *SS Cardena*. The bustle around the ship sparks an ember of excitement in me. I've always loved to travel, but the thrill diminishes when I remember George's cheeky grin, next to me on this very dock, only a few months ago. I swallow hard — once again, I'm running away.

The wind swirls and I raise the collar of my oilskin jacket, then clutch a hand atop my sou'wester and follow my luggage up the gangplank. I show my ticket and realize with a start that James must be travelling on Thomas's fare. We booked a two-man cabin for this trip, but I won't bunk with James. Hopefully, he's not dim-witted enough to think I'll let him in.

Down on the dock, James is still talking with a worker. When the ship's steward directs me to the room, I decide the first step in avoiding James is claiming the berth. Unlike my trip up-island, when I stayed on the lower starboard level, this cabin is on the upper deck, right at the bow. The view is brilliant. I hang my bag on a hook, shaking the rain off my hat and jacket out into the hallway before hanging those too.

With a heavy sigh, I collapse onto the narrow bunk, tears welling. After a few moments of self-pity, I straighten. I can hide here the whole trip if I grab sandwiches and snacks from the kitchen now. The thought of being alone for hours, with a comfortable bed, my knitting, and another of Edith's *Anne* books, sounds delightful.

In the tiny mirror, my reflection is hardly recognizable. Stark purple circles under my red-rimmed eyes stand out against my pale skin. My dark curls are a frizzy mess from the rain and my hat. Oh well. I lock the door and leave without fixing my appearance. This ship's no place for a beauty contest.

I walk down the narrow front stairs to the lower deck. As I round the bow, my footsteps falter, remembering. On this spot I had felt Ruby's first movement, had finally understood what the books meant by the quickening. At that moment, there was no denying I carried a new life. I lean against the ship, closing my eyes, fingernails curling into the wall behind me. These damn memories live everywhere. Even getting a sandwich reminds me of poor past decisions.

Inhaling deeply, I head to the kitchen. Then, with the needed supplies clutched to my chest, I return to my cabin, retreating from the world. I deserve some solitude.

Chapter 46

Two days after clambering into the speeder by the lake in a downpour, I awake in my childhood bed. There's a rumble from the furnace in the basement as it pumps heat into my carpeted room. I'm tucked under a fluffy snow-white eiderdown scented faintly of lavender, staring up at the geometric bronze and glass electric light hanging from the painted plaster. The insulated attic space of this vast house muffles the torrent outside. I instantly picture Thomas, lying alone in our tiny bunkhouse on grimy sheets, blinking at the rough-sawn rafters. The rain would be pelting on the shingle roof, the damp air cold inside.

Rolling toward the wall, I groan. I don't want to be thinking about Thomas. Don't want this heaviness in my chest. Coming home was supposed to remove this weight from me, but I suppose it'll take some time. Twelve hours here can't possibly solve problems that took months to create. Downstairs, the breakfast china clinks, and again I exhale heavily, my teeth grinding. Mother's marathon of interrogation begins today.

The trip south had been exhausting. With every pulse of the train's wheels, doubt crept in. Farther and farther south, the rail carried me, and with each gentle sway of the carriage, my uncertainty grew. I napped, knit, and read, but nothing relieved the quiver in my stomach whenever I thought of Thomas, and by the time I arrived I was a mess of misgivings.

Father had picked me up at the railway station late last night. He moved unsteadily, his hair and beard greyer than I remembered, and his lips tinted a concerning shade of blue. His frailty rolled a wave of protective worry over me, my mind skipping ahead to possible conclusions. When James, rather than Thomas, escorted me out of the station, his eyebrows had furrowed. By the end of the exhausting trip south, my resolve to ignore James had weakened enough that I let him collect our luggage. The concern on my father's gaunt face, as he crushed me against his rough wool coat, had hardened another lump under my breastbone. No matter where I go, guilt follows.

James had shaken Father's hand, introducing himself as a colleague, explaining the mill fire, and Thomas's need to stay up north.

"It's been a pleasure to escort your daughter, sir," James had said, his words sincere. My father had nodded and held my gaze until I turned away. He had questions, but I wasn't ready to unload my heartache on him. Not yet.

Outside the station, James disappeared among the dirty snowbanks lining the parking lot. A severe cold snap had hit Seattle, creating a picturesque white Christmas. The two week deep freeze had also caused its share of chaos, which Father shared with me once the porter hoisted my trunks into the Buick. As we slid our way onto the main road, I silently thanked my lovely father for not asking questions on our drive home. He knows me well, detecting the chinks in my emotional armour, and sensing I was on the brink of tears. Instead, he filled the stillness with news of his car lot sales, how long he had to wait for a plumber to fix the frozen water pipes, the cost of heating fuel during this cold spell, and how, for once, Mother is thankful for the rain, since it means the temperatures are finally above freezing again.

Now, the scent of bacon drifts into my room, and although dread fills my roiling gut, it's time to get dressed and face my mother. I step onto the soft carpet and open the mirrored wardrobe, staring at the neat stacks of undergarments, rows of sweaters, and line of hanging hats, all just as I had left them. As I dress, it dawns on me that I never once missed this luxury. From the closet opposite, I choose a navy blue silk sheath with a modest neckline. When I step into it and tug the straight, fitted sleeves over my arms and shoulders, the dress is snug. The wood-chopping muscles Thomas teased me about, strain the feminine silhouette of the garment. But it buttons easily, my waistline trimmer than when I left. The north island has been good for my figure.

At the wardrobe, I peek at my reflection. While my eyes are no longer red-rimmed, they still look hollow and haunted. My hair is an untamed mess, so I wrangle it into a half-up style with a tortoiseshell comb. No matter my appearance, Mother will find something to criticize. I pull back my shoulders and lift my chin a little, then open my bedroom door, steeling myself for the inquest.

Downstairs, the woodsy, jam-like scent of the Christmas tree draws me into the front room. Red candles in fluted silver clips weigh the ends of each *Abies amabalis* branch, interspersed with Mother's fragile gold and green Kugels, keepsakes from the old country.

Fingering a satin ribbon I recall a Christmas years ago. Tony and I had shattered one of the teardrop-shaped ornaments while roughhousing. In the stunned silence that followed, Mother had stiffly left the room. Father had gathered us close, kneeling down to our eye level to convey his disappointment in a measured tone.

Even today, those three Kugels, no longer a perfect set of four, twist a thread of shame through me. We had carelessly destroyed something Mother held dear. I sigh, stepping back to envision more pleasant memories of carols and gifts. Tonight I'll ask Father to light the candles. There's nothing more beautiful than the flickering candlelight reflected in the aged patina of these old glass decorations.

A spoon clinks against china in the dining room. I straighten and move toward the sound. My father sits at the head of the table, a plate of scrambled eggs and bacon in front of him. He beams, waving me in as I pause in the archway of the luxurious room. I pass behind him, where I stop impulsively. Placing both hands on his shoulders, I lean in to kiss his pale cheek. He swallows and his eyes close for a moment, the lines on his face appearing deeper today under the bright electric chandelier. A clatter draws my gaze to the kitchen, where Mother stands in the doorway. Instinctively, I stand straight, giving my father's shoulder a squeeze. I notice simultaneously the bony frame under Father's starched shirt, and how exhausted Mother looks.

"You've lost weight." Her tone is accusatory, and as I approach, she shifts the plated breakfast to both hands, holding it out and keeping me at a distance. "Don't Canadians eat?"

"Good morning, Mother," I say, smiling, my tone light. There's comfort in her consistency. Ignoring her question, I take the plate, and for an instant I'm tempted to lean in and kiss her cheek, too. But I've never done that. Displays of affection between us do not exist. I wonder suddenly if she ever hugged us as children, the way Grace cuddles Daisy. If my mother did, I have no memory of it. She's always been distant and firm, her smiles and laughter reserved for her country club friends.

"You look exhausted. Are you sleeping?" Mother's lips purse. Since the fire, George has haunted my nights. In my dreams, I hear him telling me to mug up and see his big ears surrounded by flames. Now, when I don't respond, my mother turns away, yanking off the apron that protects her emerald silk sheath. The dress pulls against her too-thin frame. She's lost weight as well.

I take my seat on my father's right, and when my mother comes back with her own plate of food, she sits across from me. In Tony's spot. My eyebrows raise and my fork pauses mid-air.

"Your father needed help cutting his meat." Mother answers my unspoken question, her tone defensive. "When he was... ill. So I sat here. And I... I just never moved back." She juts her chin toward the far end of the table.

"I like you right here." Father lays his hand over hers, diffusing some of the tension. "Nice and close." He grins and Mother softens, her lips twitching into a smile, as she unfolds her napkin onto her lap. This open affection between them feels different, new. Something has shifted.

I stare at Father's purplish fingertips, anxious to hear how his health has been since their last letter to me, but the relaxed glances they share make me unwilling to darken the mood. We eat in silence for a moment, then I ask Mother about her bridge club. As expected, her response fills the next ten minutes as we finish our meals. While I'm curious about the lives of her friends, women who have watched me grow up, none of the news carries the gravitas Mother attaches to it. My thoughts wander as I nod along to a tale about a hideous wall colour.

When Mother's monologue pauses, Father clears his throat and struggles out of his chair, leaning heavily on the armrests. She puts down her cutlery, moving to help, but he stops her with a small wave. Father heaves himself up, his legs shaking a little, his balance off. But he smiles at me, then kisses us each on the cheek, saying he'd best be off to work. We wish him a good day and are left in the quiet of his absence.

Mother and I have always avoided being alone with each other, but here we are. With the polished silver knife, I spread store-bought blackberry jam onto a slice of toast. When I take a bite and look up, tears are streaming down Mother's face. She snuffles, dabbing at her cheeks with the napkin. My hand hovers over the tablecloth. I've never seen my mother cry. She's never shown emotion in my presence, and I don't know what to do. Should I comfort her? No. Mother would not want to be hugged or consoled. So I sit, unmoving, until she takes a shaky breath.

"He was just so sick, Eva. You have no idea." Her voice cracks as she sniffs loudly.

I nod my head, leaning in, my voice soft. "It must have been hard to watch." Caring for Edith and Grace is a fresh memory. It's painful seeing someone you care for suffer. "Tell me what happened. And what the doctors say now." And so, as we move into the kitchen to wash the dishes, my mother recounts every doctor's visit, medical prescription, and blood pressure reading my father has had since the day he collapsed.

When she's done sharing, it's clear Father has a heart condition, but his prognosis is vague. The doctors say he could go on in his current state for years. Or he could have another attack tomorrow. Mother's eyes are bright and her lips tremble with fear.

"I don't know... I... can't..." She fingers her gold necklace, biting her lip, her anxious words trailing off. I see she's imagined losing him, pictured her life without my father in it. And she's afraid. I wish I could find words of comfort or share a nugget of wisdom to ease her mind, but the months I spent away from here have cemented how easily, and unexpectedly, death interrupts life. This family has already weathered enough. Without Tony, our clan of four is forever fractured, just like the mismatched set of Christmas Kugels.

"He'll be fine. You'll see," I say finally, willing it to be true. She nods, and we drift into silence again. As I dry the gilded trim of the last china plate and carefully stack it in the cupboard, my mother turns to me.

"I don't know why you're here without Thomas. Or what's gone on up in that... place. But you need to open your eyes. That man loves you. Everything about you." There's a tightness in her eyes and a hard edge to her words. "Don't waste time... good years... chasing the wrong dream." She pulls her apron over her head without disturbing a strand of her manicured hairstyle, turns on her heel, and strides out of the room. Her heavy footsteps echo up the stairs and above me the floorboards creak as she enters their bedroom, leaving me alone to ponder her words.

CHAPTER 47

An hour later, I'm driving a bright red Buick coupe to Millie's. The engine's growl and the world whizzing by bring a smile to my face, clearing heavy thoughts as I focus on steering and shifting. The roads are still wet, but the skies have cleared. Sitting low on the horizon, the sun glints off the pavement and icy lawns.

On Millie's road, plowed dirty snowbanks hide the sidewalks that were freshly placed the last time I was here. Across the street, her neighbour's house is fully built, with a wreath on the door and wicker furniture on the porch. The rhythm of the builders' hammers is a distant memory.

I get out of the car, stepping carefully through a shovelled gap, and gaze up at Millie's place. A row of snowmen lines the salted concrete path, their carrot noses and gravel eyeballs scattered on the ground, their scarves and hats still clinging to their melting bodies. Sunlight flashes off the windows and a toboggan leans on the stairs. A picturesque family home. Millie is so happy here. My life would be simpler if I wanted this. A suburban house, a working husband, and children scurrying underfoot. My stomach clenches and I bury the thoughts. It's too risky to want this — it can hurt so, so much.

Then the front door bursts open, and Millie bounds onto the covered porch, the baby in one arm, exclaiming greetings and reaching a hand toward me. Eddie and Lizzie follow behind her, still in their pyjamas, both inches taller. I bound up the stairs, throwing my arms around Millie, and hugging her tight. Flora grabs my curls in her chubby fist and Millie holds us both, one on each shoulder. Her cheek is warm against mine and her perfume envelops me in a bouquet of amber and vanilla. Millie asks questions in rapid succession, her chatter leaving no break for me to answer anything. Finally, we push back from each other, extricating my hair from baby Flora's fingers, laughing.

"It's so good to see you!" Millie pulls me inside, herding the two toddlers ahead of us.

"It's good to be here." To my surprise, before I even hang my jacket, I burst into tears. The foyer blurs into a swirl of brown and white. I've craved having a girlfriend to talk to, one who knows me to my core. Grace and Edith are lovely, but they'll never understand the way I grew up in this bustling city. Most of me is foreign to their rugged, small-town lives.

But Millie... Millie knows me. I've missed being with a friend who implicitly understands how frustrating my mother is, how many things changed when Tony died, and how hard I worked to earn my degree. Sniffing, I try to settle myself.

"I'm sorry. It's just..." I trail off, considering how to describe my thoughts. I'm disappointed I let myself get pregnant, angry I had to give up a career to marry Thomas, heartbroken my daughter died, and guilt-ridden about George's death. And now, on top of all that, there's the worry about my father's illness. "It's just... too much."

"Oh, honey! Come. Sit. Tell me." Millie cups my shoulder and leads me into the kitchen. "So. What's happened?" I sit, dropping my hands on the sticky table, twisting my wedding band. Millie slides Flora into a wooden highchair beside me, then bustles around, fixing coffee, waiting for me to start. Millie knows about Ruby, although the letter I wrote shared only a veiled version of my grief and the wedge it thrust between Thomas and I. But Millie doesn't know about George.

"We lost a dear old friend last week." I rub my fingers into my temple, George's red cheeks, deep crinkles, and his wide smile flashing before me. "He was the camp cook. A gentle old-timer. With big hands. Big ears. Made the best sourdough bread ever." Millie spoons ground coffee into the percolator and sets it over the gas burner. "The sawmill burnt down. And he was in it. That's why Thomas didn't come down."

"Thomas isn't with you?" Millie's eyebrows raise in surprise. "When is he coming?" I shake my head, tears welling again.

"I don't know if he is... coming. We're..." I take the tissue Millie hands me, blowing my nose. "We're not doing so well." Once the percolator boils, we drink cup after cup of coffee, as I unload my heartaches on Millie.

Two hours later, we're eating lunch, Eddie and Lizzie on either side of me. The toddlers add smears of jam to the already-tacky table, talking over each other as they describe every new Christmas toy they got. Millie sits across from us, spooning mashed peaches into Flora, whose little hands reach eagerly toward her mother each time she finishes a bite.

I feel lighter, having shared my problems with Millie, but still rudderless. All my life, I've been on someone else's schedule. Routines set by family, school, and camp. Now that I'm back in Seattle, there's nothing to fill my days. To move away from my mother's house, I need to get a job.

"I can't believe you and Thomas are having troubles." After everything I've told her about Ruby and George, Millie's focused on my marriage. "You two are so well suited. We've said that for years. And we were so thrilled when you ended up together." She drains her third coffee and places the cup gently on the table so she doesn't wake Flora, who's fallen asleep in her arms. "Thomas adores you. Always has." She shakes her head in disbelief.

Millie knows everything except the truth about Ruby's father. Everyone assumed it was Thomas, and I'll never correct them. I imagine the turmoil honesty would cause for our families and the Company, a shudder shaking me. No, that night with James will remain my secret, but its weight is hard to carry on my own.

A clatter from the front room, followed by Eddie's cries, raises Millie from her chair. She passes a floppy Flora to me, rushing out of the kitchen.

From the other room, Millie's soothing words fade as I gaze at Flora. She's warm and soft and heavy in my lap. I take her hand into mine, letting her plump fist wrap around my forefinger, lifting it gently. Tiny fingernails, indented knuckles, a hint of peaches. So unbelievably perfect. Flora squirms, her eyelids fluttering open, her lips suckling, and she snuggles into me with a wee sigh, resuming her nap.

My throat closes, and I shut my eyes, trying to keep tears from falling again. My tiny Ruby never opened her eyes, never pursed her lips to sigh. Remembering my daughter brings on a tumble of Thomas thoughts, too. The devastation written on his face when I held the motionless Ruby. His dimpled smile when he proposed, kissing me under the tree in the graveyard. The wonder in his eyes when he felt the baby kick. His deep respect for my work on the bridge design. And just days ago, his hunger for me as he peeled off my red Christmas dress.

Now Flora stirs, and I pull her close. The weight pressing on my chest is unbearable. I won't go through this again. The world is too unpredictable. Any more loss and I'll break in two. I've tried to be strong, but I have nothing left.

My heart cracks as I breathe in Flora's baby-fresh scent. I know what I need to do. After the holidays, I'll find work. And an apartment. Once we've celebrated New Year's, the next chapter of my life starts. And it doesn't include a man or children.

My chin lifts a little and I wipe my eyes as a beaming Millie walks back in, holding a tear-stained Eddie. This life is perfect for her, but it isn't my path. For much of the trip south, I'd second-guessed leaving Camp 2, but in this moment, my decision feels right. For now, I have a plan of my own.

Chapter 48

New Year's Eve is dark and stormy. Rainfall has reduced the snowbanks to grimy bumps of solid ice, giving Seattle a gloomy, ominous feel. I brake outside Millie and Leo's house late, around ten o'clock. The front window glows, guests' shadows milling about, laughter and music reaching me over the clatter of rain on the coupe's hardtop.

I almost didn't come. But ringing in the New Year with my parents and their country club friends felt bleak, so I finally pulled myself together and came.

Unable to get parking nearby, I drive farther up the hill to an open spot. It's umbrella weather, but when I couldn't find one at Mother's, I donned my oilskin slicker and sou-wester instead. Not party attire, but a practical defence against the deluge, which made me feel strangely at home. I slam the car door, then hop over the rushing gutter and hurry toward the house.

The street lamps illuminate the streaking raindrops, swirling in wind gusts. As I turn onto Millie's path, another guest arrives from down the hill, shielding himself from the downpour with a newspaper. I nod a greeting but don't stop before hurrying up the stairs ahead of him. On the porch, I take off my hat and slicker, carefully shaking them off, away from my silk sheath dress. When I step to the front door, I freeze, my eyes widening. The other guest standing beside me is James, folding a soggy newspaper.

"What are you doing here?" Emotion warbles my voice and I feel dizzy, stunned to run into the one man I strive to avoid. Had I known he was coming, I would have stayed home with Mother's unbearable friends.

"Good to see you, too, Eva." James chuckles, shaking his head. Light glows through the door's glass, illuminating his steely blue eyes and damp, shaggy blond hair. We both wear the outfits we wore last week, to Camp 2's Christmas dinner. That evening in the rugged cookhouse feels a lifetime ago and a world away. A time and place when George was alive.

Behind us, two vehicles rumble past, blaring their horns in the downpour. The din of the city is unrelenting. I turn toward James, my back against the door, searching his bloodshot eyes on Millie's porch as the rain thumps on the roof overhead.

"Look, James. Really. Why are you here?" A damp wind gusts between the deck columns, and I shudder. "Do you know Millie? And Leo?" James nods.

"I'm an old mate of Leo's. We went to high school together, and when he heard I was back in town, he invited me." Just my luck.

"Did you know I was going to be here?" I ask, finding it strange our paths haven't crossed before. James nods once, eyes softening as his hand clenches briefly. Then he tugs up his pant leg, pulling a curved container of Canadian Club from inside his black kip leather boot. He takes a swig, fingering the etchings on the short-necked bottle and swallowing hard.

"It's why I'm here, Eva. You must know that by now." He suddenly looks less confident, clearing his throat, staring at his toes, kicking at the coir doormat. He steps toward me, hand out to touch my arm, but I move away, holding up a palm, my back pressed against Millie's front door. James pauses, then leans down until our noses are inches apart. He smells of aftershave and Listerine and bootlegged whisky. My heart beats in my ears, every muscle tensed, ready to push him off.

"I know what I want." James breathes the words into my face and heat rises in my cheeks despite the cold. "You need to decide what you want, my barefoot diva." He steps back now, turning to the road before continuing. "We could have some good times together. Here in the city. If that's what you want." I imagine myself in a grand house, two shiny cars parked next to an immaculate green lawn, children playing inside a white picket fence. Again, my skin prickles as James continues. "Thomas would build you a house, with that big company paycheck of his, if you asked. He'd do anything for you. And you'd have plenty of time to come fishing and skiing..." My stomach churns as it dawns on me that James isn't asking me to tend a home for him. He's asking me to be his bit of fun on the side.

I stiffen, lifting my chin, rage consuming me. Then, a giggling, intertwined couple stumbles out the front door, pushing me into James. I suck in a breath and straighten quickly, forcing some space between us. Across the porch, the young man leans the woman against a pillar, his hands moving over her hungrily as she smiles and kisses his neck. I wrench my eyes from what should be a private scene and find James gazing down at me, stroking his throat, his lips parting.

James tucks a loose curl behind my ear. His fingertip barely brushes my cheekbone, and it sends sparks through me. But it's revulsion I feel, and anger, not attraction.

"Never," I say, twisting from him, my teeth grinding. Words explode through my mind, but before I can verbalize my jumbled thoughts, James speaks.

"I'm done here," he says, spinning away. He staggers down the stairs and into the rainstorm, leaving behind the soggy newspaper. I watch him go, one trembling hand on a pillar, until he's out of sight. Tension leaves me and I slump to my elbows on the rail, aching to be held, to feel arms around me. Thomas's arms, I realize.

With a sigh, I turn, setting my shoulders, and walk into the party's warmth, pushing away thoughts of my husband. Tonight, I ring in a new year with my best friend Millie, and tomorrow I start the new life I'm so driven to craft.

Chapter 49

Three weeks later I'm driving toward my parents' house from yet another job interview, hunched over the steering wheel, every bone in my body heavy with disappointment. The first meeting I had was worse than the one with Mr. Howard, who at least acknowledged my skills. The next four appointments have progressively deteriorated. Today, after I shared my background and education, the interviewer peered over his wire spectacles at me with beady eyes and voiced what all of them seem to think.

"But Mrs. Clark, you're a woman. Married to a manager at a rival company. No one's going to take a chance on you." I hadn't been able to answer, a coldness coursing through my veins. He continued as I stood, a flush rising in my cheeks. "I'm not trying to be unkind. Just realistic. You're wasting your time." He walked around his paper-stacked, glossy desk offering a manicured hand, but I had backed away. "My advice to you is go back to your husband and be a good wife." My pulse pounded in my ears as I clenched and unclenched my fists, then turned without a word, refusing his handshake.

I'm still twitchy and on edge a half-hour later, as I guide the Buick along the familiar streets of my childhood, dread gripping me. To support myself, I'll need to switch fields. That's becoming clear. Even the government interview last week had gone poorly, once the hiring manager realized I was one of *those* Clarks.

"You come highly recommended by your professors, Mrs. Clark. But we can't be seen playing industry favourites. You understand, of course," he'd said, shaking his head and ushering me out.

A few weeks ago, I had felt control over my situation. Now, that confidence is rapidly dissolving. Living with my mother has become unbearable and without an income, I'll need to dip into my gold stash to fund moving out. I ponder how to cash it in. The challenge sucks the energy from me. I'm a caged animal, searching for an escape, but encountering solid steel on all sides. For the millionth time, I wonder why I ever expected anyone would hire me. The world isn't ready for a lady forester, much less one that's a Clark.

These thoughts bring Thomas to mind. At least he values my input. A slight smile builds on my face, and my eyes prickle with tears. I miss him. It's been years since I've gone this long without seeing Thomas. Throughout university, he was a steady colleague and friend. These days, everywhere I look, I see things I want to share with him. A funny quote in the newspaper, a beautifully stubborn *Crocus chrysanthus* poking through the snow, a new method of replanting in *The Modern Forester* magazine. And last week, when Ruby's due date came and went, it was Thomas's arms I yearned to be in. But the thought of returning to the north island triggers a tug in my throat. Amid nature's grandeur, Camp 2 echoes with calamity. Ruby. George.

I park behind a sparkling Ford Model T pickup, dragging my feet up the walk, dreading the inevitable once-over from Mother and the sympathetic looks from Father. Both are certain to follow the news of yet another unsuccessful interview. I hesitate before opening the front door, then take a deep breath and step inside.

The house is quiet and there's a vaguely familiar coat on the rack. I hang mine beside it, hushed voices drifting from the dining room. Mother appears at the end of the hallway, her face drawn, her slim hand stroking her necklace as she walks toward me. I freeze, gripping the carved banister. Something has happened. Something bad. Oh Lord, don't let it be Father. I can't bear it.

To my horror, my mother, who has never once touched me in affection, brushes my cheek gently, her gleaming eyes never leaving mine, as she bites her lower lip. My thoughts freeze and my vision clouds.

The voices from the other room silence and a chair scuffs, then footsteps shuffle toward us. I rip my gaze from Mother's, finding James in the archway, rubbing his jaw and staring at the floor. Behind him stands my father. A gasp of relief leaves me. Thank goodness. He looks no worse than this morning.

So, why is James here? His expression is flat, and though he's looking my way, he won't meet my eyes. I see pity in his frown. And something else. Hope? I haven't moved a muscle since Mother touched me, and now she reaches a shaky hand toward my father. He wraps a protective arm around her as they share a sad glance.

James stops a few feet from me, clearing his throat, his stare downcast.

"I had to come tell you myself." An icy shiver runs down my spine. It must be someone in camp. Oh please, not Daisy. Not Grace. Not another one of the crew. Haven't we all had enough loss? "There's been an accident. It's Thomas." Now my ears ring and my heart thumps so hard the beats must be visible through my blouse. I collapse onto the stairs, my legs giving out and my fingers trailing along the banister. Thomas. No. Not my invincible rock. My world tilts as the rushing in my head slowly subsides.

"...retrieving George's body." James is explaining something I don't hear, crouching next to me.

"Wait. What? How is he?" My voice cracks as a deep chill hits the base of my spine.

"We don't know for sure." James glances over at my parents and looks up at me, swallowing before he continues. "He fell into the lake, Eva. At the booming grounds. He and the boys were retrieving George's body. And it was windy." I picture that water on a gusty day, logs pounding together in the rolling whitecaps, and shudder. There are afternoons when thirty-knot gusts rip the tops from rollers, covering the lake in a fine mist. Getting caught in the bight on such a day would be lethal. "The boys got him out right quick. But he broke his arm." James clears his throat again, and I can see there's more he's not telling me.

"Just say it, James. What is it?" I wrap my arms around my belly, trying to stop shaking.

"Thomas was unconscious when they got him back onto the dock. Far as we know, he hasn't woke yet." Oh God. My hand moves to my gaping mouth.

"I need to see him. Where is he?" I get up, but James gently pushes me to the step.

"Slow down, Eva. Sit for a minute. You're barely breathing." Concern fills his eyes. "We think he's still in the hospital in Alert Bay. You know how hard it is to get news from up there." My mind races as I nod. I last saw Thomas a month ago, outside the speeder car in the pouring rain beside the lake. His dark eyes wincing in disappointment, a stranger's stony expression on his face. That can't be the way I leave it with him.

"I need to see him." I repeat the words more firmly, but my voice breaks. "I need to pack, get a train, and steamship ticket, and go to

Thomas." There's a hint of hysteria in my words, but I'm suddenly sure of my next moves, and I take the steps two at a time. Up in my room, I yank clothes from the wardrobe, flinging them onto my bed to be packed.

Thomas is my compass, my gravity. I can't conceive of a world without him. He isn't my back-up plan — he's my first choice. Nothing has ever been clearer. And I need to get to him.

CHAPTER 50

Mother follows me upstairs, perching on the covers in silence while I pull a single worn suitcase from under my bed. No heavy trunks for this trip — I'm just taking the north island essentials.

"I haven't been a good mother," she says when she finally speaks, pulling a handkerchief from under her sleeve. I stop stuffing clothes into my luggage and stare at her, running a hand through my hair. This isn't a subject our family discusses. When I start to respond, she holds up her palm for silence. "No. Let me speak." And then, as I bustle around the room packing, Mother tells a layered tale, beginning in Austria when she was a child. "I've told you my mother died when I was twelve. You remind me of her, Eva. She fought for her beliefs." She pauses, a tight smile flitting across her face. "And I was so angry with her... we all paid a price for her sense of justice. She battled for better working conditions, for my father and his friends. But her tactics... her group's tactics, got her killed by a policeman during a strike protest."

There's bitterness in my mother's voice. "Her death nearly killed my father. He drank... he... he wasn't equipped to care for me... or hold a job. Not without her." I'm only half listening, as I yank at the wardrobe and drawers, wondering why she's opening up now about the grandparents I never met. But my distraction doesn't deter Mother's storytelling.

After hastily fleeing Austria for America, my mother and her father moved west during her teen years without a plan, money, or grasp of the language. By the time they reached Seattle, my mother was sixteen and had learned enough English to get by. That summer, she dated the handsome son of a bicycle salesman, who lived in the apartment above them.

"It was all just a bit of fun. But he fell for me. Hard." Her eyes gleam in remembrance, her stern expression softening before her face darkens. "But I didn't feel the same." Our gazes lock as my brows furrow. Heeding Mother's narrative while checking off my mental packing list makes my head hurt. Somehow, I need to get my tin of gold into my suitcase without her noticing. My gaze darts away from Mother and I return to my wardrobe, shielding her view with my body. I reach into its depth, wrapping my gold into a wool sweater, lifting the whole bundle.

Tucking my stash into my luggage, I ponder again why she's telling me all this now. I need to get to Thomas, not hear about ancient family history. As I gather my knitting and notebook, piling those into Tony's haversack, her words spill on.

"And when my father died in a motorcycle crash, I did what I thought I had to. To survive in this country without him." Mother shakes her head almost imperceptibly, her chin dropping. Then she squares her shoulders and her eyes bore into mine.

"What do you mean?" I blink rapidly, not quite following her.

"Your father proposed... and I accepted. Even though I didn't love him." She sucks in a breath, her mind far away. She blows her nose gently into the embroidered handkerchief, the shame of her admission burning her cheeks.

"But you... and father... you care for him now, don't you?" I slam the suitcase lid closed, pushing a trouser leg inside the bulging case, then force the latches shut. Sitting next to her on the edge of the bed, my restlessness forgotten, I consider how similar our stories are. We both accepted marriage for reasons other than love.

"I do..." Mother looks at me, blowing her nose again. "But I wasted so much time being angry. All through my teens, I was angry with my mother for forcing us to leave Austria. Then, once we got to America, I was angry with my father for his wanderlust and job-bouncing. And when your father came into my life, I... I treated him as if he were replaceable." She shakes her head and puts a hand on my knee, turning to face me. "I was hurt, early in life, by losing people. And I... I never let myself love... not fully... again. Until now... when I almost lost him."

The bedroom door taps open and Father peeks into the room, his brows raised. Mother's face lights up, and she crosses over to him, her hand out. He wraps an arm around her and they share an intimate glance before turning back to me on the bed. After a moment, Mother clears her throat again, twisting the handkerchief in her fingers.

"Look. I resented getting married. Resented having Tony... and you. Thought I deserved more than this." She glances around the room and up at Father, who squeezes her shoulder. "And I... I see you making the same mistake." My mother's words tremble in anger. "I didn't let myself see how good my life is... and what a wonderful man I have... until..." She sucks in a shaky breath. "...until I almost lost him." She turns and crumples into my father's chest, heaving with sobs. Father envelops her gently, rubbing his thin hands up and down her back. I look away, dragging the suitcase off the bed, and jerk it toward the door, my lips pinching together.

"Stop... I know! I'm going back, aren't I?" My words are a plaintive wail, and I can barely breathe, feeling like I deserve the pain that fills my chest. "I see it now..." My shoulders curl, my voice barely a whimper. I just hope I'm not too late.

"Thomas is a good man," Father finally says, clearing his throat, his tone gruff with emotion. "We're just so glad you're going back to him." I lift my chin, swiping at my tears. The love in my father's eyes melts the icy rebellion growing in my chest, and without hesitation, I step toward him, collapsing into his other shoulder. He holds us both close, and when our trio finally pulls apart, he has a sad smile on his face.

"I gotta go." I wipe my eyes, picking up my luggage. Downstairs, James silently lugs the heavy suitcase out to my father's Buick, thudding it into the back seat, then kicks a tire, stuffing his hands in his pockets.

"Look... I... I came today myself... so I could know... could see how you reacted to this news." His lips twitch into a thin line, and he stares into the bare branches of the maple tree in our yard, exhaling audibly. "Thomas is a lucky man." When he turns back, his gaze is icy, and I'm haunted by his vile proposition on Millie's porch weeks ago. Today's events have crystallized how deeply I cherish my steadfast, dependable Thomas compared to this shallow flirt. "Goodbye, Eva." With that, James hops into his shiny Ford pickup and peels away from the curb without a backward glance. I slump against the Buick, shaking my head. Good riddance.

Behind me, Father hobbles down the stairs, leaning heavily on the handrail. My mother follows, head erect, her reddened eyes now dry. They move along the path toward me, hands linked. My father clears his throat as James's truck disappears over the horizon.

"Ready?" he asks, stepping off the curb to the driver's side, dropping Mother's hand. "I'll drive."

"Ready." I nod, and before I can turn away, my Mother steps forward to cup my cheek. I lean into her palm, my eyes fluttering closed, taking a contented breath. When I look up, my mother smiles through tears. She drops her hand, steps back, and nods. Grinning, I hop into the Buick.

We lurch down the street and a sudden lightness fills me. I twist in my seat, waving to Mother, her words echoing through my mind. Reaching for the stars can wait. I'm going to reclaim my Thomas.

CHAPTER 51

We don't speak on our drive downtown, except for a terse exchange about our route. Before going to the train station, I direct my father to stop at the Clark Company building. I need to know if Thomas's father has heard from him. As we clatter over the cobblestones, I twist my wedding band, feeling lightheaded. It's all too much. I take a deep breath and close my eyes. Clanging trolley bells, shouting street vendors, and distant notes of jazz fill the city's smoky sea air. Seattle's bustling rhythm forcing my retreat.

When we lurch to a stop outside the office on 2nd Avenue, I hesitate before threading through the lunch hour crowd on the sidewalk. I pull open the heavy glass door to the building, taking the stairs to the second floor rather than waiting for the creaky elevator. When the secretary announces me to Mr. Clark, he comes to the reception area immediately, pulling me into a long, powerful hug. The faint scent of cedar drifts from his wool suit, proof of Thomas's father's personal oversight of the local sawmills. He sounds and smells so much like my husband that tears streak my cheek when he lets go and leads me into his office.

"It's so good to see you, Eva." Settling into a plush velvet chair across the desk from him, I sit tall, dabbing the wetness from my cheeks. "I can't believe all this bad luck," Mr. Clark says, shaking his head sadly and running a hand through his silver hair. I look away, studying the imported rug, knowing I could have prevented all this, had I been watching Daisy. It wasn't bad luck, it was negligence. My negligence. Taking in Mr. Clark's dull expression, I vow to make it up to him, and the Clark Company, somehow.

"How's Thomas? Have you heard anything?" I chew on the inside of my lip, hoping there's good news, my heart pounding. But he shakes his head.

"The hospital sent a telegram this morning. He's stable. That's all they wrote. Stable. It could mean anything." He speaks with forced restraint and we gaze at one another, swallowing hard, knowing this doesn't bode well. If Thomas were able, he would contact his parents. He knows they're concerned, and I wonder for an instant whether he would send me a message too. I've allowed us to drift apart, and the uncertainty brings on more tears.

"I'm going back," I say without a preamble. Mr. Clark's eyes widen in surprise, but he nods, forcing a smile.

"That's good. Good. I was going to come see you myself, but James insisted he deliver the news to you." His eyebrows furrow, and he looks like he's going to ask me something, but cuts himself off. "That young man still struggles. He's doing better, but..." Mr. Clark shakes his head.

"James, you mean? What... struggles?" I ask, unable to contain my curiosity.

"Oh. He hasn't told you?" Mr. Clark pauses, pulling at an ear and spinning his leather chair away to gaze out the window. When he turns back to me, his expression is sombre. "James... he lost his younger brother... in the war. They were close, and ever since... well, I know the liquor's been a problem. He's been difficult to reach. Hard to help."

"I... I had no idea." For a moment, I feel a kinship with James. It leaves a desperate void, losing a brother, and I understand his reckless need to fill the gap.

He pauses again, shifting in his chair, letting out a heavy sigh. "But he'll always have a position with us. His father is one of my oldest pals... and it's breaking his heart. All of it." He clears his throat. "Parents will do anything for their children." He gives me another smile that fades quickly.

"I'm so glad you're going back, Eva." Mr. Clark smiles broadly now. "Actually, I have something for you."

"Oh?" Now it's my turn to frown.

"Thomas has told us how much work you've done on the bridge and setting layout." I nod, unsure why we're talking shop. "He feels you should be compensated for your time." Mr. Clark reaches into a drawer and pulls out an envelope, sliding it across the desk. "We were going to mail it, but since you're here..." I stare at my name, typed onto thick cream paper, the scripted print of the Company logo stamped in the corner. After glancing up at Mr. Clark, who waves encouragingly, I carefully open it.

Inside is a cheque for $100. My jaw drops. Not counting my secret stash of gold, now wrapped in a sweater in my suitcase, this is more money than I've ever had. I do some quick math, comparing it to the men's earnings. One hundred dollars is fair value for my limited hours.

I stare at Mr. Clark, unsure how to react. He sits silent, a grim twist to his mouth, and I know Thomas arranged this. Thomas knows I need money to move away from my mother, but the payment feels illegitimate given the damage I've caused. I tuck the cheque into the envelope and slide it back across the desk, my hand lingering over it. Then I clutch my fingers in my lap, shaking my head.

"Thank you, Mr. Clark. That's very good of you. Of Thomas." I imagine my unconscious husband lying bandaged in the drafty Alert Bay hospital. His kindness and foresight puts a lump in my throat. He knows I have no money of my own and understands living with my parents will drive me batty. Despite everything, he's arranged this to help me.

I swallow hard, blinking back more tears and lifting my chin, a bold solution taking shape. "But I'd rather be on your payroll. As a forester. A proper position, with a proper salary." Mr. Clark chuckles, and I feel a familiar chill run through me as I look up. Why do these powerful men always dismiss capable women? But his eyes sparkle with amusement, as if I've told a joke.

"My son knows you so well!" Mr. Clark slaps his palms on his lap, then stands and walks around the desk. "He said you'd never accept this payment. And he encouraged me to offer you a job. You have a deal, Mrs. Eva Clark." Mr. Clark extends a handshake, and I stand, taking it limply.

"Thank you." My vision blurs as I mumble my gratitude. "You won't be sorry." In the middle of the room, I go still, arms hanging loosely at my sides, my thoughts blank.

"Of course not." Mr. Clark moves to the ornately carved sideboard, pouring us each a finger of whisky from a heavy crystal decanter. "It's no time for celebration. Not until we know Thomas is well. But I need a drink, and I won't drink this contraband alone." So I join him, swirling, then sipping the amber liquid, its heat sparking a little hope in me. Thomas's father winks at me over his drink. His expression darkens as he replaces the decanter's square stopper. "Now. Go find my son. Get him healed up." He drains his glass, a bittersweet smile on his face. "Send me news. And be good to one another. That's an order." Some of the usual life returns to his eyes with his last words, and I promise I will. Then I shake his hand once more before leaving.

Outside, as I climb back into the passenger seat beside my father, a tingle spreads through my chest. I wonder if it's from the whisky, or because I just got my first proper job. Or maybe this feeling of lightness, of things being... right... stems from admitting Thomas and Camp 2 are where I belong.

"Everything okay?" My father raises an eyebrow as I grin to myself, his face lighting up with love and pride.

"Not everything," I say, wishing we knew more about Thomas's condition. "But I'm starting to see the treasures right in front of me." Reaching across the bench seat, I put my gloved hand over Father's on the Buick's steering wheel. "Take me to King Street." I squeeze his thin, blue fingers, and a hint of sorrow clouds his expression. He's going to miss me. We pull into the midday traffic, rumbling toward the train station. Toward home.

CHAPTER 52

The Vancouver-bound afternoon train is less than half full, and I settle into a window seat, pulling out my knitting. By the time we cross the border into Canada, darkness speeds by, and my reflection stares back at me against the inky backdrop. The track's rhythmic clatter replays my mother's counsel. And to my surprise, as I think of her now, a soft affection blooms in my middle. She was once young, like me, treading through an ocean of hardships, finding her way. Seeing her in that light shifts my view of her.

The train car door rolls open, filling the cabin with a blast of frigid air, the clickety-clack of the rails drowning out the hushed conversation around me. A tall, well-dressed man escorts a woman inside. With a satisfied smile, he follows her slim figure down the aisle. Thomas has always looked at me that way, with pride and love, but my ambitions blinded me to the value of that look.

Unlike this train, its path bound by the track, life can take you on detours. Those detours hold wonderful surprises and tragic setbacks. Despite the past months' losses, I never imagined a world without Thomas — until this afternoon. Now, the thought chills me.

The lights of New Westminster trundle by, the reflection of my trembling lips flashing on and off in the cold window glass. A cold tremor snakes down my spine, the fear of losing Thomas weighing heavy. The train arrives at Vancouver Station with just minutes to make the steamship. I navigate the chaos of the bustling port, clinging to the hope of reuniting with Thomas, apprehension and excitement knotting my middle.

The *SS Cardena* arrives in Alert Bay on a blustery, dark grey morning. I'm eager to disembark, bundled in all my warmest layers, pulling my oilskin hat down and flipping my collar. I fidget impatiently, waiting with the rest of the passengers under the ship's breezeway, clutching my pack and absently twisting my wedding ring while our luggage is unloaded.

Stepping off the lurching gangplank and onto the solid wood dock, I smile at a couple of local boys huddled in the rain, who hope to make a little money serving passengers. I catch the eye of a dark-haired lad and drop a quarter into his mittened hand, asking him to deliver my suitcase to the hotel.

"They expectin' ya, ma'am? Can I tell 'em yer name?"

"No, they're not expecting me," I say, shaking my head at the wide-eyed young man. "But tell them to hold a room for Mrs. Thomas Clark." I savour every syllable of my married name and tell the lad I'll return to the hotel once I've checked on my husband in the hospital. The boy nods, brushing rain from his face, then he lifts my suitcase onto a homemade dolly atop a crate of groceries. He tugs on the frayed rope handle and the swivel casters squeak shrilly, lurching over the gaps between the dock boards.

Lifting an eyebrow, I hustle down the boardwalk toward the hospital. Six months ago, I would have followed that boy, worried he'd topple my luggage, or just wander off with it, leaving me without my precious belongings. In contrast, today, I trust the young man will deliver my goods to the hotel, where the clerk will expect me shortly. I glance across the strait, aching to return to Camp 2 with Thomas where Grace's gentle smile, Daisy's giggle, and Edith's sarcasm await.

In the downpour, the town's boardwalk is deserted. The occasional resident rushes from one open door to the next, shoulders hunched, eyes on their footing. Through the sheets of windy rain, the smokehouse's savoury scent, tinged with an undertone of rotting fish, reaches me as I pass the processing plant.

The wooden walk turns to gravel as I near the hospital, muddy streams running over the path. The murky water disappears under piles of driftwood on the beach to my right, where the ocean's foamy white waves boil. I step carefully around the deepest puddles, then finally turn up the walk leading to the hospital. Once under the shelter of the balconies, I shake off my jacket and stomp my boots clean, but when I try to enter the main doors, they're locked. I peer through the glass, my rapidly blinking reflection staring back at me. A handwritten sign is taped to the inside, stating that this wing is closed because of fire damage.

I vaguely remember someone talking about a fire at the hospital on my trip down island in January, but with George's loss so fresh, I hadn't heeded the news. Now, I follow the sign's directions and walk around the building, the totems across the road in the burial ground looming in the haze.

As I finally open a side door, a flutter of anxious excitement vibrates through me. Will Thomas be pleased to see me? Or does he blame me for his accident? Will he even be conscious? The last telegram was vague. My whirling thoughts anchor me in the empty hospital hallway. Although it's mid-morning, the corridor is dim, lit only by grey streaks of daylight entering through the door glass at either end. Without the typical reception desk, I have no idea where to go.

Halfway up the hall, a harried nurse steps from a room. She rushes toward me, the crisp white cotton of her uniform swishing at her ankles. Holding her glowing kerosene lamp overhead, she looks me over.

"Can I help you?" Her tone is brusque, but not unkind. I nod.

"I'm looking for my husband, Thomas Clark." Tension leaves my shoulders. I'm so close to seeing him again and my heartbeat races. But the nurse's brow furrows. Instead of pointing me to a room, she's shaking her head, her bouncing white cap casting long shadows on the adjacent wall.

"He checked out. Last night, I believe." A heaviness grips me, and I drop my chin.

"Oh." My single syllable conveys the surprise and disappointment I feel. "How is he?" I ask, in a lighter tone. Thomas's departure from the hospital suggests improvement. The older woman's features soften.

"I'm not sure. My shift started this morning. But let's go check his chart. He wasn't expecting you, was he?" Without awaiting my reply, she lowers the lamp and motions for me to follow her. Our footsteps echo through the hall, as a gust of wind makes the walls groan. A breeze touches my cheek, and with it, the acrid odour of charred wood and antiseptic wafts around us. I shiver as the nurse opens the door to a hospital room and motions me inside.

"Since the fire late last year, we've been scrambling to keep going. We've blocked off the damaged ward, doubling up the beds in each of our remaining rooms. And we're using this as our reception and nurses' station. And break room." She glares around the makeshift office, where lunch bags and winter coats clutter a row of filing cabinets. "Moving into the new building in the summer will be a relief." She places the lamp on the edge of a single desk, shuffling through a stack of charts. "Ah. Here it is." Her glasses hang from a chain around her neck, and she settles them on her nose, scanning the pages and clucking her tongue.

"Well?" I say, impatient now. Although it's rude, I can't stop myself from pushing for an answer. She clears her throat, squinting at me.

"He was unconscious when he arrived. Broken arm. Plastered that up... Hypothermic... But it was the bump to his head that had Doc worried." She frowns at the chart, lifting a page, then placing it back down again. "Looks like your husband checked out against the doctor's advice. Should have stayed longer, to be sure his head injury is stable." She peers at me over her reading glasses, her expression stern, and I nod. It doesn't surprise me that Thomas left as soon as he felt able. He has work to do, and a crew to lead.

"Do you know where he went?" I ask, uncertain and directionless, as my mind races. I assumed I'd find Thomas here, stay at the hotel until he recovered, and figure out together what we were going to do next. Instead, life is presenting another detour.

The nurse shakes her head, placing the chart back on her desk. "Not me. The night shift nurse might know. But we don't ask or record where a patient is off to." She looks at me pointedly, as if not knowing my own husband's whereabouts is some kind of failure. Which, I suppose, it is.

"Thank you," I say and turn to the door.

The nurse sidesteps, blocking my way. "Wait. Your husband should be resting. Avoiding strenuous activity." She shakes her head, glancing out into the greyness, sounding far away. "The men up here all think they're invincible. Until they're not." She turns back to me, holding my gaze. "When you find him, have him rest. And get him back here right away if he loses consciousness, has any weakness, or seizures. And watch for unequal pupil size and discharge from his ears. Blood or clear fluid." I feel my eyes widen and my mouth drops open, a lump knotting my stomach again. The older woman reaches over and squeezes my arm. "I hope he'll be fine, Mrs. Clark. But the doc wouldn't have asked him to stay for no reason." Then she opens the door, letting me out into the dim hallway.

I hurry away, wanting distance between me and this bad news building. Outside, the totems glare down at me and raindrops jump from the puddles as I hustle back toward the centre of town and the hotel, hoping that wherever he is, Thomas is looking after himself.

Chapter 53

Unlike the grandeur of Seattle's Olympic, the Bay Hotel on this secluded island boasts no opulent features. Where the city's hotels flaunt shiny, ornate entrances, the paint on this hotel's weathered door peels away. I step inside and a bell announces my arrival, although the loud creaking floorboards make the chimes unnecessary. Here, there's no polished terrazzo or dancing palm fronds, no staff in crisp uniforms. Instead, the old clerk limps from his living room beyond the front desk, his moccasins padding over a worn rag rug.

He leans against the counter, thick twisted fingers curled below the cuffs of a pilled cream-coloured cable knit cardigan. Tearing my eyes away from his deformed hands, I glance around the warm room, pulling off my soaked hat and jacket. Stacked on the left, my suitcase crowds the tiny reception area. Across from it, a wood stove crackles, emitting a golden glow, my dampness already fogging the windows.

"Can I help you?" The clerk peers over the desk at me, the whites of his milky grey eyes rimmed with red. His skin is deeply wrinkled and his bushy white brows lift as he rubs a ruddy cheek with a crooked thumb.

"These are my things." I gesture at my luggage. "But my husband isn't here. What I mean is, he isn't at the hospital anymore." My words topple out, sounding scattered, and the clerk's unruly eyebrows furrow together. "Did he come here? Yesterday? His name is Thomas Clark." Thomas had to stay somewhere last night after leaving the hospital, and I can't think of anyone he'd impose on. But the clerk shakes his head.

"No ma'am. No customers yesterday, not even off the steamship. Not unusual for the southbound runs, but..." He drifts off, shrugging and shaking his head sadly, then glances at the numbered brass keys hanging in an unbroken row behind him. His mention of the ship spins my thoughts in another direction. It's possible Thomas went south. Maybe he felt poorly and travelled to Vancouver. We'd promised each other, after Ruby, that if we were ever seriously ill, we'd seek medical help down in the city. The doctor here performs well when he's sober, but larger hospitals are better for many things.

I wonder if Thomas would have gone south, or back to Camp 2. Biting the inside of my cheek, my mind races through the possibilities. The hotel clerk watches me patiently as I twist my wedding band and sigh.

"Did ya check with the store? Or the lads on the docks?" I shake my head and ask if I can leave my suitcase here while I inquire around. He nods his agreement, then slowly lurches back into his living quarters on a limping gait.

For the next half-hour I hustle through town, but no one I speak to saw Thomas yesterday, which is strange. Everyone knows about his accident and thinks he's still in the hospital. In a tiny place like this, it feels odd to find nothing. It should be impossible to just disappear.

I end my search at the docks, with no news. But I'm offered a ride across to Camp 1 in a fishing skiff if I can be ready in fifteen minutes. It's a better option than waiting in a hotel room, so I rush to the post office to send a telegram. After double-checking the transcription of our names and addresses, the operator types out the short message to Thomas's father:

THOMAS LEFT HOSPITAL. LOCATION UN-
KNOWN. I AM HEADING TO CAMP.

I retrieve my suitcase from the hotel and call a hasty thank you to the clerk, then arrive at the skiff as the skipper pulls his mooring line. He takes my luggage and offers me a rough hand to step into the boat. When we reach the bay, I question my decision. The seas are rougher than I've ever seen them, and this skiff is hardly bigger than a rowboat. Soon we're bobbing and dipping. Saltwater splashes over the bow, soaking me and the pile of fishing nets I'm clinging to.

An hour later, I struggle to keep my breakfast down as I step onto the dock at Camp 1. The tumultuous journey has left me lightheaded and off-balance, and I gladly take the skipper's hand as he helps me off the boat. He plunks my dripping suitcase beside me, then silently pushes off to wherever he's going. Rain and seawater have left me drenched, and I shiver. I smooth the front of my skirt and inhale the cool, damp air, hoping to quell my queasiness. But when I stoop for my luggage, the world wobbles. Pausing bent over, I take three more steadying breaths before standing upright, still focused on keeping my last meal down.

From the end of the dock, a figure jogs toward me in the rain. It's a young worker I don't recognize, rubbing his chin as he looks me up and down, before taking the suitcase from my chilly hand. He turns, striding away, motioning me to follow. The wind howls around us, and even with the 800-foot breakwater providing protection, the logs in the booming ground jostle and moan. Below me, the bark peels off a large cedar log, revealing the naked flesh of the underlying wood as it bashes against a boomstick. I shudder, imagining Thomas's fall into our lake's booming grounds, my stomach roiling at how lucky he was to escape with his life.

I'm suddenly consumed with an urge to see Thomas, to know he's alright. Blinking back tears, I swallow the lump in my throat. My body now aches to hold him, to run my hand through his wavy dark hair. My mother's words linger in my thoughts. I need Thomas to know how much I love him. Before it's too late. I need to get to him.

When I open my eyes, the worker and my luggage are already on the muddy gravel road. He turns, expecting me right behind him, so I give my head a quick shake and hustle along the dock. I'm exhausted, nauseous, and anxious. When I catch up to him, the shuffling young man shouts over the wind, asking where I want to go. I point straight ahead, to the big white two-storey, where Thomas's uncle lives. The worker's eyes widen, but he shrugs and carries my suitcase to the front step. He drops my things onto the small covered deck before tipping his hat and running up the road dodging puddles, then disappears into a bunkhouse.

I take a deep breath before knocking on the painted front door. The sound of my knuckles on the wood is barely audible over the weather, but after a moment, Thomas's tall, stern-faced uncle yanks open the door. A gust of wind ruffles his white hair as he frowns. His dark eyes peer past me, scanning the path, looking for my husband. Without a greeting, he takes my luggage, leading the way inside.

After closing the door behind me, I scan the dim living area. It's sparsely furnished, and like the bunkhouses, lacks a woman's touch. Soup simmers somewhere, its hearty scent mingling with tobacco smoke. I've never been inside the big house, but met Thomas's uncle once in passing, during a shopping trip to Alert Bay. Where Thomas's father exudes an air of kindness, his brother has steely eyes, his lined face etched into a perpetual frown.

"So?" He puts down my case and faces me, his thumbs hooked into the suspenders of his suit pants. "Where's Thomas?"

"I... I don't know." His question makes my heart sink. If he's asking, Thomas hasn't come through here. "I was just at the hospital. He discharged himself last night. I thought... I hoped he came back to camp. No one in town knows anything." Mr. Clark's gaze is harsh, and as my coat drips a ring of rainwater on his floor, I realize this unfriendly man is now my boss.

"Haven't seen Thomas since they brought him through after the accident." He shakes his head. "Costing us a pretty penny... all this downtime." I feel my shoulders stiffen and I cross my arms across my chest. George's death and Thomas's injury aren't an accounting problem. These are... and were... human beings. Lives. Lost and altered. This man is heartless.

"Yes. I'm sure." My reply is curt, but I hold my tongue. If I say anything more, I'll get myself in hot water. I stand up a little taller, itching to leave. "When's the next train to Camp 2?" He pulls out a pocket watch, furrowing his brow.

"Should be down within the hour. I imagine the reload is rougher than usual." I nod, biting my lip, unsure of what to do. "Take off your coat." Mr. Clark waves at the hooks beside the door. "You'd best wait here. Dry up a bit."

"Thank you." I let out my breath, shivering, then shake off my things and hang them, steeling myself for an hour with my new boss. Maybe this is a grave mistake. Working for Thomas's father seemed like a grand plan. But most of my dealings will be with Thomas's uncle. I consider sharing I've been hired, but decide it's best if he hears it from his brother. I don't need to endure this man's scorn about my skills. Or assumed lack thereof. At least not right at this moment.

Doubts swirl through me as the rain splatters the front windows. I'm surprised when Mr. Clark presents me with a bowl of soup, which I decline, accepting just a glass of water to settle my stomach. He reads a paper in the kitchen while I sit out on the stiff living room sofa, silently finding patterns in the wormwood plank coffee table. My fingers trace the darkened holes and tunnels left in the wood by the *Teredo navalis*, while the nurse's warnings replay in my mind. I hope, wherever he is, Thomas is resting and healing.

Chapter 54

Three hours later, at Camp 2's rail spur, I step out of the cramped engine room of the old 5-Spot locie. Billy passes me my suitcase, but I hesitate, the icy terror of my last days here gripping my insides. Despite the rainstorm, the acrid hint of charred wood reaches me from the sawmill. In the descending dusk, I carry my luggage toward our cabin, my footsteps crunching on the gravel. The warm glow of lantern lights floods from the camp windows up the way, but I'm not ready to see anyone.

I let myself through the unlocked door of our dark cabin, where signs of Thomas's time here without me litter the empty room. His wool sleepwear is flung over the foot of the unmade bed. The washbowl below the mirror sits half full, snippets of beard shavings floating on the scummy wash water. I brush a fingertip across the razor's handle propped near the basin, the scent of Thomas's soap closing my throat.

The open box of bull's-eye mints rests on the table, surrounded by a scattering of pencils and erasers. I step closer and lift the unlit lantern, recognizing the layout of the next setting. Opposite me, the bridge drawings lie exactly as I left them, and set at my seat is a vase filled with evergreen boughs. The winter arrangement is fresh, and a flutter of emotion stirs in my belly. Thomas has been bringing the outdoors inside, anticipating my return.

A creak from the doorway shoots a jolt of hope through me as I turn, aching to see my husband's familiar form stride through the door. Then I chide myself. It's only a gust of wind shaking the cabin. Thomas is gone, sailing south on yesterday's steamship. It's the only explanation left. Both his uncle and Billy agree he must have headed toward Vancouver. There's nowhere else he'd go. And I'm here, still alone and no closer to reuniting with Thomas.

I sink into a wooden chair, heavy with disappointment. Shoving the pencils away, I fold my arms across the table, my head collapsing onto the cool dampness of my oilskin sleeves, and I cry. Loud, shuddering sobs fill every corner of the tiny cabin, while outside the storm rages, echoing my desperation.

Sitting in our home, surrounded by the echoes of our laughter and the sting of our tears, it's clear to me — all I want is my husband. Thomas. That's it. I've wasted so much time pushing him away, my brain scrambling my true feelings. I just hope I haven't taken too long to find my way. A man has his limits, even if he loves you. Keeping Thomas at a distance, letting his affections fall flat, may have driven him south in frustration. He's a strong, handsome, and kind man. A man any of my university mates would be grateful to land. My heartbeat quickens as I picture a slim city girl running her manicured hand through Thomas's thick hair, and jealousy pulls at my gut.

I've been so blind! Clenching my curls with both hands, I throw my head back and growl at the rafters in frustration. Then I thump my fists onto the table, rattling the lantern, just as there's a pounding from outside. It's not the wind this time. Without awaiting an invitation, Edith bursts in. She slams the door behind her, taking in my wild eyes and tear-stained face. In two strides, she envelops me in a long, powerful hug. She still smells of liniment and whisky. I sob against her thick frame as she pats my hair and rubs my back as if I were a child.

For the first time since we lost Ruby, I let the pain roar out of me. I moan for my baby. For Thomas, and our marriage, our ruined family. I weep for George, for the time I've wasted pushing Thomas away, and for the mess I've made of the best friendship I've ever known.

As I gasp for breath, I feel selfish and guilty for indulging in my pain. Edith, who props up my trembling body, has lost her George forever. Recalling her stoic grief, I pull away, looking out across the lake, wrenching off my jacket and hat, throwing them both onto the floor in a childish tantrum. My ragged snuffling echoes the rhythm of the wind outside as I take in the view I've grown to love. This wild, beautiful, inhospitable place has dug its harsh claws deep into me. I can't imagine living anywhere else, or with anyone other than Thomas. I'm so afraid I've blown my chance at that.

I wrap my arms around myself, my breath coming in shudders and I can feel Edith's eyes on me. Neither of us has said a word. She should be upset with me for leaving without saying goodbye, and for the part I played in this mess. But she's here, wordlessly welcoming me home. With a steadying inhale, I turn to the older woman, wavering. She frowns a little, tilting her head to one side.

"Well. Are ya comin' for supper? Or what?" Her eyes bore into me, full of love and sadness, but her tone leaves no question about what my answer must be.

"I could eat." My voice quivers, then I nod weakly and clear my throat, blinking back another round of tears. "Let me get cleaned up."

Edith grunts, shaking her head. "You ain't there in ten minutes, I ain't holdin' it for ya," she says, but she squeezes my arm as she pushes past me, winking. "Food first. Then we talk." She steps out into the rainstorm, slamming the door without looking back. A smile spreads across my wet cheeks. Edith's world logic is comforting, like a warm wool sweater on a gloomy day.

CHAPTER 55

The next morning, I file into the cookhouse for the first seating. No one here knows it yet, but I'm a paid crew member now. Soon, I'll work directly with the men instead of assisting Thomas behind the scenes. Everyone greets me somberly, and tension fills the gaps in table chatter. For most of the meal, it's unclear if the crew's unease is caused by me or something else. Then Roy pushes back his plate and assigns the day's tasks, doing his best to fill in Thomas's role.

"Donkey, Crank. Get the cars lined up so Tetley and Paul can load you. Grinder, Slim. You come with me. We'll start clearing the next rail spur." Roy looks around the room. All the men, except Donkey Donny, keep their eyes down, studying their plates or tying a bootlace. But Donny has something to say.

"We should all be goin' with ya today, Roy. There ain't more'n half a load out there now. We don' ship half loads." Donny's words are calm, measured. And also correct. When Thomas first started here, this was his biggest challenge. Everyone wanted to run the locie continuously. It felt productive to see the big timber leave the landing, but Thomas had me do the math. Between the cost of coal and labour, we realized quickly that shipping anything other than full loads on the train raised the costs per cubic yard so high it was nearly impossible to make the target margins. He'd struggled to convince the men, not to mention his uncle and father. Thomas's way led to higher profits after just one month. They took longer to bring in enough timber to fill the train, then shipped loaded cars intermittently.

At first, the railmen, Donkey Donny and Crank, protested. Running the engine was less labour intensive than the hand falling out in the cut block, but now, here's Donny, challenging his young foreman. I watch with interest as Roy stands, leaning his thick hands onto the oiled tablecloth.

"Look. I don' need yer lip, Donkey." Roy's jaw clenches and the cookhouse is silent except for the clatter of dishes from Li Wei and Edith in the back. Without thinking, I lay my napkin beside my tin plate, sliding off the bench to stand opposite Roy at the other end of the table. His narrowed eyes glare past me as he focuses out the window, but Donny and two other men look up when I rise.

"Thomas would…" With all eyes on me, I falter, the cookhouse in complete silence. Even Edith and Li are motionless. I clear my throat and decide this conversation with Roy is best done without an audience. "Maybe the crew can wait outside?" Roy stares at me, drawing in a breath. Pushing off the table, he directs the men with a chin jerk.

They take a few minutes to collect their lunch pails from Edith at the counter, then don their jackets, casting furtive glances at me. Roy shrugs at the men, lifting his eyebrows to suggest he will humour the boss's wife, and be right out.

I lean against the log wall, my hands behind my back, considering the best way to approach Roy. I could tell him they've hired me, to give my words some official weight, but I'm not sure how Roy will react without Thomas as the middleman. By the time the crew shuffles out into the cold January dawn, I have a plan.

Roy stands opposite me, arms crossed and chin lifted. "So?" he asks gruffly.

"You know I helped plan this setting," I say, and Roy nods. He's seen me in the office with Thomas enough times. "And if Thomas was here, he'd want us to work Donny's plan today?" Roy hesitates, but nods again, his eyes downcast. I see uncertainty in his face as his shoulders droop, and address it directly. "What is it, Roy? What are you not sure about?" Still, he remains silent, his lips clamped in a tight line. "Maybe I can help." It's with these words that his jaw unclenches.

"Thomas didn't..." Roy glances up, rephrasing his thoughts. "I didn't go over the long-term plan with him... before..." Again he pauses, averting his gaze, avoiding mention of the accident. I simply nod.

"No. You wouldn't have." Thomas shared enough information so his crew could make good decisions throughout the day, but it doesn't pay to have them thinking too far ahead. They must focus on the present during their dangerous, hands-on tasks. Thomas's role was to plan months in advance. Now, with Thomas gone for the past week, Roy is struggling.

"I got no layout up on the spur. An' the fellas from the mill are needin' work, too." Roy shrugs. "I'm just tryin' to keep everyone going until... Thomas..." Now he looks straight at me. "How is he, anyway? When's he back?"

At dinner last night, I had been evasive. It would alarm the camp if I admitted I didn't know how Thomas was, or even where he was. But now, looking at Roy's earnest face, I share the whole truth.

"Look. Roy. I'm going to level with you. I don't know where he is." My voice breaks, but I clear my throat and stand tall. Roy's eyebrows knit as I tell him about the fruitless search for Thomas in Alert Bay. "But I do know what his plans are for that spur." We outline the crew's day together and agree Roy will come by the office cabin before dinner so we can discuss the upcoming week. I ask Roy to gather details about the setting, equipment location, and current workers, then give him a smile. "You good now?" I ask.

He nods a few times and grins. "Yeah. Yeah, I'm good for now." He grabs his lunch pail from the counter, waves at Edith, and pulls on his jacket. "Better get a move on. The fellas are gettin' restless." Then, before he ducks outside, he steps close and lowers his voice. "I'm bettin' Thomas went south to getcha. He was beside himself after you left." Roy grins again and slams out the cookhouse door, saying over his shoulder, "He'll be back. You'll see!"

As Roy's good-spirited shouts to the men fade away toward the landing, a flutter of hope spreads through me. Maybe it's not too late to save my marriage. While I figure out if I should go after Thomas, or just wait here for news, I'll keep Camp operational. And profitable. I owe everyone here that much. As I watch the crew accept Roy's confident direction outside, I silently vow to prove my worth. To the Company. And myself.

CHAPTER 56

Almost three weeks later, I rouse well before the jangle of Thomas's alarm clock. Outside, the fluting song of the Swainson's thrushes begins. First one bird, then more, join the melody of upward-spiralling whistles. Somewhere under the floorboards, the industrious scratching of a deer mouse joins the morning music. I lie on my side, hands tucked under my down pillow, savouring another tranquil awakening alone. Up in the brush, something scares the *Catharus ustulatus*, their songs ending in an abrupt *whit*. When the clock's luminous minute hand jumps for the third time, the birds' whistles return. I crawl out from under the sheets onto the creaky floor, and my steps silence the chewing of the Peromyscus maniculatus below. Whispering a good morning to Tony's photo on the nightstand, I wish I had a picture of Thomas, and a familiar weight settles in my heart.

The cabin air is frigid, last night's fire long burnt out. Since returning, there's no reason to light it in the morning — I spend no time here. I eat with the crew, work in the office until noon, join the families for lunch, return to the office, and only go back to my cabin after dinner. Most evenings, after I light the fire, I sit in my rocker overlooking the lake, reading or knitting by lantern light, until I roll into bed, exhausted.

I still can't believe I've been here this long without Thomas. Once we knew he had headed south, I wanted to follow him. But my first week back was filled with stormy weather, so travel was impossible. Then a reply from Thomas's father reached us, stating simply:

"T ARRIVED. RECOVERING WELL. WILL HEAD NORTH SOON."

I'm still puzzled by that telegram. Why did it come from his father and not Thomas directly? We've heard nothing more since then, and I worry Thomas has aggravated his head injury, like the nurse warned. Or maybe he's so apathetic about me it hasn't occurred to him to update us.

Twice I've asked Donny to check in with Thomas's uncle at Camp 1. Donny's there most days while the logs from the train get unloaded down at the booming grounds. Both times Donny came back with a curt message from Thomas's uncle — when he hears anything, he'll tell us.

"An' I ain' askin' again, Mrs. Eva." Donny had knitted his brow and shaken his head. "That Mr. Clark, he gets mean. He don' like bein' disturbed."

If I don't go south to find Thomas, I at least need to send a telegram and wait in Alert Bay for a response from him. It's the only way to get out of this limbo. I've talked it to death with Grace and Edith, and they both agree it's me who needs to act. They frequently remind me of Thomas's goodness and urge me to make a move. We know Thomas would return if he was well enough. So every day he doesn't come, makes us worry about his health.

"You's dumber than Sammy if you's don' go get 'im back," Edith says to me daily. Until recently, I had hoped Thomas would show up in a few days. Lately, Grace has been gently pointing out things could have changed since the telegram.

"What if he isn't recovering? He loves you. You love him. Don't wait too long, Eva. If he's unwell, you need to be with him." As I get out of bed, I can hear my friend's wise words in my mind, and my stomach clenches. We expected him up here by now, so I should probably just go after him. I change quickly, pulling on my camp version of office attire: an all-wool vest and drawers under a cotton blouse and long skirt. At the door, I lace my worn leather work boots, supple and smelling musky from yesterday's waterproofing treatment.

After a damp trip to the outhouse, I walk the length of the camp to breakfast, a chattering squirrel scolding me from a high branch. I keep my gaze averted from the charred skeleton of the sawmill that still dominates the foggy lake shore. I can't imagine a time when my heart won't clench making this trek. Near the cookhouse door, the voice of the *Tamiasciurus hudsonicus* fades away and the rich, earthy smell of strong coffee greets me. I make a mental note to ask Thomas's uncle for permission to have the crew demolish the burnt mill remains. There's no reason to have this daily reminder looming in the mist. Even when we rebuild, the damaged structure can't be reused.

Inside, a haze drifts high in the cookhouse rafters from the thick cuts of bacon crackling in a huge cast-iron skillet. Edith smiles, waving a spatula as I pull a stool up to the counter, then she pours me a steaming cup of coffee from the percolator. Today, I'm the first one in, and I wrap my hands around the tin mug, watching Li pull a tray of fluffy biscuits from the oven. He bows his head deeply and grins at me too, his dark eyes disappearing into the folds of his unwrinkled skin.

Li, a transplanted sawmill worker, has adapted well to the kitchen. In practised movements, he opens the firebox, stoking the orange glowing coals with a steel poker, just as George used to. Then, Li places the chopped wood inside, slams the door shut, and adjusts the draft regulator so the oven will heat perfectly for the next batch of biscuits. He wipes his forehead with the back of his hand, his blunt-cut thick black bangs brushing his brows as he dumps the baking into a huge stainless bowl, then sets it in front of me on the counter.

As I reach for a flaky biscuit, the cookhouse door opens, and the crew files in, hanging their coats. These days, every worker nods or waves, many of them commenting on the weather or the kitchen smells, making friendly small talk as they slide into their usual spots on the benches. I take my seat opposite Roy, who catches my eye.

"How's yer mouse doin'?" Roy raises his eyebrows at me as he tears open his biscuit.

I chuckle. "Sounds like he's building a mansion down there."

Laughing along, the crew chides my refusal to trap the little critter. It isn't the words the men share with me that fill my heart, it's the tone of their voices and the sincerity in their eyes. In the past three weeks, I've gained their respect and trust. To a man, I've won them over. And I can hardly believe it.

Our chatter quiets as Edith delivers heaping plates of crisp bacon, scrambled eggs, and Li's special spiced hash browns. The next few minutes are still, other than the sound of utensils scraping and lips smacking. My mind drifts to the day's agenda as I plan roles to recommend to Roy.

When I arrived, Roy doubted my abilities, but was overwhelmed enough to accept help from anyone, even a woman. We battled each other that first week. He kept prioritizing the easy tasks, sacrificing long-term efficiency. I persevered stubbornly, believing that if I allowed Roy to take some wrong turns, he would eventually realize I had been right. And that's how it had gone.

On my sixth day here, Roy had stormed into my office, thrown his cap in the corner, and collapsed onto the bench opposite my desk, scowling. I had put down my pencil, placed my palms on my page of notes, and lifted my brows at him. Intuition warned me anything I said would give him an excuse to shout. So I'd sat quietly as Roy's eyes flashed and he looked out across the lake, arranging his thoughts.

"Well. The boys got to the end of the cut today. Now our access is bungled." Roy looks at me with lowered eyes. "Nowhere to go tomorrow." His voice drops a note, and he shakes his head. "Just like you warned."

I nodded, suppressing a smile, and laid out a plan to fix the crew's impending bind. From then on, Roy had listened. Really listened. He never apologized for not taking my advice to start, but his acknowledgement that the bottleneck I had predicted days ago had indeed occurred was enough for me. That and his commitment since then to implement my plans.

Often, I'm not right, and Roy points out operational constraints I'm not aware of. The rest of the crew also trusts me enough to share their thoughts. Not just about work, but also other parts of their lives. Last week, Slim had come into my office, holding out a scrap of paper, asking whether I had a pen to write a birthday letter to his ma. When I'd offered him my fountain pen, he waved his oil-stained hands at me.

"I'm filthy, Mrs. Eva. You mind doin' it?" But Slim's flushed face and downcast eyes hinted at something else. As I searched his expression, he silently conveyed his inability to read and write. Hiding my surprise, I had held his gaze, nodded, and asked what he would like to share with his mother. Then Slim, who usually saved his breath for laughing, smiled with relief. He spoke more words than I've ever heard from him, to get a letter out to his beloved mother.

Next, Donny had shown up, asking for help with some payroll paperwork he didn't understand. Then Grinder brought in the new Eaton's catalogue, wanting my opinion on which bracelet to mail his sweetheart. And when I noticed Tetley didn't eat Edith's omelettes, he shared that mushrooms make his mouth itch. Although she grumbled about it, Edith now keeps the *Cantharellus cibarius* separate for him.

These small, caring interactions have built a solid bond between all of us these past few weeks. By working together, this camp is now just as productive as under Thomas's leadership. The knowledge makes me sit up a little taller, but I push away my empty plate and stare into my coffee mug.

Thomas. Every day, I wonder what's keeping him away. Sometimes I'm angry with him, but more often I'm just worried. It's so unlike Thomas to leave his crew floundering, which makes me think there's something wrong. On those days, I long to go to him. If only I knew whether he would welcome me.

Around me now, the men move to collect their lunches, stirring me from my thoughts, and I look across the table at Roy. He's watching me, and lifts his brows, wordlessly asking if I'm alright. I nod, then take my cup of coffee and slide in next to him. As the men leave the cookhouse, we review the day's details, like every morning. Roy confirms a trainload of logs will head to Camp 1 first thing. There won't be much to haul when it returns this afternoon. He shrugs, nodding gravely and leaves, saying he'll focus on getting timber down today. With a sigh, I drain my mug, placing it on the counter for Edith, then wave to her as I pull on my coat and follow Roy out into the crisp day.

A thickness builds in my throat, the solitary peace I felt when I awoke now replaced by a gnawing in my gut. I must go to Thomas, but there's something I have to handle first. Rather than going to the office, I make a quick stop at my bunkhouse before trudging down to the point to talk to George, who's buried next to Ruby. It's silly, but sitting with him and my baby girl always clears my thoughts.

On a frosty log across from the graves, I hold the Lucky Strike tin between my palms, my breath a lingering white cloud in the chilly air. There still isn't anyone who knows about the gold I discovered here. I have considered using it to fund more reforestation research, but my seedlings are doing well — Grace and Daisy took good care of them in my absence. The research requires my time, not cash for supplies, so I'm hopeful Thomas and the Company will support it. In any case, sharing my gold find would destroy the life I love. This is my home now. I'm here to stay, so I don't need this treasure. Hiding it will protect this place.

"You'll guard it, won't you, Boss?" I smile meekly, removing George's cross and digging a two-foot deep hole in its place. Then I plunk the tin down into the steaming earth, replacing the tall white cross, tamping the ground with my boot. I tear some old man's beard from a nearby bush and scatter the Usnea longissima and some twigs over the base, masking the disturbed soil.

Sitting back on my haunches, my mind drifts to Thomas. It's been too long. Something feels off, and I can't shake the need to go to him. But without me, the camp work will suffer. Standing, I wipe my hands on my skirt, resolving to come up with a plan. Crafting a two-week schedule with Roy should ensure things run smoothly while I'm away, searching for Thomas in the city. Salvaging my marriage and finding my best friend fills me with hope, and makes my breath catch. What if he doesn't want me anymore? A last glance at the white crosses brings peace, and I'm bolstered by George's spirit. He'd say mug up and get going.

As I plod back to the office, I decide going south for Thomas feels right. I need to be brave enough to move forward, not cower here in limbo. I stare at my feet, shaking my head. So I'll go. In three days, after a bit of planning with Roy, I'll go reclaim the missing piece of my life.

CHAPTER 57

It's late afternoon when Daisy bursts into my office, bringing with her a trail of muddy boot prints and the sound of the locie puffing into the landing.

"Look what I found!" Daisy holds up a glass canning jar, peering through the bottom at a treasure inside. "It's huge. Lookit!" she says, placing the container on my papers, pointing at a big black beetle. I put down my pencil, hoisting Daisy onto my lap, both of us craning over her prize.

"Strange," I say. "It's a European ground beetle. *Carabus nemoralis.* Shouldn't be active this time of year." Daisy taps on the glass and the insect wiggles its antennae, moving away from the sound. "Where did you find it?"

"Our place. In the corner. Beside the woodbox," she says.

I nod, stroking her hair. "You woke it up, Daisy-girl. It should be hibernating." The insect's wing cases are a beautiful metallic purple and both of us watch, mesmerized, as its horned legs slip on the smooth surface inside the jar. I hold Daisy's waist with one arm, leaning over her to point out the insect's body parts. The segmented abdomen, the shiny compound eye, the breathing holes, or spiracles, under its gleaming elytra. She digests the information and repeats it back in her sing-song voice, unwrapping each new word like a treasure.

Daisy kicks her boots against the legs of my chair, clumps of mud falling onto the roughly hewn floor. I breathe in the loamy sweet aroma of her tangled blond curls as she leans into me, her weight a warm comfort. Gazing up at me rosy-cheeked, her wide blue eyes sparkle with the joy of discovery. A yearning for my own child hits my heart with an unexpected violence. I swallow the lump in my throat, bending to kiss the top of her head. This illogical ache needs to be crushed — I've vowed to avoid the heartbreak of having children.

The office door opens again, and Daisy looks up, pushing her curls against my lips.

"Oh, hi!" Her voice squeals with excitement as she wriggles off my lap, taking the glass jar with her. Mispronounced beetle anatomy tumbles from Daisy as I look up at our visitor.

And there he is. Thomas. His oilskin drapes open, a plaster arm cast slung across his wide chest as he crouches on his haunches next to Daisy. The fingers of his broken hand graze the canning jar, his head nodding at her words. But his gaze is locked on me. I stand, then collapse back into the chair, my breath abandoning me, my heart pounding. All the while, Daisy explains how beetles breathe through holes in their stomach and isn't that odd?

Thomas's eyes search mine with an unreadable expression. He's here. My Thomas is really here. A slow, incredulous smile lifts my cheeks, but his face remains stony.

"Hey, Thomas! Where you been anyway? I gotta know!" Daisy's narration of beetle wonder stops when she realizes she doesn't have Thomas's attention. She places a small palm on his stubbled cheek, pushing until he's compelled to look at her.

"Sorry, Daisy-girl. Your bug is just grand." He gives her a forced smile and places the jar in her hands before standing. "Will you do a big job for me?" Daisy inspects the beetle again, before nodding at Thomas gravely. "Will you go tell Edith to make up the guesthouse? And tell her I said you could have a cookie." Daisy grins and runs out toward the cookhouse with boundless energy, the poor insect getting a shaky ride. Thomas holds the door open, watching her go, then pulls it closed, staring at the doorknob for a beat before turning.

His jaw clenches and he rocks onto his toes stiffly, almost imperceptibly. Although my heart has settled its pace, my mouth is suddenly dry. I push back my chair and rise to my feet, brushing my palms down the front of my skirt, my smile fading as the silence lengthens. Why would he need the guesthouse?

Thomas finally clears his throat. "Look," he says, his jaw clenching. "You need to go. I dragged you into this marriage. To this godforsaken place." He flinches, his dark eyes sad. "I took you away from everything... and everyone you know. And I won't hold you here." He pauses, looking out the window behind me, over the lake. "I won't... can't... do this... have you leave me... again..." Now his voice cracks and he winces, pain flashing across his features as he stares down at his hands, his shoulders slumping. "You need to go," he says again and strides outside before I can say a word.

For the second time in minutes, I slump into the hard wooden desk chair. My vision blurs and I sit with a palm pressed against my breastbone in stunned silence, my heart hammering. This isn't the reuniting scene I had imagined, and as I contemplate returning to Seattle, my shock melts into a blazing rage. Damn him! He doesn't get to decide this.

Surging to my feet, I grab my jacket off the hook and slam outside. The icy February wind seeps through my layers and tugs my curls into unruly tangles as I search the camp for Thomas. I spot him near the guesthouse, down at the far end. He waves at the crew coming back from their day but takes no time to talk to them, quickly disappearing inside with his suitcase.

My teeth grind as I stride through camp, the frosty gravel crunching under my feet. Even with the wind etching my cheeks, my face feels flushed. I acknowledge Roy and the crew with an absent wave, not slowing my pace, ignoring their curious looks. When I reach the guesthouse steps, I shove my shoulder into the door, but it's latched from the inside. With clenched fists, I pound on it, my fingernails biting into the flesh of my palms, and I shout at Thomas to let me in.

Thomas yanks open the door, towering above me. His furrowed eyebrows and blank stare put a cold knot in my stomach. Loose hairs blow into my eyes, but I don't move either. Our gazes lock. Thomas glances over my head, his frown deepening. Behind me, the entire crew has paused their walk home, their curious stares eager to witness our exchange.

"For god's sake. Come inside then." Thomas exhales an exasperated breath and steps back, letting me through, slamming the door behind us. The man opposite me in the dim cabin feels like a stranger. He stands stiffly, a flat look in his narrowed eyes. He's taken off his oilskin and boots, the bright white sling across his rib cage a reminder of the damage I've done here. My words dry up and I turn away, unable to bear this version of my husband. He wouldn't be injured if I had been watching Daisy. Guilt tightens in my chest, but it's his indifference that squeezes me until I can hardly breathe.

Leaning against the countertop, my eyes focus on a perfect spider's web stretched across the top corner of the dusty window frame. Dozens of radial spokes of fine silk thread connected by parallel concentric circles shimmer in the gloomy dusk, and in the centre sits a large garden spider, head facing down, legs held wide. Waiting. I envy the *Araneus diadematus*'s ordered environment. If I were to draw my life as a spider's web, it would be a jumbled mess, like a cobweb wrapped around a feather duster. Some parts are beyond repair, but I need to untangle what I can.

"You didn't drag me into this marriage, Thomas." When I speak, my words are hoarse with emotion. "You saved me with it. I see that now." I look out past the spider web, where fir branches dance gently. Outside, the wind pushes against the guesthouse and the waves lap the shore in a hushed chorus. "When I was back in Seattle, all I could think of was you... and this place. Last year, you took me away from everything I knew. But you brought me to a place I didn't even know I needed." Remembering the bombardment of the city smells and sounds, I shudder. I finally turn to face Thomas, willing him to see, to understand all I've learned since we separated. His posture is less rigid, his eyes widening. "And when I heard you were hurt..." My voice chokes, but I hold his gaze, blinking back tears. "When I heard..."

Again, I can't finish the sentence, reliving the anguish I felt when James delivered the news. A tear rolls down my cheek, but I make no move to wipe it. "Look," I say, choking out the word and cracking a small smile. "I love you. You're my best friend. Have been for years. There's no one else I want to be with... spend my life with. I'm just sorry it took me so damn long to figure it out." I take a step toward him, one hand out, biting my lip. But Thomas shakes his head and closes his eyes, slumping onto the bare mattress of the guesthouse's twin bed. He puts his head in his hands, staring at the dusty wood floor, and I wish I knew what he was thinking. When he looks up, his eyes are bright, and he swallows.

"James?" His one-word question is barely audible above the wind and waves outside, and Thomas's jaw sets as he stares at me, his brows narrowed and expression full of questions.

"There's nothing!" I take another step forward, my fingertips reaching for him, but when he remains motionless, his eyes seeking more detail, I stop again. "Nothing happened. Not since…" My palm involuntarily touches my middle, as I do whenever I think of Ruby. I tilt my head at Thomas, wondering if he's guessed. He's never asked me who I made my mistake with, but I've always felt he knew it was James.

"He's a bastard." Thomas's fists tighten. "For what he did to you."

I nod. So Thomas knows. Briefly, I wonder what gave us away, but I focus on relieving Thomas's doubts, my explanation tumbling out.

"He came to tell me about your accident. I'm not sure what he was hoping for, but he knows I'm yours. He won't be back." At these words, Thomas's eyes crinkle in that way I've always loved, and I cross the room in two quick strides. He stands and I bury myself against him. My lips kiss his neck, above the frayed collar of his knitted sweater, and I nuzzle my forehead under his chin. His skin smells of shaving soap, and I push him hard against the wall next to the bed. Thomas lets out a choked groan, wrapping his arms around me and lifting me onto my tiptoes.

Then he leans me back, the rough edge of the plaster cast under my chin, his thumb grazing my lip, his stare intense. At his belt, my fingertips tingle with the urge to touch his face, caress the soft beard he's grown, trail my hand through his damp curls, pinch his earlobe. But I don't move, my desire for him building in the stillness. Thomas's eyes narrow just a little, a question flitting across his dark eyes as he holds my gaze. Asking muted permission for the one part of me I've been withholding for so long.

"I love you." My heart flutters as my fingers clench the fabric at his hip pockets. "And I... want... you." With those words, Thomas exhales a groan, kissing me roughly.

"God. I've loved you since I first laid eyes on you." His voice is a soft growl in my ear, and he looks around the dingy guesthouse. "You got the fire going at our place?" And when I nod, he slips into his boots, and without putting on a jacket, grabs my hand. A warm thrill courses through me as I follow my husband across the road. To our place.

Chapter 58

An hour later, the sun reaches the mountaintop and a band of gold streams through the cabin window. It highlights an angry red scar running across Thomas's bare chest. I pull the tangled sheets over my breasts, protection from the chilly room and my husband's possessive stare, but Thomas pulls the covers down with a mischievous grin, tracing his finger around my nipple. A shiver runs through me as I arch against the comforter and moan softly.

"God. You're beautiful." He echoes the words he's expressed countless times during our intimate exploration. I smile up at him through lowered eyelashes, still breathless with desire. While our wedding night had been a tender adventure, tonight was a tempestuous storm, bursting with unbridled passion and raw intensity. Thomas's hunger and curiosity have transformed our connection. Amid laughter and teasing, we explored each other thoroughly. I've never felt so close to someone, so complete. Depriving myself, and him, of this delightful coupling is, in hindsight, regrettable. But maybe the wait has made it this wonderful.

Nestled beside him now, with my body softened by climax, the world feels flawless. As the golden light fades to darkness, we share all that's happened while we were apart. I tell him about the dirty, snow-covered city, and how odd everything had felt. Waking up to the rumbling furnace, the confinement of fancy silk dresses, the frenzied streets milling with people, the stench of coal smoke, and the constant clanging of traffic. All of it had felt foreign.

"The city is the same as ever. But I don't belong there anymore," I say, realizing the truth in those words.

"So you've turned into a country mouse?" Thomas asks, pulling me against him with his good arm, until I'm lying on my side, my cheek nuzzled into his shoulder. "Tell me about your meeting with my father. And how the crew's doing." He's curious about all of it, and I talk until the full moon rises and the wind dies. "So. You think we can work this camp together now?" Thomas peers down at me, his eyes sparkling in the blue shadows as he teases. I elbow him with a grin.

"The only change is I'm finally getting paid for my interference." At this description, Thomas guffaws, kissing the top of my head again.

"And how were your parents? Your father?" His concern melts my heart.

"They look older. Thin. Worn out," I say, describing Father's gaunt frailty and the perplexing tenderness between my parents. Then I roll onto my back, away from him. "And Mother's opened up. Told me a bunch about her past I didn't know." I recount the history she shared with me. When I finish, Thomas's eyes search mine tenderly, and he leans onto his elbow, taking my hand.

"Well... it explains some of how she... is. How did all that come up?"

"My first day back, when she told me about Father's heart condition, she... she cried, Thomas. I didn't know what to do... how to react. She cried. And got pretty angry with me, before she stomped upstairs. Accused me of chasing the wrong dream." Thomas squeezes my fingers. "Then, as I was packing to leave, she got all nostalgic. Told me she should have seen how good her life was... and how wonderful my father is. Warned me not to make the same mistake with you. That was after James came to tell us about your accident." I stare at the ceiling, knowing this mention will lead our thoughts to James.

"Eva..." Thomas clears his throat, hesitating before speaking. "You should know..." His tone sends a flicker of fear through my stomach, but he doesn't take his eyes off me. "James told me." The muscle in his jaw twitches. "Bragged about it, actually. The morning after you... you two..." His voice trails off and I suck in a breath. "He watched me drop you off that night... at the party... and he..." Thomas's eyes squeeze shut, his expression pained. "I... I should never have left you there... like that."

"He told you? You knew?" My mind races. "But you... you proposed to me that week." Thomas sags back on his pillow.

"I did. It didn't change anything for me." He shrugs, his eyes flashing. "The opposite, actually. My father has always had a soft spot for James. Even more so since his brother was killed. But the man is..." He lets out a breath. "You're too good for him. I wanted you. Needed to fight for you." Thomas shakes his head, squeezing my fingers. "I figured I had nothing to lose by asking."

I close my eyes, grappling with this revelation, taking a deep, shaky breath. "I'm glad you told me." Rolling onto my side, I trace circles on Thomas's chest. "And maybe Mother's story helped straighten me out. I'm sorry it took me so long to catch up to you." I smile and Thomas meets my gaze, his eyes twinkling. He kisses me, and I run a finger from the raised scar on his ribs to the rough cast on his arm. There's one more big topic we need to talk about.

"Tell me... how this happened." The whispered words snag in my throat as I tap the plaster. I don't want to hear about how they found George, but I have to know.

"Oh, Eva." Thomas tries to sit up, to pull away. He wants to protect me, but I wrap my arms around his solid chest, keeping him close.

"Tell me. I've already imagined the worst." I kiss his neck as I say the words and Thomas exhales, groaning.

"You don't play fair, girl." His tone is gruff, but he sinks into his pillow and stares at the rafters. Then he clears his throat. "I don't remember all of it. But it was Tetley who found George. Wedged between two logs, floating out in the booming grounds." His voice shakes, and I'm glad it's too dark to see his expression. The sound of his pain makes my chest ache. "It was rough, windy. Too rough, really, to be out in the rowboat. But we had to get him." Beneath my palm, Thomas's heart beats faster, his breaths shallow as he continues. "He was stuck. We couldn't tell on what. But when we pulled and pulled on him... his body..." Thomas's words choke and he pauses again, then sucks in a breath. "Anyway, I leaned too far out of the boat and there was a wave and... well, that's about all I remember. Woke up two days later in Alert Bay with a helluva headache and this thing." He lifts his broken arm a little, gripping my hand.

"Does it hurt?" I kiss his chest, the muscles rippling beneath my lips as he shifts under me.

"Not much anymore. Aches a bit if I move a lot."

"And your head?" I rise onto my elbow, running my fingers behind his left ear where a patch of stubbly hair surrounds the rough threads of seven stitches. The nurse's warnings echo in my head and a shudder runs through me. It's by chance we didn't lose Thomas that day.

"I'm fine, Eva. I'll be fine." His words flood my body with a tingling need. I throw back the sheets and boldly straddle him, moaning as he fills me. Closing my eyes, I sit tall, my hair cascading. Thomas grips my hips with gentle strength as we move in breathless rhythm. When

I collapse onto him, shuddering in fulfilment once more, I giggle through tears.

"Why haven't we been doing this?" My teasing evokes a groan from Thomas and his fingers run the length of my body, making me tremble again.

"Worth the wait. We can make up for lost time." He chuckles, and the sound fills my heart. With a reluctant groan, Thomas pulls his arm from under me. "I should stoke that fire." As I watch him cross the room, I smile at how quickly we return to our conventional roles. It feels lovely to be taken care of.

At the table, he lights the lantern. The flames' glow reflects off his bright white plaster cast and paints shadows on his naked frame. He raises the lamp, turning to the woodstove, then pauses.

"What's this?" He points to a grey sweater draped over the back of his chair.

"Try it on," I say, rolling up onto my elbow.

"Is this…" His words trail off. He fingers the soft silver grey sweater I've been knitting and stares over at me.

"Yes," I whisper. "It's the yarn from…" My throat catches, but my face softens and I inhale. "It's the yarn from Ruby's layette. I just finished it. Still need to weave in the ends. Go on, try it on." I smile as I repeat the words impatiently, a lightness filling me.

"So. You finally decided I'm knit-worthy. I'm honoured." He grins, his eyes twinkling. Thomas puts down the lantern, then carefully pulls the sweater over the cast and over his head. "How does it look?" he asks, turning around once in the dim light.

"Perfect," I say, stretching out on the bed. "It's perfect."

As he returns my grin and stokes the fire, a deep sense of peace settles over me. Difficult things have happened here, at a fast pace. Yet there's nowhere I'd rather be.

When Thomas snuggles under the covers, his warm body curling alongside mine, my skin tingles with the force of our love. This kind of devotion leaves us vulnerable, open to the pain only loving deeply can cause. But as I stroke the sweater stretched over Thomas's scarred chest, I know it's worth the risk.

CHAPTER 59

The sweet forest scents greet me along my trail, every bush and blowdown a familiar friend after five years of hiking this route. My soft leather work boots and rifle bump gently against my hips. Both are slung from my backpack, which holds two of Edith's delicious sandwiches and my old Thermos filled with chamomile tea. Under my bare feet, the earth is warm, and the moss crunches. Dappled sunlight dances through the forest canopy as I pop late-season huckleberries into my mouth, savouring their tiny bursts of tartness. This Vaccinium parvifolium roots on a rotting cedar stump, surrounded by the thick leathery leaves of dense salal.

A thrush's flute-like voice competes with a chattering squirrel in the underbrush. In the treetops, the rustling morning wind builds. When I look up at the circle of Douglas firs surrounding me, they dance dizzily high against the blue sky. I reach out to a tree's thickly grooved bark to get my balance, which is harder these days. I blink rapidly, staring straight ahead where a swarm of no-see-ums hovers around the moss-covered trunk of a broken alder, snapped off by last month's windstorm.

Chewing on a handful of berries, I continue slowly to where Thomas will meet me. It's a secluded spot, a good hour's hike from camp, down the east side of the lake. Somewhere above me stands the bridge I designed, completed three summers ago. A quiet grin widens on my face and I take a deep, satisfied breath as I picture it. The trestle is an engineering feat, towering over the ravine. It provides access to another decade of timber for our camp, including the active setting where the crew is now, just half a mile above the shore.

The whining chug and occasional metallic clang of our latest up-grade, a Caterpillar Thirty tractor, echoes through the woods now. Like kids with a new toy, the men devoured the forty-page manual and debated who would move the shiny machine to the setting. Even I was taken by the squirming Caterpillar logo on the front grill, taking a charcoal rubbing of the arching word before the tractor left the landing. Technology continues to improve our safety and production.

Also up there, close to where Thomas shot the buck, is our first hand-planted setting. It's doing better than the areas that were natu-rally seeded, but there are still plenty of improvements I want to make. We're tracking which trees produce the best seeds, how to amend the soil for better germination, and how to boost seedling survival over winter.

Each season we learn more, and there have been failures, too. Three years ago, none of the seeds sprouted. And last year, we lost almost half our seedlings to a fungus. But the Company supports our efforts, which is validating.

Now, I emerge onto the rock shore from the dim forest, squinting against the lake's glare. Thomas is already in the water. I pause, catch-ing my breath and watching my husband from under a red cedar, the smooth rocks underfoot providing a welcome chill to the soles of my swollen bare feet.

Thomas has waded in to his waist, wearing only his undershorts, splashing the frigid water up his arms and chest. His tanned skin glints golden in the sunlight and I shade my eyes, mesmerized by his toned physique. I'll never tire of watching this man. He dives under, swimming a few powerful strokes, then emerges from the waves, whipping his hair and sending a sparkling spray of water in an arc over his head. When he turns, I wave, and he strides toward me, grinning. I pick my way carefully across the beach cobbles, stepping around worn driftwood logs. As Thomas nears, I stumble, and he shouts at me.

"Stop! Just wait a second." His eyebrows furrow with concern.

"I'm fine. It's okay." With a smile, I swat at him as if he were a no-see-um. But he insists on helping, slinging my backpack over his shoulder before tucking a chilly hand behind my neck and kissing me deeply on the lips. My eyes close and I shudder, a rush of desire flooding me. With a satisfied sigh, I lean into him, my palms exploring his wet, sculpted forearm and chest.

Then I push him away, laughing. "Cut it out. It's only lunchtime."

Thomas grins at me mischievously and takes my hand, guiding me to a large log and dropping my pack beside his pile of clothes. "Do you want to cool off first?" I nod, unbuttoning my cotton skirt, the band pulled high on my waist.

Thomas's eyes roam my body as I undress. He steps close, wrapping his arms around me from behind, and places his palms on my swollen belly. He kisses my neck before resting his chin on my shoulder with a contented sigh, and I snuggle into him, my eyelids fluttering closed in the warm sunshine. His heart beats against my back as we sway in the wind.

"I can't wait to meet this little one," Thomas murmurs into my ear, and as if in response, our baby kicks against my insides under his hand. Relief flickers through me, as it does whenever I feel this child move.

I've carried this baby two weeks longer than Ruby, and the stretches between those tiny kicks seem endless. The heaviness in my chest eases only when the little one stirs. Even in beautiful moments, a fog of dread grips me, and it's exhausting to fight it off and conceal it. I'm still terrified I won't be able to carry this precious bundle to term.

After the first flutters of quickening, Thomas insisted I stop working. But I refused, fearing boredom. It's part of a cherished routine, to wake up early with the crew and contribute to camp life. He's been relentless, and we finally compromised on my working half-time. These days, I rise and eat with him. Then I help start everyone's day, after which I pack lunch and explore trails alone until midday. Sometimes, like now, Thomas joins me.

"How've you been today?" Thomas lifts the thin white cotton of my undershirt, rubbing the tight skin of my belly slowly, his lips pursed in concern. Since the doctor reminded us how important mild exercise and relaxation are to the developing fetus, Thomas has been obsessed with my health. Movement is easy — I walk miles every day — but I'm still hesitant to share my deepest fears with him. There's nothing we can do to change the outcome. So on most days, I verbalize only my positive thoughts.

"Good. The little one's been busy, lots of kicking this morning." I open my eyes, relishing the rippled reflection of the green mountains and the bright blue sky. Then I finally pull away and ask Thomas to take me for a swim.

Almost two hours later, I round the point, refreshed and deliciously relaxed. After swimming in the frigid crystal waters, we shared a lunch, and dozed while the sun dried us. We dressed, debating the crew's next work front, before parting ways with a tender kiss. Now, with the clanking of the reload in the distance, I veer off toward the point, my bare feet silent on the warm trail.

At Ruby's grave, I blow her a kiss. Beside her small white cross, standing guard over my baby and my tin of gold, are three taller crosses.

I place a huckleberry branch on George's grave, then say hello to Arthur and Tetley.

At seventeen, Arthur had been our youngest employee, whom the kids loved to 'beat' in the nail driving contest on Dominion Day. Two summers ago, he was killed by a widow-maker. It was a heart-wrenching day — the accident still haunts Grinder and Slim. And we all miss quiet Tetley's solid presence. He drowned falling off a boom in a storm last autumn, right near the spot he hauled George's body from the lake.

I perch on a small stump, cocking my head to one side, my unfocused gaze on Camp 2's growing graveyard, and remember them all. As if on cue, two loons hoot behind me, their haunting calls echoing back and forth. My grief for them all hasn't diminished, but life has filled in the spaces around it.

With a thickness in my throat, I pull my stockings and boots over my calloused bare feet. Then a slight smile spreads across my face. This responsible adult needs to set an example for the children, and wearing shoes in the work areas is a good rule, even if I'd rather run barefoot. Standing, I blow the crosses a kiss, and with a shallow sigh, turn toward camp.

In the five years since I first saw this place, Camp 2 has seen progress. Four additional bunkhouses line the east side, housing men who work the new sawmill and extra setting. They all have families, so we now have seven women, all with children, living here. Not yet a balanced demographic, but our settlement is no longer resolutely masculine.

The community's edges, barren when I arrived, are flush with the ridged green stems of Scotch broom. It invades every inch of unforested land, filling the camp with the sharp vanilla scent of their pea-like golden blooms each spring.

On my left is our most precious addition, the schoolhouse I'm so proud to have wrangled here. It sits beyond the reload, between an outhouse and the office, backing onto the lake. The weathered bunkhouse planks are painted a vibrant red. Over the entrance, a lovingly carved wooden archway with the words "Camp School" welcomes all who enter. The front door is bright white and a cast iron bell hangs beside it, where Miss Long, our copper-haired young teacher, rings it twice a day, to summon the children in the morning, and to get them back again after their lunch break. Inside, youthful voices recite multiplication tables and colourful alphabet cut-outs hang in the windows.

I enter the office which Thomas and I have shared since my hiring, glancing at the clock. Almost an hour before Adeline gets home. Without taking off my pack, I lean over the desk, jotting down a few notes for Roy and Thomas to review after shift. Exhaling fully, I stand tall, trying to stretch the ache out of my lower back, and feeling suddenly exhausted. My body craves a nap, which is a decadent luxury in our hardworking community. But the familiar camp sounds tell me things are running fine.

From the reload, the rhythmic creak of cables over pulleys, and the hiss of the locie set a steady backdrop of production. Across the tracks, the rebuilt sawmill resonates with the clang and shouts of shingle bundles being loaded onto railcars, adding to the camp's hypnotic heartbeat. All is well on the work fronts.

So I head home, past the cookhouse, where smoke furls from the chimney. Muffled snippets of Edith and Li's friendly banter seep outside, mingled with the savoury aroma of fried onions. I stifle the urge to join them — if I don't rest now, my family will get a cranky Eva this evening.

I hoist myself up the steps using the handrail Thomas built. When Addie was born, we moved to this spacious double bunk at the river mouth. Inside, I eject the rifle cartridges before placing the gun in the rack, then throw my pack on the cluttered counter. After shuffling through scattered toys, I fall onto our bed covers, still wearing my boots. I really should tidy. The pain in my back fades as I lie on my side and the mattress hugs my belly. I close my eyes, sinking into the cool cotton cover on the feather pillow. The wind rustles the sun-drenched curtains in the open window, and I savour this moment alone, deciding the perfect time for chores is later.

Chapter 60

Through the fog of sleep, the school bell rings. I inhale sharply, startled, and squint into the bright afternoon. With a measured effort, I ease to the edge of the bed, planting my feet on the floor. I feel so heavy these days. The dishevelled bunkhouse draws a dejected sigh from me. Turns out children are messy. And I'm a terrible housekeeper. I really should tidy. If I stay, Miss Long or Grace will bring Addie to me. But I frown and bite the inside of my cheek. Chores don't warrant missing my favourite part of the day.

I hoist myself off the sheets, placing a steadying hand on the bunkhouse wall, then wade through the sea of wooden playthings to grab a picture book off the table. Outside, children scatter from the schoolhouse onto the gravel path. Grace stands in the shade, chatting with the other mothers, bouncing a fibre reed baby carriage, and waving me over. I smile back, scanning the group for Addie. She's perched on the steps beside Roy Junior, their heads bent over something in his hands. They laugh, their animated chatter and glowing faces putting a warm tingle in my chest.

The mothers, other than Grace, choose their words carefully around me. I hired their husbands, and the power imbalance has been a hindrance to building friendships. But hiring families has improved our camp. In the past, applicants willing to come this far were either desperate drifters or adventurous young people. Neither made a great long-term worker. Drifters seek a place to hide their demons, and adventurers soon yearn to move on.

So I now focus on families when hiring, asking the wives to attend the interviews I host. These couples are here on purpose, taking pride in their homes and work. We have less turnover and better production than ever using this recruiting strategy.

"How are ya, Eva?" Rosie Miller is as pregnant as I am, carrying her fourth. With a hand on her lower back, she watches her three boys churn up dust as they play a lively game of tag with Daisy, who's now almost as tall as I am.

"Not bad, Rosie. You?"

"Feelin' like a beached whale, honestly." She grins shyly and I laugh, handing her the picture book I brought. She runs a palm over the shiny front cover, a grateful smile lighting her face. Addie got the book from my parents, her Oma and Papa for her birthday last year, and she's finally agreed to share it with the youngest Miller boy. I do whatever I can to help the wives thrive in this camp. A big part of why we hired Rosie's husband, who came with a brood, is because we needed more children for the school.

While Thomas and I had convinced the Company to build the schoolhouse at their cost, the province required a minimum enrolment of ten students to fund the teacher's salary, room, and board. Since Addie was two, I've worked hard to establish this school and its teacher. I waded through the provincial regulations and set up an elected school board in a location that, according to the government, isn't a town. Then, with the trustees and schoolhouse in place, we waited eleven months for the Department of Education to send up a school inspector to certify the building and supplies.

I twist my wedding band with a churning stomach when I recall how the portly inspector in his city suit measured the schoolhouse windows, finding them four square feet shy of specification. Edith had plied the old bureaucrat with huckleberry pie, while Thomas and Roy sawed another square through a side wall. They had taken a window from the sawmill, so they could add the required square footage of glass to the schoolhouse. The satiated official had finally given us a pass on final inspection.

Recruiting a teacher had been the ultimate challenge. Young, single, females weren't rushing to apply for a position in a place like Camp 2. So I travelled to Vancouver in person this spring to find us one, and Miss Long has proven to be a good choice. She grew up in Rock Creek, no stranger to logging and mining and steam trains. The children love her, and she rooms with Edith, who's noticeably softer around the tiny freckled scholar.

We banter in bubbly voices as we follow the kids to the shore, helping Grace haul the wood artillery wheels of baby Jane's carriage down the sloping gravel path. The mid-September day is pleasantly warm and the lake shimmers with the iconic Pinder Peak towering in the distance. Boys wade in and cast lines over the lake's drop off. A screeching fishing reel still reminds me of James, but he's become a meagre memory. Thomas sees him down in Seattle once in a while, but James hasn't returned to Camp 2. So I haven't seen him since Thomas's accident, when he sped off in his shiny Ford outside my parents' house, all those years ago.

When the dinner bell chimes, the kids squeal, racing ahead of us. I lumber up the bank from the beach, running into Billy near the outhouse. He grins a greeting, dropping his wheelbarrow of firewood. We exchange a few work-related words as he rubs a handkerchief over his scarred brow, the honey-sweet scent of chopped fir filling the air. He's busier than ever as our bull cook, maintaining our growing camp's facilities.

The one building that never lacks Billy's attention is the schoolhouse. On the front steps, Miss Long struggles to reach a 'Welcome Back' banner she hung last week on Labour Day. While we speak, Billy's stare lingers on the teacher's petite hourglass figure. When he finally looks at me, he laughs nervously, his gaze darting to the schoolhouse again.

"For god's sake, Billy. Go help the poor girl." I laugh and he nods, his eyes glowing as he grips the wheelbarrow handles. "And Billy? Do us all a favour and ask her out." His step falters. Without looking back, he lifts his chin and stands a little taller, striding toward a beaming Miss Long.

I pull open the cookhouse door, still grinning, the chili's savoury scent and the children's chatter nourishing my soul. When I offered Miss Long this position, I knew Billy would take to her. But I've only admitted my matchmaking to George — I know he'll keep my secret.

Later that evening, I sit in a rocker on our back porch, a blanket wrapped around me, my palms cupping the mug of tea balanced on my belly. Down by the river, Thomas crouches beside Adeline, who's examining something in her palm. Our precious Addie, almost four now, has a shock of curly black hair that, like mine, is impossible to comb. Her excited voice drifts up the bank, but I can't make out her words, so I wave at them, smiling. Watching Thomas with his daughter fills my heart.

He smiles at Addie, who's walking carefully along the gravel path toward me, hands cupped. Thomas trails behind her, his suspenders dangling at his sides, brown breeches rolled up below his knees. His thin white shirt, untucked and unbuttoned, flaps against his tanned chest in the warm breeze. They're both barefoot, their soles toughened by a summer of exploring rugged ground. Addie wears her favourite sleeveless sky blue cotton shift, chosen for the pretty ribbon work stitched along the neck and armholes. She stops directly below me, extending her arms.

"Look, Mama. Fish!" Addie glances over her shoulder, her dark eyes wide. "Papa, lift up." Thomas chuckles. The steps of the porch are too tall for Addie's short legs, so he swings her onto my lap. I pass my mug to Thomas and wrap an arm around Addie to examine her treasure. Her palms cradle a small threespine stickleback, its tail fluttering weakly.

"*Gasterosteus aculeatus.*" The scientific name rolls off my tongue.

"Gaster-rockus. Gaster-rockus-tus." Addie's brows knit together and Thomas grins as she struggles with the mouthful of new words. The stickleback's iridescent scales shimmer in the dimming light. "Fish." Addie settles on the single syllable, pronouncing it easily.

"Yes, love. A stickleback fish." I pick a salmonberry leaf out of my daughter's hair before placing a quick kiss on the top of her head, my eyes fluttering closed as I inhale her soft, sun-kissed scent.

After a thorough examination of the squirming fish, Thomas returns it to the river. Addie snuggles under my blanket and nestles into the curves of my warm lap. With each rhythmic rock, Addie's eyelids sink lower. Her breathing slows and a soft sigh escapes her tiny red lips as she sinks into slumber.

Thomas steps onto the porch, the faded scar on his chest a reminder of how close we came to losing this moment. He buttons his shirt and pulls on the pilled silver-grey sweater he's worn every day since I gave it to him. As Thomas settles into the chair beside me, he brushes his calloused fingers down my cheek before extracting a pinch of tobacco from a soft leather pouch. He crumbles the fragrant leaves in his palm, the rich earthy aroma filling the night's cooling air.

Thomas tamps his pipe and strikes a match, the flickering flame dancing to the rhythm of the river below. He inhales and leans back, slowly exhaling, his face softening as tension leaves him. I pull my arm from under the dozing Addie, reaching for Thomas. We hold hands, rocking in unison. Beyond the rustling bushes and reed grass, a king-fisher's rattling call fades downriver as it flaps low over the water. In the distance, the marine fog creeps toward the tree-covered mountains, softening their soaring silhouettes in its hazy embrace.

With each quiet evening ritual, amid the wildlife and weather, I'm reminded of the abundance we've discovered here. There are no white picket fences, bone china, silk dresses, or pianos. Instead, mice scurry below the floorboards, a rifle hangs by the door, and wind whispers through towering firs.

Thomas and I rock, hands clasped, with one child on me and one in me. Four entwined heartbeats. Together, here, now, in this gorgeous, rugged place. We've traded luxuries for richness. And it's perfect.

NOTE FROM SYLVIA BOURGEOIS: Thank you for going on this adventure with me! If you enjoyed *Here, Now,* please consider telling a friend or posting a short review. It would mean a lot to me. Then, turn the page to read a FREE excerpt from another book in this series, *True Moxie*!

Island Echoes Series

Sylvia's **Island Echoes** novels are stand-alone stories featuring strong women in untraditional roles, celebrating the vibrant setting and industry of the Pacific Northwest, past and present.

Turn the page for a FREE excerpt of *True Moxie*!

True Moxie - Chapter 1

The day starts in the usual way — wet and windy. Rain drums on the roof and gurgles in the downspouts. I lie still, cozy under my down , straining to hear the clatter of breakfast dishes downstairs. But other than the racket outside, the house is silent. Then, as the fog of sleep lifts, I remember. The raw hollow of my mum's absence envelops me. Every morning, it stops my heart and takes my breath away, like plunging into an icy lake. Even now, over six months later.

I swing my legs off the bed and onto the soft carpet before the memories hold me under the covers. Grabbing my robe, I walk across the hall to shower, then pull on a pair of faded jeans, a t-shirt, and a hoodie. Downstairs, I flip on the lights and start a pot of coffee. As the brew percolates, I open the almost empty fridge. A stick of butter on a plate. A liter of whole milk. Four eggs. A crisper full of red apples. And a two-four of lager.

After sniffing the milk, I dump the last of the granola into a bowl. Someone needs to get groceries today, but there's no movement from upstairs. A glance at the clock spurs me to hurry, packing a lunch between bites. I stack my dishes in the sink with yesterday's and pour a travel mug of caffeine. Out in the mudroom, I cram the brown paper bag next to a folder of blank university applications. I'm jerking the zipper of my backpack closed when footsteps shuffle down the stairs.

"There's coffee." I force a bright tone and look up at my dad. He's paused on the last tread, a four-day stubble and dark eye circles match his gloomy expression. "Will you go shopping? We're out of everything." I shrug on my jacket, willing him to respond. Eventually, he nods silently. On his way to the kitchen, he stops to gaze into the living room; a room we haven't entered since The Last Day. The slump in his posture tells me he won't make it to the store today.

The door slams behind me and I step out into the downpour, avoiding murky puddles in the rough gravel driveway. He needs to get his shit together. It's been long enough. If he's still in ghost mode when we start work next week, it won't go well. My throat tightens as I hurry along the faded center line. The rain blows in sheets up the asphalt road and the backs of my jeans are drenched by the time I reach the bus stop.

When the yellow school bus lurches to a halt in front of the leaning shelter, I bound up the stairs and nod at Nancy, the driver. She pulls the door shut behind me, the rowdy interior reeking of musty, wet children.

"Hey, Raptor Claw!" Robbie, a little shit in Grade 7, yells at me from the back row. The chatter on the bus suspends, waiting for my reaction. But I ignore them all and silently slide into my spot above the wheel well. I've endured twelve years of bus ride dread, but since The Worst Day, this stuff feels farther away. Big problems block out petty problems. And Robbie's taunting is definitely a petty problem.

I slouch low, my knees riding up the seat back in front of me. My hood shields my temple from the cold, fogged-up window. I rub a slow circle in the condensation, bigger and bigger, and watch the bright green salal bushes roll by outside.

At even spacing, gravel driveways interrupt the overgrown brush, giving glimpses of our neighbors' homes. I know part of everyone's story. The double-wide where I babysit on Friday nights, the parents just weeks from divorce. The giant log house where the twins and my used-to-be best friend Nora celebrate their parent's anniversary with the fervor of those deprived of birthday parties and Christmas. The sad house where Old Man Henry walks his big chocolate lab by driving beside it in a rusty maroon Oldsmobile. The crazy house. The bunkhouse. The pink house. And in turn, people know my name, who my father is, and dozens of so-called facts about me.

The bus seat creaks as I shift, the wet cotton of my jeans sticking to both the black plastic and my hamstrings. A screech from the backseat makes me turn. Robbie is holding his cupped hands high, declaring he has 'a ginormous daddy longlegs' today. He threatens to dump the spider onto the sisters sitting in front of him. The girls shriek in fear, spilling toward the window and out into the aisle. I lean my head against the glass, my pulse pounding, hating that we all just stay out of things.

The crowd snickers as the girls beg Robbie to stop. He cackles again, and it snaps the last thread of patience in me. Enough. I push by the other kids, holding onto the seat backs as I stumble to the back of the bus and stand over Robbie.

"Heeeey!" He protests as I squish his hands together, staring into his flinty eyes above flaring nostrils. "You cooow! No faaaair!" Robbie whines as he opens his empty palms, revealing his bluff about the spider. I push him firmly into his seat and nod at the sisters, surprising myself. Getting involved means Robbie will focus on me tomorrow. And the next day. But it actually feels good — sticking up for the girls. Somebody needs to. Nancy peers into her rearview and shouts, "Stay in your seats, puh-leaze!"

The bus speeds up as we pass the gas station and merge onto the two-lane highway. The arcing beats of the telephone lines flash by against a backdrop of second-growth. When we've rattled past precisely fifty-three wooden power poles — yes, I've counted them piles of times — the bus turns off the highway into town. Asphalt rumble strips and a 'Children Playing' sign remind drivers to slow down as the first houses come into view. Next to the police station, the bus takes another jerky right. Today both Mounties are parked below the flagpole, where the red maple leaf flaps wildly above the cruisers in the pouring rain.

As we near our first stop at the elementary school, the bus bounces over a speed bump. The little kids grab their lunch boxes and backpacks, their chatter and rustling reaching a crescendo. They jostle off the bus, scattering across the concrete schoolyard. I don't react when Robbie gives me the finger from the aisle, hoping I can handle whatever revenge the little punk is planning for me. My head knocks against the glass as the bus cuts the corner beside the sports field, where a wide ditch surrounds the turf.

I grin to myself, recalling the hours I used to spend in those ditches hunting frog eggs in my little red gumboots. The ditch was always deep with slimy green muck. During recess and lunch, I would push aside the reed grass with a stick, searching for gelatinous sacs of eggs. I'd keep the slimy masses in a Mason jar outside the back door of my classroom. After school, I would carefully carry my live treasures home. My mum would sigh, but smile gently and find a shady spot on the deck where I could watch the little gel balls grow from egg to tadpole to frog.

I drop my chin to my chest. Every memory of my mother still aches so, so much. Why is it the more you try *not* to think about something, the more those images cycle through your thoughts? My mum's brown wavy hair. Her gray-blue eyes, just like mine. Her mischievous smile and chipped front tooth. Comfortable shoes. Elastic-waist cotton pants. The striped wool sweater she knit herself.

My mother had been background music. Someone who washed my sheets, cooked our dinners, did the shopping, and asked me how my day was. Ever there, but not... not really notable. With that background music now suddenly gone, I'm realizing how much my mother touched every heartbeat of our lives.

I pull the worn sleeve of my gray hoodie over my knuckles, over the scar where my pinkie and ring finger should be, and wipe away a tear. Damn! With the little kids gone, the bus is quieter as it pulls back onto the main street. Across the aisle, Josh, one of the double-wide twins, swiftly moves his gaze to the window when I look over. I know from his sister Nora, my now ex-best friend, he has a crush on me. Or at least he *did* six months ago. Even if he saw my tears, it's unlikely he'll blab.

I can't get used to these waves of memories. They run shivers down my spine, stab me in the stomach and make my heart beat all wacky. The thoughts come from nowhere. Like yesterday, I was walking along the sidewalk to the library, when suddenly, my feet froze. My ribs clamped onto my insides as my brain flashed back to last year, when my mum was teasing me about something between the bookshelves. Will these vivid bursts of time traveling ever stop? Then again, do I want the memories to end? I'm already forgetting parts of her, details fading.

We ramble down the hill, past the Rotary park no one uses. At the high school, the bus parks in the roundabout, near a totem pole. Nancy opens the doors with a mechanical clunk and twists in her seat to watch us file off onto the half-moon stairs which lead to the front entrance. In a few short weeks, as is the town tradition, our graduation class will arrange itself on these steps for our last school photo together. By now most of the girls have gone down-island to buy their grad dresses, at one of the big wedding boutiques. The boys have it easier. A shop from down-island came to measure them for suit rentals. They only needed to pick a style and match their cummerbund to their dates' dress color.

I have a lot of sewing left to do on my grad dress. My mum had been an excellent seamstress, and we bought the pattern over a year ago. It was perfect for me. A simple A-line dress with a scoop neck and absolutely no lace or ruffles or frills. Then, two days after picking out the dress pattern, my mum got The Diagnosis. She wanted to start the dress, but lacked the energy. So my dad drove me to the fabric store, where I had really tried to make all the decisions myself. Should I get blue, my favorite color? Or green, which my mother said looked best with my face? And which type of fabric? The choices had bewildered me.

Surprisingly, my dad had stepped in to help. Back when we all still had hope, he had been his take-charge self. After waiting in the truck for over an hour, he came into the fabric store where he found me baffled. First, he asked about the fabric type. We knew my mum would want a natural fiber and together we had eventually decided on a thick brushed silk.

"It... you know... flows real nice." My dad had observed the fabric. "If you ever twirl... or whatever."

We had chuckled at this thought. I am not a twirler. Under the harsh fluorescent lights, we had draped a few different jewel tones of the silk across my chest, finally agreeing the emerald green color suited me best.

It's only four weeks until grad now, so my dress will need to be ready. And I still don't have shoes. Anyway, graduation is totally overblown. Most girls have looked forward to it for years. But not me. Time spent with people we don't really like to celebrate something that isn't much of an accomplishment! All their fuss about dresses and shoes, hairdos and manicures, is hard for me to understand.

I slide into the bus aisle ahead of Josh and smile at Nancy as I step out into the downpour. With my pack over one shoulder, I take the stairs two at a time. I head up the ramp to my locker, shaking the rain from my blond hair, willing today to be a little easier.

Grade 12's get the best lockers, near the central ramp that connects the upper east and the lower west wing of the school. Amid the chatter of the hallway, I twirl the dial to enter my locker combination, shielding my hand from curious stares with my body. A crowd of hockey players lunges down the hall in their athletic jackets, shoving each other and narrating a step-by-step replay of a 'beauty goal, man!'. A couple in ripped jeans walks by, hand in hand, dragging with them the acrid scent of the smoking area. Cheap perfume mingles with the stale smoke as a clique of popular girls saunters down the ramp behind me. Their furtive glances and loud whispers used to fill me with uncertainty. Since The Worst Day, their opinions mean nothing to me. "Only twenty-two more days," I whisper to myself. "You'll make it. Only twenty-two more days."

I know my schedule without looking. Calculus and physics before lunch, then art and gym. I also have a session with Ms. Wells, the school counselor, over the lunch hour. Ugh. What a waste of my break. She's nice enough. As far as adults go, Ms. Wells is a favorite. But she won't understand how things have changed. Not at all.

Calculus and physics flash by. I love these classes. There is something so comforting about equations. One correct answer. No personal opinions. No gray areas. Just right or wrong. In physics, I sit alone now, near the back. Nora slides into a desk up front, as far from our usual seats as possible, avoiding my gaze. People can be so disappointing. The rhythmic focus of the calculations leaves me calm and in control. The memory waves of my mum never hit me while I'm doing math. When the bell shrills, I pack my books, file into the flow of students in the hall, and weave my way back to my locker, still talking to no one.

I pull my lunch and the folder of applications from my backpack. In the brown paper bag are the same three things I now eat every day: peanut butter and raspberry jam on wholewheat store-bought bread, cut diagonally and wrapped in plastic; a big red Fuji apple and two Oreo cookies. I unwrap half the sandwich and put the rest back on the top shelf, then slam the locker shut and stride down the ramp toward the school office and tiny counseling room.

Ms. Wells looks up when I tap on the open door. "Come in, Maia. Come in!" she says, motioning me to sit in the padded chair across from her desk. "How are you today?" She shuffles through a pile of folders.

"I'm fine," I respond. "Fine." The office is bright and tidy, and Ms. Wells has a couple of healthy plants behind her on the ledge below the windows. Outside in the courtyard, the rain is still pounding.

On the office walls, Ms. Wells has the typical inspirational counselor posters. Over the past six months, since the school and my dad decided I should see her every week, I've seen the whole rotation. This week, near her desk, above a cluttered bulletin board, hangs one of an enormous mountain with the quote "Tough times never last, but tough people do". On the wall, an orange sun setting over a rocky beach proclaims "Believe & Succeed". And alongside it, another poster shows a close-up of a drop falling into calm water making circular rings, with the quote "Attitude is a little thing that affects everything".

"Good God," I think, "does this shit work on anyone?" Ms. Wells hands me an application and I consider my name, typed into the first line. Maia Müller. No one else in this town has an umlaut in their name. And hardly anyone has parents whose English is their second language. My parents had only been a bit older than me when they left Europe for a farm in Quebec. They had moved west through Canadian mining towns, reaching for higher-paying jobs and more comfortable living conditions. When they ended up here, on the northern tip of this west coast island, the place stuck. For some reason.

Finally, Ms. Wells gets started. First, she congratulates me on my grades. Straight A's. Again. Still. Whatever. Next Ms. Wells moves to the fast-approaching deadlines for university applications. She's seen none of my forms. Nor have I asked any teachers to write recommendation letters — Ms. Wells has inquired. What exactly is my plan?

I think about this. Going to post-secondary school has always been the plan. I don't know what I want to do with my life. Not precisely. But I was going to finish high school, work the summer and then head to school in September. My mum had been the one who encouraged me to look at all the options. She believed I should love my career... and love to learn about it. But it's hard to imagine... picking a direction and committing to a single type of work *forever* is totally overwhelming. How do you *know*?

Anyway, my plans to leave for school are gone now. My dad made that clear. He will not be funding my post-secondary education. No money for my school. End of story. Instead, he needs me to work with him for a year. And although he hasn't said it out loud, I sense he wants me to take the business over from him and make it my own.

"I'm here to help, Maia." Ms. Wells interrupts my thoughts. "How can we get these applications out the door?"

I'm not sure how to answer. Telling Ms. Wells about my dad's current position regarding university will kick off a series of unpleasant conversations. Ms. Wells had been a friend of my mum's. And she's still a family friend and neighbor. When my parents needed to travel down-island for my mum's endless treatments, Ms. Wells would feed me dinner in her bright little kitchen. If she finds out now that my dad is not supporting my education, Ms. Wells will be pissed. And when Ms. Wells is pissed, she isn't quiet about it. So it's really better to avoid telling her the whole truth.

"Could you help get one teacher to draft a reference letter?" Pretending to apply to universities will cause the least amount of upset right now.

"Of course!" The corners of her brown eyes crinkle under her glasses as she flips some pages and makes a note in her daily planner. "Let me get Mr. Buckley to write one for you." Her eyes shift back to me and she grins. "He's your best bet out of all the math & science teachers. The rest of them, well, let's just say they're better with numbers than letters. Plus, your physics mark is spectacular. Yes, I think Mr. Buckley is a splendid choice for a reference letter!" Ms. Wells beams at her own cleverness.

She pulls out an application from my file, then scans through the pages.

"So. What's your topic for extracurricular activities? Your guiding work?" she asks.

Four years ago, when my dad lost his forestry job, my parents started a kayak wilderness guiding company. It was my mum's idea — something she had dreamed about for years. And together they built a decent business. It doesn't pay what my dad made out in the bush, especially since the weather up here limits the tourist season to the summer months. During school vacations, I would join them, doing the daily setup, cooking, and other chores on the trips. My parents had worked together, sharing their reverence for nature with clients, and it made them happy. For a short while, at least.

"Yes. Where they ask about 'an experience that taught me something about myself and the world.' I can talk about meeting new people... and about guiding work, I guess."

"I agree. And you should touch on your love of nature. Universities love that stuff." She nods, flipping to the next page.

"Yeah. That should work." I consider how to weave all those points into an essay.

Working as a guide is fun. I keep to myself at school, but with visitors from faraway places, I'm pretty open. Their lives fascinate me. Most clients are from big cities, used to viewing the landscape through glass from inside climate-controlled spaces. They come on these adventure trips to experience the raw beauty of the area, always excited to discover wildlife up close. It's normal to see wolves and bears, deer and elk, seals and otters, orcas and gray whales. These creatures are gorgeous and fascinating. But I enjoy our clients' reactions to the wilderness as much as I love the nature itself. The unspoiled vastness up here impresses these strangers. We can go for days without seeing another human. Some of our clients love the isolation, while others are totally unprepared for it. "Wait. What? No cell service? You're kidding!" they'll ask incredulously, stunned their newest gadget doesn't work everywhere.

"And what about this next question?" Ms. Wells asks. "'Explain how you responded to a problem and/or an unfamiliar situation. What did you do, what was the outcome, and what did you learn from the experience?'" Her eyes soften as she reads from the application. "Have you considered writing about your mum?".

I ponder those days: The Diagnosis, The Summer of Hell, The Worst Day, and The Last Day. Could I write about them? Sure. But will I write about them? No. Definitely not.

"I dunno," I say. "It's not really anyone's business, you know?"

"I don't disagree, Maia, but you can honor Maxi by writing about her. She'd be very proud of you." Ms. Wells yanks a Kleenex from the box on her desk, lifts her glasses, and wipes her eyes as she remembers her friend.

"I'll think about it."

"Can I ask, Maia, is there something else going on? You're less excited about going to school than you were during the fall. What's up?"

"I'm not really sure I want to go in September," I lie. "I think my dad would be really lonely if I leave. And he needs me to help on the guiding trips. Our season starts Thursday." I'm looking forward to skipping school, but I'm also apprehensive about this first trip back. My dad is doing better. Last week, he got the boat in the water, then ran up the coast to check on the trails and restock our supply cache. But when he starts the day in a trance like this morning, I worry it's too soon for him to work.

"Oh, Maia! I really hope you decide to go. You are so smart... so capable!" Ms. Wells folds her hands on the desk. "This year has been hard... terribly hard... for you... and Lars. None of this is fair." I can't argue and stare down at the carpet. "Getting back to work will help your dad. And you." She might be right. And if I keep saving my pay and tips, maybe —

"How are you and Nora, by the way?" I shake my head. There is no me and Nora. Not anymore. "I'm sorry, Maia," Ms. Wells says.

"Friendships can be hard. And moving away from your parents..." Her voice falters as she corrects herself. "... your dad... and the life you've always known takes a lot. It takes courage. And belief things *will* work out," Ms. Wells says. "And I know it's even harder to take those first steps... to leave when you don't have full support from home."

I feel the heat rising in my face. Does she know my dad's stance? This talk needs to stop.

"I'll finish the applications, Ms. Wells. I promise. And I'll send them in. That's all I can say for sure right now, okay?"

The rest of the counseling session flies by. Together, we brainstorm ideas for my essays. I even find the courage to mention the technical school program I researched the other night. Ms. Wells seems skeptical because someone with my grades "really belongs in university". But she also promises to check out the program outline.

When the bell rings, ending the lunch hour, I leave Ms. Wells' office, hope rekindling. Something I haven't felt in months. I was looking forward to going to school, and talking about it reminded me. I walk back to my locker, excited to give the applications my full effort. If I work all summer and get a couple of scholarships, I might have enough money to make it to Christmas break. It would be a start. Now I just need to get my dad on track. I have no idea how to help him, but I'm going to try. Harder. I have to.

TRUE MOXIE - CHAPTER 2

Full sun, blue skies, and calm waters. A rare day, almost making me forget we're one of the rainiest towns in our province. From the F350 back seat, I drag a bright yellow dry pack. After heaving it onto my shoulder, I hoist the gray and white cooler with both hands. As I head to the dock, I wonder if our clients will be on time.

I know little about them. They're a family of three, the Baldwins, from the big city. The mother's name is Anna, the father is Carl and their eighteen-year-old son is called Jack. They booked the first four-day trip of the season. It's what our brochure calls a 'combo trip'. A boat run up the coast, drop-off at the south trailhead with the kayaks, two days of kayaking, and a two-day hike over to the north trailhead, where we'll get picked up by a van shuttle.

Early June is always a crapshoot with the weather. It can be beautiful. And it can be torrential. The forecast for the next few days is unsettled. I'm hoping the rains hold off, so I can ease back into this adventure work. I've missed being out on the ocean and in the forest. But the work is physical and often uncomfortable. Shitting in the woods isn't for everyone, and I hope this first group isn't too high-maintenance.

My eyes crinkle as I think of Margo, a bleached blond, who came with her new husband, Jeff, last year. He was prepared — over prepared — with outdoor tools and technical clothing and an encyclopedic knowledge of our flora. Margo, on the other hand, wore knee-high leather boots with a wedge heel, insisting they were great for walking in. My dad took one look at her footwear and refused her access to the boat. Margo got dragged to the general store, where the unsmiling owner found a pair of proper hiking boots and some plastic clogs that fit. She wrinkled her nose at her comfortable, but unfashionable feet, the entire trip.

Margo had needed help with everything. I checked her tent for insects, cleared the spider webs before she squatted and threaded her manicured fingers into her pack straps so she wouldn't break a nail. High-Maintenance Margo. But the extra effort had been worth it when we got Jeff's tip. I still wonder how anyone can pride themselves on being helpless, the way Margo did. People can be strange.

I drop the cooler to the dock and step onto the swim fin of the twenty-six-foot aluminum boat, glancing down at *Moxie* painted on the transom. When my dad bought the boat from a bankrupt logging contractor, it was named *Ruby Tuesday*. Ruby, the guy's ex-wife, still lived in town and we felt awkward keeping the name.

Deciding on the new name for the boat was easy. Before I was born, when my parents first moved to town, a neighbor commented how well mum's name matched her personality. With my dad's accent, the neighbor heard 'moxie' when my dad called her Maxi. Once dad looked up the definition of moxie, it became an instant nickname. And my mum had lived up to her nickname — always bold and gritty.

To rename the boat, my mum had been adamant about conducting a proper name purging and renaming ceremony — anything less was bad luck. So, to avoid the wrath of the gods, we had first removed every physical trace of the old boat's name. *Ruby Tuesday* was scrubbed from the transom, life ring, bow, ship logs and floating key chain. Then my mum wrote *Ruby Tuesday* on a metal garden tag with a water-soluble marker. According to legend, the name of every vessel is recorded in the 'Ledger of the Deep', and known personally to the sea gods. To expunge the name *Ruby Tuesday* from the gods' ledger, my mum stood on the bow, grinning with a twinkle in her eye, and recited the timeless declaration:

> "Oh, mighty and great ruler of the seas and oceans, to whom all ships and we who venture upon your vast domain are required to pay homage, implore you in your graciousness to expunge for all time from your records and recollection the name *Ruby Tuesday* which has ceased to be an entity in your kingdom. As proof thereof, we submit this ingot bearing her name to be corrupted through your powers and forever be purged from the sea."

Then she dropped the tag into the ocean and poured a bottle of Champagne overboard, from East to West, saying,

> "In grateful acknowledgment of your munificence and dispensation, we offer these libations to your majesty and your court."

Apparently, this gets the sea gods drunk, so they forget the old boat's name.

She had continued the renaming ceremony with mischievous formality. First, we appeased the sea gods by pouring another bottle of Champagne into the ocean from West to East, introducing the *Moxie* to their ledger. Then we appeased the four wind god brothers by facing each of their four compass directions. She poured a generous amount of Champagne into a flute and flicked it overboard in each direction while addressing the gods by name.

I smile at the memory. The ceremony had been ridiculous. And fun. As we had toasted the renamed *Moxie* and taken sips of bubbly, my dad had grumbled about wasting three bottles of Champagne. Mum smiled playfully, stood on tip-toe, and kissed his scowl away, saying, "You'll thank me when this boat has a long, lucky lifetime."

The boat is a converted crew boat, seating ten. I drop the bag of food from my shoulder onto the colorful pile of supplies already on board. Then I lug the cooler full of perishables onto the deck. Later, we'll divide the food between the kayaks for the first leg of our trip. By the time we get to the hike, we'll carry freeze-dried meals to keep the weight down. Besides the food, there are five orange dry packs, one per adventurer, on the pile. Each pack holds a sleeping bag, mat, and tent. The guests will add their belongings to these bags when they arrive.

A car door slams in the parking lot and a short, plump woman opens a silver Range Rover's hatch. She's talking to a dark-haired young man. Her movements are quick and excited. He leans in, listening, then helps with the bags. I wait for the father to get out of the vehicle, which would confirm my hunch these are the Baldwins. But no one else appears. Well. Now what?

I re-stack the bags, buying time and hoping my dad gets back, so I can avoid the whole greeting ceremony. Right on cue, my dad's voice calls out from across the gravel lot. He towers over Anna as he shakes her hand and then Jack's. They're too far away to make out words, but Anna says something to my dad. He looks down at the dock, then turns back to Anna and nods once. He motions in the general direction of the boat with his head and he picks up two of their bags, walking toward me. When he doesn't slow down or look back, Anna glances over at Jack. They shrug, then Jack grabs the last bag from the Range Rover and they both stride to catch up. My dad is a man of few words.

With the gear stacked on the deck, I climb up on the narrow ledge beside the cabin to the roof rack, holding four fiberglass touring kayaks. I check the ropes on each one, stalling, so I'm away from the guests for the introductions. In the past few months, I've learned a few tricks to avoid handshakes.

Their footsteps thump on the dock's wooden planks and I sneak a look at Jack from behind a kayak. Maroon hoodie, dark gray jeans, brand new skater shoes, and a frayed ball cap. He's tall, almost six feet, and athletic. He looks bored and unhappy. That could make this trip difficult. The worst clients are those who are high-maintenance or don't want to be here.

"This is us." My dad drops the bags and looks up at me on the roof. "This is my daughter, Maia. She's our cook, nature expert, and all-around helper. Maia, this is Anna. And Jack." He gestures at each of us. It's been weeks since I've heard him say so many words at one time. Maybe this trip can be the start of getting back to normal... our new normal.

I smile tightly and give them a quick wave. "Nice to meet you both." Jack's dark eyes catch mine for an instant and my throat closes. Nope, he does not want to be here.

Anna's wearing runners, khaki nylon pants, a pink fleece, and a white ball cap with her brown ponytail threaded through the back closure. Clearly, she read through our brochure and followed our directions that warn against wearing cotton. Anna has a smile that hits every part of her face. I'm going to like this lady. One bright spot on this trip so far.

Jack is another story. He now avoids my gaze, standing off to the side, fiddling with an iPod connected to the cord of his earbuds. He either hasn't read the brochure or, more likely, didn't listen to Anna's rules about clothing. Everything he's wearing is cotton. In our Conservation and Outdoor Recreation course we were reminded daily that "cotton kills" because it absorbs more water than other fabrics and loses its ability to insulate when wet. I groan inwardly — having people who won't follow directions makes a trip so much harder.

But you're getting paid for this, I remind myself. And you get to miss school to be here. These people don't need to be your friends. Just smile, be helpful and go the extra mile for the guests like mum taught you. Then maybe, just maybe, there will be a gratuity in it for you at the end of the week. Judging by their vehicle, this family can afford to tip us!

Once the kayak check is finished, I climb back down onto the deck. "Where's Mr. Baldwin?" I glance toward the parking lot again.

"As it turns out, Carl won't be joining us." An odd expression crosses Anna's face. "He got tied up at work and was going to join us this morning. But he's..." Her eyebrows knit together in a flash of pain. "... He's still tied up." Anna glances toward Jack. He looks back at her without saying a word. Something's off, but I can't tell what. Doesn't matter. Not my business.

"Four is a good number," my dad says. "Pass me the extra pack, Maia." I pick one of the guest packs and pass it to him. "We'll still bring all the food," he says. "Don't want hangry teens."

I give Anna and Jack each their dry pack and instruct them to move their clothes into them. The dry packs are a rugged waterproof fabric with a water-resistant roll-top closure. Useful when we have water on all sides of us. Anna is pretty minimalist for a city girl. She lays her bathroom kit on the deck as she folds her belongings into the pack. It's a clear zip-top bag with travel-sized toothpaste, dry shampoo, sunscreen, and soap; a toothbrush, and Tylenol. Impressively light.

Jack stuffs a new-looking pair of hiking boots into his dry pack, then adds his socks, underwear, T-shirts, one pair of pants, and a clear bag of bath supplies with even less in it than Anna's. Jack finishes first and I turn so I'm able to grab the pack from him with my left hand.

When Anna is also ready, my dad waves her over and says, "Let's take the extra bags up. Then we'll go." Together they walk to the vehicles, Anna chattering and my dad answering in short syllables.

Jack stands on the dock, studying me with a look of... what? Curiosity, maybe? "Come on board," I motion him over. I have to talk to him at some point.

"Huh?" he says, taking out an earbud.

"Come on board," I repeat. He nods and steps onto the side rail. But as he jumps, his foot gets tangled in the dock line. Jack is flying toward me, about to take a face-plant on the gritty deck. I grab for his arm with both hands. My help slows Jack's fall, and only his other hand skids across the deck.

"Shit!" Jack says. I pull him upright and he glances at me, cheeks flushing. He smells of spice and coconut suntan lotion. Nice. Then his gaze drops to my right hand, still pulling on his arm. His eyes widen, taking in the gnarled scar and missing fingers. He pulls back and I spin away. I'm still not used to seeing people's shock. Most of the town has seen my injury by now. But strangers struggle with an appropriate reaction.

"Are you okay?" I ask, my back to Jack, watching Anna and my dad walk down the ramp. Her bright colors dazzle in the sunshine next to my dad's faded and grimy attire.

"Yeah," Jack says. But a sharp intake of his breath from behind me tells me otherwise.

"What happened?" Anna hops on board.

"I'm fine. I tripped," Jack says. My dad assesses Jack's minor wound and reads Anna's reaction from where he stands on the dock. I take an ice pack from the cooler, wrap a clean fish towel around it, and pass the whole thing to Anna.

"Thanks love." Anna examines Jack's hand. "You're fine." She closes Jack's palm around the towel-wrapped ice pack. "You'll be fine." My dad nods once, satisfied with her underreaction.

Get your copy of **True Moxie** *now. Scan the QR code below to go to Sylvia's website. Or search your favourite app or bookstore.*

Thank you for being a reader!

A Note on Canadian Spelling, eh?

Dear reader,

Here, Now adheres to Canadian English spelling and usage conventions, so you may spot some quirky words. We Canadians have a charming habit of spelling things our own way – not quite British, not quite American, but 100% Canuck!

So, don't be alarmed if you come across these differences:

- The retention of the letter "u" in words such as "colour," "favour," and "honour"

- The use of "-re" instead of "-er" in words like "centre" and "theatre"

- The doubling of consonants in certain words like "travelled" and "counselling"

These aren't typos – I'm just honouring my roots. Happy reading!

About the Author

 Sylvia Bourgeois grew up on northern Vancouver Island, in some of British Columbia's most beautiful small communities. Sylvia now lives in Fanny Bay and considers her family, friends, and time outside to be most important to her. When she isn't working her day job or on a boat with her husband, you can find her creating fine foods in her kitchen. She loves to hear from her readers. Visit her at www.sylviabourgeois .com and click now on her Instagram for a colourful glimpse into her life.

BOOKS BY SYLVIA BOURGEOIS

True Moxie

Here, Now

instagram.com/sylviabourgeois/

Get a FREE copy of the *Here, Now* maps by visiting me at
www.sylviabourgeois.com